Christopher Fowler is the author of several Bryant & May mysteries, including the award-winners *Full Dark House* and *The Victoria Vanishes*, plus the acclaimed memoir, *Paperboy*. He lives in London's King's Cross.

For more information on Christopher Fowler and his books, see his website at: www.christopherfowler.co.uk

BRYANT & MAY AND THE MEMORY OF BLOOD

CHRISTOPHER FOWLER

BANTAM BOOKS

LONDON • TORONTO • SYDNEY • AUCKLAND • JOHANNESBURG

TRANSWORLD PUBLISHERS
61–63 Uxbridge Road, London W5 5SA
A Random House Group Company
www.transworldbooks.co.uk

BRYANT & MAY AND THE MEMORY OF BLOOD
A BANTAM BOOK: 9780857500946

First published in Great Britain
in 2011 by Doubleday
an imprint of Transworld Publishers
Bantam edition published 2012

Addresses for Random House Group Ltd companies outside the UK
can be found at: www.randomhouse.co.uk
The Random House Group Ltd Reg. No. 954009

The Random House Group Limited supports the Forest Stewardship
Council (FSC®), the leading international forest-certification organization.
Our books carrying the FSC label are printed on FSC®-certified paper. FSC
is the only forest-certification scheme endorsed by the leading environmental
organizations, including Greenpeace. Our paper-procurement policy can be
found at www.randomhouse.co.uk/environment.

Typeset in 11/13 pt Sabon by Falcon Oast Graphic Art Ltd.
Printed in Great Britain by Clays Ltd, St Ives plc

2 4 6 8 10 9 7 5 3 1

This book is a small wedding gift for
Martin Butterworth,
wishing you a universe of merriment and joy.

PUNCH: I shall be feared. I shall be the Bogey-Man that frightens children in the dark.

BLIND MAN: Children will love you. And the more people you kill, the more they will laugh. (*To audience*) Now you have seen our little puppet play, here is a moral you may take away: Suppose tomorrow's sun should rise for *you*, give you the power for a single day, how would you use it? Would our tale come true?

ACKNOWLEDGEMENTS

Old (and new) readers will notice that Bryant & May books aren't like other detective series – they can be read out of sequence (in fact, they sometimes benefit from it), and I cheekily incorporate suggestions from readers. I have a feeling that if I tipped Bryant & May over the Reichenbach Falls they'd find a way to climb back up. Every time I prepare to send them to their deaths, they win a reprieve and fight on.

This time I owe their survival to my US editor, Kate Miciak, who always believed in the characters and willed them back into existence, and to my UK editor Simon Taylor, who has consistently and wholeheartedly supported the series. I'd like to thank my agent, Mandy Little, for remaining, without question, the truest of true believers. These are interesting times for publishing, and authors need all the help they can get. On that score, I'd like to thank book clubs and library groups everywhere for championing these adventures and providing a lifeline for authors like me. In particular, I'd like to thank Jan for her inside knowledge of London, and Stephen 'Stalky' Groves, who knows more about my movements than I do.

As always, the least-likely sounding facts in this novel are, in fact, true. For further information, visit: www.peculiarcrimesunit.com and my daily blog www.christopherfowler.co.uk

The following undated document appeared on Wikileaks and is now the subject of a government investigation. It may be read before the case which follows, skipped, or used for reference.

A GUIDE TO THE PECULIAR CRIMES UNIT, ITS STAFF AND AIMS

This is a restricted communication. No part of the following personnel report is intended for public release. No reference copies may be reproduced from this document, and reading may only take place within the Records Office upon the receipt of signed approval.

AN EXPLANATORY NOTE ON THE ORIGIN OF THE PECULIAR CRIMES UNIT, 231 CALEDONIAN ROAD, KING'S CROSS, LONDON N1 9RB

The Peculiar Crimes Unit is not like other police divisions.

It was founded soon after the outbreak of the Second World War, as part of a government initiative to ease the burden on London's overstretched Metropolitan

Police Force. In this time of desperation most able-bodied men had been taken into the armed forces, and seven new experimental agencies were proposed by the Churchill government. The Peculiar Crimes Unit was one of them.

Its aim was to tackle high-profile cases which had the capacity to compound social problems in urban areas. The affix 'peculiar' was originally meant in the sense of 'particular'. The government's plan was that the new unit should handle investigations into those situations deemed uniquely sensitive and a high risk to public morale. To head this division, several young and inexperienced students were recruited from across the capital.

The crimes that fell within the Unit's remit were ones that could potentially cause social panics and general public malaise. Its staff members were outsiders, radicals and freethinkers answerable only to the War Office, and later the Home Office.

The Other London Units

One of the other experimental units created at that time was the Central Therapy Unit, set up to help the bereaved and the newly homeless cope with the psychological stresses of war. This unit closed after just eleven months because bombed-out residents continued turning to their neighbours for support rather than visiting qualified government specialists.

A propaganda unit called the Central Information Service (later to become the COI) was set up to supply positive, uplifting news items to national newspapers in order to combat hearsay and harmful disinformation spread about our overseas forces, and to fill the void left by the blanket news blackouts.

A further unit based at the War Office employed a number of writers and artists, including members of the

Royal Academy and novelists Ian Fleming and Dennis Wheatley, to project the possible outcome of a prolonged war with Germany, and to develop stratagems for deceiving the enemy. The most famous wartime deception created by this unit was Operation Mincemeat, in which the corpse of a dead Welsh tramp was disguised as a drowned naval officer, planted with false plans and left for the Germans to find.

The most successful of the seven experimental units launched by the Churchill government in wartime was the cypher-breaking division based at Bletchley, where Alan Turing and his team cracked the Enigma Code, and in doing so laid the foundations for modern computer technology.

THE PCU SINCE 1945

The PCU remained in operation through the war and has continued in one form or another ever since that time. In the past two decades, reorganization of the national policing network has aimed at reducing the influence of individual units and creating standardized practices operating from guidelines laid down for a national crime database, subject to performance statistics.

The PCU unofficially aided a number of high-ranking politicians in the past, and as a consequence has remained exempt from these measures. Subsequently, a series of high-profile embarrassments has placed the Unit on a cross-governmental blacklist of Organizations of Potential Detriment, which is the reason for this ongoing internal surveillance.

The following notes are supplemental to official PCU personnel career details (see attached D/SC12–649). They are not intended to be comprehensive and represent public observations made by various co-workers. As such, they are provided to act as guideline opinions only.

RAYMOND LAND
Temporary Acting Head of the PCU

Raymond Land's original PCU contract was intended to last for eighteen months but was extended indefinitely after no other applicants could be recruited. He has applied for a transfer from the PCU on no fewer than seventeen separate occasions, which gives some indication of his dissatisfaction with the Unit.

Land comes from Luton, which says it all. He's never really lost his suburban temperament. He finds it hard to work with his detectives, who appear to pay no attention to his directives and treat him with amusement and disdain. His attempts at discipline go unheeded.

As a former graduate of the Central London Criminal Biology Unit, Land has on occasion proven himself to be intelligent, driven and meticulous, but I once heard it said about him that 'he could identify a tree from its bark samples without comprehending the layout of the forest'. Most members of the PCU seem to share this flaw.

In the past he has shown himself to be a strong government ally, but he can't be trusted to toe the party line, and has switched sides on more than one occasion. He could probably be easily manipulated with a promise of relocation/early retirement.

ARTHUR ST JOHN BRYANT
Senior Detective

Where do I start with Arthur Bryant?

Bryant is the original thorn in the side of the establishment. I could point out that he managed to blow up his old headquarters, that he released illegal immigrants into the underground system, infected a Ministry of Defence outsource unit and offended a member of royalty, but let's stick to the more salubrious facts.

Bryant was born in Whitechapel, East London. Formerly

of Bow Street, Savile Row and the North London Serious Crimes Division. In policing terms, Bryant has really covered the waterfront. He's handled just about every type of case, including multiple murder, kidnap, vice, burglary, public affright, terrorism, the disappearance of a pub and the theft of forty cats. Typically, it was the solving of this last case that most endeared him to the general public.

Formerly of Hampstead and Battersea, he's currently sharing habitation in Chalk Farm with his landlady, one Alma Sorrowbridge. His brother died on a Thames barge, parents lived in Bethnal Green, father was a street photographer and a drunk. Bryant had a French wife, Nathalie, who died after falling from a bridge. He was devastated and never remarried. A loner by nature, he's rumoured to sleep no more than four hours a night. Has commited numerous driving offences, incurred in an ancient Mini Cooper apparently called Victor (187 TWR).

Bryant is past Civil Service retirement age and his health is far from good, but despite having had a heart attack and needing a walking stick he seems surprisingly robust. He's extremely eccentric, offensively rude and is known to smoke cannabis, supposedly for his arthritis. We could probably get him for that.

Bryant's success rate in investigations is far above the capital's average, and this is the main reason why Whitehall continues to sign off on his budgets. Arthur Bryant and John May have a long history of refusing promotion, and the loyalty this engenders allows them to maintain control of the Unit. They are still well connected in political circles.

Bryant garners much of his information from a loose network of psychics, healers, New Age fringe-dwellers, police time-wasters and anarchists, many of whom have lengthy arrest files. He is also an expert on the subject of London and its history, and conducts guided tours of the capital in his spare time.

Bryant's oddly lateral thought processes remain a total mystery to us. University College London is currently offering a course that attempts to explain his methods. Whether deliberate or inadvertent, he has a habit of making us look bad. He has broken local, national and international laws on numerous occasions, but somehow always seems to get away with it. He remains entirely beyond the reach of influence. I simply wouldn't go there, if I were you. Personally, I find him incomprehensible and utterly ghastly.

JOHN MAY
SENIOR DETECTIVE

Bryant's partner was born in Vauxhall, South London. He's the human face of the team, and could be considered to be Bryant's alter ego. There's one sister, Gwen Kaye (married name), living in Brighton, married with two children. May moved from Hampstead to St John's Wood, and now resides in Shad Thames. He was married to Jane Upton, now divorced, has an estranged son, Alex, and had a daughter, Elizabeth, who also worked for the PCU until her death on active duty.

The source of the estrangement between May and his son is not known. May's ex-wife was declared mentally unstable soon after their divorce. His granddaughter, April, suffered from agoraphobia until she had resolved issues about her mother. She worked at the Unit for a while, but we understand she now lives with her uncle in Canada.

May is a pragmatic, determined worker well liked by his colleagues, but, like Bryant, he has a few secret anti-government contacts we're not happy about. On a personal level, he's fitter, friendlier and certainly a lot more pleasant to deal with than his partner. He is three years younger than Bryant, drives a silver BMW, knows a surprising amount about new technology.

On a personal level he has loneliness issues, and continues to date women the department classifies as high security risks. May suffers from high cholesterol and has a history of lower back pain. His continuing loyalty to Bryant is complete and unfathomable; there seems to be little likelihood that he could ever become an ally of the department.

JANICE LONGBRIGHT
DETECTIVE SERGEANT

Longbright's parents were Gladys Forthright and Harris Longbright, both highly respected former Metropolitan Police officers. She was once an Olympic javelin hope until an injury ended her career. Janice Longbright has been employed by Bryant & May for almost her entire adult working life, and is fiercely loyal to them, largely because of their relationship with her mother.

She dated DCI Ian Hargreave for ten years, but inexplicably chose not to marry him. Her last partner, Liberty DuCaine, died on active duty. She lives alone in Highgate. Not to be underestimated. Lately there have been odd rumours about her supposed clairvoyant abilities, although perhaps someone is pulling our leg on this. There was also some kind of scandal involving her role in the running of a Soho burlesque club, but we haven't been able to uncover any details.

GILES KERSHAW
FORENSIC PATHOLOGY

Kershaw was a child prodigy who dropped out of Queen's College, Oxford, after his wealthy family became newly impoverished, but he subsequently took his medical degree at UCL. He has now left the Unit to become the St Pancras coroner, but continues to work with the PCU on special investigations. By a peculiar coincidence, an earlier St Pancras coroner, Sir Bentley Purchase, was the supplier of the corpse for Operation Mincemeat (see above). When a government representative had trouble finding the coroner's office, Purchase famously suggested that he would get there quicker if he got hit by a bus. Kershaw's brother-in-law was the last Home Secretary. His reputation is unimpeachable, and his loyalty to the PCU is also entirely unfathomable.

DAN BANBURY
CRIME SCENE MANAGER/INFOTECH
Banbury is the only staff member who seems completely normal. Born in Bow, London. Married with a ten-year-old son. Lives in Croydon. He's a solid worker, eager and enthusiastic and reputed to show intuitive brilliance at crime scenes. He's a dyed-in-the-wool tech-head who once ran afoul of the Official Secrets Act while still a teenager. The case file on that incident appears to have been mysteriously erased. Another loyal supporter of the PCU, despite the fact that his wage level has remained unchanged for nearly three years.

JACK RENFIELD
SERGEANT
Formerly a duty sergeant based at Albany Street police station, Renfield's a bit of a thick-eared old-school copper, and has a reputation for playing it by the book. He's on record as being an outspoken critic of the PCU, but lately appears to have been won over and has started siding with them, which turns him into a liability. I'd love to know what Bryant & May put in the water that makes their staff become so doggedly loyal.

MEERA MANGESHKAR
POLICE CONSTABLE
This one's a tough South Londoner from a large Indian family, hardworking, responsive, with a strong sense of duty. She has argued with her superiors and lodged complaints against them in the past, but things seem to have gone quiet on that front. However, there are rumours that she's not happy in her current position. Has anger management issues. Could be exploited.

COLIN BIMSLEY
POLICE CONSTABLE
Another inherited employee; his father and uncle were both former members of the PCU, so he's pretty much bound to the Unit for life. By all accounts decent enough, he suffers from Diminished Spatial Awareness (DSA), which made him a liability at the Met. Trained at Repton Amateur Boxing Club for three years until suffering a head injury. Maybe Health & Safety could look into this?

FRATERNITY DUCAINE
POLICE CONSTABLE
This chap appears to have joined the Unit without any Home Office approval. It seems Bryant took it upon himself to offer the lad a job. Can somebody do some digging on him?

NB There have been numerous Health & Safety infringements at the Unit, including unsecured weapons in the Evidence Room, illegal wiring and dangerous chemicals stored on-site. There also appears to be a cat called Crippen (a surviving relative from Bryant's feline investigation) wandering around the place. Unfortunately, although the Caledonian Road building is unsafe, it was privately rented by Bryant in a deliberate attempt to exploit a legal loophole, and therefore does not technically fall under the jurisprudence of the Home Office.

Although it is entirely possible that the HO could find a way to close the Unit down, the basic problem continues: so long as the PCU is useful, it remains a necessary evil.

On a personal note, I find it astonishing that these officers are allowed to remain on active public duty. If Bryant and May were removed, the place would collapse like a house of cards. Just a thought.

This report commissioned by Leslie Faraday (Home Office Liaison) for Oskar Kasavian (Internal Security)

I

CHAMBER OF HORRORS

Arthur Bryant stood there pretending not to shiver. He was tightly wrapped in a 1951 Festival of Britain scarf, with a Bloody Mary in one hand and a ketchup-crusted cocktail sausage in the other. Above his head, a withered yellow corpse hung inside a rusting gibbet iron.

'Well,' he said, 'this is nice, isn't it?'

His partner, John May, was not so consoled. The great chamber was freezing. Rain was pattering into an array of galvanized buckets. The smell of mildewed brickwork assailed his nostrils. A few feet behind him, the Witchfinder General Matthew Hopkins was stabbing a thin-bladed knife into a screaming priest, looking for the marks of the Devil. On the other side of the detectives stood a torture rack and several members of the Spanish Inquisition clad in crimson robes, armed with flaming brands and scourges.

'You could have made an effort and put on a clean jacket, instead of that ratty old overcoat,' said May. 'You look like a character from *Toad of Toad Hall*.'

'This is Harris Tweed,' said Bryant, fingering a frayed

hole in his soup-stained sleeve. 'It was handed down to me by my grandfather.'

'Was that before or after he passed away?'

'Funny you should say that. He died in it. Gave himself a heart attack trying to get the lid off a jar of gherkins. My grandmother thought it was a pity to waste good fabric.'

A distorted tape loop of chanting monks began to play once more from hidden speakers, adding to the chamber's pervasive gloom.

May sighed. 'Of all the things you've put our unit through over the years, this has to be the strangest. Hosting a cocktail party in a house of horrors in order to catch a murderer. If you ever say a word about it in your memoirs, I'll kill you.'

'I didn't hear any better ideas from you,' Bryant reminded him cheerfully. 'This is absolutely our last chance to break the case. At midnight we'll be forced to unlock the doors and we'll lose everything, unless we can flush him out in the next hour. Keep your eyes peeled for anything unusual.'

May looked around at the kidnapped party guests, most of whom were glumly wedged between rotting corpses. 'Unusual,' he repeated, trying not to lose his temper.

Bryant sucked his celery stick thoughtfully. Somewhere above the stalactite-spiked arches of London Bridge station a train rumbled. The bricks trembled and soot sifted down. The shunting mingled with the thunder outside. Rain was pouring under the front door and pooling around the sodden shoes of the guests, all of whom were underdressed for the occasion. In the silences between rain, thunder and trains, May saw the group's breath condensing and imagined he could hear their teeth chattering. A waitress passed them, bearing a tray of bloody eyeballs on sticks. On closer inspection, these turned out to be dyed pickled onions.

'Masks,' said Bryant, apropos of nothing.

May turned to him. 'Explain?'

'They're all wearing masks. Look at them all nodding and drinking.' He waved his sausage at the partygoers. 'You wouldn't think we had to bring them here under sufferance and lock them in. They were as jumpy as cats when they arrived, but they're attempting to pretend that everything's normal. Middle-class people with upper-middle incomes. They come alive at parties, no matter how strange the circumstances. They discuss house prices and holidays and restaurants, and give opinions on the plays they've seen. But after all that's happened in the last few days, they know they've been brought here for another reason. What do you think is going on behind those forced smiles?'

'I imagine they're morbidly curious, the way people are about watching traffic accidents.'

'But they're careful to keep up the illusion of appearing unconcerned. An interesting phenomenon, isn't it?'

'That's the English for you,' said May, studying the gathered guests. 'We're great pretenders.'

'Yes, an odd mixture of exaggerated politeness and thoughtless cruelty. The true mark of English conversation is not being able to tell when you've been insulted. I think the more sophisticated society becomes, the more it hides behind the masks it manufactures.'

'Do we have to discuss this now, Arthur? We're on a bit of a deadline here.'

Bryant ignored his partner. 'It's just that we seem to be so good at hypocrisy. I always think when an Englishman says "We really must get together soon", he's telling you to piss off. We bury ourselves so deeply inside complex personas that it's amazing we remember who we really are. Which makes this room, for example, very hard to read. You know me, I don't play those games. I prefer honesty.'

'Yes, but you're downright rude to people,' retorted May. 'And I do know you. It's a class thing. This lot make you feel uncomfortable. You're from a working-class background. Your mother cleaned cinemas for a living. You hate the idea that one of the guests might get the better of you tonight.'

'No,' said Bryant firmly. 'I hate the idea that one of them thinks they can get away with murder.'

'Well, our legal priority over the investigation ends in exactly' – here May checked his Rolex – 'fifty-five minutes. You're cutting it a tad fine.'

'I know. We have to watch for the smallest signs, an odd look, any betrayal of emotion that might cause one of them to give the game away.'

'Arthur, an odd look isn't going to secure a conviction. We need concrete evidence before the clock strikes twelve.'

'Well, whose idea of a shindig was this?' said a tipsy blonde woman in a tight black Lycra dress that had made her tanned breasts rise like golden loaves. She turned her attention to May while ignoring his partner. It was her habit to address only men she found useful or attractive, a trait that made her thoroughly unlikeable.

'How did you get in?' asked Bryant. 'This is a private party. No riffraff allowed.'

Rudeness had no effect on Janet Ramsey. As the publisher of *Hard News*, the capital's gossip daily, she was used to having the door metaphorically slammed in her face. 'Actually, Uncle Fester, I'm here as a guest,' she rejoined airily. 'And you're up to something. I can smell it. I can see it on that old tortoise face of yours.'

'I'm surprised you can see anything through that face-lift,' Bryant harrumphed. 'If you print a single word about this, I'll send so many uniforms around to your office it'll look like you're staging *The Pirates of Penzance*.'

Ramsey gave him a blank look.

'There are a lot of over-zealous policemen in *The Pirates of Penzance*,' May explained to her.

'I don't know why you hang around with Rip Van Winkle here,' said Ramsey, walking frosted fingernails up May's lapel. 'He's holding you back, John. He always has. Tell me the truth. Give an old newspaper gal a break. What's this party all about? Why are the guests locked in? Why does everyone look so anxious? What exactly are you two up to?'

'You wouldn't believe me if I told you, Janet.'

'I recognize some of the people in this room.' She narrowed her false eyelashes at the assembly. 'This wouldn't have anything to do with the murders your unit has been investigating, would it?'

'You can't print conjecture,' May warned.

'I see the time has come to let you in on our little secret,' said Bryant, trying not to grimace as he took Ramsey's arm. 'Come with me and I promise all will be revealed.'

Ramsey knew she couldn't trust Bryant, but her curiosity got the better of her. She stumbled after him, into the chill shadows of the cobwebbed chamber. There was a short silence followed by a yelp and a clang of metal, and Bryant came back alone.

'What did you do?' asked May. 'Where's Janet?'

'I think I managed to spike her story,' he said cheerfully. 'I shut her in the Iron Maiden.'

'That thing's just a stage prop,' said May with a hint of regret. 'There are no sharpened nails on the inside of it.'

'Really?' Bryant's eyes widened in innocence. 'I had no idea. What a pity. I'll let her out after midnight.'

'OK, what do we do now?'

'We know that our killer is in this room. I just have to come up with a way of drawing him out.'

'You mean you haven't thought this through?'

'How could I? From the very first moment, this entire

investigation has been an unmitigated disaster. Nothing has gone according to plan.' Bryant peered up his sleeve. 'The little hand's fallen off my watch. How much time do we have left?'

'Fifty-two minutes. This is the last time all of our suspects will be in one room together. It's the only chance we have to put things right. We're so close now.'

'John, we're no closer than we were a week ago,' said Bryant. 'God, it feels like we've been working on this case for a lifetime. Come on.'

The pair set off into the penumbral chamber of horrors, determined to catch an impossible murderer. Last week had felt like a fresh beginning. Now they could see it might have been the beginning of the end.

2

CLAIRVOYANCE

'A fresh start!' said Raymond Land, striding into the Unit's smart new open-plan office in the warehouse at the corner of Caledonian Road. Over the weekend it had been painted arctic white and filled with furniture, admittedly secondhand, but it provided the staff with a pleasant communal space.

Land was pleased to see that the holes in the floor had been repaired. The workmen had almost finished redecorating the building. Broken windows had been replaced. There were no longer bare wires hanging down from the ceiling. There was a door on the toilet and a banister on the staircase. The coffee machine was finally working. The funny smell had gone from the Evidence Room. He slapped his hands together with an approximation of good cheer and beamed hopefully around the place.

His joy was not reciprocated.

'What are you so bloody happy about?' asked Jack Renfield, not bothering to look up. The sergeant was crunching indigestion tablets and checking his emails, attacking his keyboard with great bearlike paws.

Land looked pathetically expectant. 'It's the start of a new week, the sun's out, summer's on the way, nice new paintwork everywhere, we haven't been blamed for anything awful in nearly a month. Makes you feel glad to be alive.'

'There's a bad storm coming,' said Meera Mangeshkar. 'It's going to be chucking it down by noon. We'll have to put the lights on.'

Land felt he had every reason to be in a good mood. He and his wife, Leanne, were going on a sailing holiday around the Isle of Wight at the end of the week. His desk had already been cleared in readiness. His monthly budget had been met. The Home Office was leaving him alone. The crime figures were down. Only the staff seemed fed up, but they always looked like that when he came into the room. A more sensitive chap might almost doubt they were pleased to see him.

'Come on, you lot,' he jeered, 'perk yourselves up a bit. You should be thankful. You've got a nice new office, and the mean streets of King's Cross are quiet for once.'

'We'd rather be busy,' grumbled Mangeshkar, flicking a rubber band at the cat. Colin Bimsley was making a paper sculpture of a flamingo from old witness statements. Dan Banbury was reading *Forensic Analysis in the Home – Volume 4: Drains*.

Land found it hard to share Meera's sentiment. Being busy at the PCU usually meant risking his career, health and sanity. He still fantasized about running a police department in a sleepy Spanish village, the kind of place where the most exciting thing that ever happened was a cow wandering into a shop.

London was not much smaller than New York but averaged around 130 murders a year, compared with the Big Apple's rate of over 460 in the same period. Most of the London cases were handled by the CID, but the more troublesome crimes were reluctantly placed in the hands of the PCU. Raymond Land had inherited the worst of both worlds; the cases that the Home Office preferred the CID not to handle were the most awkward and unsolvable, and were also the least likely to win public praise for their solution. The PCU received no help from the Met divisions, which meant that they effectively operated in a vacuum.

Land liked order. He liked graphs and bar charts and Venn diagrams, and Excel spreadsheets of policing figures, even though he didn't really know how to use them. He didn't understand waffling academics and weirdos, and disorganization and mess, and strange, elliptical ideas that led to investigative dead ends.

He didn't understand the PCU.

Sticking his hands into his pockets, he wandered over to the window and sat on the ledge. 'I thought you'd all be happy,' he said plaintively. 'For once, everyone thinks we're doing a good job. You can take it easy. You don't have to spend the week going through someone's rubbish or sitting in a car all night staring at a front door. You can go home at the normal time, catch up on your emails, watch some telly, cook a meal that doesn't come in a plastic tub. For once, you can get on with your lives.'

But as soon as he said that, Land realized he had made a mistake. Working at the PCU meant surrendering all thoughts of a normal private life. It meant abandoning loved ones, working unsociable hours, falling out with friends, never having time to do the comfortingly habitual things civilians did. His staff barely existed beyond their working lives. Their refrigerators remained empty, their bills piled up, their houseplants died and their voice-mails were never played back. Even their pets gave up on them. Apart from a brief, disastrous stay at Raymond Land's house, Crippen had spent his entire nine lives in the office.

'Well, I feel good about today, and I'm not going to let you lot put the mockers on it,' Land said, rising and turning.

He looked back and found that suddenly everyone seemed to have brightened up a little. Perhaps his positivity had proved inspirational after all. Bimsley was trying to suppress a laugh. Meera was smiling and shaking her head. 'Right,' said Land, 'we're going to use this week to get organized and learn to behave like a proper police unit.' He looked down to discover a thick arctic-white stripe across the seat of his new black trousers. 'You can start by getting the workmen to stick a bloody Wet Paint sign on this ledge.'

Bimsley burst out laughing.

A dark thought crossed Land's mind. 'And where are Bryant and May?' he demanded to know.

'Look here, can somebody give me a hand with this?'

Bryant appeared in the doorway right on cue. If Land hadn't known better, he'd have suspected that his most senior detective had been waiting outside to make an entrance. Bryant moved to reveal a crimson-painted wooden case. It was about five feet tall and covered in cobwebs. 'I found her in the attic.'

'What is it?' asked Land. 'How did you get it down the stairs? Must you bring it in here?'

Bryant leaned against the case with a mischievous smile. He removed his battered trilby, leaving his hair standing in a frightened white tonsure. 'I hear we've got no work on – this is total disaster. What are you doing about the situation, Raymondo?'

'Don't you understand, Bryant, it's good news. Nobody's doing anything they shouldn't be doing.'

'Of course they are, it just means the Met are picking up the cases before they get to us, which will make us redundant.'

Redundant. Land rolled the word around in his head, savouring it. *Redundancy pay.* An image sprang to mind; he was lying in a beach hammock in the Maldives with Leanne serving him a cocktail in a coconut.

'So I suggest you get on the phone to your opposite number in Islington and find out how we can be of use,' Bryant was saying as he halfheartedly attempted to haul the case into the room.

'Here, Mr Bryant, let me give you a hand.' Colin Bimsley sprang up to help. Together they manoeuvred the dusty object into the centre of the floor. The box was on squealing casters, and the top half of one side was covered in filthy glass. Bryant pulled a large chequered handkerchief from his pocket, dipped it into Land's tea mug and, before the Unit chief could protest, started to wipe the window clean.

John May appeared from behind the case, patting cobwebs from his suit. 'I couldn't stop him once he'd seen it, Raymond,' he said apologetically. 'He had to bring it down here.'

'It's Madame Blavatsky,' Bryant proclaimed. 'Not a terribly good likeness I'll admit, but it's clearly meant to be her.'

Land sniffed at the box and recoiled. 'Who the hell is Madame— Who is she, and what's she doing in our attic?'

'Madame Blavatsky was a noble-born Russian spiritualist who founded the Theosophical Society. She was a Buddhist who believed in reincarnation and the spirit world. She died right here in London.'

'What the bloody hell's she doing upstairs?'

Bryant ignored him. 'Her followers thought she was steeped in the wisdom of the ancients, whereas I'm more of the opinion that she was a barking mad fascist, and a racist to boot. And she's been living in our attic for donkey's years. Remember I told you the history of this place? About Aleister Crowley's Occult Revivalists' Society of Great Britain using the building for their meetings until the 1930s? Well, I was up in the attic looking for my first edition of *Nachtkultur & Isolationism*, and found her under a blanket. There's all sorts of weird stuff up there, including a spirit horn and an electromagnetic field detector, the kind geologists used to use. They were popular in spiritualists' circles. I think there must have been many other occult societies here before Crowley's, because most of the stuff hasn't been touched for the best part of a century. We're at the centre of several ley lines, you know. They cross underneath our basement floor.'

'Are you sure this is something to do with our previous tenants?' asked Land suspiciously.

'Indubitably, old trout.'

Land thought for a moment. 'Is it worth anything?'

'Good Lord, it's not about the monetary value.' Bryant had conducted some research about the PCU's new home just after Raymond Land had discovered an alarming mural of a witchcraft ceremony hidden under the paintwork on his office wall. 'The Occult Revivalists' Society split from the Hermetic Order of the Golden Dawn and lived here with some ladies from the Lodge of the Isis-Urania Temple until they all fell out with each other. I think there was something saucy going on between them. The real Madame Blavatsky stayed here on her way to India, and the poet William Butler Yeats held his first séance in this building. It all turned nasty after Yeats materialized a terrifying spirit calling itself *Leo Africanus* in the room – right where you now have your desk, Raymond. Apparently the creature claimed to be Yeats's Daemon or Anti-Self, and threatened to kill everyone and drink their blood.'

Land looked appalled. Bryant was enjoying himself.

'Because of his experience, Yeats adopted the motto *Daemon est Deus inversus* – commonly translated as *The Devil is a God Reflected*. The occult order became a Satanist society in the Second World War, and it all ended very badly in the mid-1950s. I'm writing a brief monograph on the history of the building at the moment. I'll give you a copy when it's finished.'

Arthur Bryant, as you may have gathered by now, was capable of holding forth on virtually any subject for any amount of time. This made him initially interesting, then exhausting, and finally annoying. He had an aloof and self-contained manner, as if he never quite heard what most people said to him (and often he didn't, depending on whether his hearing aid was switched on).

His partner John May knew this, and was usually on hand to head him off from conversational culs-de-sac. But when the two of them were alone, Bryant could banter on about everything from geomancy to abrakophilia, and May would simply tune in and out of his friend's lectures, remembering to interject the odd 'yes', 'no' or 'really', because that was what old friends did.

The rest of the PCU had grown accustomed to his ramblings, but Bryant's erudition – albeit an erudition of the most abstruse kind – always made Raymond Land feel duped and dull-witted. He was convinced that Bryant deliberately tried to undermine his authority at every available opportunity. He was wrong about this; Bryant had no interest in power games. He simply soaked up knowledge and sprayed it back out, hoping to breed enthusiasm in others, like a gardener cultivating ideas instead of flowers.

May found some cleaning fluid and squirted it on a sponge, wiping away the grime on the glass. The round pug-nosed face of Madame Blavatsky slowly appeared. She was made of beige wax that had taken on the translucence of dead flesh. She had green eyes (one slightly sunken) and an ebony hair-clip, and was dressed in the grubby black crinolines of a dowager duchess. Her right fist was raised to her formidable bosom. She wore a cameo brooch and had golden earrings. Her hair looked suspiciously real.

Gladdened by the distraction, the staff moved in for a closer look.

'Have a shufti around the back, John,' Bryant instructed. 'There should be a plug somewhere.'

'There's just a lead with bare wires,' said May, crouching down.

'Well, stick them in the wall socket.'

'There are only two wires and there are three holes.'

'Jam a fork into the earth, that's what I do at home.'

'Wait – you're not going to plug that thing in here!' Land protested.

Too late. May flicked the switch and the case started buzzing. There was a smell of burning hair. Slowly the medium's eyes glowed into life. The figure was life-sized, constructed with what appeared to be opticians' glass eyes and cracked rubber lips.

'But what exactly is it?' asked Meera, who had been trying to look uninterested.

'I might be mistaken, but I believe she's an automaton. She tells your fortune,' said Bryant.

'We'll need an old penny,' said May. 'Anybody got one?'

'Don't be so ridiculous,' Land snapped. 'The government got rid of pounds, shillings and pence in 1971.'

'I've got one,' said Bryant, pulling a handful of illegal tender from his overcoat pocket. 'Let's see, a threepenny bit, a florin, a couple of conkers, half a crown – ah, here we are.'

May took the huge brown coin from him and inserted it in the slot at the front of the machine.

'You don't honestly think that ridiculous contraption is still going to work after all these years, do you?' Land stood back and folded his arms, refusing to be drawn in.

'Now give me your hand,' said Bryant, grabbing Land's wrist, 'and place it palm down on the brass panel.' The automaton was humming with errant electricity.

The rectangular plate beneath the wax figure was dotted with a hundred tiny holes. Unwilling to appear a spoilsport, Land placed his hand over it. Pins shot out of the holes in a ripple, stinging his fingers. 'Bloody hell!' Land shouted, trying to pull his hand free, but Bryant held it in place. He had a surprisingly strong grip.

The medium's eyes flickered more brightly and she jerked forward, as if trying to examine Land's palm. Inside the case, gears groaned and unoiled pistons squealed in discomfort. 'I'll get some WD-40 on that later,' said Bryant.

Land's hand was tingling – the metal pins had delivered a mild shock. 'I've just been electrocuted,' he complained dramatically.

'Yes, some automata do that,' said Bryant with interest. 'The Victorians thought it was very health-giving. Wait a minute.'

Madame Blavatsky's eyes dimmed, then flared. Her right arm swivelled forward and her fist partially opened to drop a white oblong card, which rattled into the slot at the front of the machine. Rubbing his fried hand, Land retrieved it and examined the stamped-out lettering.

DEATH WILL REPAY ALL DEBTS

'What kind of fortune is this?' he exclaimed.

'It's a paraphrased quote from *The Tempest*,' said John May. 'Even I know that.'

'Well, it's a bloody depressing thought for a Monday,'

Land said, tossing the card onto his desk. 'Get this thing out of here.'

'Fine,' said Bryant. 'I'll have it beside my desk.'

'Must you? The office is already starting to look like your old space in Mornington Crescent.'

'But of course. It's the contents of my head.'

'Well, it certainly contains the contents of a head, unless you've had the brainpan of that stinking Tibetan skull cleaned out.'

'No, I mean it acts as my excess memory. It contains all the things there's not enough room in my head to hold. Clutter, either mental or physical, is the sign of a healthy curiosity.'

As Bimsley began rolling the automaton towards the door under Bryant's guidance, Raymond Land looked back at his own bare office space and tried to figure out whether he had just been insulted again.

3

INDISCRETION

'Madame Blavatsky?' said May as they headed downstairs later to a newly opened tea shop just beneath the Unit. 'You're the last of your species, you know that, don't you? One day you'll be in your own glass case in a museum. Label: the London Eccentric, *Londinium insolitum*, shy, hardy, solitary worker, difficult to breed, uncomfortable out of its native habitat – an area extending no more than five miles either side of the Thames, liable to bite when provoked.'

'You missed out my key attribute,' said Bryant. 'My eidetic memory. It's unconventionally arranged, but more useful than any of your fancy computers. The world seems so intent on erasing its past that someone has to keep notes. That's why I'm good at my job. I make connections with my surroundings. It's like throwing jump leads into a junkyard and sparking off the things you find there. No one else can do that. It's why we're still in business.'

Bryant was being a little disingenuous, and knew it. In truth, his mental connections were extremely haphazard and just as likely to short out. Moreover, he was unable to function without his partner. John May was indeed the acceptable face of the PCU, friendly with officials, kind to staff, linked to the zeitgeist. May had never allowed himself to become an institutional officer, the kind who blankly processed criminals through the system. He believed in the innate decency of humankind, and Bryant's innocence kept his belief alive. Such an old-fashioned approach to teamwork was not encouraged in the league-table mentality of the new century.

'I want you to meet someone,' said Bryant, pushing open the door of the Ladykillers Café. The new tea shop had been named after the famous 1955 Ealing film that had been shot in the neighbourhood. It had begun life a few weeks earlier as a pop-up shop, but the owners, two sisters who dressed in identical postwar fashions, had taken up the lease and now served teas in a setting that perfectly replicated a period neither of them was old enough to remember. The girls were in their early twenties, and had adopted the café's styling as an ironic pose. Instead, they had attracted the wrong clientele: older locals who took the environment entirely at face value.

Bryant made his way to the blue Formica counter and studied the merchandise: Battenberg cake, quiche Lorraine, Bath and Banbury buns under glass.

'Hello,' said one of the girls, 'can we help you? I'm Brenda and this is Yvonne.'

'That seems highly unlikely,' said Bryant rudely. 'Those are working-class names and judging by your accents your families are from the stockbroker belt, Thames Valley, probably. Any blue-collar customer would find your prices outrageous.'

Yvonne looked at Brenda nervously.

'It's all right,' May explained to them, 'that means he likes you. We're from the police unit upstairs. I'm Mr May and this is Mr Bryant. A pot of English Breakfast tea and a couple of those buns, thanks.'

Now the girls studied the men; appearances had proved deceptive in both directions. 'There's a lady over there waiting for you,' said Yvonne. The pair set about serving.

'Anna Marquand is editing my memoirs,' replied Bryant, waving an ebony walking stick in the direction of a thin, oval-faced woman of around thirty-five, seated alone at the furthest table.

'I thought your editor was male,' said May as they made their way over.

'I had to fire that one. He accused me of being inconsistent. I told him it wasn't true, because he had annoyed me from the outset, so we parted company. Anna was recommended by my old friend Dr Harold Masters, at the British Museum. She called to tell me she's got proofs of my first volume of memoirs. I thought you might like to meet her.'

May was slightly puzzled by this, as his partner rarely asked him to meet friends. Anna Marquand rose and removed her pink plastic spectacles, shaking their hands with an air of grave formality.

'Anna transcribes for the historians in the Classical Studies department, and freelances for Icarus, the specialist publishing house that has taken the book. Anna, this is my partner at the PCU, John May.'

'You're younger than I was led to believe,' Anna remarked as they seated themselves.

'You were doubtless expecting someone more decrepit,' said May.

'Well, Mr Bryant's description—' She stopped awkwardly, then dug into her plastic shopping bag. 'I have the finished text, Mr Bryant. They told me it's not likely to be a big print run, but it's going to be a nice-looking volume.'

'Hopefully the first of three,' Bryant beamed, thumbing through the proofs.

'Wait, let me see,' said May, snatching it away. 'Where does this go up to?'

'It's not chronological; rather it's a selection of our more eccentric cases,' said Bryant carefully. 'I've covered the Leicester Square Vampire, that business with the Belles of Westminster, the Deptford Demon, the Shepherd's Bush blowtorch murders and the hunt for the Odeon Strangler.'

'I'm afraid I had to take out some of the more politically sensitive passages,' said Anna apologetically. 'Your boss was very concerned about showing the Home Office in a bad light. Also, I checked with a lawyer and found that three of the sections fell foul of the Official Secrets Act. I excised those, but I couldn't make all the minor changes you wanted. I mean, you sent me an awful lot of revisions, and many of them contradicted each other. There simply wasn't time to include them all, and the deadline was so tight—'

'There's nothing in here that's going to upset anyone, is there?' asked May, riffling the pages. His partner had a reputation for being appallingly indiscreet.

Anna Marquand glanced uncertainly at Bryant. 'Well, um, there are one or two passages that could be construed—'

'What has he said? Arthur, what did you put in this book?'

'So many sections were blue-pencilled and then re-inserted that I don't honestly remember,' Bryant admitted. 'But I think I mentioned Raymond's wife.'

'What did you say about Leanne Land?'

'I might have pointed out that she was having an affair with her flamenco instructor. But I only did it to explain why Raymond was going bald and was so hopelessly inefficient at work.'

'Mr Land wanted to read it for himself,' Anna explained, 'so I sent him the section on disc.'

'Oh, Arthur,' May admonished. 'Did it never occur to you to spare Raymond's feelings?'

'Not really, no.'

'When did you do this, Anna?' asked May.

'About a week ago.'

'Then there's still time to get it back. Raymond's not good with books. He virtually moves his lips as he reads. He probably hasn't got around to looking at it. You two stay here. I'll go back and find it. It was very nice meeting you, Anna.'

'I didn't mean to cause any trouble,' said Anna when May had gone. Bryant looked at her anxious brown eyes and his heart softened. He could see her history laid out before him as neatly as parts in a model aircraft kit. Erudite and quick-witted but nervous and lacking in confidence, afflicted with apology, generous but broke, partnerless, the renter of a small flat in Stepney or Bermondsey, a solitary drinker, underpaid and underappreciated, she was probably still dominated by her mother.

All this could be easily read by anyone with a vaguely Holmesian turn of mind. Anna Marquand's plastic shopping bag was from a cheap supermarket usually situated at the wrong end of a high street, where the rents were lower. In the bag he could see a loaf of white processed bread and a half-litre of Gordon's gin – if she lived with a partner, she'd probably have bought a full-sized bottle. There was also a packet of menthol cigarettes in there, but Anna wasn't a smoker. Not a man's brand, but one popular with older women starting to worry about their health. She had recently given money to charity – there was a sticker from the National Society for the Prevention of Cruelty to Children on her jacket. There was also a slim paperback of Robert Browning's poetry collection *Men and Women* in the pocket. Her hair was a mess and the ballpoint pen she had laid on the table was badly chewed. There was something inexplicably South London about her. Bryant wanted to clasp her hands and tell her to be as strong as she felt inside.

'I can't stay long, I'm afraid,' she told him. 'Since my father died I've been looking after my mother, and she doesn't like to be left alone. Our area – well, there's been trouble before. You said you didn't want to keep the original notes and documents, so once I'd inputted them I made a single copy on disc and wiped my hard drive. I usually just return the material, because I don't like to leave potentially sensitive documents lying around on an old computer somewhere.' She removed a clear plastic slipcase from her shopping bag and handed it to him.

'Have you got a pen?' Bryant asked. 'I'll forget what it is otherwise.' She handed him a felt-tip and he scribbled his name across the disc's label. 'Mind you, I'm just as liable to leave it on the bus. I got a terrible ear-bashing for losing the cremated remains of our coroner.'

'I keep a safe at home. My academics are paranoid about their work, so I always shred their annotated copies once I've retyped them and file away my version. You'd be surprised what I get sent – Ministry of Defence work, big oil companies . . . I feel like a spy sometimes. Except it's mostly boring technical stuff. I enjoyed doing your book, though. A breath of fresh air for me.'

'Then perhaps you'd better keep hold of this.' Bryant handed the disc back. 'Your hands are clearly safer than mine.'

Anna rose to go. 'I must be heading home. My mother will worry.'

'Well, I'll see you at the launch party. I mean, it'll just be a drink in a scruffy old pub, but—'

'I'd like that very much.'

'So would I,' said Bryant, offering up such a genuine smile that his false teeth nearly fell out.

On his way back up to the office, he realized he had really taken quite a shine to Miss Marquand, and decided he would try to find a way to help her. Perhaps Raymond Land could be persuaded to employ her in some freelance capacity – provided he didn't stumble across her exposure of his wife's extramarital sex life first.

4

ATMOSPHERICS

'There's nothing more exhausting than an entire roomful of people calling each other *darling*,' declared Mona Williams. The veteran actress cast a jaded eye around the crowded penthouse apartment. 'God, when I was in Brecht's *Caucasian Chalk Circle* the conversation was a bloody sight more enlivening than tonight's, and I was playing a goat farmer. Is there any more red wine?'

'They've probably run out. You know how cheap our host is. Oh, he's clever, of course, but so unbearably common.' Neil Crofting ran a hand ineffectually around the crown of his head, a habit he had lately picked up to indicate that his hair was real, although everyone knew it was not. Before curtain-up it sat on a false head in his dressing room and was carefully brushed prior to every performance. Neil and Mona had once been a successful song and dance double act, but by the eighties they were cajoling uninterested punters through lounge sets in third-rate supper clubs. They continued to audition with grim dignity, but now listed only Shakespeare and Noel Coward roles on their CVs. After her third drink, Mona would reminisce about the time Olivier coached her through 'Gertie' in *Hamlet*. After his third drink, Neil would reach for a fourth.

'What time do you make it?'

Mona squinted at a tiny gold watch. 'Eight-thirty. I shan't be staying late. I'm voice-coaching in the morning, teaching a class of Essex girls not to use glottal stops. They hardly need elocution to work in nail salons, but the money's good.'

The vast semicircular lounge had a sweeping curve of glass overlooking the Palladian streets below Trafalgar Square. All along the blue silk back wall were arranged dozens of theatre souvenirs: playbills, autographed headshots, programmes and props. At any one time there were over two hundred plays booking in London, and their convoluted histories were well represented here. The Duchess, the Duke of Yorks, Wyndhams, the Garrick, the Aldwych. Gielgud, Olivier, Richardson and Bernhardt, they all smiled down at the guests. There were Indonesian silhouettes and Chinese shadow puppets, Italian harlequins and French Guignol dolls.

On one side of the lounge door stood a grotesque cast-iron minstrel that grinned and rolled its eyes when fed coins. On the other side was a Jolly Jack Tar in a wooden case. The Victorian seaside amusement was a museum piece that seemed designed for the specific purpose of giving children nightmares. Its skin was just plaster, its rictus smile mere painted wood, but it looked leathery and cancerous, like an embalmed corpse. When a ten-pence piece was inserted, it rocked back and forth squealing with laughter while a crackly organ recording of 'I Do Like to Be Beside the Seaside' played. The sailor grinned and eyed the guests from the side of its moulting head, as if to say *I know what you're up to*.

It was, everyone agreed, an extraordinary apartment.

But then, it belonged to an extraordinary man, the host of this evening's event.

'I used to love the theatre,' Mona Williams said. 'So many British playwrights wrote eloquently about the human condition. Griffiths, Ayckbourn, Brenton, Nichols, Barnes – they created proper parts for real women, but where are those parts now? These days I'll settle for a play that's got a practical meal in the first half and a sofa in the second, so long as it's closer to the West End than Harrow-on-the-Hill.'

Always bitching, thought Neil Crofting wearily. *She's hardly been off the stage all her acting life, and still she complains about being hard done by. The West End is full of dreadful old musicals starring teenagers from TV talent shows. She should be glad she's still working.*

A dull rumble of thunder tinkled the glasses on the sideboard, like an approaching earthquake. A moment later, rain drummed against the great windows of the penthouse. The conversation lowered its volume for a moment, as if in respect to the gods above.

A knife rang out against the side of a delicate Lady Hamilton wineglass.

'Ladies and gentlemen, if I could have your attention for a moment.'

The host, Robert Julius Kramer, glared at the room's inhabitants until they became more stilled by him than by the storm outside. 'Thank you all so much for joining me here tonight in celebration of our first production, *The Two Murderers*. As you know, we took the unprecedented step of providing the critics with a special matinee today, in order to guarantee simultaneous reviews for the production. So far their advance comments have been, shall we say, *unequivocal*.' A ripple of uneasy laughter pulsed through the room; the reaction of the critics as they filed glumly out into a miserable afternoon on the Strand had been absolutely horrific. 'However, our producer, Gregory Baine, has just handed me a spreadsheet of the advance bookings, and I can safely say that we already have a guaranteed three-month run ahead of us. A clear indication that the public has much better taste than the critics.'

Everyone turned around and stared at the critics in the room, who squirmed awkwardly. When it came to creating nervous tension, the party's host was a master of his art.

'It matters not,' Kramer continued, 'because there's always a new *Hamlet* at the National for the critics to enjoy, and there's always something in the West End to please the sensation-seekers, so everybody wins. Although I'd happily stage Shakespeare with pole dancers if I thought it would get more bums on seats. I'm a showman, not an intellectual.'

'You can say that again,' murmured Mona.

The embarrassed amusement turned to forced applause. Kramer air-patted his congregation back into obedient attention. 'As you know, my plan is to establish a permanent company at this theatre, starring in at least three repertory productions throughout the next winter season, four if we can manage it. And I am pleased to announce that we will begin casting for the second of these productions within the next few weeks. I'd like to thank our wonderful leads, Della Fortess and Marcus Sigler; my producer, Gregory Baine; our director, Russell Haddon, who has guided us through perilous seas; our brilliant set designer, Ella Maltby; our genius writer, Ray Pryce; and especially my lovely wife, Judith, whose handbag habit requires that I continue working later in life than I had intended. Oh, and to the critics here who were happy to take our bribes, stay and enjoy your free champagne. Now, I'd like you to charge your glasses to *The Two*

Murderers – long may they continue to bring death and destruction to the West End.'

'*The Two Murderers!*' Thirty-five champagne flutes were raised aloft, and the casual conversation resumed, more excited than it had been before.

'I notice we didn't warrant a mention.' Mona Williams sniffed. 'My agent told me I'd be required for the second lead, not a character part. I shall have a word with Robert about that.'

'Perhaps you should have a word with your agent,' said Neil Crofting, turning aside to talk to a spectacularly endowed young lady who was shaking herself out of a wet jacket.

The thunder rumbled, and a sharp crack of lightning turned the room into a dazzling tableau. The wall puppets stared down at the crowd with shining dead eyes. The room unfroze and glanced uneasily towards the windows. Chatter faltered. The storm had moved directly overhead.

'I haven't seen you before.' Crofting directed his attention to the attractive girl who had just arrived. 'I take it you're not part of our disreputable production.'

'Not yet, no,' replied the girl, smiling pleasantly. 'Mr Kramer hired me to start on Monday as the ASM.'

'But we already have an assistant stage manager,' said Crofting.

'She's leaving to have a baby?' The girl looked at this pair of old actors as if she were their carer. Crofting noticed that she inflected her sentence upwards, as so many young people did these days. He vaguely recalled seeing an assistant stage manager hovering in the background, complaining about the players' timekeeping habits, and struggled to conjure up a face. The stage manager, a hateful old haystack called Barnesly, gave the impression that he detested actors, and never socialized with them. 'You know, I never even realized she was pregnant. She's so thin. The director drives us all so hard that we never get time to eat. I'm Neil Crofting.' He held out his hand and waited for a glimmer of recognition from the girl to show that she had seen him in the BBC's recent Sherlock Holmes series, but none came. Admittedly, it had only been a small part.

'Gail Strong.' She shook his hand and peered over his shoulder, already anxious to move on.

'Well, I daresay we'll be seeing a lot of each other in the weeks ahead – welcome aboard.' But Gail Strong had already slipped away.

'She was in a rush,' he complained to Mona. 'The young always are, aren't they?'

'Only when you talk to them,' said Mona, draining her red wine. 'Don't you think there's an odd feeling in here tonight?'

'What do you mean?' Crofting was immune to sensitivities. In his experience, most actresses went mad after they hit fifty and started believing in all sorts of New Age rubbish.

Mona sniffed and studied the guests. 'Is there any trouble among the cast that you're aware of? Apart from the usual old bollocks, I mean.'

'Not that I know of. Why?'

'There's a bad atmosphere in the room. A kind of tension. I don't like it.'

'Storms always put people on edge.'

'Only if you're doing Regent's Park open-air theatre. No, this is something else. It's hard to explain. You truly don't feel it?'

'No. Honestly, Mona, I don't know why you can't just relax and enjoy yourself like everyone else, instead of worrying about – atmospherics. Not everything has to be theatrical, you know. Shakespeare was wrong. All the world is not a stage, not really.'

As if to disprove him, an immense bellow of thunder sounded, like a tumble of boulders rolling across the roof. A woman shrieked and Mona started, but the shriek turned into a laugh.

'You must learn to accept, Neil, that some people are more sensitive than others. We all feel things differently. The older we get, the thinner the wall between life and death becomes.' Mona was suddenly serious. 'I can sense when someone is about to die.'

'And you can sense that now? You can feel death in the air tonight?' Crofting looked around. 'Who's giving you this feeling? Where is it coming from?'

Mona glanced down at her shoes and shook her head. 'I don't know. Everyone's being thoroughly ill-tempered; they're just pretending things are fine. Robert's over there saying hateful things about his first wife. Our writer is talking about moving to Australia where the money is apparently better. I overheard Russell complaining that he thought everyone's performances were off this afternoon.'

'Oh, he's just the director. Everyone ignores him.'

'I'm sorry – take no notice of me, darling. It's been a long day. I didn't think the matinee went especially well. Marcus was put out when that woman's mobile went off, did you notice? He lost a whole page in the fourth scene. He doesn't seem to care that it throws the rest of us off.'

'You know matinees never get the reaction they're supposed to. It didn't help to look out and see a row of critics sitting there making notes. I wonder if Robert really did try to bribe them. I wouldn't put it past him.'

'Do you mind if I sit down for a minute? I'm tired and it's hot in here.'

'Really? I was just thinking how oddly cold it was,' Crofting replied. 'There's a draught coming from somewhere.'

'Someone just walked over your grave,' said Mona, raising her glass. 'Be a darling and get me another drink, would you?'

5

OMINOUS

The great glass lounge cast a buttery glow across the street. The Kramers' two-storey penthouse apartment occupied a key position on Northumberland Avenue, the elegant, underused thoroughfare that extends south of Trafalgar Square towards the Embankment. The terraced floor of ground-to-ceiling glass was topped with a minstrel gallery and four en suite bedrooms. The views took in the London Eye and the Royal Festival Hall. There were few more desirable properties in central London.

Robert Julius Kramer, the host, was a self-made man who had come up with the bright idea of buying all the private car parks that had existed on former bomb sites around the city. The sites had made fortunes for their owners in the postwar years, until the city's public transport system improved and London's congestion charge kicked in.

Kramer realized that the old property rights were mostly still attached to these derelict open spaces and warehouses, so he applied for planning permission to erect office buildings, offsetting his costs with funding provided by city regeneration schemes. He had become a millionaire before his twenty-fifth birthday, and celebrated the occasion by informing his loyal girlfriend that he was now rich and was dumping her. That was when he added the name Julius. Now he was in his forties, and his second wife, Judith, had recently given birth to their first son.

Beneath the building's portico, the liveried doorman glanced out at turbulent clouds and watched lightning crack the sky apart. All thirty-five of Robert Kramer's guests had been checked against his list. No one had failed to show up, even on a night like this. From what he'd heard, they wouldn't dare to stay away if they valued their jobs. He settled back in the doorway to await their intoxicated departures.

Up in the penthouse, Gail Strong, the new ASM, was working the other side of the room. Robert Kramer had suggested she should come along and meet everyone, but they were all wrapped up in private conversations. She passed a broad-shouldered man with a luxuriant cascade of glossy black hair and heard someone call him Russell, so that had to be Russell Haddon, the play's director. Pretty fit, but he was wearing a flashy wedding ring. She spotted an anxious-looking, bespectacled but oddly pretty young man with thin blond hair and a reticent attitude, seated alone beside the food display.

'Hi, I'm Gail Strong, do you know anyone here?' she asked, sitting down beside him. For a moment he seemed not to hear. When he turned to study her with faraway eyes, something prompted her to ask, 'Are you OK?'

'No, not exactly,' he replied, breathing out. 'I hate being here.'

'I grew up accompanying my parents to parties like this almost every night. My father—'

'—is the Public Buildings Minister. I know who you are. You've been in the papers quite a lot lately.' He removed his glasses and wiped them. He had tiny black eyes, like a mouse. 'I'm Ray Pryce. Pleased to meet you.'

'I've just joined the company as the new ASM?'

'Then we'll be working together.'

'Cool – I'll be the one fining you when you're late for rehearsals. What do you do?'

'I'm the writer.'

'Oh, my God, I'm like so embarrassed!' She threw her hands to her face. 'I thought you were one of the cast. You're so young. I saw the dress rehearsal of *The Two Murderers* last week. I thought it was totally amazing?'

She had a way of moving her hands around her face that made him think of a deaf person signing. She had the studied elegance of a model. He fell for her, trying not to remember that everyone who met her fell in love – at first.

'The critics don't seem to agree with you.' A note of annoyance crept into his voice. 'There's an old Chinese proverb: *Those who have free seats at a play hiss first*.'

'Oh, who cares about them? You heard what Mr Kramer said, it's a critic-proof show.'

'*He* doesn't seem to think so.' Ray Pryce pointed through the gathering at a portly, bald man in his late thirties who was attacking a plate of salmon sandwiches. 'That's Alex Lansdale; he's the theatre reviewer for *Hard News*. One of the critics Kramer couldn't buy.'

'I hate that paper. Their photographer took a picture of me coming out of the Ivy and said I was drunk, but I'd just broken my heel.' In fact, Gail had broken her heel *because* she was drunk, but she felt it was important to rail against the gutter press whenever possible.

'Lansdale wrote an incredibly insulting piece about the play even before the New Strand Theatre held its press event. Nobody does that; it breaks a longstanding un-spoken rule of the West End. Now he has the nerve to turn up here for the party. If I was the host I'd have him thrown out. After all, Robert Kramer holds more power in this room than everyone else put together. The rest of us are just his players, but at least we're here because we have skills. Theatre critics are just wannabes.'

'Yeah, well, it gives you all a common enemy.'

'We already have a common enemy.' Pryce glared in the direction of a smarmy-looking City type with slicked reddish hair and a supercilious smirk. 'Gregory Baine. The producer.'

'I'll never remember who everyone is,' said Gail.

'It doesn't matter – you'll soon get to know them, trust me.'

'What's the problem with him?'

'Baine stopped our salaries and put us on a profit-share, says it's better for us that way. He and Robert know they'll be able to fiddle the books and prove the show hasn't made enough money to pay us scale. We should never have signed our contracts, but I guess we were all desperate to work. What about you?'

'I'm really an intern. This is my first professional job. I haven't worked in a West End production before. My father thought it would be a good way of keeping me out of the papers for a while.'

'Well, don't expect to be recompensed for your labours.'

'I guess Robert Kramer has plenty of money,' said Gail, looking around. 'This is a pretty cool penthouse.'

'He bought the New Strand Theatre outright in order to indulge his hobby. Owners don't use their own cash for shows any more.'

Gail didn't have much of an attention span, and Pryce was already beginning to bore her. 'What else have you written?'

'This is my first full-length play. I took it to Robert because I was sure he'd buy it. The subject matter suits him down to the ground.'

'It's about betrayal, seduction and murder.'

'Exactly.' He threw her a meaningful look, then turned away.

'Well, I was looking forward to working here,' said Gail, annoyed with Ray Pryce for painting such a gloomy picture of her future. 'I'm going to get myself a drink.'

Glad to be away from the archetypically angry playwright, Gail allowed her champagne to be topped up and took small sips from the glass as she watched the room. Robert Kramer had issued his guests with a warning that no photographs were to be taken at the party. The door security had taken their mobile phones, as if they couldn't be trusted to follow instructions.

Mona Williams had been ignored by the waiter and was forced to head for the bar, where she poured herself a large glass of appallingly bitter red wine. Her companion seemed to have disappeared, so she stood admiring a framed set of Victorian music hall posters: Marie Lloyd in her torturous corset and feathered hat, Little Titch leaning forward on his elongated boots, Vesta Tilley, George Robey and Harry Champion photographed against Elysian backdrops. The apartment was a shrine to the world of artifice.

Mona wondered how Kramer's new wife coped with it all. The woman clearly had no interest in the theatre. She seemed a class above him. It was hard to imagine why she should have married such a man, if it wasn't for his money. He was physically unattractive, loud and apparently brutish in his treatment of females. But Judith had given him a son, something Kramer had craved for a long time.

Nearby, the object of Mona's thoughts, the theatre owner's new young wife, was attempting to discuss the earlier performance with Marcus Sigler and Della Fortess, the show's two leads.

Marcus was absurdly handsome, and knew it. He had positioned himself opposite a wall mirror, and had trouble avoiding its gaze. The atmosphere between the three of them seemed uncomfortable. Mona assumed this was partly because Judith Kramer had influence over her husband and could impose upon him to get rid of anyone she disliked, and the others knew it. But she suspected it was also because Judith knew absolutely nothing about the stage apart from the shows of Andrew Lloyd Webber, whom she adored, and therefore had nothing to bring to the conversation – not that this stopped her from holding court.

Mona studied the trio more carefully. The leading lady was staring hard into her martini. The leading man was looking at their hostess in ill-disguised pain. Had they all just had an argument?

Mona stepped a little closer and listened.

Judith Kramer had clearly said something that had upset the other two. And in trying to put it right, she had changed the subject by doing something unthinkable: she was discussing *Macbeth*. You simply didn't mention the Scottish play in front of the company. Marcus Sigler was looking particularly uncomfortable.

A huge peal of thunder, the loudest yet, made everyone jump. Mona's glass leapt in her hand and she spilled a little on the pristine white carpet. She glanced guiltily down at the scarlet splash of Rioja and could not help noticing that it looked like blood.

The skin prickled on her bare forearms. It felt like an omen of something terrible about to happen.

6

FRACTURE

Anna Marquand hated the litter-strewn alleyway. It ran behind Jamaica Road to the back of her terrace and was the fastest way to get from Bermondsey tube station to her back door. The problem was that she had to pass the sons and daughters of the Hagans.

The Hagans were a four-generation criminal family who lived in the street's corner house. They often hung around at the mouth of the alley, watching and waiting for trouble to ignite. Three hard little girls with angry, feral faces and armour-plate attitude, two dim-eyed drug-flensed brothers in baggy bling and a morbidly obese child of indeterminate sex. They lurked in varying combinations depending on the night, as if on sentry duty.

The oldest boy worried Anna the most. His eyes followed her from beneath the arch of his baseball cap, defying her to return his stare. Anna had always presumed herself immune from the attention of men, but Ashley Hagan made a point of noticing her. He licked his lips as she passed.

'Don't be intimidated,' said her mother. 'They're all bad

apples, those Hagans, flashing their drug money around and behaving like they own the street. The old man used to sell stolen goods after the war, and now his great-grandchildren are still doing it. The police never touched them, not then, not now.' But it was easy for Rose to say; she never went out any more, and waited at the window, watching for her daughter to arrive with the groceries.

Tonight the alley looked grey and empty. Two of the streetlights were out. Anna had a very good reason for not wanting to meet any of the Hagans. A week earlier she had argued with Bunny, the youngest daughter, over the McDonald's containers that were nightly discarded on her back doorstep. The conversation had quickly escalated into threats from all three sisters, who had warned that they would stab her if she complained again. In one respect Anna's mother was right: going to the police was likely to exacerbate the problem, so for a week she had avoided the alley.

But now a storm was breaking overhead and she had no umbrella, so she had taken the shortcut.

And someone was walking fast behind her.

She knew that looking back would represent an acknowledgement and continued to face forwards, but increased her pace.

Ahead, an unruly spray of buddleia had sown itself into the masonry in a thicket, the dense panicles of its pink flowers laden with raindrops. As she skirted around it her shoes slipped on the paving stones, nearly tipping her over. It took a concentration of balance to right herself and continue. The sharp footsteps behind briefly stopped, then quickened, closer now.

The Hagan girls always wore grubby pink tracksuits and trainers – a man, then, but which one of them? Someone in shoes, so an older member of the family. Anna told herself this knowledge was a safety mechanism, not paranoia, and that there was no reason to be afraid. As she walked, she located her house keys. She clutched them tightly in her right hand, swinging her shopping in the left.

Nearly home now.

She had reached the back door of number 14 Hadley Street, had unlocked it and dropped the keys in her shopping bag when she felt a sharp tug on the handles. In the four years she had lived with her mother in Bermondsey, she had twice been mugged for her mobile. She wasn't about to lose another one, so she yanked back hard and felt the plastic bag stretching.

It was like pulling a Christmas cracker and knowing you had the half without the toy inside. She did not want to see into his eyes, in the same way that you would not stare at a dangerous animal. He was just waiting for something to fracture.

This was what life had become for Anna – an endless tug-of-war between her mother, her employers, the government, even strangers in the street. Suddenly sick of it, she let go. Let him keep the damn groceries.

The move caught her mugger by surprise. The bag dropped between them and was quickly snatched up by unseen hands. Anna dared to raise her eyes and look. Through splinters of rain she saw a baseball cap, a black jacket, a pale face lost to shadow.

The neon panel above the back door flicked on, casting a harsh mausoleum light; her mother must have heard the commotion and come into the kitchen. Anna used the moment to throw herself inside the house, locking the door behind her. She stood behind the barred glass and listened, her heart thumping, but heard nothing. Surely he should have run off?

'Call the police,' said her mother, but Anna knew there would be no point. Instead, she instructed Rose to go back to the lounge. She stood in the middle of the kitchen waiting for her pulse rate to drop. Then she did what so many British do after a moment of crisis. She made herself a strong cup of tea.

The rain fell harder, rattling the gutters and spattering the windows. Anna sat in the bright, empty kitchen with her steaming mug and tried not to think about anything. Her doctor had shown her how to do this whenever she was stressed. Now, though, something made her rise – a drop in the wind, a sudden silence – and she needed to see.

Quietly, slowly, she opened the back door and looked out. Her spilled shopping bag was still on the step. Gathering it up, she brought it inside. Her wallet, work folders, shopping – it was all intact.

The only things missing were her mobile phone and her keys.

7

ENTROPY

Gail Strong glanced at her watch. Eight forty-five p.m. It was too early to leave the party. She had no intention of going home yet. Her father was still furious with her for skipping the Irish embassy dinner at Grosvenor House and staying out all night, and the atmosphere in the house was frostbitten. Besides, she wanted to have some fun. She was feeling horny.

She looked around the penthouse lounge for available men and found the pickings pretty slim. It was a theatre crowd; surely they were meant to be attractive?

There were two cute young actors handling the play's smallest roles, but they were obviously gay, and the only other members of the cast she hadn't met were women. The stage doorman was ancient, at least forty-five, and the show's producer looked like a total creep. A group of dull men in off-the-rack suits were clearly bankers. One of the waiters was quite fit but – well, a waiter.

Which just left the lead, Marcus Sigler, who was in his mid-twenties and totally hot. But he was still talking to Della Fortess, his leading lady, the one with the big sixties-style hair and the false eyelashes like garden rakes. At least they had managed to ditch the theatre owner's wife, who was now having one of those don't-let-every-one-see-we're-arguing conversations with her husband.

Gail headed across to the windows overlooking the length of Northumberland Avenue and watched the rain coursing down the glass. Marcus was standing directly behind her. She glanced at his reflection and noticed that he was wearing low-cut Dsquared jeans and a River Island khaki T-shirt that showed off his muscular arms. She could price a man's wardrobe from thirty paces. She wondered if he was screwing someone here – there were quite a few attractive single girls in the room.

Four old guys in D&G suits and patent leather Ferragamo shoes were hanging around by the door, eyeing the ladies lasciviously; they were obviously backers, and had been invited along out of politeness or because the director wanted to squeeze more money out of them. She had seen their type lurking around near her father at official functions so often that she could tell what kind of watches they would be wearing.

She knew she was looking good. She had great legs, and the tight little black skirt always caught men's eyes. As she adjusted it, she noticed water pooling around the base of the window, coming through a seam in the glass. Moments later it had enveloped the left heel of Marcus's trainers.

'Oh my God,' she said, touching him on the back, 'your shoes are getting wet.'

He turned around, and now she caught the full effect of his eyes, a startling ocean green. He stared at her in surprise and looked down, lifting his feet from the water. 'Hey, a bit of a leak. Thanks. I guess it's hardly surprising with this weather.'

'I'm Gail Strong. I just joined the company.' She shook his hand.

He smiled. 'I'm—'

'I know who you are. I saw you when you took over the role of Emmett in *Legally Blonde*. You have a great singing voice.'

'Well, thank you.'

'I went twice, actually. Had a bit of a crush on you.'

'Did you now.' Marcus had a soft Irish accent that made her melt. His smile widened. 'I'm glad you could make it tonight. Are you having fun?'

'Not really, no. I don't know anyone.'

'Well, it's a bit of a meet-and-greet for the investors, but these things have to be done. I guess if you're here it means that Robert Kramer has just employed you.'

'He's taking a chance. I'm standing in as ASM.'

They chatted easily for a few minutes. 'Actually,' Marcus confided, 'I'm dying for a cigarette. It's because I've got a drink in one hand. They go together.'

'God, me too, I'm gagging. I think I saw a fire escape on the way in. I was wondering if it's protected from the rain. I just had my hair done.'

'Come on then,' he said, brushing his fingers against the back of her hand.

That was when she knew she had him.

They found their way to the back of the room, then out into a corridor that led to the rear exit.

Marcus pushed open the fire escape door and stepped out. Rain sprayed through the diamond grating of the black iron staircase above them. It cascaded down the brickwork, rumbled through pipes, bounced from gutters and thrashed into drains, as if the world had sprung a leak and was subsiding into aquatic depths. The building had once been offices, but had been carved into residential apartments. The dead windows of other offices looked down on them, but everyone had gone home hours ago.

They had slunk from the party like thieves, propping

open the door with an empty cigarette carton in case it closed and locked them out. Marcus sat on the stairs and inhaled deeply, funnelling blue smoke up into the damp air. 'I love it,' he said. 'Anyone who tells you they don't is a liar. All that attention – of course acting is an ego trip.'

He handed the joint back. Gail had found it in her bag. She had got it from a Spanish waiter at an embassy dinner the week before. Her father would kill her if he thought she was smoking dope, which was why she always asked the waiters where she could score.

'But you'll be playing a murderer every night. How do you get the audience to like you?'

'That's an interesting question,' said Marcus. 'Of course, every night is different. You never know who you'll get in. I was in California last summer and I saw this teenage girl being interviewed on television. She had burned down her parents' house one night because they wouldn't let her watch her favourite TV programme, something like *The X-Factor*. They had died of smoke inhalation and she'd been arrested on suspicion of murder. And this is the terrible part – I remember thinking she was really sexy, even though she was probably a killer. It was the way she looked straight into the camera, and I could tell she was enjoying the attention. She'd realized she could become a celebrity. And she did when the interview appeared on YouTube. She got offered all kinds of modelling jobs. That's the thought I hold onstage. Plus, I keep the top three buttons of my shirt open.'

Gail sucked on the joint, held the searing smoke in her lungs and tried not to cough as she exhaled. 'I think you're a little too pretty to make a convincing real-life murderer,' she said finally. 'But you're very good in the role.'

Marcus reached forward and slipped his hand around her waist. 'I think you're too pretty, too.' A moment later, she moved forward between his jeans-clad legs and kissed him, pressing down hard on his open mouth. Unbuttoning his jeans, she climbed the step and lowered her bare thighs onto his as the rain fell with renewed vigour.

Back at the party, Robert Kramer had noticed the water coming in through the window frame and had snapped at a waiter, ordering him to clear up the mess.

'What's the problem?' asked Judith, joining him. She looked a little drunk.

'You're supposed to be the hostess.' Kramer eyed his wife with fresh disappointment. 'That means keeping an eye on everything. Christ, it's not a very difficult job. You should be able to manage that.'

'I thought my job was to look beautiful and encourage those disgusting old men to hand over their cheques,' she bit back. 'When can we get rid of them?'

'It's too early yet. Did you check on Noah?' Their eleven-month-old son had almost taken his first tottering step unaided this week, and was asleep in his cot in the upstairs nursery.

Judith took out her pager and showed Robert the screen. 'See for yourself. Not a peep.'

'That's because it's not switched on – look.' He turned the pager round and showed her the *Inactive* symbol.

'Damn. It's not my fault. It keeps turning itself off in my pocket.'

'The window isn't open, is it?'

'No, of course not.'

'Well, there's a draught coming from somewhere. Go and check on him. You should have made Gloria stay this evening. It's her job to look after him.'

'I couldn't, Robert, her mother is dying. She has to get all the way down to Kent. She'll be back by eleven.'

'Hurry up – I'll see to this mess.'

Judith pushed away through the crowded room as the waiter came running with a bucket and sponges.

Out on the fire escape, Gail Strong pushed Marcus Sigler back against the metal staircase and licked his lips. They were now both naked below the waist, their clothing shoved down to their calves in a hampering tangle. Rain spattered through the trelliswork of the stairs above, dampening their clothes. Marcus bucked and Gail tightened her hold over him, and the staircase rattled, and something fell or slid – like a can of paint being pushed across a floor – and their bodies shook, and they saw nothing, felt nothing except the core of heat that joined them.

Judith closed the lounge door behind her and climbed the stairs, thankful to be away from the party for a moment. With so much forced laughter and so many guests working their private agendas, it was hard to know if anyone really liked her, or whether they simply saw her as the boss's wife. And to have all the actors here in the flat, seeing how lavishly they lived, surely that wasn't a good idea.

She paused on the stairs and listened – something fell, an odd sort of sound. She stopped before the nursery door, a queer feeling tilting her stomach. Thunder rolled across the rooftops once more and the lights momentarily flickered. She depressed the handle and pushed, but the door refused to move. It wasn't locked, so what was wrong?

She tried it again. Nothing. She called to the child, but there was no sound inside the room. Total silence. What to do?

She knew she should use her initiative, but her ability to make her own decisions had been excised when she agreed to marry Robert. So she turned and ran back downstairs.

'It's not possible,' said Robert flatly. 'That door is never locked.' His disbelief felt accusing.

'Then try it for yourself.' She grabbed his hand and led him away from the horde of investors.

They returned to the baby's room and Robert tried the door. He pressed his ear to the wood and listened, hushing Judith. 'This is ridiculous,' he grumbled finally, straightening. 'You left it unlocked?'

'You know I did, Robert. There's no way of locking it without removing the key from the other side. I kept telling you to sort the door out.'

'Maybe Noah—'

'For God's sake, he's not even able to get out of the cot!'

'Then I'll have to break the door open. I don't know what the guests will think.'

'I can't believe you're even thinking about them at a time like this – just do it.'

Robert placed his shoulder against the wood and pushed, but the door barely moved. 'All right, stand back.' He raised his foot and kicked as hard as he could against the lock. The wood cracked a little but held. His second kick split the frame, and at his third the door popped open, swinging wide.

The first thing they saw was the window. It had been raised. The white net curtains were apart and billowing, and the rain was soaking the carpet.

'No,' said Judith, softly. She ran to the cot and saw the covers thrown back. 'He's gone. How could he—' She turned and searched the floor, panic blinding her.

'Judith—' Robert's sudden command struck a chord of fear. He was standing at the window, looking down into the street. They were on the sixth floor.

She could barely bring herself to walk across the room. When she finally did so and looked to where her husband was pointing, he had to catch her. He was still holding her in his arms when the guests began to crowd into the room.

8

PUNCH

John May parked his silver BMW behind the ambulance and got out, opening the passenger door for his partner. Arthur was no longer allowed to take the driving seat since he had sent Victor, his Mini, straight across the round-about on the north side of Westminster Bridge, ploughing through the flowerbeds without even noticing, because he was busy explaining the history of Dutch microscopes.

Northumberland Avenue was dank and deserted. The tourists stayed on streets that connected restaurants and theatres. Bryant could smell the chill rush of the river from here. He clutched his hat and looked up into the rain. 'Sixth floor? Quite a drop.' Thumping his walking stick against the black railings, he peered down into the base-ment area, where a couple stood beside a small blue plastic frame that had been pegged to the ground. 'Body found down there. Poor little bugger. At least it was quick. Who's securing the place?'

'Renfield's already up at the crime site. Janice, Colin and Dan are in the lounge with the guests. Local chap down there. Want to go down?'

'I'm not good at consoling the bereaved, but I'd better have a look. I hate this part.'

'Corpses?'

'No, stairs.'

May opened the gate and led the way down.

'You took your damned time getting here, didn't you?' Robert Kramer had been standing in the rain for almost half an hour, awaiting the senior investigators' arrival. Judith had refused to leave the spot where her son had fallen. Their guests had been prevented from leaving the flat by an officious bull-necked sergeant. Now Kramer needed someone to vent his anger on.

'Westminster isn't our jurisdiction, sir,' May explained. 'Your local division felt that the situation would require specialist expertise, and their assistance unit contacted us. I understand how terrible this is for you and I'll do everything within my power to make this part bearable, but you must also consider that a crime may have been committed. Perhaps you could come inside now.'

May brought them inside the building, took the lift to the apartment and found a quiet room where they could be interviewed in comfort. Judith Kramer was in a bad state. He called in a female medic, who administered a mild sedative.

DS Janice Longbright and Dan Banbury, the Unit's crime scene manager, were concluding the basic formalities. 'Take Dan up with you,' Longbright told May. 'Colin and I can handle the rest.' With seamless efficiency, she took over from the detectives and outlined the next stages of the investigative process to the distraught couple.

On the staircase to the top floor the detectives were met by Jack Renfield. 'Some of the guests are getting restless and making noises about calling lawyers,' he warned. 'We're taking standard witness statements and contact details. They're expecting to be released as soon as they've talked to us.'

'I don't care what they're expecting,' snapped Bryant. 'This looks like a murder investigation. Hold them here until we've examined the nursery.' He headed up with May and Banbury. Renfield taped off the stairs and followed them.

'You're putting on plastics, both of you,' said Dan, handing them gloves and shoe covers. 'I know what you're like.'

'I'm not wearing a hairnet,' Bryant warned. 'You know my hair type. You've found enough of it scattered around past murder sites.' Carefully skirting around the splintered door, he entered the room.

'Robert Kramer says it took four hard shoves to break in,' said May.

'You can see why, too,' Banbury replied, kneeling to study the door. 'Quality wood. Look at that.'

A standard brass Yale key was inserted on the inside, with the lock bolt still protruding into the displaced strike plate. 'It was definitely locked on the inside. Why would the nursery have an internal key?'

'They've only been living here a short time,' said Renfield. 'According to Mr Kramer, the previous tenant had a lodger. This was the lodger's room. He fitted the lock, and they hadn't got around to removing it. The baby was less than a year old, so he wouldn't have been able to accidentally lock himself in. One thing's for sure. He didn't throw himself out of the window, even if he could have climbed from his cot and got up to the sill.'

The window was still wide open, the curtains sodden. The cot stood at least three feet from the exterior wall. Bryant leaned out for a good look. 'Come away from there,' Banbury instructed. 'You're making me nervous.'

'I'm not going to touch anything, all right?' Bryant shot him a scowl.

'Mrs Kramer insists the window was down and locked when she last came up,' said Renfield.

'When was that?'

'About half an hour earlier.'

'Whoever did this didn't come in from outside the window. The rug's soaking, but I can't see any footprints.'

'With all due respect, Mr Bryant, your eyesight isn't anything to write home about. Let me do some tests.'

Banbury dusted the door lock and handle for prints, but they were completely clean – there was not so much as a single sweat whorl on the hasp. 'At a guess I'd say someone wiped up.'

Bryant leaned back out of the window and looked above. 'Even assuming someone had come up with a way to enter the room from outside, he couldn't have come from the roof. There's a sheer wall above. That's got to be a ten-foot gap. And there's no way of climbing down, no handholds, nothing.'

May came around the other side of the cot, where the shadows fell from the window. He froze in his tracks. 'What on earth is this?'

He knelt and examined the sprawled shape on the floor. About two and a half feet long, the hunchbacked figure had jointed limbs and was garishly dressed in a striped red velvet suit with a great paunched belly, yellow pom-poms and a white ruff collar. It wore a pointed crimson hat topped with a bell and had the curled yellow slippers of a sultan. The scarlet parrot nose was so hooked that it almost met the chin. Its gimlet eyes stared wide and were tinged with madness.

'Hello, what have we here?' said Bryant, brightening up. 'Mr Punch. Dan, may I?'

'All right, but be careful,' said Dan, who was tired of

dealing with the problems of tainted evidence that occurred whenever Bryant tramped merrily through a crime scene.

Bryant lifted the figure into a standing position. 'It looks like a Victorian original. Stuffed with kapok, wooden hands and feet, papier-mâché head. There'll be a little bell in his cap. What's it doing beside the cot?'

'Over here,' called May, who was standing by the opposite wall. An entire collection of Punch and Judy puppets was arranged along it at head height. Only one was missing from its hook.

'Looks like Mr Punch decided to go for a walk,' said Bryant. 'How did it get off the wall and over to the cot inside a locked room?'

'The parents had probably been amusing their child and forgot to put it back,' said May.

'Rather a grotesque thing to wave at a baby, isn't it? After all, it's a very valuable antique, not a kiddies' plaything. It would probably have made him burst into tears.' Bryant knew a thing or two about making children cry. 'So what's it doing on the floor?'

'Don't read too much into this, Arthur.'

'I can't help it.' Despite Banbury's look of horror, Bryant raised the figure high and wiggled it. The puppet's movements were unnervingly realistic. 'After all, what's one of the first things Mr Punch does in the play?'

Renfield and May looked at each other.

'He throws the baby out of the window,' replied Bryant.

9

SHAKEN

In the great glass lounge, the mood had turned to confusion and a determination among the guests to be seen to be behaving properly in extraordinary circumstances. Coffee had been served and groups had formed in various parts of the room, seated on extra chairs supplied by the waiters. For now at least, the attitude was one of civilized calm, as if they were commuters in a stalled train.

Unsurprisingly, Arthur Bryant and John May were greeted with curious looks. Bryant was wrapped in a seaweed-green scarf and had his ancient soaked trilby pulled down over his ears. John May was tailored with inappropriate elegance, from his white Gieves & Hawkes shirt to his Lobb Oxford shoes, but both men were of retirement age and bore no resemblance to traditional officers of the law.

'May I have your attention?' May called. 'This is Mr Bryant, I'm Mr May. I know it's getting late, but we hope to be able to release you just as soon as we've established the order of tonight's events. First of all, let me explain why we're here. We belong to a specialist unit that has taken over from the Westminster Metropolitan Police, owing to certain unusual circumstances connected with this investigation.'

'And what are those?' asked Russell Haddon, the theatre's director.

'We're not able to give you full details, but we can tell you this. It is highly unlikely that Noah Kramer's death was an accident. He appears to have died as the result of a vicious and callous attack. However, it's very unusual to have such a specific margin of opportunity occurring in this kind of situation.'

'Meaning?'

'There's no easy access from the outside of the building. The front door was locked and answered by a security guard who admitted only those who had been invited to the party. He checked in a total of thirty-five guests, plus the waiters and a chef. It appears no one else came in or left. Now, we know that Mrs Kramer checked on her son at around eight-forty p.m., and that the discovery of her tragic loss occurred just before nine-twenty p.m. We now need to establish whether any of you left this room in the intervening forty minutes.'

'You're saying we're all suspects,' said Mona Williams loudly.

'Well, obviously,' snapped Bryant, rolling his eyes. 'We didn't come around for cocktails, did we?'

'I think that's a very inappropriate remark to make under the circumstances.'

'Let me handle this,' May told his partner before turning to the assembled gathering. 'Naturally the enquiry will be treated in confidence. If any of you left the room tonight for whatever reason, we need to know when, why and for how long. You can provide us with the details on these extra pages.' He held up a sheaf of notepaper. 'As soon as you've done that, you'll be able to leave.'

Gail Strong accepted one of the sheets as they were handed out. She glanced at Marcus Sigler, making sure that he understood she was about to lie. The actor sent the faintest of nods in her direction, and turned to providing his own alibi.

The gabled gingerbread house behind the graveyard of St Pancras Old Church was finished in orange bricks and maroon tiles and appeared to have been designed by the Brothers Grimm. Plane trees and rowans hung over it with branches like claws that scrabbled at the windows, leaking sap and dripping rainwater so that moss and lichen grew in abundant clumps about the eaves, gradually consuming it. A miserable-looking heron balanced forlornly at its gate, and a pair of moorhens had bundled themselves against the downpour inside a bucket by the door. This bucolic night tableau was all the more remarkable for being just two miles from Piccadilly Circus, and no more than a three-minute walk from Europe's largest railway terminus.

'I suppose Mrs Danvers is still on the door,' muttered Bryant, checking his watch. 'Giles should get rid of her before she goes mad and burns the building down.'

'The poor woman spends her day surrounded by opened corpses,' May reminded him.

'Didn't Giles's predecessor die in mysterious circumstances? Maybe she killed him.'

'You wish. It would make a good case for you, wouldn't it? Let's get inside.'

Bryant furled his umbrella and rang the bell, then jumped back as the door swung open, revealing Rosa Lysandrou, Giles Kershaw's housekeeper. As usual she was clad in a shapeless knee-length black dress and had pulled her thick dark hair back in a severe bun.

'She must have been standing behind the door,'

whispered Bryant as they entered. 'Hello, Rosa,' he said loudly, 'you're looking particularly effervescent this evening – is that a new shroud?'

'He's in there. He's expecting you.' She raised a stiff arm and pointed.

'It probably takes a major traffic accident to bring a smile to her face,' groused Bryant as they passed along the dimly lit corridor.

Giles was in the autopsy room of the St Pancras mortuary, still dressed in the green plastic apron he was required to wear while working. Mercifully, the tiny body of Noah Kramer had been filed away. 'Dear fellows, good to see you, although these are awful circumstances. The babies are the worst – one always wonders what lives they might have led. I've finished here. Let me get out of this and wash up. Rosa will make us some tea. Trust me, you'll need it after hearing my report.'

They entered the octagonal room beyond the chapel of rest and found refreshments neatly laid out beneath the stained-glass windows, tea and plates of warm chocolate cake. Rain cascaded from the eaves, rippling the light.

'Rosa is passionate about baking; you must eat.'

'No, thanks,' said Bryant. 'I remember what happened to Hansel and Gretel.'

'Oh, she's all right once you get to know her.' Giles flicked back his mop of blond hair and dropped into a deep sofa. He always seemed to bring sunshine into the room. 'I thought we'd have a chat away from the morgue. Rosa believes that children keep on listening after they die. She lost a child herself, you see. It changed how she saw the world.' He helped himself to cake, then checked his notepad. 'I'll spare you the main list of injuries. They're what I would expect, entirely consistent with a fall from a window of that height. However, I'm afraid the fall doesn't appear to have been the cause of death.'

'Why, what else did you find?' asked May.

'I think we've got a case of SBS, except that here there's evidence of external injury.'

'Shaken Baby Syndrome? I thought it was difficult to diagnose.'

'Well, it is, because there's no single definable symptom. There can be multiple fractures in the vertebrae, retinal haemorrhages, subdural hematomas – bleeding in the brain – it's a rotational injury generally associated with child abuse, but really I suppose it's about the frustration of someone ill-equipped to deal with a crying baby. The real problem, of course, is that it's hardly ever a pre-meditated action. This was a particularly violent example. Noah Kramer's larynx was ruptured, and there are bruises on either side of his throat. Broken blood vessels near the surface were caused by severe restriction. He was shaken violently, then strangled. It was an act of rage, which probably means a lack of prior intention to kill.'

'So, manslaughter.'

'Obviously it will depend on the *mens rea* – criminal culpability based on the perpetrator's state of mind.'

'Do you have any idea how long before the fall this might have occurred?'

'I imagine the two acts, the shaking and the defenestration, were virtually concurrent, the second happening moments after the first, but of course I have no proof.'

'So whoever did this plucked Noah from his cot, attacked him, then opened the window and threw him out.'

'Yes, which is problematic from a legal point of view.'

'Because the perpetrator stopped and opened the window, which would indicate a level of premeditation.'

'Exactly. But I'm afraid it's a little stranger than that.'

'What do you mean?'

'Dan Banbury brought me the Victorian doll you found

beside the cot. I got a very bothersome feeling in my stomach the moment I examined it. Dan can't do any DNA matches – I gather you don't have the budget to send samples away for such things – but you know how he gets a sense of what happened. Well, he suggested that the odd pressure bruises on Noah's throat might match the dummy's wooden hands. I'm afraid it looks like he's right. The fingers are coarsely carved and grooved. They leave a pretty unique mark.'

'Oh, please don't say this,' groaned May, passing a hand across his face.

'I did some tests. The hands exactly fit the bruises on Noah Kramer's neck. There was even a tiny wooden splinter stuck on the surface of the infant's epidermis. I talked with Dan, and he says he can't find any evidence that anything human touched the baby. What's more, there was no forced entry to the nursery. So far he's found no signs of anyone apart from Mrs Kramer and the nanny having been in there.'

'So what you're telling me is that after the baby was left alone, Mr Punch climbed down from his hook, turned the key in the nursery door lock, crept over to the cot, took his rage out on Noah Kramer and fulfilled his mythical destiny to become a murderer,' said Bryant, genuinely shocked.

10

POLARITY

The senior detectives felt it was important for the PCU staff to be able to share time together away from their desks and laptops, so they had set aside the newly designated common room. May thought it would be an area where they could form impromptu gatherings at various times of the day and night to share their ideas about ongoing cases.

Instead, they usually found Bimsley there with his boots off, eating cheese and onion crisps while thumbing through the latest issue of *Gadgets*. Now it was heading towards midnight, but the lights were still ablaze in the common room and all was far from well.

'Oh no,' said Raymond Land, studying the photographs Sergeant Jack Renfield had taken. 'No, no, no.'

'I'm afraid that's who she is,' said John May. 'I assume that's why we've been given the case.'

'The daughter of the Minister for Public Buildings,' said Land. 'Gail Strong is working for this troupe?'

'It's a theatre company. A troupe refers to the actors. She's on the production side. Assistant stage manager, I believe. A perfectly reasonable explanation for what she was doing on the premises.'

'Yes – but the murder of a baby? And she's a potential suspect? That phone is going to start ringing any minute now. My God, the implications are appalling!'

'The only appalling thing is that an infant has been brutalized,' said May, annoyed. Land worried too much about his job and not enough about the victims of tragedies.

'Yes, yes, babies die all the time, but the involvement of a minister's daughter is unthinkable. I suppose you know that Gail Strong fled the country after a pregnancy termination earlier this year? She told the press she has a horror of babies. She also has a habit of disappearing whenever the spotlight gets too strong. Her father usually pays the press to hush everything up. What if she killed Noah Kramer in a fit of jealousy or something? No, even worse, suppose Bryant starts thinking she's guilty? Her father's department has been under fire lately. This could be a lethal blow for him.'

'I'm glad you've got your priorities in the right order.'

'I look at the broader picture. You just have to deal with the aftereffects of the crime. I've got to keep the money coming into this unit. If the budget dries up, cases like this will revert to the Met's jurisdiction, and we know what that means. You might as well give them to the cat.' He threw a poisoned glance at Crippen. 'I'm sorry, I don't mean to sound callous. Coming in this morning I thought to myself, this is a good start to the week. I had a bit of trouble at home and was glad to get back to work. And now this.'

'It's not Leanne again, is it?' asked May solicitously. Land's wife was bored and showing renewed signs of unfaithfulness. She had taken a suspiciously large number of flamenco lessons lately, and was now attending sherry-tasting evenings in the company of a twenty-three-year-old Tio Pepe representative from Jerez. She had already suggested going on holiday with Paco instead of their customary cycling fortnight in Wales.

'I think it's some kind of midlife crisis. She's dyed her hair blonde and wants to buy a sports car. It's all these late-night women's TV shows about fulfilment she's been watching. She's suddenly got it into her mind that she should be enjoying regular sex. But enough of my troubles. Get this sorted out as quickly as possible, will you? And try not to involve Gail Strong. She wants to be a singer or something. She's hired a PR consultant to manage her, but he has to spend the whole time covering up her indiscretions.'

'I'm surprised you know all about this,' said May.

'I saw it on television,' Land admitted sheepishly. 'One of Leanne's programmes.' He eyed the overcoat he had hung on the back of his chair, and knew there would be no likelihood of slipping into it until midnight at the earliest.

'I don't know what more I can tell you, Mr Bryant,' said Dan Banbury. The detectives had returned to the Unit after visiting Kershaw because they knew Banbury would be back from the crime scene. 'It appears that Noah Samuel Kramer was removed from his cot at around nine p.m. tonight. Giles has told you he was shaken and strangled to death, and his body sustained further injuries from a fall, and I'm telling you he was thrown from the end of the cot through an open window into the basement area of the building. There are no footprints on the wet rug beneath the sill. There are faint depressions on the other rug that the cot stands on, because that's where everyone has to stand in order to reach in and pick the baby up.'

'But no definable prints.'

'No. It's a hardwearing cord that doesn't hold heel

marks. The door of the nursery was securely locked on the inside, with the key still firmly in place. The key turns easily enough but it's tricky to actually get out, so I guess they just left it in the door. There were no signs of tampering with the lock, and Mr Kramer had been forced to kick the door in. A couple of minutes after he did this, the noise, and Mrs Kramer's scream, attracted the attention of the party guests, eight of whom came upstairs to see what the problem was. They saw the damage and naturally entered the room, but Mr Kramer sensibly realized that a crime had been committed and stopped them from coming all the way in. He could see that the rug beneath the window was wet and that the rails of the cot might hold prints. As it was, there weren't any.'

'What, none at all?' asked May.

'Well, I got prints from the nanny and Mrs Kramer, but that's all. As for the floor, it's hardwood and hadn't been cleaned in several days, so there are a few scuff marks which we'll try to identify by matching against the shoes of the guests and those belonging to the Kramers, but there are no water marks. I'm bothered by the fact that there's nothing on the rug, because the killer had to have left the room by the window and it would be physically impossible to do so without putting a foot down. There's simply no other method of exit unless we find some kind of secret panel in the room—'

'There are quite a few houses in London with secret panels,' Bryant pointed out.

'I was joking, Mr Bryant. The house was converted into flats from offices three years ago, it's not Gormenghast. All the walls are new and solid. So the killer had to climb out of the window, and unless he could fly he would have had to place a foot on the rug. Likewise if he came in that way.'

'Is there any way he could have scaled the building

and entered from the outside?' asked Meera Mangeshkar.

'The toilet window is about fifteen feet away and the nearest drainpipe is at least seven feet away,' said Banbury. 'I don't see how that would be possible.'

'Parkour,' suggested Longbright. 'That jumping thing kids do.'

'I think you'll find that's defined as the art of overcoming obstacles in your path by adapting your movements to the environment,' Bryant recited. 'I've watched lads doing it down the South Bank on a Sunday morning.'

'They can climb a wall just using their fingertips, can't they?'

'That still leaves the closed and locked window, the print-free rug, the lack of raindrops shaken onto or around the cot – it was bucketing down outside, remember – and so far no witnesses from the buildings opposite or the street below. Have we got any CCTV cameras outside?'

'A couple mounted at either end of the avenue but not in the middle,' said Longbright. 'We're checking them for coverage at the moment. Westminster has an e-map of every CCTV in central London.'

'And no unexpected fingerprints anywhere? You checked the whereabouts of the nanny?'

'At her mother's bedside in Kent. And Mrs Kramer was downstairs in the lounge at the estimated time of Noah's death,' said Banbury. 'I want to run checks on fibres from the floor and rugs if we can scrape together the lab costs, but I've got nothing out of the ordinary.' He sat back with his thick arms folded, defying anyone to come up with a theory.

'Mr Punch,' muttered Bryant, fishing about for his pipe.

'I'm sorry, Mr Bryant?'

'Well, he seems to be the obvious culprit. If Mr Punch

had killed the baby, there'd be no conflicting evidence, would there?'

'That's right, Mr Bryant. The only thing Mr Punch lacks is the motor movement that usually comes from muscles controlled by the human brain.'

Sarcasm had no effect on Bryant. He located his pipe and calmly attached the stem to the bowl, patting down his pockets for tobacco. 'Remote control,' he said through clenched false teeth. 'Take it apart.'

'Where is the puppet now?' asked Longbright.

'It's still with Giles,' said Banbury. 'He and I are going to pull it to bits first thing in the morning. Robert Kramer's already warned us that it's valuable and we're not allowed to cut it open, but I chucked him a bit of legal and he shut up sharpish. Makes you wonder if he cares more about a bloody toy than his own flesh and blood.'

'OK, let's see what we've got.' May indicated that Longbright should hand out copies of the witness statements. 'Everybody take a few and we'll start going through them. We're going to be here most of the night.'

'Whoa, I'm not spending the night in this building,' said Meera. 'There's something wrong with it. Bad karma.' There had been a number of complaints about strange late-night noises in the Victorian property since the staff had discovered it had once provided a home for the society of black magic practitioners.

'Don't worry, I'll protect you,' Bimsley said with a laugh. He was more than prepared to, as well – if only she wanted him.

'Yeah, right, that's reassuring.' Meera shot him a sour look and slumped back in her chair to study the pages. 'It looks like a third of my witnesses left the room to use the bathroom at some point during the forty minutes. This guy, Marcus Sigler, went outside for a ciggie twice.'

'So did some of mine,' said Longbright. 'I don't

think these are going to be detailed enough for us, Dan.'

'All right, I'll fix it, but until then we'll draw up a chart,' said Banbury, turning over a whiteboard. 'Time line along this side, guests at the top. Mark every absence to the minute, see where they cross over, get them to verify each other's movements.'

'It doesn't sound very scientific,' said Meera.

'Well, I'm sorry I can't nip over to an American forensics lab and split everything into nucleotides and mitochondrial DNA, Meera, but we're just a small experimental unit in North London operating on a budget that wouldn't keep a string quartet going.'

'I'm going on the balcony for a ponder and a puff,' said Bryant, 'unless I'm allowed to enjoy my pipe in here, seeing as it's raining and I'm a fragile senior with a dreadful chest.'

'No!' said everybody in the room.

'That's a pity, because I was going to share my thoughts with you.'

'I'm not sure we're ready to hear your theories on ambulatory puppets,' May warned.

'No, this is about premeditation.' Bryant hovered in the doorway, shamelessly playing his audience, waiting to be called back. 'Yes?' He raised his eyebrows and listened for a response.

'Oh all right then,' May said finally. 'Tell us.'

Bryant darted back in and lit up. 'It's all right, I'm on the herbal stuff. Old Malahyde's Tincture of Rose-Mulch.' It smelled suspiciously like grass. 'Well, the crime is bizarrely polarized, isn't it? On the one hand we have factors that point to an act of violence occurring in a flash of temper – the shaking, the throwing – but on the other, everything seems planned – the locked room, the lack of prints suggesting gloves or at least a cloth to wipe up with, the waiting for the perfect opportunity. The party, by the way, provided the perfect cover, because the Kramers' house is alarmed, so it was the easiest way to gain admittance when the baby was sure to be there. And the window was opened. If it was simply an act of murderous temper, why not hurl the baby to the floor? Why not dash its brains out on the head of the cot? Why go to the window, avoid stepping on the rug, open it and throw the baby out? It really is the most contradictory set of circumstances. And the theatricality of the whole thing smacks of actorly behaviour – you know, a grand dramatic gesture.'

'What do you think it tells us about the killer?'

'I think the intention to do harm had been harboured for a while, but something happened at the party to flush it into the open. We need to look at the evening's events far more carefully. Janice, can you organize that?'

'All right, ladies and gentlemen,' said Longbright wearily. 'Let's go back to the beginning and see how much more we can wring out of the statements. I suggest we form pairs and keep switching until they're all covered.'

'OK,' said Meera, 'but I don't want to sit next to Colin.'

'Why not?' asked Bimsley.

Meera wrinkled her nose at him. 'You smell like you fell in a vat of cheap scent.'

'That's Lynx.' Bimsley sniffed his right armpit.

'What are you, fourteen?'

'It pulls the chicks, this stuff.'

'I can tell you right now that it doesn't.'

Longbright watched her teammates bickering like schoolchildren and wondered how they would ever make any headway. She hoped they would remember that at the base of the investigation was the tragedy of a child's lost life.

11

PARALLELS

Just after nine o'clock on Tuesday morning at the St Pancras mortuary, they went to work.

'OK,' said Giles Kershaw. 'Hold it steady, I'm going in.' He raised his scalpel above the steel dissection table, sprayed the blade with a neutral oil-based lubricant and inserted it beneath the neck of the prone Mr Punch, just where his hump began.

'Try to keep it to the stitching,' Dan Banbury suggested. 'This one's worth a fortune. Most of them are in the hands of private collectors or in museums, and Mr Bryant told me this one is part of a complete set from the 1880s, which makes it very rare.'

'I open bodies, Dan, I can do this, OK?' Kershaw's blade snicked the stitches apart. He reached the dummy's legs and carefully began to remove the kapok-and-horsehair stuffing inside. A jointed brass skeleton was gradually revealed, still gleaming. 'Amazing bit of workmanship, this. Beautifully put together. The Victorians really made things to last, even toys.'

'It's not a toy, Giles; it was crafted like that because it

was a way of earning a living. According to Mr Bryant, the Punch and Judy men were masters of their craft and could make good money. There was one appointed to Buckingham Palace for garden parties. He was granted the royal crest – *By Appointment* – it's on this one's back.'

Giles shone a penlight into the puppet's cranium. 'The head and hands are made of carved wood, hollowed out but heavy things to lift, performing with your arms raised all the time.' Kershaw set aside another handful of brown horsehair and peered deeper inside.

'I think there were usually two men working in the booth. The later models are papier-mâché over a wire frame. See anything?'

'Nothing out of the ordinary. No electrical wiring, no pistons, certainly nothing that could allow the thing to stand up under its own power. There would have to be some kind of support in here. The Japanese currently have a couple of robots that could do it, although I think even they would draw the line at building one that could strangle a baby. There goes the Golem theory.'

'What do you mean?'

'In the sixteenth century, the Chief Rabbi of Prague brought a huge creature made of clay to life to stop anti-Semitic attacks, but the Golem eventually turned on his creator. I get crazy thoughts while I'm working. It comes from hanging around old Bryant too much. You start to think like him, and then pretty soon no self-respecting CID officer will talk to you.'

'OK, what do we do now?'

'Stitch it back up,' Giles replied, studying Mr Punch's angry red face. It seemed the creature was staring at him, its eyes filled with murderous intent.

A Stab in the Back

Alex Lansdale

The classic murder thriller used to be a staple of the West End theatre. Plays like *Maria Marten, or The Murder in the Red Barn*, *Sweeney Todd*, *Wait Until Dark* and *Sleuth* proved popular with the public, but lately this genre has gone into decline, with only Agatha Christie's *The Mousetrap* still hanging on for grim death at the St Martin's Lane Theatre, where the director is still required to follow the original moves laid down in the play's first production sixty years ago, preserving the whole ghastly farrago in amber for the undemanding non-English-speaking tourists who inexplicably keep it running.

I was reminded of the play while sitting through *The Two Murderers*, a farcical drama in which a young woman (soap actress Della Fortess – dismal) is beaten by her husband and falls into the arms of hunky gardener Bert (former boy-band singer and model Marcus Sigler). Together the pair hatch a plot to murder the bullying captain of industry, but plans go awry and soon the stage is drenched in Kensington Gore.

Despite some brief and painfully hammy support from veteran actors Neil Crofting and Mona Williams, the show belongs to the young leads, who'll have no appeal whatsoever to older audiences. Ella Maltby's superbly evocative Gothic set designs and extravagant period costuming from Larry Hayes notwithstanding, the overmiked sound makes it unbearable for anyone above the iPod generation, especially when the absurd plot twists start kicking in after the intermission.

The fault lies largely with the New Strand Theatre's Russell Haddon, whose misjudged blood-and-thunder direction renders the actors' Grand Guignol posturing ludicrous and turns the plot into some kind of teenage multiplex action movie. First-time author Ray Pryce provides clever dialogue that bristles with ironic epithets, but his lines are lost under a welter of overblown effects that include a stabbing, torture, nudity and a grotesquely realistic hanging.

None of this will make a jot of difference to the youngsters who will flock in droves to see this monstrously distasteful catalogue of lurid thrills, especially as the second half features a scene in which Miss Fortess dances naked for her lover in the most gratuitous nude scene I have ever witnessed on stage. The soap star's ample charms will doubtless prove a useful distraction from the play's many faults. Meanwhile, the company has already announced a new production, God help us, and at least author Pryce will once more be on hand to ensure that the script provides frissons, even if the director is unable to rise to the occasion.

The Two Murderers *New Strand Theatre, Adam Street, WC2 Perfs 7:30pm (exc. Sundays, Mats: Weds, Sats)*

'The bastard has the nerve to show up at my house, witnesses our private grief and then prints these two items right next to each other!'

In the manager's office above the New Strand Theatre, Robert Kramer threw the newspaper across the desk to Gregory Baine, his accountant and producer. '"Unable to rise to the occasion" – Lansdale knows we had trouble conceiving because of my low sperm count. My wife was stupid enough to tell him.'

'Oh, I'm sure he didn't mean it to read like—'

'Of course he bloody did!' Kramer bit back. 'Read the second piece.'

Baby in Horror Fall

An 11-month-old baby boy fell to his death from an open sixth-floor window in central London last night. Noah Kramer, son of millionaire theatre owner Robert 'Julius' Kramer, 47, and his second wife Judith Kramer, 26, were hosting a lavish first-night party to mark the opening of their play *The Two Murderers* when tragedy struck.

An ambulance was dispatched to the £3.5 million penthouse at around 9:30 p.m. Officers are at a loss to explain how baby Noah reached the window, which the parents insist was securely locked, or why it had been opened during the torrential rainstorm that hit central London last night. 'The couple had given their nanny the night off and were downstairs celebrating with celebrity guests when Noah somehow found his way to the window,' said a close friend. 'Judith is devastated.' The police want to know why the baby was left alone by an open window, and will have no choice but to treat the death as suspicious.

Kramer's first play at London's newly opened New Strand Theatre is a gruesome horror-drama that is not for the fainthearted, and has received a critical drubbing.

'You can see what he's implying, can't you?' said Kramer. 'That the show is somehow paralleled in our private lives. And that we deliberately neglected our own child. "Left by an open window", "celebrating with celebrity guests", "Judith is devastated" – no mention of *my* grief. And putting our ages and the price of the property in the bloody article! Apart from anything else, the place is worth four million at least. This is obviously Lansdale's work, although I don't know what they think they're doing, getting a bloody theatre critic to write the news. I got him his first job on the *Telegraph* and this is how he treats me. Well, I want him kept out of my theatre from now on.'

'How's Judith doing?' asked Baine. He wasn't really interested, but felt that Kramer would expect to be asked.

'How do you think she's doing? She's inconsolable. She's been dosed to the gills with Valium and has taken to her bed. I can't go to the theatre while this is going on. We can't even plan the funeral until some coroner has finished poking about with the body. It's a bloody nightmare! And now the press are working some kind of neglect angle, things can only get worse.'

'Everything's under control at the theatre. We had a bit of a flood after the storm but we're working on that. The box office is healthy. I hate to say it, but the coverage of the accident has raised your profile.'

'My wife has just lost her child. Show some bloody respect.'

Baine shrugged. 'I'm an accountant, Robert, it's how I see the world. Bad for you, good for business.'

'What are we going to say?' asked Marcus Sigler. 'They're going to find out that we were together on the fire escape when they compare notes.' He and Gail Strong were seated outside a coffee shop on Upper Street, Islington. Gail was wearing absurdly huge Audrey Hepburn glasses that drew attention to her.

'You don't need to sound so worried.' She took a drag on her cigarette and jetted smoke away from him. 'I lied to that stupid policewoman about the timings, the one who looked like a model from the sixties. I told her I was out there after you, and passed you coming in as I went out.'

'Christ, what if somebody else saw us and contradicts your testimony? When were you going to tell me this? You know my situation. They've got everyone else's times. If there's a mismatch, they'll know something's wrong.'

'Grow yourself some gonads, Marcus. I'm just going to stick to my story. No one can prove we were outside together, and so what if we were? Strangers take cigarette breaks in each other's company all the time.'

'They'll know something was going on. Judith will know. Women can sense these things.'

'Judith's virtually in a coma, in case you haven't heard.'

'She's probably been prescribed something to calm her down. You can't imagine how bad I feel about this.'

'It didn't seem to bother you at the time. That's what cracks me up about men. You never think things through.'

'If this gets out I could have my contract cancelled.'

'I forgot, it's all about you, isn't it?'

'Well, it rather is in this case.'

'What do you mean?'

'Give me one of those.' He pointed at her Marlboro Lights. 'I thought you understood. I thought that was the whole point.'

'Understood what?'

'Well.' Marcus fussed about trying to light the cigarette. There are few sights as spectacular as a handsome man embarrassed. 'That Judith and I are an item.'

'No, somehow you never got around to mentioning that.'

'We met at her best friend's wedding in Gloucester and spent the night together. In the morning, she told me that Robert had already proposed to her. I tried to stop seeing her, but it's kind of still going on.'

'Kind of? How could you have let that happen if she was about to marry someone else?'

'I don't know. We really do care for each other. I guess it was just bad timing for both of us. I mean, I made love to her the night before her wedding to Robert. But since then things have got even weirder. I'm starting to get this feeling he knows something's going on.'

'So, what the hell happened between us on the fire escape?'

'I was a bit drunk, and you came on to me.'

'Is that all it takes to make you unfaithful, Marcus? God, at least I'm unattached. Poor Judith. Do you really think her husband knows something?'

'Probably not. I don't see how he can. He'd kill me if he did. At the very least he'd make sure I never worked again.'

'I suppose it's struck you how similar your situation is to the character you play in *The Two Murderers*. It sounds like you're living the part.'

'I've been feeling uneasy about that for a while, but lately the sensation's been getting worse. It's like some kind of shadow play.'

'God, if it follows the play we're all in trouble.'

'You don't know Robert Kramer. He's a dangerous man. He manipulates everyone.'

Gail removed her dark glasses. She was wearing no eye makeup and suddenly looked like a child. She rubbed at her nose with a tissue. 'I joined this company because my father thought it would keep me out of trouble. If the press finds out I was there when a baby died, they'll ruin everything for me. I've had a few problems in the past. And they'll start digging around. Who knows what they'll turn up about the rest of the cast?'

'Sometimes productions take years to gestate, and all kinds of things happen to the casts in that time. Actors get promoted or replaced, they marry, divorce and die, kids get born. People always look for parallels between the plays they're in and the lives they lead . . .'

Something in his manner made her pause and stare at him. Without her sunglasses she could see that Marcus had purple shadows beneath his eyes. 'What else do you know?' she asked.

'Look, there's some stuff you shouldn't get involved in. In fact, I think we should try to avoid each other's company. It wouldn't be healthy to be seen together. I'm trying to protect you.'

Gail did not feel protected. Either Marcus was simply trying to brush her off after an ill-advised liaison or he was genuinely terrified, and for once she decided not to ask any more questions.

For Arthur Bryant, the case was starting to evoke a different parallel. London has nearly fifty major theatres and countless fringe venues employing hundreds of people, so it was hardly surprising that occasionally crimes occurred within these very public spaces. The Unit's first investigation had involved the gruesome death of a dancer in the Palace Theatre, and still fascinated the elderly detective. The theatre was where a great many of Bryant's obsessions intersected. The heady combination of artifice, obsession, esoterica and intrigue fired his synapses. As a child he had sneaked into theatres via their open scenery docks and would be allowed to watch performances. He watched in open-mouthed awe while Hamlet goaded Claudius and Richard III schemed. Walton's masque from *The Tempest* and the sprites of Arden seduced him into an impossible world, taking him away from the poverty and bitterness of his childhood home. He still visited theatres whenever he could, but had become disenchanted with the Disneyfication of the West End, which had lured audiences away from thoughtful plays to witless family extravaganzas.

Bryant clambered onto his library steps and pulled down various musty volumes on the history of British theatre, hoping to find some answers to the elliptical questions that flittered about inside his head.

In a book on the lives of Gilbert and Sullivan he found a quote: 'London's modern skin has settled easily over its Victorian heart. Far from erasing the old and replacing it with the new, the city seems to encourage paradox, just as it always did. The high-born and the lowly, the wealthy and the poor, are kept as separate as they have always been.'

How true, he thought, recalling Lord Lucan, the missing seventh earl of Lucan who in 1974 allegedly murdered his nanny and fled the country, apparently protected by a coterie of wealthy friends. Bryant knew that if Robert Kramer operated in similar circles, he would never get to the truth of the boy's death. There were areas of London society where even the law was powerless. The gap between rich and poor was not just one of wealth but of accountability.

However, Kramer could not be protected by any altitude of birthright. He had few friends in high places. He was an opportunist, a financier, a self-made man. His protection was based solely on money, and that made him a little more vulnerable. What's more, he ran a new and already disreputable theatre company. Something about the play and the death resonated, and as Bryant searched the shelves, he found what he was looking for. He pulled down a rare French volume from 1887: *The 'Rosse' Vignettes of Oscar Méténier*.

Laying it carefully on his desk, he began to read. Méténier's lurid little plays had given horrified Parisians a glimpse into the lives of desperate men and women laid low by birth and circumstance. His stage was filled with cackling whores, violent alcoholics and graphic executions. Some of his work was labelled an affront to public morality because of its shocking street jargon and was promptly banned. In *La Casserole*, the writer even hired real criminals to play themselves. It seemed the play-going public always loved to witness gruesome tragedy, so long as it didn't involve people of their own class.

Artifice and reality, he thought, examining the photographs and drawings, *they combine more easily than we realize. TV shows pretend to offer realism but they hide as much as they show. Fiction, on the other hand, can contain fundamental human truths. And sometimes it's possible to step back and forth between these two worlds just by opening the correct door, by finding the key that will unlock mysteries. So much of London is masked; unspoken rules protect the privileged, unseen codes hide the guilty. What a crafty lot we are!*

This, then, was Arthur Bryant at work, his furrowed forehead bowed beneath the yellow light of the desk lamp, a shambling Prospero presiding over the desiccated pages of his literary arcana, stirring fresh knowledge into the heady stew of ideas that filled his brain.

As he sat at the chaotic centre of his office-cum-library, blowing the dust from one forgotten volume after another, scribbling notes and teasing out tenuous links, he began to build a structure of evidence in the case.

Bryant had no interest in the common grounds of detection. He refused to be swayed by plausibility or likelihood. Human beings, he knew, were capable of acting in extraordinary ways for reasons that extended into the realms of the bizarre, and the best way to uncover their confidences was to match the strangeness of their thinking.

As he unfolded a series of grotesque etchings from the works of Charles Baudelaire, Jules Verne and André de Lorde, he wondered if the shroud shielding London's deepest secrets was about to lift for him once more. In the miasma of his mind, dark ideas began to swirl and take solid form.

12

RICTUS

The following guests were present in the lounge at the house of Robert and Judith Kramer, 376 Northumberland Avenue, WC1, when Noah Kramer's death was discovered, and came to the nursery to see what was wrong when they heard the door being broken down by Robert Kramer.

Della Fortess (Actor)
Neil Crofting (Actor)
Mona Williams (Actor)
Marcus Sigler (Actor)
Russell Haddon (Director)
Gregory Baine (Producer)
Ray Pryce (Scriptwriter)
Ella Maltby (Set designer)
Larry Hayes (Wardrobe)
Alex Lansdale (Theatre critic, HardNews.com)
Gail Strong (ASM)

The list had been scrawled out by DS Janice Longbright on a whiteboard in the common room and the staff were now adding witness statements against the names of each of the guests. The giant schematic concentrated everyone's attention in the simplest manner possible.

Interviews were now also being entered into the PCU's system via a new application developed by Dan Banbury called WECS (Witness Evidence Correlation Software), and the pattern of the night's events was recreated in a single spreadsheet of insane complexity.

When Longbright stared at the list of names, the times they arrived, who they knew, when they entered and left the lounge, their relationships to their hosts and to each other, all she saw was a data grid that detailed everything and explained nothing. The problem with traditional witness statements was that they sometimes obscured important facts, but WECS just seemed to make her job harder.

She wanted to know something far more fundamental: who among these people could kill a child? Who could act with such violence towards one so innocent, and then return moments later to make small talk at a party? Clearly, it was possible; many killers described a sense of blankness descending upon them, removing their ability to feel any kind of remorse. But she and the other members of staff had met these people and noticed nothing untoward.

'John, do you think actors lie more easily than people in other professions?' she asked.

'I don't know enough about them to judge, but I wouldn't think so.' May looked up from his notes. 'Arthur's your best bet for a question like that. You'd be better off looking for the distinct emotional characteristics common to homicides. Dissociative states of mind, stress snaps from long-gestating problems. Killers supposedly undergo something called an "aura phase". Their senses become heightened, skin becomes more sensitive, they experience sights and sounds more vividly. You might discreetly check our suspects for the appearance of such a state.'

'I suppose it's possible the perpetrator doesn't even remember what happened.'

'True. It could help explain the anomalies Arthur pointed up.'

'Why would somebody strike in such a public place? It seems to be inviting extra risk.'

'About a third of all killers strike in public. And they often become very depressed after they've acted, but we can't monitor all our suspects all of the time – the system isn't built for it.'

More confused than ever, Longbright went back to work. She was still inputting everyone's movements when the call came in a few minutes later. She rose and left the room.

Bryant was poring over a huge old book entitled *Folk Myths & Legends of England*. On top of this were a limited edition of Calthrop's *Punch and Judy*, published by Dulau & Co Ltd, and a slipcased original playscript, *Punch & Judy*, edited by Rose Fyleman for Methuen.

'I've got some bad news for you, Arthur,' said Longbright. 'Do you know someone called Anna Marquand?'

'John and I had tea with her yesterday,' said Bryant without looking up. His unlit pipe was clenched between his teeth, a sure sign he was concentrating. 'She's the editor of my memoirs. I'm thinking of bringing her into the Unit in some capacity. Why?'

'She's dead.'

Bryant stopped what he was doing. 'What do you mean? How?'

'Her mother just called. She found the PCU's phone number in her daughter's jacket. Apparently Anna

Marquand got home last night, was going to make herself a toasted cheese sandwich, cut up the bread and passed out in the kitchen. Her mother was in the other room with the TV up loud and didn't hear anything. Fifteen minutes later she found her on the floor, blue in the face. The medics reckon it might have been some virulent form of blood poisoning, perhaps tetanus. She died in the ambulance.'

'Blood poisoning?'

'Bacteria in the bloodstream.'

'For God's sake, Janice, I know what it is. How did it get there?'

'The mother says she nicked herself with the bread knife.'

'Is that all? Seems very sudden. Are they sure?'

'It's not as uncommon as you'd think. I had a cousin who died in exactly the same way.'

'But Anna – what a terrible waste.' Bryant looked genuinely horrified – not a common sight.

'That's not all. The mother, Rose Marquand, reckons there was something odd about it. Her daughter was attacked on the way home by some local hooleys, kids from a criminal family. They snatched her mobile on the front doorstep, not for the first time either. She'd been having a running battle with them for a couple of years. Rose says her daughter was terrified and couldn't calm down after. She thinks maybe her heart gave out and the doctor misdiagnosed.'

'Frightened to death? Sounds unlikely.'

'I suppose that's what she's implying. She didn't want to talk to the local constabulary, says they were aware of the problems Anna had been having but never did anything about them. Mrs Marquand didn't know who else to call, but Anna had talked about you.'

'Where did they take her? St Thomas's?'

'I believe so. Want me to talk to the doctor?'

'Good idea. But let me ring the mother first.'

With a heavy heart, Bryant made the call. As much as Rose Marquand was upset about losing her only daughter, it seemed to him that she was more fearful for her own future. Anna had been caring for her mother since her father died.

Bryant explained that he would be sending Longbright to visit her. Perhaps his detective sergeant would be able to help in ways that the Met had no time for. Something about Anna had penetrated his heart; clever, shy and somehow lost, she had not been able to find her place in life, and now that confused existence had ended. If she had been bullied by a local gang, he needed to see the wrong put right.

He had an ulterior motive in offering his detective sergeant's services; Longbright was to reassure Rose that she would be looked after, but he also asked her to collect the notes Anna had excised from his memoir. They were, after all, of a sensitive nature and, as Anna had indicated, their publication was banned by the Official Secrets Act. If the local service visitors came in to assess Rose, Bryant didn't want them stumbling across incendiary material.

He sat back in his cracked green leather chair and rubbed his red eyes. He hadn't been sleeping well lately. The excitement of moving the Unit into new premises had worn off as soon as he realized they would face the usual uphill battle against budgets and bureaucracy to keep the place alive. An infanticide; it would probably not turn out to be much of an investigation, but it would keep them ticking over until something meatier came along. The case wouldn't have turned up at all if it hadn't been for Gail Strong's ministerial connection.

Bryant wiped his filthy computer screen and tried to

understand Banbury's WECS spreadsheet. He was annoyed with himself; it should have been obvious who was responsible for the child's death. He felt sure that the matter would be wrapped up in a day or two. The crime was bound to have been committed by someone close to the baby or his mother – domestic investigations, even those that took place among the wealthy, were usually the easiest to solve.

The Mr Punch element intrigued him, though.

He could afford to indulge himself and study it from a more esoteric angle, safe in the knowledge that it would all have blown over in a day or two.

And yet. The lurid rictus of Mr Punch grimaced out at him from its hand-coloured plate in mockery, daring him to find a darker solution, and a shadow passed across his soul. The puppet on the floor had the laughing face of someone who knew they had killed and could get away with it.

If they were capable of taking the life of an innocent child and hiding the crime in plain sight, what else might they have the confidence to do?

13

THEORIES

Police officers are social drinkers. They have to be. The stresses of shifts are washed away with pints, and debriefs turn into scandalmonger sessions at the backs of boozers where the landlady can be relied upon to keep her barrels bled and her mouth shut. The alcohol is soaked up with carbohydrate-laden pub grub, but the cruelties of criminals are not so easily absorbed.

DS Janice Longbright and Sergeant Jack Renfield had detested each other at sight, but the death of a colleague had recently drawn them into a cautionary orbit. Longbright was lonely. Statuesque and physically imposing, she scared off men who wanted their girlfriends to behave like Barbie dolls, and as her conversation frequently revolved around the tragedy of sudden death, few civilian women remained in her circle for long.

Renfield, on the other hand, was the kind of Arsenal-supporting, beer-hammering mate who would never be alone in a North London pub. But there was something about Longbright that made him want to ditch his friends and be alone with her.

However, as Renfield settled into a corner at the King Charles I with his pint, that thought was cut short by the arrival of Meera Mangeshkar and Colin Bimsley. Sometimes the group liked to meet and chew over the day's events without the senior detectives. They dealt with the grim practicalities of crime, and occasionally enjoyed leaving the abstruse thinking to their bosses.

The King Charles I was the oldest pub in King's Cross. It had The Smiths on the jukebox, animal heads on the walls and a clientele that often ended up on the floor. It was home to a number of obscure games played by drinkers, including Mornington Crescent, the Drunk Shakespeare Club and the Nude Alpine Climbers Society of London, an inebriated challenge that involved making your way around the bar naked except for a coil of rope, a pith helmet and crampons, the loser being the first one to fall and touch the floor.

'We just had Gail Strong's old man on the line,' said Meera, chucking packets of pork scratchings onto the table. 'He went nuts at Raymond, warned him to keep his daughter out of the tabloids or he'd personally oversee the axing of our budget. Says it's bad enough she's working on this play without getting mixed up with a negligence case.'

'You think that's what it is – negligence?' asked Longbright, taking her gin from the tray. 'Giles reckons it's murder.'

'Even though he can't issue a death certificate, he's going to give us the nod tonight,' said Renfield. 'It's going to be Unlawful Killing, wait and see.' In the case of an infanticide verdict, the sergeant knew that the inquest would have to be adjourned until the conclusion of the criminal proceedings. He'd heard that the Kramers had hired a solicitor and sent him to the opening of the inquest, but they had stayed away. Mrs Kramer was apparently in a bad way.

'It'll be an open verdict,' said Longbright. 'Not enough evidence.'

'It's premeditated, though. Prints wiped clean, window opened. Opportunity is everything.'

'You reckon someone knew the only way they'd get into the house would be by invitation?'

'Like a vampire,' said Colin.

'Well, I don't buy it,' said Meera, stirring her drink.

'You don't buy anything. You're the most cynical person I've ever met.' Colin had a new plan. He figured if he argued with Meera often enough, then suddenly withdrew his attention, she would realize she missed him and finally fall in love with him. He argued with her a lot. She had been raised in the urban war zone of an Elephant and Castle council estate, where open spaces were navigated in cautious silence and family combat took place at a high decibel level.

'Dan checked the CCTV in Northumberland Avenue this afternoon,' said Colin.

'Where is he?' Longbright asked.

'At his nipper's school play, *Murder in the Cathedral*.'

'Did he find anything?'

'There's a camera mounted on the wall of the opposite building, an insurance company, but its screen height is cut off just below the window ledge because the Kramers' property is a private residence. Invasion of privacy policy. But Dan reckons it shows nobody could have left the building that way. Turns out there's also CCTV coverage of the area either side of the front door to the apartment building, so we're able to corroborate the doorman's timings on when the guests arrived and left.'

'I think the answer's obvious,' Meera began. 'Robert Kramer killed his own son.'

The drinkers fell back in surprised protest. 'Come off it, why would he do that?' asked Colin.

'Maybe he didn't want to be tied down with a kid. Someone should ask Judith Kramer if it was a planned pregnancy when she wakes up.'

'Great, that'll be your job, then, Meera.'

'Look at it logically: he had the opportunity. He waited until the house was full of people, nipped upstairs for a moment—'

'Hang on, love.' Renfield raised his hand. 'How'd he get in and out of the bedroom?'

'Don't call me "love", Jack, OK? Has Dan really checked every inch of the room? Kramer's a theatrical type – he could have built in some kind of mechanism to remove the door hinges or something.'

'Dan's had the door to pieces,' Longbright pointed out. 'It's an ordinary Yale lock and key with a regular handle and mortise and ordinary over-the-counter door hinges, no funny stuff. That just leaves the window, and we know he couldn't have climbed outside after because the rain had soaked the rug and there were no prints. So unless he drilled a hole in the ceiling, dropped down into the room, killed his own son and then hoisted himself up, replastering as he went, it looks to me like some kind of simple timing trick.'

'What do you mean?'

'Maybe we've been led to believe that the kid was chucked out of the window and he wasn't at all, did you think of that? He could have been taken from the nursery earlier and had his brains dashed out in the basement, then the room was prepared to look like he'd been attacked in his cot.'

'How do you prepare a room without setting foot inside it, Janice?' Renfield asked.

'I don't know. Theatrics.' She fell silent and sat back.

'And why the hell would you?' said Meera. 'I don't see who gains from any of this.'

Colin thought for a moment. 'Someone who wants to hurt the mother very badly by destroying the thing she loves most of all.'

'If that's the case, Mrs Kramer could be in danger. We need to put a watch on her, or at least make sure she's not left alone.'

'Her husband's looking after her,' Colin pointed out.

'What if he's Mr Punch?'

'What are you talking about? Please don't start calling him the Mr Punch Killer.'

'The old man's got it in his head that the Punch puppet was put beside the cot to leave some kind of warning. You know what happens in the story. After Mr Punch kills the baby, he goes after his wife and beats her to death.'

'Someone's been reading too many supermarket thrillers,' said Colin. 'Stuff like that just doesn't happen in real life.'

'But it has, hasn't it?' Meera drained her gin. 'And it does happen, Colin. In Indian communities men go to incredible lengths to hide honour killings.'

'Robert Kramer's not Indian.'

'No, he's a millionaire sleazebag businessman working in the theatre.'

'And that's exactly what makes it unlikely,' said Colin. 'When it comes to settling scores, men like Kramer have plenty of legitimate means. My dad once paid to have a boxing referee's ankle crushed. They spend all their time on their feet. Ended his career, it did.'

'And you seriously wanted me to go out with you before admitting that, did you?' asked Meera.

The squabbling continued late into the rainy night.

14

RELATIONSHIPS

On Wednesday morning the June weather grew worse, and the pleasant, airy start to the week faded to a memory. Charcoal clouds punched down over King's Cross and drizzle drew a shroud across the streets, staining brickwork and shining roads. The working population dragged itself to offices in the knowledge that the London summer had once again failed to materialize and would probably truncate itself to a halfhearted four-week period starting in late July.

John May arrived early at the warehouse on Caledonian Road to face a mountain of old-fashioned glue-staples-and-scissors paperwork. In his spare evenings and weekends away from the PCU, he had been building an experimental programme based on witness responses that would work as a supplement to Banbury's. Now, looking at the forest of forms before him, he was starting to wish he hadn't.

Traditional witness statements often failed to garner as much information as they could. On one side of the usual chequered MG 11 form there was a consent request about the provision of medical records, a disclosure for the purposes of civil proceedings and an agreement to allow details to be passed to the Witness Support Service. The other side simply left room for a statement made in the knowledge that falsehoods would be liable to prosecution.

May's new supplementary questionnaires were informal and oblique, dwelling largely on moods and feelings, but he thought they could prove useful in understanding the mind-sets of those who had been suddenly exposed to criminal activity.

Although the new forms could not be officially recognized in a court of law, he was planning to try them out with the guests who had attended the party at 376 Northumberland Avenue. Accordingly, he arranged for everyone to visit him in the informal atmosphere of the PCU staff common room, and sorted the appointments into three main groups.

At nine a.m. he saw the party's waiting staff and the downstairs doorman. Immediately it was clear that the questionnaire could provoke surprising responses. One waitress, a ghostly, slender Estonian girl, remembered overhearing an urgent whispered argument in the kitchen between Mrs Kramer and the handsome young actor Marcus Sigler, but her English was not fast enough to follow the conversation. A Polish waiter recalled which of the guests were smokers and which were not. He also knew which ones were heavy drinkers, who had appeared agitated and who had left the room to use the bathroom.

'They don't see us,' he explained. 'We're invisible when we move among them, so we see everything.'

The doorman remembered who treated him with politeness and who regarded him disdainfully. In May's experience, staff usually made good witnesses because they were focused, silent and watchful.

At ten a.m. May met with Robert Kramer and his financiers and went through the same exercise. Now, though, the recollections were about business conversations, not body language and shielded slights.

Kramer was frank about his reasons for throwing the party. His producer had asked him to raise further finance and find new backers for the show. The company needed to be seen as a new force in the world of commercial theatre. He had discussed mergers and acquisitions, copyright and licensing issues. But there were others in attendance who spent the evening vying for his attention.

For Kramer, hosting the party had been an important display of power, and he was convinced that someone in the room hated him enough to harm his only child. He freely admitted that he was disliked, but was reticent when it came to providing a reason. His employees were even less forthcoming. May learned the least from this group.

Finally, at eleven-thirty, May saw the actors and production crew. At first they politely refused to discuss the other guests, but it didn't take long for most of them to crack and start enthusiastically chipping in with scurrilous information. This group proved to be the most interesting, but a new problem emerged: May could not tell who was telling the truth and who was exaggerating for effect. The responses on the questionnaires were colourful but largely constructed from surmise and gossip.

'Judith Kramer doesn't love her husband,' confided Mona Williams, the older lady who was playing the handsome actor's grandmother in *The Two Murderers*. She had insisted on being interviewed with Neil Crofting, her onstage partner.

'They've only been married a short while,' said May. 'What happened?'

'She told me that Robert had deceived her.'

'How?'

'She was seeing someone else when they met, but Robert was extremely persistent in his attentions. He bombarded her with gifts, turned on the charm, flew her to India to propose. He pushed her to marry him. She says he wanted a hostess, not a partner. Look at her, she's a classic trophy wife! After they were married he completely changed. Treated her like a servant.'

'How do you know this?'

'Judith and I have had quite a few heart-to-hearts.'

'Why did she go through with the marriage?'

'She told me her parents divorced when she was seven and her mother was left penniless, and I think she was frightened that the same thing might happen to her. She did what a lot of insecure women do. She married for security and saw someone else for love.'

'Do you know who this "someone else" was?'

Mona shot a meaningful glance at her old friend Neil Crofting.

'You might as well tell him, seeing as you've gone this far,' said Neil, with a sigh.

'So long as it goes no further,' said Mona. 'It's Marcus Sigler, our leading man.'

'When did she stop seeing him?'

'That's the thing. I don't think she has. I don't know for sure because she won't tell me, but apparently the last ASM walked in on them in his dressing room, which we think is why she left the company. She knew too much, couldn't face seeing them after that.'

'And Robert Kramer really has no idea?'

'God no, he'd never have hired Marcus for the play if he had! If he ever found out, I don't know what he'd do. He has a terrible temper. He was married before but his first wife couldn't take any more of his behaviour and it all ended badly. He never talks about her.'

What would it take, May wondered, for a man to kill

his own child? Could Robert have murdered Noah to spite his wife for her infidelity? And if so, how did he do it in his own flat, surrounded by his friends?

'There's something else,' said Mona, always happy to be a harbinger of ill will. 'Gail Strong, our so-called ASM, was giving our leading man the come-on from the moment she set eyes on him at the party. I'm RADA-trained, you know. I miss nothing.' May made another note.

The corpulent Alex Lansdale had been a restaurant critic, a film critic, an art critic and now a theatre critic. He explained that he had been born to criticize others for a living, and made more money than any of those he lambasted. His ultimate ambition was to become a TV talent show judge. Lansdale sat back in the sofa, his tiny grey eyes lost in a basin of unhealthy flesh, and held forth to his audience.

'You must understand, Mr May, that Robert Kramer is a terribly clever man when it comes to money, and an imbecile when it comes to art. He knows what the public wants, but he couldn't tell Nijinsky from Stravinsky. Basically, he's a property developer with no taste. Have you seen *The Two Murderers*? Oh, it's smartly written, I suppose, but pure sensation, gore and sex for the masses. It'll make a fortune, but in my opinion it's meretricious trash.'

'So it's safe to say you don't like Robert Kramer,' May pushed.

'I'm not paid to have an opinion about him one way or the other,' Lansdale replied. 'I'm paid to cover the show.'

'You broke ranks to stab the play in the back. Yet you still showed up to the party. Why was that?'

'I'm as entitled as anyone. My readers expect me to be rude, and I try not to disappoint them. Besides, I had a—' He stopped himself.

'You had a what?'

'Nothing. Please go on.'

May switched tactics. 'Who do you think killed his son?'

Lansdale puckered his dimples, thinking. 'It's usually the mother, isn't it? Postnatal depression. I think the wife's positively unhinged. You hear all kinds of rumours about her, how she married him because she'd heard how much money he'd made and found herself stuck in a hellish relationship. Maybe she was pushed to the end of her tether. She's out of her depth, pretty as porcelain and a lot more fragile.'

'Judith Kramer is a saint,' said Gregory Baine a few minutes later. 'You have no idea what she's had to put up with.' The producer helped himself to fresh strong coffee, which was probably a bad idea. His fingers fluttered restlessly in his lap and brushed at his shirt. He kept pawing at the iPhone on the next sofa seat, as if expecting momentously bad news to arrive at any second.

'How's the general atmosphere between you all?' May asked. 'Amicable? Fractious?'

'I'm sure you'd like to hear that we're all at each other's throats, but we're not,' Baine replied. 'It's one of the most ego-free productions I've ever worked on. We all have our designated roles and we stick to them. Outsiders always assume we're either friends or rivals, but that's not true these days. Modern theatre is a business like any other. You draw up contracts and budgets, take meetings, put in your hours and go home at night. But money's a problem. Cash flow is a nightmare, and I'm the one who takes the blame if anything goes wrong.'

'Do you think what happened to Noah Kramer is a personal affair? Nothing to do with anyone else at the party?'

'This is a private matter between Robert and Judith. The rest of the company is hardly known to them. They're just employees.'

'You don't count yourself in that group?'

'No. I've known Robert for years.'

'I understand Mr Kramer was primarily a property developer. What made him get into the theatrical business?'

'He fell in love with the building, and when the property report came in he found out that it still had a theatre licence, simple as that. He saw a way to make easy money on a relatively small investment. But he wouldn't have been able to do it without Ray Pryce.'

May checked his notes. 'The playwright.'

'Ray went to Robert with the play already written. Robert's an astute businessman but he hasn't got a creative bone in his body. Luckily, Robert listened to his advisors and Ray chose to stick with him.'

The director, Russell Haddon, agreed. He had nothing but compliments for his team and the company. But May noticed they were all being careful when it came to discussing Robert Kramer's relationship with his wife. The detectives were being politely but firmly treated as outsiders. The theatre company had closed ranks against them.

Flicking back through the pages on his desk, May became aware that the case was starting to point in a single direction. To all appearances it seemed that Robert Kramer had found out about his wife's affair and had killed their child in a fit of uncontrollable anger.

Marcus Sigler looked uncomfortable from the moment he sat down. He glanced around and dropped his voice, as if expecting to be spied on. 'Am I being singled out?' he wanted to know.

'No, we're talking to everyone.' May held him with a level gaze. 'The main reason bad things happen to loved ones is that someone close to them gets angry, and I wondered how angry you are right now.'

'I don't think I know what you mean.'

'Let's start with your relationship to Judith Kramer. I understand you met her before she got married, and began an affair with her that's still continuing—'

'Oh, Jesus—'

'Who initiated it?'

'It was a mutual thing.'

'Did you ask her to leave her husband?'

'Oh, Christ.' Marcus pushed back in his seat and covered his face with his hands. 'No, you don't understand. I care for her but I'm glad she married Robert. She is too.'

'Why?'

'Because she got what she always wanted. The best of both worlds.'

'A successful husband and an attractive lover.'

'She also became a mother, something else she'd always wanted.'

'Don't you think it was a dangerous idea to continue seeing her?'

Sigler stared silently down at his perfectly manicured nails.

'How does it work, in the practical sense? You wait for Mr Kramer to go to the theatre, then say you're heading off somewhere on business? You send Mrs Kramer a coded telephone message? What?'

'Look, it just happens. We find ways. Theatre people work unusual hours. It has to be like this.'

'No, it doesn't. You could have stopped seeing her.'

'You have no right to judge me.'

'I'd agree with you if I were a regular police officer, but I'm not. I'm paid to hold opinions. You could be the cause of what's happened, have you thought about that? Robert Kramer might have done this to get back at his unfaithful wife. And he might want to hurt you too.'

'No. Until Monday at least, I thought he couldn't know about us.'

'How can you be sure?'

'He's not the kind of man who can bottle up his emotions. You should hear him in the theatre sometimes. When he gets angry everyone knows about it.'

'OK, let me run another situation past you. You killed Noah Kramer to hurt the man who has been mistreating his wife – your lover.'

'No!'

'Why not?'

Another silence extended into discomfort. 'I could never harm a child. *Any* child.'

'Give me a reason, Mr Sigler. Eliminate yourself from the inquiry, or we'll be seeing quite a bit more of each other.'

'You mean I'll remain under suspicion if I don't tell you?'

'It's looking that way.'

Sigler glanced around, then leaned closer. 'How can I be sure that what I say in this room remains in the strictest confidence?'

'You can't. It will stay within the confines of the investigation, but I'm not a priest.'

Sigler took a deep breath. 'The boy was mine.'

'Noah Kramer was your son?'

'Yes. Judith told me that she and Robert had had trouble conceiving. They went to get advice, and Robert found out he has an abnormally low sperm count. He thinks he got lucky with Noah, but the hospital told Judith it was unlikely he would ever be able to give her a child. So I did. OK, it was an accident, but that's what happened.'

'How did Judith feel when she discovered she was pregnant?'

'She was happy about it. She wanted to keep the baby – for Robert's sake.'

'And Mr Kramer has no inkling about this either?'

'No, of course not. And now Noah's dead, so you need to look for someone who wants to hurt me, not him. You wouldn't have to look very far.'

'What do you mean?'

'I would have thought it was obvious. Something happened at the party. Somebody must have told Robert about us, and he put two and two together. He took his revenge by killing our child. I don't know how he covered his tracks, but I'm sure it was him.'

This idea crystallized an uncomfortable sensation that May had felt since the start of the investigation; everything turned on the conversation at the party. It made the investigation trickier, because Bryant was chronically unable to empathize with the victims and witnesses of crime. This was a problem only May would be able to solve.

He released Marcus Sigler. As they walked out into the corridor, May collected Ray Pryce from the bench that had been set there. 'I just have a few questions for you,' he explained, ushering the playwright into the common room.

Pryce flattened his hair in an attempt to smarten himself as he sheepishly entered, clearly uncomfortable with being in a police office, even one that looked like a cross between a student bedsit and a junkyard.

'I need to get certain facts clear in my head,' began May. 'You went to Robert Kramer with a play you'd written. I can't find any previous CV for you. Have you always been a playwright?'

Pryce looked embarrassed. 'No, before this I was working for the government.'

'As a playwright?'

'No, I was in the parks and gardens department. I'd excelled at English at school. But I didn't think I had any talent. I wrote for my own amusement, at evenings and weekends. I finished this play, *The Two Murderers*, and didn't know what to do with it. I didn't have an agent, so I sent it direct to Robert Kramer. He forwarded it to Russell Haddon, and the director hired me.'

'How did you know who to send it to?'

'I'm sorry?'

'If you didn't have an agent.'

'I read in *The Stage* that Kramer was opening the New Strand Theatre. It's a hard field to break into.' Pryce seemed unsettled in his skin, the kind of man who transmitted his discomfort to others. 'I thought because he was new to the business himself he might have more of an open mind about hiring someone with no previous experience.'

'I haven't seen the play but I hear it's incredibly gruesome. Like that kind of stuff, do you?'

'The audiences do. And actually, yes, I do too. I've always been a big fan of horror films. Theatrical styles come and go, but a good scary plot never goes out of fashion.'

'People keep telling me that there are parallels between the events of the play and the performers – I mean, in terms of jealousies, rivalries and so on. That true?'

'I hate to disillusion you, Mr May, but I understand that actors say this about virtually every production. The truth is, I wrote the play before I'd ever met any of the performers, and I didn't have a say in the casting. That was down to Russell Haddon.'

'Isn't there a puppet that comes to life in the show or something similar?'

'It's a dummy – a wax dummy comes to life at the end of the first act and murders a girl. It's a traditional image that has precedent in many films and plays of the past. I'm new but I've done plenty of research on the subject.'

'I see. Perhaps you'd better let me have a copy of the script. Just in case anything else happens.' May found himself taking an irrational dislike to the little writer. There was a paradoxical arrogance in his humility that irked the detective.

'Sorry, I don't have one on me,' said Pryce, folding his arms. 'Is there anything else?'

'I've got one in my bag you can have,' said Larry Hayes, the young wardrobe master. 'I always keep a script on me.' He worked closely with Ella Maltby, the set and props designer, and had asked to be interviewed with her. Together, they had been responsible for creating a brooding, Gothic feel to the play. Larry was pierced and tattooed in every visible spot, with a splayed pack of playing cards stitched in red and blue up his right arm and a chain of Asian tigers running around his left. He proved friendly and helpful, but could add no further insights into Robert Kramer's relationships with the members of his company.

'Yeah, I'm in charge of bringing the dummy to life,' Ella Maltby agreed, 'but that doesn't make me a suspect, does it?'

'Why would you think you were?' asked May.

'Because there's a rumour going around that the kid was chucked from the window by a walking Mr Punch puppet. Which rather puts me in the frame, don't you think?' Maltby's tone suggested a prickly, aggressive personality. She was solid-framed and crop-headed, the self-consciously creative type one usually saw in Camden Town or Hoxton.

'I'm more concerned with motive, Ms Maltby. This doesn't appear to have been a premeditated act, so I'm looking for people who have some kind of grudge against Mr Kramer and his wife.'

'Then that rules out most of us,' said Larry Hayes. 'I mean, unless we had a death wish about our careers. If we upset the boss we could kill the show.'

'Fair point,' May conceded. 'Any idea who might want to do that?'

'None whatsoever. I'm production, which means I'm basically backstage staff. If you're trying to find someone who bears a grudge, you'd be better off asking Mr Kramer himself.'

Finally, May saw Robert Kramer for a second time. The theatre owner was displeased at being retained and impatient to be on his way, but submitted to May's questions with the resignation of a man who was used to attending long, dull meetings. He perched on the common room's ratty sofa, his ankles crossed at his red socks, and watched with distaste rain leaking through the warehouse's rusted window frames. May knew it was impossible to mention what he had discovered without incurring further threats of lawyers, something he was anxious to delay for as long as possible.

'Enemies,' he said instead. 'Family stresses or people you meet in the course of your working day. I need an honest appraisal from you. Anyone you might consider a risk?'

'Plenty, in financial terms,' answered Kramer. 'You don't rise in business without making tough decisions. But there's no one so upset with me that he'd shake my son to death and throw him from a window.'

'So what do you think happened?'

It was the first time Kramer looked less than confident. His gaze lost its focus, as if he feared what he might imagine. 'I don't know. Something evil. Something cruel. I can't understand how anyone could visit such horror upon us. I honestly can't. Maybe our lives were too perfect and something terrible had to happen. I watched my wife sleeping this morning, and I thought *this will destroy us*. You don't get over the death of your only child, not when you've tried so long and hard to bring him into the world. I haven't always been a good man, but I don't deserve this.'

May kept his counsel, but wondered how long it would be before the lie of the Kramers' marriage escaped. Secrets had a habit of slowly becoming visible, like images appearing on photographic paper. Crime often exposed hidden shames to the light.

He watched from the window as Kramer left the building. Standing on the edge of the pavement searching for taxis in the rain, the tycoon seemed a bewildered, lonely figure. May wondered what his partner would have made of these people, but Bryant had chosen to hide himself away in the office, preparing an archive for his rare books. The last time May looked in on him he appeared to be dismantling a bookcase and searching behind it for something. He showed no interest whatsoever in the interviews, and rudely sent May away to carry out what he considered to be the prosaic end of the investigation.

It was no good. May knew he would have to find out what was going on by himself.

15

STORYBOOK

Arthur Bryant couldn't handle cases that required an understanding of human relationships, and would take off into lunatic new directions if left unchecked. Someone had to keep an eye on him.

May peered round the door of their office and watched Bryant knocking the contents of his pipe into the brainpan of the Tibetan skull on his desk. Half a bookcase had been emptied and two immense stacks towered on each side of the desk, framing the old man with playscripts, manuals, comics, art books, histories, encyclopedias, miscellanies and a number of surprisingly sleazy pulp thrillers.

'I knew it,' May said with a sigh. 'You've been thinking again.'

Bryant widened his watery blue eyes in surprise. 'Ah, there you are,' he said. 'I'm attempting to archive some of my more esoteric but occasionally useful research volumes. Now that you've finished holding your little chats, we can talk. Do come in, and shut the door behind you.'

'No loopy diversions this time, OK?' May warned, settling himself in another overstuffed armchair that had appeared in the room. Bryant seemed to accumulate furniture wherever he went. 'It's a fairly straightforward case, despite the circumstances of the death.'

'What do you mean?'

May pointed to the nearest stack of books on the desk. He could see spines which read: *The History of Icelandic Hospitals*, *Confessions of a Soho Call Girl*, *Phrenology for Beginners*, *The Role of Duty in the Operas of Gilbert & Sullivan*, *A Treatise on the Correlation Between Victorian Dental Care & Naval Policy* and – open on top of the pile – *Poetic Justice: The Morality of Dramatic Puppetry*. 'I mean there's no point in going through all this stuff, hidden meanings about puppets.'

'I was reading it because I had some ideas about the case,' said Bryant cheerily. 'I know you think you're going to make an arrest in the next day or so, but you won't.'

'How do you work that out?'

'There were thirty-five invites to the party, and fifteen guests left downstairs in the main lounge at the time of Noah Kramer's death, plus the waiting staff, the chef in the kitchen and the doorman. Eleven of these guests went up to see what the fuss was about when Robert Kramer kicked in his nursery door. That's a surprisingly high number of curious people, don't you think? I assume you've talked to everyone now, and have some idea about their feelings for one another.'

'It certainly helped to sit down and talk to them. Why wouldn't you sit in on the interviews?'

'John, there's nothing for me to do there. I never ask the right questions. You're better with people. You know what time they all arrived, which ones left and when they did so. You have all their timings and statements. You've got graphs and that computer thing.'

'It's a new application. You should try using it.'

'I don't need to. I mean, surely this is just a matter of elimination, and then putting the screws on the remaining likely suspects.'

'I know a lot more than I did this morning, and you would if you'd come in to help me. I thought you were going to give me the benefit of your wisdom.'

'My money's on the husband. He's got shifty eyes. Far too close together for my liking.'

'Motive?'

'Oh, I'm sure one will come up.'

'I was rather hoping you could bring a little more insight to the case than that.'

'As it happens I can, but you wouldn't like it, particularly as it involves a paradox worthy of Gilbert and Sullivan. I think I'll wait for a while, until you've given it your best shot. I still have more reading to do. Begone with you now.' Bryant wrapped the arms of his bifocals around his ears and returned to his books.

'Wait,' said May, 'am I missing something here? You're annoyed with me because the investigation is likely to prove more mundane than you hoped it might be, is that it? You honestly thought Giles might find some kind of mechanical equipment inside the puppet that could control it?' May was furious. 'I'm sorry the world isn't weird enough to keep you interested. You know what's wrong with you, Arthur?'

'No, but I have a feeling you're about to tell me.'

'You see words on pages but you never see beyond them to the heart. If this was a story in one of your grubby old books you'd be interested, wouldn't you? Imagine: a rich, successful couple think they have everything, but the one thing the father wants most of all is denied to him, so his wife provides him with a son from her lover on the condition that she can continue the affair, and he silently endures the arrangement so that he can raise a boy of his own, with the complicity of his wife and the man she prefers. But the triangle fractures, and the reason for the arrangement is removed. Now a mother is comatose with grief over the death of her only child, her husband doesn't know what to say that can comfort her, and the lover remains trapped on the outside, suspicious that tragedy might somehow strike again. That's boring old real life for you, is it? Their worlds have been overturned not once but twice, and we have a chance to give them closure—'

'Closure – *phffft* – ridiculous term thought up by psychotherapists to justify their jobs.' Bryant waved the idea away.

'Yes, closure – by finding out why this happened and ensuring that justice is done.' May jabbed a forefinger back in the direction of the common room. 'Life is going on out there, not in here in your books. And if that isn't enough for you, maybe it really is time to retire.'

Bryant watched his partner storm from the room with a heavy heart. He was not himself today; the news of Anna Marquand's death had upset him more than he realized.

As for the case, he could sense a greater tragedy at work, and as much as he hated to deceive John, he was powerless to act until he had some proof. Part of the answer lay right in front of them, but May needed to reach the same conclusion independently before they could act together.

He picked up the phone and punched out Banbury's number. 'Dan, are you terribly busy? I want to examine the layout of the Kramers' penthouse, right now if possible. Could you come with me?'

'Of course, Mr Bryant.'

Bryant rose and rubbed his back, then jammed his shapeless trilby onto his head.

They pulled up outside 376 Northumberland Avenue in Bryant's old yellow Mini Cooper. Banbury had been alarmed to find that he needed a bent teaspoon to keep the seatbelt in its clasp. Bryant squinted up through the smeary windscreen as he tried to avoid hitting the kerb. He had refused to be dissuaded from driving this time. 'The doctor says Mrs Kramer's in her bedroom asleep and can't be disturbed under any circumstances, but I need to take another look at the nursery.'

Banbury got out and peered down. 'You can't park here, it's a double red line.'

'What are you talking about? I'm elderly, I can do whatever I want. Here. I had Renfield knock it up.' He threw a forged disabled card onto the dashboard.

'You're not allowed to do that.'

'I'm colour-blind. That's a disability.'

'There's been a huge rise in senior citizen crime in the capital lately, you know,' said Banbury.

'Quite right too. There should be some compensations for the horrors of getting old. Come along.'

'I don't know why we're back here. I gave the place a thorough going-over. There's no more evidence to lift.'

'I don't want to gather evidence,' said Bryant. 'I want to understand.'

'So do I. Usually I get a sense of what went on, but this one—' Banbury shook his head. 'I didn't pick it up at all.'

They made their way up to the front door and were admitted by the Kramers' nanny, who showed them to the great glass lounge.

Seating himself, Banbury opened his laptop and pointed to the design he had created. 'This is the layout of the place.'

'Oh, I don't need a computer program to see that,' said Bryant. 'Here, I made my own drawing.' He unfolded a damp piece of paper and tried to lay it flat. 'How's that for draughtsmanship?'

'Incredible,' Banbury admitted. 'It could be anything. It looks like a henhouse drawn by Picasso.'

'I was trying to capture the building's spiritual resonance.'

'It would help if you put the doors in. Let's work from my layout, shall we? OK, it's a corner property on two floors with windows on both sides. Two-thirds of the lower floor is given over to the lounge, with kitchen, loo, TV room and utility room coming off the corridor from the front door, main staircase and lift. The rear door opens onto the fire escape at the back, which is where the guests went to smoke. A single staircase goes up to the floor above, where there are three bedrooms and three bathrooms. The bedrooms are as follows: main double, guest double, smaller guest room. It's this last one that was made into a nursery.'

'No fire escape on the top floor?'

'No. The idea is that if there's a fire you'd make your way down one floor and use the rear exit.'

'Can you get onto the roof?'

'There was access before the conversion, but it was removed.'

'How long does it take to get from the lounge door to the nursery door?'

'I timed it climbing the stairs at a reasonable pace. Seven to ten seconds.'

'The nursery is at the end of the hall, so you pass the other two rooms and the toilet first. In theory, someone could have been hiding in one of the other rooms.'

'Unlikely. Although they aren't lockable, Mrs Kramer closed them before the party because she didn't want anyone going into the private areas, and hers are the only prints on the handles.'

Heading upstairs, Bryant stood before the toilet door and tapped its window with his walking stick. 'Smoked glass. You can just about see if there's someone inside.' He reached in and turned on the light, checking the level of visibility from outside. Then he tried the door handle, examining it carefully. 'There's something wrong with the inside bolt.'

'Funnily enough, it's the one room you need a lock on and it doesn't work properly. Someone painted over the hasp. You can get it shut, but you have to push hard.'

Bryant stepped into the toilet and looked around. 'Another exit,' he noted.

'Yeah, the door on the far side opens into the guest double, so it functions as another en suite bathroom or as a stand-alone toilet if you're having a party.'

'Righty-ho, so if the culprit had been hiding in there, anyone queuing for the loo would have been able to make them out through the glass.'

'I understand a number of people ended up waiting out here in the hall, because they couldn't access the locked en suite bathrooms. Now, let's check out the nursery.' Banbury led the way and opened the door. The cot had been left in position. 'Nothing has been moved. The Mr Punch doll came down from its hook and was found by the side of the cot that faced away from the window.'

'Just as if it walked over, opened the window, picked up the baby and hurled it out.'

Banbury threw him a look. 'I think we need to establish something, Mr Bryant. The doll did *not* climb down from the wall and commit murder. I can't work from that supposition.'

'That's fine,' said Bryant. 'I'm keeping an open mind.'

'No, you're not. You're talking about the supernatural. I have to be more realistic.'

'I appreciate that. You gather up your spoor – your skin flakes and hairs and particles of food – and ship them off to a company who'll tell you what they mean. I'll attempt to communicate with the spirits of the departed.'

'You don't mean that literally.'

'Most certainly. Everyone leaves a trace, Dan, you should know that.'

Banbury tried to work out whether he was being teased, but as usual it was impossible to read Bryant's thoughts. The detective's phone bleeped, but by the time he'd removed the bits of string, rubber bands, coins, conkers, boiled sweets, keys and pencil stubs from his pockets, the caller had rung off. 'Bugger. Do you know how to retrieve a call?' he asked. 'I'm sure it must be in there somewhere.'

'Give it to me.' Banbury snatched the mobile from him and studied it in amazement. 'Where did you find this?'

'I bought it from a splendidly moustachioed Russian gentleman in the Edgware Road. I accidentally microwaved my old one. There's something odd about it, though. I keep getting crossed lines with angry-sounding foreigners.'

'That's because it's a State Security Agency phone from the Republic of Belarus. It's illegal to possess one of these. Don't ever press the red button.'

'Why not?'

'You'll accidentally call the Russian secret police.'

'Really?'

'Try it if you want to watch your credit cards get cancelled in under thirty seconds. It's been reconditioned, but I can't imagine what made you buy it.' He handed the phone back. 'There's your number.'

'Thank you. Now what do I do?'

'Press that one.' Banbury indicated a button, and watched as Bryant fudged and fuddled his way around the keypad.

'Hello? Who am I speaking to?' Bryant bellowed.

'Hello?'

'Yes, I can hear you, hello?'

'What do you want?'

'You called me. I mean, I called you but only because you called me first.'

'I'm sorry, who are you?'

'I'm Arthur Bryant. What do you want?'

'You called me.'

'No, you called me.'

'Dear God, if I ever get like you when I'm old just shoot me,' Banbury muttered.

'You just rang this number a minute ago.'

'Ah yes,' said a mature Germanic voice. 'I was given it by a lady at your division. My name is Irma Bederke. I work in the Human Resources Department of Farcom. It's a telecommunications company.'

'If you're trying to sell me broadband, you're wasting your time,' said Bryant. 'I'm broke.'

'No, I'm in the building opposite the apartments at number 376 Northumberland Avenue. I was working late on Monday evening.'

'You mean you witnessed what happened?'

'Well, I certainly saw something. One of your officers called on me but I was out. She left her number.'

'Are you there now?'

'I'm in my office, yes.'

'Can we come over and talk to you?'

'I am on my lunch break so I suppose it will be all right.'

Bryant and Banbury left the penthouse and made their way across the road. Ms Bederke was waiting for them in the company's blankly corporate reception area. A small-boned, elegant woman in her late sixties, she led the way to a conference room at the front of the building. 'We shouldn't be disturbed in here,' she told them.

'Do you mind if I record a statement?' asked Banbury, holding up his phone.

'Please go ahead. There's not an awful lot to tell, really. I didn't realize what I'd seen at the time, but I heard about the death on the news last night, and thought back about it. I was going to report it anyway. First I called the Westminster police, but I couldn't speak to the right person. Then I got your message.'

Banbury repeated Ms Bederke's contact details, then asked her to explain what she saw.

'I was required to work late on Monday night. The company is restructuring and we're short-staffed. I've been here longer than anyone else in the organization and know where everything is. I had hoped to finish by eight-thirty p.m. so I could catch the eight forty-five train from Charing Cross to Dartford, but the work ran over. I was packing up to leave—'

'What time was this?' interrupted Bryant.

'A few minutes after nine, perhaps ten past, maybe a little later. I don't wear a watch but there's a clock in my office. I put on my coat and walked to the window to see if it was still raining. I'd heard the thunder, but you know what London rain is like, you can usually get away without taking an umbrella. I could see there was some kind of party going on because there was a doorman standing at the entrance to the building, and I could see lots of people in the big semicircular room upstairs. The floor above that is level with my office window. I was idly looking across, wondering who they were – as you do – and while I was watching, the window suddenly opened. It went up with a bang.'

'Did you see who opened it?'

'No, but then I wasn't properly looking – and it was raining very hard. There was no light on in the room – I suppose I noticed because I usually go home before the tenants arrive, and it was interesting to see who lived there. It looked like a very glamorous party. While I was watching, it appeared.'

'What appeared?'

'Well, I don't want you to think I imagine things – I'm really not the imaginative type – but I couldn't help but think it odd.'

'Please, go on.'

'There was this – thing. A horrible old gnome with yellow striped arms and a bright red face. It had a fat stomach and was wearing a pointed cap. Just under a metre tall, I suppose. It suddenly appeared at the window. It was carrying something wrapped up in its arms. It threw the bundle from the window and stepped back into the dark. I won't forget the face, because it was so creepy.'

Bryant dragged out a pencil stub attached to a ring-bound notebook and handed it to her. 'Do you think you could draw what you saw?'

'I'm no artist but I can try.'

For the next few minutes, Ms Bederke worked on her sketch. Finally she tilted her head and approved. 'That's what it looked like. It reminded me of something from one of my childhood storybooks.'

She handed back the pad with a perfect rendition of Mr Punch on it.

16

MISERY

DS Janice Longbright alighted at Bermondsey tube station, stepped out into the drizzle and made her way up Jamaica Road towards Rose Marquand's house. Here, pale cohorts of low-income houses were arranged in regiments beside the dual carriageway, their front doors turned away from the traffic. Longbright saw the problem at once: residents had to walk twice as far to reach the main entrances of their homes. It would be easier to cut through the alleyways behind the terraces, but a lot less safe. The grim utility design of Hadley Street was an architectural admittance of defeat. As she rang the bell of number 14, she wondered if the planners had ever bothered to visit their designs. A heavyset, tracksuited girl with a blonde ponytail and cheap hoop earrings opened the door. She stared without speaking, her weight hefted to one considerable hip.

'I'd like to see Rose Marquand,' Longbright told her, indicating her unit badge.

'She can't move about much,' cautioned the girl. 'I'm looking after her. I've had to move her bed into the lounge. It's a bit of a mess in there.'

'Don't worry about it,' said Longbright, thinking, *You should see my flat. I haven't tidied the place up since Liberty died.*

The house smelled of stale fried food. It had been lived in too long with the windows sealed. Rose Marquand was younger than she had expected. Her dyed auburn hair had been newly permed, and as Longbright studied the pyjama-clad figure seated before her, she suspected there was little wrong with Anna's mother apart from obesity and a desire to be waited on.

'I was reliant on my daughter for everything,' said Rose, clearly reluctant to thumb the off switch on her TV remote. 'I don't get around to the shops much. The plumbing's packed up in the other bathroom and I can't fix it. And the magpies are nicking all my nice seaside stones from the garden. The place is falling down around my ears.'

'What's actually wrong with you?' asked Longbright, nettled.

'The doctors don't know. I stay well away from them – they're no bloody use at all. Anyway, I've got Sheena to look after me now.' *I bet they told you to eat less and get some exercise*, thought Longbright. *You certainly didn't waste any time replacing your daughter.*

'She seems like a good kid,' said Rose. 'They don't feed her properly at home so she's staying here.'

'I understand Anna had trouble with the local youths. What happened?'

'The Hagan family, they live in the corner house, grandparents, parents, kids and their kids. None of them ever had a job in their life, all on the fiddle, all ex-cons. Ashley Hagan, he's the oldest boy, he's the worst. We had our car broken into and the radio nicked, had to get rid of it in the end. And Anna had her phone nicked twice, once from the counter in the kitchen—'

'You mean someone broke in?'

'No, she left the back door unlocked by accident. It don't pay to leave anything unlocked around here.'

'Did you tell the police?'

'Yes, of course, and Anna told them who did it, but they did nothing.'

'Did she have proof that it was Ashley Hagan?'

'She didn't need proof, everyone knows that when someone gets robbed in this street it's always the Hagans.'

'The problem is that she would have needed a little more evidence to pursue the matter further,' Longbright explained. 'I checked with your local constabulary and they agree the Hagans are most likely involved in much of the crime that goes on around here. But they also get blamed for everything else that happens.'

'Seems to me the police are on the wrong bloody side.'

'They've conducted raids on the house looking for stolen goods several times in the past, but haven't found anything.'

'That's 'cause the Hagans keep it in a lock-up on the estate.'

'Do you know that for a fact?'

'Common knowledge, isn't it? Ashley found out that my Anna had reported him, and after that she was given a really hard time by the whole family. It was stressing her out. She couldn't sleep from worry. Then on Monday night she came home and one of them attacked her right on the doorstep.'

'Did you see them?'

'No, I was in here. But who else could it be? She had to go right past their house to get home. They're always hanging around outside. She got her shopping bag back but they'd got her phone again, and her keys. I've had to change the locks. Anna hadn't been feeling well for a couple of days, and this only made her worse.'

'What happened after she was mugged?'

'She came in, made some tea and started slicing up bread for toast. You know, for her supper. That's when she cut herself. She showed me – it was just a little nick on her thumb, that's all. I told her to stick a plaster on it. She went back in the kitchen, and I found her a few minutes later. The doctor said it was some form of blood poisoning, like I keep a dirty house! That knife had only just come out of the dishwasher.'

Longbright was used to dealing with the fallout of sudden death, but was shocked by Mrs Marquand's lack of grief. She seemed to be positively thriving on the drama of the tragedy.

'Blood poisoning can be triggered by pre-existing damage in the body's immune system, Mrs Marquand. Or by some kind of organism that's already in the blood. I looked at the doctor's notes. Anna was just very unfortunate.'

'Why had she been to see you, anyway? Nobody has explained what she was doing talking to the police.'

'She was working with my boss. Would it be possible to see Anna's room? Anna was taking care of certain documents for him, and I'm supposed to return them to the office.'

'You'll have to take a look for yourself. I don't do stairs.'

Longbright made her way to the upper floor and let herself into Anna's neat, light bedroom. Bryant had found his biographer through Dr Harold Masters, who insisted that Anna was far too good to be transcribing documents for academics at a pittance. But she was also employed by government agencies helping to prepare white papers, so she was required to keep a secure area in her office for documents of a sensitive nature.

A cheap Ikea desk stood against the back wall, with

books arranged in tidy piles. There were hardly any photographs or personal belongings on display. A small threadbare teddy bear that had probably been a childhood friend sat on colourful cushions at the head of her single bed. A window overlooked the untidy back garden. Two unlocked cupboards were filled with research folders, reference books and magazines. Apart from a flimsy wardrobe of clothes and a high-backed chair, there was nothing else.

This was Anna Marquand's small world, a haven away from her overbearing mother, a place of safety and comfort. Longbright felt suddenly overwhelmed by sadness.

She took up the frayed rag rug and found it underneath, a slim steel cabinet neatly recessed into the floor, locked with a single standard Yale key. Not exactly impregnable, but it probably fulfilled the conditions of her contracts. Dan had lent Longbright his key kit and she managed to open the safe in a few seconds. Inside were around thirty CD-ROMs labelled with the names of their clients, their contents numbered according to a system that Anna probably matched up in her notes. Simple and effective, but hardly secure. Nothing from Arthur or the PCU. Then she remembered: Anna had only just returned from town and would not have had time to refile the disc. She relocked the safe with its contents intact.

She picked the single framed photograph from the desk and studied it. Anna in happier times, with her father and mother on a bright Spanish beach. There was hope back then, and happiness. No sign of the future, of lives derailed and unfulfilled. She set it gently back down and closed the bedroom door as quietly as possible, as if Anna were sleeping inside.

'Your daughter went outside and found the shopping bag on the step,' she reminded Rose Marquand. 'Do you still have the contents?'

'No, I unpacked it and put everything away.'

'There was just shopping in it, nothing unusual?'

'No. But she'd been working on her laptop and had some discs. I think I put them on the sideboard.' Rose pointed across the cluttered lounge. Longbright sifted through the stacks of TV listings magazines and gossip papers but found nothing more.

'I don't see them here.'

'I don't know where anything is any more. Look, can you put a stop to those Hagan kids? They made the last few moments of my daughter's life a misery. She was shaking when she came in. She told me she was frightened, and I could see the fear in her eyes. It was probably why she accidentally cut herself in the first place. I should have prepared supper for her. I want you to arrest them.'

'I promise I'll see what I can do.' Janice searched through the sideboard and underneath it, but found nothing. Anna had taken the disc with her when she had gone to see Arthur, but didn't seem to have returned home with it.

'Did your daughter have another place where she kept things safe?' Longbright asked. 'Somewhere outside the house?'

'I don't know. She didn't tell me much about her work. It was just, you know, writing.' She made the last word sound absurd, like some kind of incomprehensible and pointless hobby.

'Did she mention going somewhere that struck you as unusual?'

Mrs Marquand tried to think, but looked blank. 'Only the lido. I said, what do you want to go there for?'

'A swimming pool? Which one?'

'The open-air one up in Tooting Bec.'

'Why did you think it was so odd that she would go there?'

'She used to swim every day when she was a little girl. But that was years ago. Tooting Bec's miles out of her way. That, and the weather.'

'What exactly did Anna say?'

'She called me after seeing your boss on Monday afternoon. I asked her to pick up some dinner and she said she'd be a bit late. That she had to go to the lido on the way home to see someone.'

'Can you remember who?'

'A girl with a similar name. Diana or Donna. That's it, Donna. Perhaps she can tell you more.'

'Thank you.' Longbright paused in the doorway. 'Would you say Anna was happy?'

'I don't know. I think she wanted a fella. We all do, don't we? She shouldn't have died like that. It don't seem fair. What did she get out of life?'

Longbright studied Anna's mother coldly. Rose Marquand could not see how much she had contributed to her daughter's misery. There was a bad atmosphere in the house. Sheena was watching her from the stairs.

She took her leave, stepping between the trash-filled puddles in the alley to reach the corner house where the Hagan family lived. In the unkempt front garden were two gigantic cardboard boxes that had once contained plasma TV screens, and an empty Apple Mac carton, yet the upper windows had silver tape stuck over cracked glass and there were slates missing off the roof. Somewhere inside, a large dog barked.

She was all too familiar with houses like this. Within it, all generations of the family would gather to bicker and get drunk, obsessing over each other's fluctuating loyalties. It was a hellishly closed world, but if any outsiders intruded, the family would briefly unite to make them a target for harm.

All the local beat officers could do was watch the

Hagans and wait for anything that would incriminate them. Drugs, stolen goods, a fight that resulted in physical signs of abuse. Families like the Hagans survived because they knew no witnesses would ever come forward to speak out against them, and nobody would volunteer to give evidence in court. But the Hagans were also an anachronism, a dying breed; Longbright was aware that there were over 180 criminal gangs in London, speaking twenty-four languages, responsible for a third of all the capital's murders, and their roots lay in ethnic divisions. Criminals were more likely to be bound by a common homeland now than by sharing the same house. Families like the Hagans still practised money laundering, tax evasion and handling stolen goods, but trafficking in drugs, weapons and people belonged to an insidious new order of outlaws.

Heading back to the tube, Longbright resolved to speak with one of the sergeants at Southwark police station, but knew there was little chance of fulfilling Rose Marquand's wish to prosecute them. She set off towards Tooting Bec lido.

17

HIGHWAYS

On Wednesday evening the sky cleared so suddenly that it looked as if the clouds had been vacuumed away like dirt, leaving a rich azure sky. The buildings lightened and the pavements dried. People reappeared on the grey streets of King's Cross and workers once more began drinking outside pubs. Smokers surrounded buildings. Cautious smiles were even spotted.

Inside the PCU, the Turkish workmen who were re-fitting the electrics and repairing walls had returned and were mopping up pools of water left by the holes in the building's roof. In Bryant and May's shared office, the detectives pored over the spreadsheet May had created to track the movements of everyone at the Kramers' party. Bryant was visibly bored and itching to return to his books.

'It's very attractive, all these nice coloured panels,' he said, 'but of absolutely no use. I don't know why you keep insisting I should study them.'

'Look, you can see who left the room, when and why,' said May. 'It saves you having to talk to anyone.'

'I don't need to be protected from the public, thank you.'

'I'm protecting them from you. By studying this we can tell who was missing at the time of the murder.'

'Ah, but this is where your reliance on technology lets you down. Your fancy chart is based on the memories of witnesses, which are nearly always faulty. It can't show us what we need to understand most of all. We can't know what each of them saw and heard that night. Upstairs, there was a queue outside the toilet. At the back, there were people smoking on the rear fire escape. Everyone else was either in the lounge or the kitchen. Are we agreed on that?'

'Yes, that's what I've got there.'

'Then, at approximately ten past nine, somebody heard an odd noise from the fire escape stairs. This is in the testimony of Gail Strong, who was outside having a cigarette at that time. Strong says she passed Sigler coming in as she went out, but Sigler says he only saw Pryce coming out, and Pryce only saw Sigler, did Renfield tell you that?'

'No. I'm getting confused.'

Bryant tapped the chart. 'Look at your time lines. At nine-ten Sigler, Strong and Pryce were absent from the room. Upstairs, a chap called Mohammad al-Nahyan, the theatre's carpenter, and Larry Hayes, the wardrobe chap, went to use the loo. So altogether there were five people missing from the lounge, three smokers, two full bladders, all accounted for. In the corridor we have al-Nahyan, in the toilet we have Hayes, out on the fire escape we have the others. But Hayes doesn't remember seeing al-Nahyan even though he must have passed him when he left the loo. People remember things imperfectly. If you overlap the times of the smokers, the bladders and the remaining guests, who were all within each other's sight in the lounge, there are no other suspects left to consider apart from the staff.'

'The one waiting to use the toilet and the other inside – they don't remember seeing each other?'

'One does, one doesn't. These are mundane moments – party chatter, a loo break – we don't give them our full attention. Several of the guests wandered back and forth from the kitchen to the main room, having a look around. And of course the host and hostess were absent to check on their baby.'

'OK, I agree that it doesn't seem likely they would all be able to keep tabs on each other, no matter what they told Renfield. Apart from anything else, they'd all been drinking.'

'Which is why all the charts and time lines in the world can't help us. So I've invited someone to give us a hand.' Bryant went to the door and opened it. 'Mr Pryce, can you come in now?'

The author stepped into the room with a look of apprehension on his face. He solemnly shook hands with each detective.

'I invited Mr Pryce here because of his specialist skill,' Bryant explained. 'He scripts the exits and entrances of his cast, and spends his days thinking of how they might respond in different situations.'

'Have you gone out of your mind, Arthur?' whispered May. 'Pryce is a potential suspect. He could compromise the entire investigation.'

'And if we were working out of a Metropolitan Police unit, I'd agree with you. But we're not. Our remit allows us to endorse experimental methods, although you seem to have forgotten that lately. Well, I'm putting the experimental thinking back in. As Mr Pryce is one of only three people whose movements we can reliably account for during the course of the entire evening, I think it's fairly safe to involve him.'

'Who are the other two?'

'The carpenter, Mohammad al-Nahyan, and the front-of-house manager, Jolie Christchurch. But neither of those has the kind of specialist thinking that might help us. We need to get an inside perspective on this, John. Writers have a long tradition of helping the government. Dennis Wheatley used to be employed by the war office and worked for Winston Churchill. He was hired to come up with ideas about how the Germans might attack us, although he did say they would try to use a death ray on London, which was a bit wide of the mark. Still, we have to be similarly open-minded.' He turned to the playwright. 'Mr Pryce, I explained our problem to you. Now you know almost as much as we know. Have you had any thoughts?'

Ray Pryce sucked at his teeth, thinking for a moment. 'Well, yes, I suppose I have, but it sounds ridiculous.'

'Come on, you're used to thinking of ridiculous situations, it's what you do for a living.'

The writer bristled visibly. 'Have you seen the show?'

'No, but I understand it features a murderous puppet and various gruesome deaths.'

'That's right. Ella Maltby designed some very creepy props. In fact, one of the ones she came up with for *The Two Murderers* was modelled on the puppets in Robert Kramer's Punch and Judy collection. Which makes me wonder about this whole thing. I mean, the murder site, the audience, the setting – it feels like a staged performance.'

'Staged for the benefit of whom? And by whom?'

Pryce looked down at his grubby trainers, fidgeting with discomfort. 'There's been trouble at the theatre. I mean, we've all overheard the fights. It's kind of hard to ignore them when they're happening in the stalls, right in front of you.'

'You're talking about the Kramers,' translated May.

'Robert often attends rehearsals with notes, even though it's not his job to do so. And he makes Judith come with him. He treats her in a way that no woman deserves to be treated. He's always asking her where she's been, and making her account for her time.'

May gave his partner a knowing look. 'Why do you think he does that?'

'Apparently he did the same thing with his first wife. I guess he's just a naturally suspicious man. Personally, I think he's a bully. I saw him slap her once – actually hit her, although he pretended it was an accident – and I heard him threaten to have Gregory Baine thrown off the board of his company unless he sorted out a problem with the accounts. And if Robert Kramer really wanted to hurt his wife he'd take away the thing she loves most of all, wouldn't he? My play is a revenge tragedy, and it seems to me he's following the storyline – not in terms of actual plot, but in tone. He's always asking me questions about the murderer's motivation. He takes a lot of interest in that.'

'Marcus Sigler is playing the murderer, isn't he? Don't some actors start identifying strongly with the characters they're playing?'

'If he did, that would mean Marcus was your main suspect. But actors are trained to know the difference between their roles and their own characters. It's those who *watch* who become the most obsessed. Look at stalkers. Look at the history of murderers who say they've been influenced by fictional characters.'

'Do you really think Robert Kramer could have murdered his own son?'

Pryce looked even less comfortable now. 'There are people who say Noah wasn't his son.'

'Who's been saying that?'

'I try not to listen to backstage gossip. Besides, Robert

is my employer, and if anything happens to the show I'm out of a job. But you can't be too careful. His wife's been doped up since Monday night. If it was up to me, I wouldn't leave her alone with him.'

'You say the murder was like a theatrical performance. I think most murders are acts of cowardice. Surely theatre is different. Doesn't it take bravery to act before so many people?'

'No, I think it just takes a form of anger. And it's an anger you can burn out by acting something out.'

'Thank you, Mr Pryce, you've been most illuminating. We may be in touch again.' Bryant opened the door to let the writer out. 'I think we need to put someone in there with her, John. Just in case Pryce turns out to be right.'

'I guess we could spare Meera. Right now, Judith Kramer is the person we most need to talk to, and the only one we can't get to. So?'

'What?' Bryant feigned innocence.

'Your big theory, the one I'm going to hate. Are you ready to share it?'

'Not yet. I'm revising my thinking in the light of recent developments. I still have some more tests to conduct.'

'What kind of tests?'

'Bells. Mythomania – that's pathological lying – and the cephalic index.'

'I'm sorry.' May shook his head. 'You've lost me.'

'Well, the bells—'

'No, the last thing.'

'The cephalic index is an index of head shape, the most popular component of racial studies. You get it by measuring the width of the head from a point over one ear to the opposite point over the other ear.' Bryant waggled his fingers around his face. 'Then you measure the maximum length of the head from a point in the middle of the forehead between the eyebrows to the occiput on the back of the head, dividing the width by the length and multiplying the result by one hundred. Most human adults range from seventy to eighty-five, and the range indicates whether you're brachycephalic, mesocephalic or dolichocephalic. But this measurement is different from the cranial index. Eastern European immigrants entering the United States were measured, and what they found—'

'Perhaps I could just stop you there before I go mad and kill you,' May suggested calmly. 'I fail to see what on earth this has to do with the investigation.'

'Well, of course you would, because I'm making sure you deal with all the boring bits. I get to do the fun stuff.'

'Explain this in terms I can understand.'

'Robert Kramer is a Bavarian Jew.' Bryant raised his eyebrows meaningfully.

'And what does that mean?'

'Well, one of the more grotesque racial myths is that you can separate Jews and Gentiles by measuring the shape of their heads. Officials once thought that the way you folded your arms was also an indicator of ethnicity. Whether you folded your right over your left or your left over your right could reveal whether you were a Kurdish Jew or not, because the Kurds in Israel favoured right over left.'

'OK, I think I'm going to leave you to wander the untravelled highways of your mind a little longer,' May said. 'Let me know when you have something to share that makes the slightest iota of sense, will you?'

'Absolutely, no problem at all,' said Bryant, slamming open another dusty volume, entitled *Morphological Traits & Ethnic Physiognomy in "The Arabian Nights"*. 'Feel free to call upon me at any hour, but next time come bearing brandy – I'll be here most of the night. Oh, and get ready for a train journey early in the morning. There's something we need to see.'

18

SUBMERGED

The air smelled cold and green. It amazed her how quickly the temperature fell as soon as you stepped out of the city's brick corridors. The swimming pool had closed for the night. At over ninety metres, the expanse of aquamarine water was one of the largest pools in Europe. The Tooting Bec lido was more than a century old, but still proved popular with South Londoners who loved the setting: a row of brightly coloured cubicles stood like nutcracker guards between rippling water and towering plane trees.

Longbright arrived at the entrance and flashed her ID card to the cashier, who was locking up. 'Yeah, I'm Donna,' said a dull-eyed girl who clearly spent her workdays researching hair care articles. 'Why?'

'Do you know someone called Anna Marquand?'

'We went to school together. Has she done something wrong?'

'I'm afraid she was taken ill on Monday night.'

'But I saw her Monday.'

'That's why I'm here. She died not long after she reached home.' Longbright explained the circumstances.

'I didn't see her very often.' Donna stood with one arm suspended in her jacket, shocked into stillness. 'We'd have a drink occasionally. She was seeing a guy who lived near here, some musician, but they broke up last year.'

'Did she ever use the lockers?'

Donna became embarrassed and hesitant. 'She asked me if she could use one, just for a couple of weeks. Well, there's hardly anyone here yet, it's still a bit early in the season, so I said yes. They're not for customers – the swimmers change in the cubicles. They're for the staff, somewhere to keep our bags.'

'And you gave her a key for it. When was this?'

'The weekend before last.'

'Was there an address on the key ring?'

'Yeah, in case anyone takes it home by mistake they can post it back.'

'Do you mind if I take a look around?'

'No, go ahead. She was using number seven, just under the canopy round the other side of the pool.'

Longbright headed back towards the staff area. The sun had set and a cold breeze ruffled the darkening water. Crows cawed in the tall planes, bobbing on branches as they watched her pass.

The lockers were set in a grey wall beneath a steel roof canopy open to the elements. Only the unlocked doors stood ajar. Locker number 7 stood open and empty. She was too late.

But only just so. A scuff of dead leaves behind made her turn. A young scrub-bearded man in a black motorcycle jacket and jeans was standing in the deep shadow. Without warning, he threw himself at her, slamming her against the lockers. Longbright landed hard but quickly caught her breath. *You can't wind a woman who's used to wearing a corset, pal*, she thought, punching him hard in the stomach. He released air from his thorax and doubled, but quickly righted himself and set off along the edge of the pool.

She had almost caught up with him when he suddenly turned and tripped her over, catching her off balance and sending her into the cold chlorinated water. As she felt herself fall she grabbed out at him and seized a trouser leg, hauling him in with her. His hip cracked on the pool edge as he fell. He splashed down heavily on top of her, his weight pushing her to the bottom.

Longbright had had no time to take a breath. She kicked out and twisted around him, breaking to the surface, and gulped air. Moments later, his hand was on her head and pushing down hard. They were locked together, sinking into the deep end of the pool.

He kicked down at her, connecting with her thigh, but the volume of water between them prevented him from doing any real damage. But now she had no air left in her lungs and his right fist was firmly twisted into her hair. Her chest started to burn.

I wish I was wearing my heels, she thought, *I'd perforate the bastard.* Turning herself over, she brought up her knee and connected with his groin. The impact wasn't as great as she'd hoped, but it was enough to make him momentarily release her.

She pushed away to the surface, swimming fiercely, and struck out for the side of the pool with him in pursuit. The concrete edge was wide enough to allow her purchase, but she knew that by the time she pulled herself out he would be on her again. Remembering her water polo days, she raised her body in the water, swung smoothly around and smashed her elbow into his throat.

It bought her enough time to reach the shallow end and she was able to climb the steps. She grabbed his jacket as he came close and dragged him up, but his clothes were slick and slipped beneath her fingers. Digging into his

154

T-shirt she hauled him onto the side and went through his pockets, but found nothing.

'What did you take from her locker?' she demanded. 'What did you do with it?'

She was checking his jeans when he struck out at her with his left fist, catching her on the side of the head.

She fell heavily to the pool surround. By the time she had managed to raise herself, he had taken off around the end of the pool. She scrambled up and powered across the concrete, but the gap was already too wide for her to make up the difference.

Trying her radio, she found it dead and full of chlorinated water. There wasn't much point in Dan creating new applications if he couldn't make the damned things waterproof. Hurling the useless transmitter into the pool, she ran out into the deserted street.

Longbright squelched her way back to the tube. Now, she sat in the warm carriage dripping. Her clothes and hair felt sticky with chemicals. Everyone was staring at her.

She tried to understand what had just happened. Anna Marquand had taken to using the locker presumably because she wasn't happy leaving things at home. Which meant that her mugging had not been a spontaneous act of violence. Someone had stolen her bag in order to search it, knowing that she had the habit of putting more than just her shopping inside. Perhaps her attacker had been specifically after her keyring. But what had she kept in the locker? And what had he been looking for?

The answer was far from comforting. Anna Marquand had come by the lido on her way home. And the one item that was missing from her belongings apart, from the mobile phone and keys, was Bryant's disc containing the documents in breach of national security.

19

ROPE

It was bloody inconvenient. Gregory Baine had been enjoying an excellent chateaubriand and a frankly sensational bottle of Rioja with Susan at the Square when the waiter stopped by and apologized for interrupting the meal, but sir had received an urgent message, just a few words but they were enough to send him hurtling towards a taxi – with Susan scowling furiously and asking what was wrong, and how dare he leave her in the middle of dinner? Did he expect her to get home by herself? But what else could he do? And how the hell could anyone have found out?

Cannon Street station – entirely in the wrong direction, but it couldn't be helped. As he sat back in the cab, he tried to think who might know about the problem. His accounts files were password-protected, but the sound was so strange in that bloody theatre that sometimes people came into the office without knocking and nearly gave him a heart attack. He supposed someone could have seen him, but it seemed a bit unlikely. Even so, Robert Kramer would murder him if he thought that anyone knew what they were up to. Cruikshank Holdings was their private nest egg if anything went wrong in Adam Street.

An even more alarming thought crossed his mind as the cab headed for Fleet Street. What if somebody knew about the debts? What if somebody knew that he had been robbing Peter to pay Paul, shifting cash from the pension fund to cover their expenditure? But no, he and Robert were the only account holders. How could anyone else know? Cruikshank Holdings had been kept well hidden, or so he had thought.

But it only took one person to overhear an unguarded conversation, and there had been a few of those lately.

Jaundiced reflections of the streetlights splintered across the windscreen of the cab as they passed St Paul's and cut down towards Cannon Street. The sky had veiled itself once more and it was starting to rain again. The City seemed desolate after the madness of the West End, all those crowds standing around on the street corners by Leicester Square, trying to decide which awful tourist-trap pub or steakhouse to throw their money at. But the Square Mile out of office hours was like a morgue, despite the vulgar new mall they had chucked up at One New Change.

No one about – why pick such an odd place for a meeting? And what was the point of it? A rebuke? A request for a piece of the action? Please God no, not that – it would be difficult enough once Robert discovered the funding shortfall, and discover it he would because Robert had a way of sniffing out financial trouble and making his life hell. As if they didn't all have enough problems with a murder investigation, of all things, Judith on the edge of a total breakdown, and now a leak, a spy in the camp. He was an accountant, not a producer. He should never have agreed to the new position. It came with too much bloody responsibility.

The cab stopped in the narrow street that used to be called Waterman's Walk, only now it was covered in platforms and scaffolding poles where the bridge was being rebuilt. He could hear the river below, and wondered why he had ever agreed to meet in such a god-forsaken place.

He paid the cab driver and alighted outside the station. More construction works, blue nylon sheeting and hoardings everywhere. It looked like a third-world bloody country and never seemed to get any better – so where the hell was his contact? It didn't look as if there was anyone here. Whoever had summoned him clearly wanted money. Why else would they send a message saying they knew about the Cruikshank account?

He tipped his Rolex to the light, turned about, ducked under the cover of the scaffolding as the rain fell harder.

And realized that someone was standing in the shadows beside him, a slender figure silently watching and waiting.

'Oh, it's you. I don't know what you think you're playing at, sending me silly messages through the restaurant when you could have called my mobile.'

'I didn't want to leave a trace.'

'I was having dinner with my girlfriend; she's furious. Not used to me walking out on her before dessert. You have no idea how she gets if you deprive her of pudding. And as for all this secret-agent stuff, if you wanted to talk about Cruikshank we could at least have met in a decent wine bar.'

'That's just it, Mr Baine, I don't want to talk about Cruikshank. I know it's a company you and Robert set up, and I know it holds the slush fund you just emptied out.'

'That's not true, it's just—'

'I know you're being investigated by the Inland Revenue office. And I know you're terrified that Robert will find out what you've been doing. You've been a very, very bad accountant, Mr Baine.'

'I've had enough of this. You theatricals are all the same, you think you can get something for nothing. If you want to talk further with me, make an appointment at my office like everyone else instead of playing silly games. I should never have—'

'Go on, say it: you should never have tried to seduce me.'

'That's a bit of a strong word. It was a stupid mistake. I'm not usually – Susan was away—'

'But I'm glad you tried. I went through your briefcase while you were in the bathroom. That's how I discovered what you were up to.'

'Stupid of me—'

'You can't change the past. But I can change the future.'

The spray hit Baine squarely in the eyes and snatched his breath away, burning and searing. His throat was on fire. He couldn't see. He dropped his briefcase and slipped to his knees on the rain-soaked street.

He felt sick and disoriented, the acid in his stomach curdling the rich meal he had consumed, bringing it up into his throat. Now he could feel gentle guiding hands under his arms, carefully towing him away from the scaffolding lights and into darkness. He staggered and found his polished brogues connecting with wooden duck-boards. Below, the tide was lapping at the shoreline.

His heart was hammering fit to burst beneath his ribs and he flailed dizzily, but found himself pushed blindly on until he felt sure he was over water. He could hear it lapping somewhere far below, smelled its acrid tang even through the pain of the pepper spray.

And then he felt the rope.

Coarse and thick, it dropped over his head, tightening around his neck, an absurdity in this day and age – hadn't they all been replaced with nylon? He reached up and felt it, rolls of the stuff arranged in some kind of – but of course that's what it was, a hangman's noose.

And now it was tight and getting hard to breathe, and his feet were stepping out into nothing but the updraught of damp, brackish night air from the river, and he was falling out over the Thames, and suddenly he realized that the steak and the wine and the bad-tempered girlfriend were part of the final night of his life.

20

KETCH

On Thursday morning at exactly eight o'clock, the workmen finishing the rebuild of Cannon Street station began hammering scaffolding pipes out of place. They always made as much noise as possible at this time, then knocked off at eight-thirty for a leisurely breakfast, knowing that one of the nearby Thameside residents would call the council to complain about the noise. In this way the workmen provided proof that they started on time, and as it was legal in the City of London to begin construction on the stroke of eight, the residents had no complaint upheld.

Amir Sahin slipped out of his harness and climbed out along the planks laid across the bridge scaffold. He knew Health and Safety would go nuts if they saw him, so he stayed in the shadows beneath the green painted arch as he worked his way out over the water.

He had taken to keeping his coat and tools here because someone in the team was a thief, and he wasn't going to leave his stuff back on the ground until he'd figured out who it was. Also, it was the only place where he could enjoy a cigarette; the bridge site had a smoking ban enforced upon it, despite the fact that they were in the open air and there were no flammable materials in use. Back in Dubai, where Amir had been working on the Burj hotels, they worked a hundred floors up on buildings without safety cables, and side winds could pluck you out of the construction like a doll. But here in this wet, grey little country, every move you made had to be approved by a sour-faced foreman. No wonder everything took so long to get done.

He reached up to get his tool bag, which was wedged in a junction of steel poles just below the underside of the bridge, when he saw the rope and knew that someone else had been out here. There had definitely been no equipment left out last night. It wasn't one of theirs, for a start – they used standard-issue blue nylon cord, not the kind of rough old hemp you used to find in fishing villages.

He leaned out from the edge of the gangplank and followed the rope down, over the cloudy green water of the incoming tide.

The body of a short, middle-aged white man was slowly twisting on the end of it.

He reached for his mobile and called his foreman.

'You have to wear a safety harness,' insisted Mick Leach, the burly Cannon Street foreman. 'If you slip and fall in out there, you won't surface. The river flows faster than you can swim, and the current will draw you out from the reach. Sometimes the bodies don't come back up until they beach at Richmond Lock. I don't want another death on my hands. I've already had trouble with the ambulance crew. They wanted to take the body and leave you guys with the paperwork.'

'Suspicious death, we take precedence,' said Colin Bimsley. 'I'll sort it out. Turn your back for a minute.' He zipped up his PCU jacket. 'Dan, I can haul him in before you even know we're out there.'

Banbury didn't look so thrilled with the idea. He peered out into the dark nest of cables and scaffold tubes with apprehension. 'It's not a good idea with your spatial awareness problems, Colin. Let me have a go.'

'It's fine,' Colin assured him. 'I've done this loads of times. It's only a problem when I'm on the move.' He led the way along the planks to the end of the scaffolding. Bimsley had immense upper body strength. Planting his legs astride, he was able to grab the creaking cord and slowly haul it up.

'Try not to let it touch the sides,' warned Dan. 'Site contamination.'

'You're kidding, aren't you? Seen the state of this place? You want to give me a hand then?'

The pair pulled and lowered the body onto the wet planks. The corpse was dressed in designer jeans with muddy knees and an expensively tailored navy Bond Street jacket. But the rope was the thing; it was secured round his neck in a traditional hangman's noose.

Banbury got in closer. The face was a reddish grey. It was a common belief that beards and nails continued to grow after death, but they merely became more prominent as the soft tissues around them lost their turgidity, so the skin around a hair follicle would retract. The effect was to make it look as though the nails and beard had suddenly grown. Kershaw could use the retraction to help him gauge the time of death.

The victim's open mouth revealed a swollen, blue-grey tongue. The skin of the dead man's neck had been abraded under either ear by the roughness of the tightening rope. He had lost a shoe, and was still wearing an expensive watch.

'Tricky things to do up, those,' said Banbury, snapping

on a pair of transparent gloves. 'The rope, a bit of a specialist skill I would have thought. Otherwise you'd say suicide. I don't think his neck's broken. Looks like he hung there until he choked to death. Either that or suspension trauma.'

'What's that?'

'If you get strung up and can't get down for a lengthy period of time, the blood pools in your legs and keeps the oxygen from reaching your brain. You lose consciousness, then your body slowly shuts down and you die. Takes about an hour. Faster if it's cold, and it must have been cold down here last night. My missus had the heating on, ridiculous in June. Suspension trauma, definitely. Supposedly it's what happened to Christ on the cross. Let's see what he's got on him.'

Banbury knelt and carefully opened the jacket. Fishing around in the pockets, he pulled out a wallet. 'What have we here? Nearly two hundred quid in tenners. Killer obviously not interested in dosh. Driver's licence – Gregory Simon Baine.'

'Blimey, he's the producer of Kramer's play.'

'Leave him here for the distress crew. Let's go back.'

They made their way down through the construction grid and found Mick Leach waiting for them. 'If you'd had an accident I'd have had my site shut down,' he complained.

'Well, we didn't, did we? Who found him?'

'My lad over there.' Leach pointed to a shivering Arab boy in a yellow safety jacket. 'He won't be able to tell you much more than I have. He's not exactly Stephen Fry when it comes to the English language.'

'How did you know who to call?'

'What do you mean?'

'Why did you call the PCU and not City of London?'

'We had your phone number.'

'Where did you get it from?'

'Here,' said Leach, holding up a clear plastic bag with what appeared to be a child's doll inside it. 'One of our men found it on the planks this morning, just where the rope was tied.'

Banbury glanced at Bimsley as he accepted the plastic bag and examined it. One of the PCU's cards had been folded into the top opening. He removed it and carefully tipped out the contents.

'This is going to make the old man's day, this is.' He showed Bimsley. 'Looks like we've got a little game of cat and mouse.' He held up the puppet.

'Christ, I thought it was a baby for a second.'

'No, it's not a baby,' said Banbury.

It was under a foot long, with articulated arms and legs, and was swathed in a black leather cloak and a black upper-face mask. Banbury dropped it in the largest evidence bag he had, sealed it and filled in the plastic over-hanging leaf requesting the exhibit number, OCU, customer number, CRIS ref, lab ref, ID signature, exhibit description, location, date, time, statement signature, witness signature and seal ID. Trying to do this with a ball-point pen and nothing to lean on usually resulted in illegible scribble.

Bimsley eyed the contents of the bag with suspicion. He recognized the figure from his childhood. On Sunday treats at the seaside, the silent figure had bothered him so much that his mother had stopped letting him attend the Punch and Judy show on the pier.

It was the figure of Mr Punch's hangman, Jack Ketch.

21

VICTORIANA

Arthur Bryant was sitting on the beach with the trouser legs of his frayed suit rolled up, watching a recalcitrant donkey attempting to tug free from its owner. The smelly, haggard beast kept its legs straight, its head down and pulled, showing the kind of mean determination for which the seaside town's residents were famous.

'Really, though, what on earth are we doing here?' asked John May in exasperation.

'Sun, sea, sand, summer,' Bryant pronounced slowly and carefully. 'Gruesome, isn't it? France has St Tropez, Italy has Portofino. England has Broadstairs.'

In front of him, a small boy had lost the ice cream from his cone and was attempting to pick it out of the wet ochre sand. His mother bent over him, ready with a slap. A handful of hardy visitors were wading knee-deep in the bristling grey sea. The watery sunshine had a suspicious chill in it, as if at any moment the clouds might cover the sky and revel in the disappointment they caused.

'I can't believe you insisted on coming here in the middle of an investigation,' said May. '*Charles Dickens stayed there in Bleak House. It won't just be work, it'll be fun.* One minute you're measuring my nose, the next we're heading for the coast. If this is the onset of Alzheimer's, can you at least remember enough to let me know?'

Bryant had resisted all attempts to engage him in conversation on the train down. 'This *is* part of the investigation,' he muttered.

'You said we're supposed to be meeting someone. I think it's about time you explained, Arthur. I mean, we're here now, so even if I get angry with you, I can't do much about it.'

Bryant checked his ancient Timex. 'Come on, he should be waiting for us.' He stuck out his hand and his partner grudgingly pulled him to his feet. Surveying the maritime scene before him, he waited with arms outstretched while May dusted him down. A seagull stumped past them with a ketchup-covered chip in its mouth. Several of its friends flew down to take a closer look at the detectives and decided they probably weren't worth landing on.

'Look at them,' Bryant complained. 'Virtually the only birds you can't eat. Why aren't there shooting ranges on the beach? You could make a fortune. Look over there.' He pointed to a dingy doorway with the word *Willy's Waxworks* picked out in gold against black. Next to it was a rock shop, selling hard-candy false teeth, giant baby pacifiers and plates of fake bacon and eggs. 'What would aliens think if they found themselves in the average British seaside town? All this gruesome Victoriana on display, death masks in wax and body parts made from sugar. Rickety rides and penny slot machines. Ghost trains. Clairvoyants. This is where the past truly survives.'

'That's why you like it so much,' May told him. 'You're still a Victorian at heart, aren't you? You'd like to see the return of fog and cobbled streets and tuberculosis, and sticking kids up chimneys.'

'It's all still here. Look at the grotesques wandering around us – instead of the healthy bodies and chiselled features you see in London, we're surrounded by fat people with terrifying red faces. The seaside is full of people who look like they've been carved out of Spam.' A woman in front of Bryant turned around and glared at him. After many decades of working together, May was used to his partner's rudeness, but forgot that it still came as a shock to others.

'You're saying it's a class issue.'

'Well, of course,' Bryant retorted impatiently. 'These days only the rich are thin. And they holiday in Tuscany and the Riviera. The working classes always headed for the English seaside, and were never content just to sit and look at the view. They wanted to eat and drink and be entertained. What a selection the Victorians had to choose from! Shell grottoes, sand artists and seaweed gardens, Pierrot troupes, concert parties, champion pier divers, phrenologists, burnt-cork minstrels, goat carriages, bathing machines, sword swallowers, pugilists, fortune-tellers. Come on, let's get some cockles and whelks and cover them in white pepper and vinegar.'

Neither of the detectives had enjoyed a proper holiday in years, and this little Thursday-morning mystery jaunt was the closest they were going to get to one. Their last abortive trip to the seaside had left them trapped in the winter's worst traffic jam, investigating a murder. As both were born Londoners, the strange sense of discomfort they felt upon leaving the capital mitigated any real desire to travel.

Most of the lightbulbs edging the Las Vegas Amusement Arcade were broken and corroded by the salt air. A less Vegas-y venue was hard to imagine. The illuminated machines in its cavernous interior blinked and shook in the gloom, tawdry treasures awaiting discovery by some third-rate Aladdin. The sharp scent of brine mingled with the pungent reek of stale doughnut fat and candy floss.

They passed a battered bandstand with an octagonal roof of oxidized green tiles and a row of blue and white public deckchairs awaiting the arrival of summer's senior citizens, who would turn to follow the path of the sun like ripening tomatoes before folding up at five for tea. A large red sea mine had been converted into a charity box for guide dogs and had been draped with a plastic banner that read *Ho-Lee-Fook! The Best Chinese Restaurant In Broadstairs!* A sign above the serving hatch of a tea hut read: *Half Price Cream Teas For Pensioners – No Seconds*.

'*Pensioner* is such an ugly word,' said Bryant vehemently. 'How quick we are to give everyone labels. In London I like to think I'm regarded as an expert, an authority, a man with experience to impart. Down here I'd be treated as a child or ignored as a *pensioner*.'

'Don't worry, Arthur, no one's expecting you to retire,' May replied, reading his thoughts. 'We all know you'll die in harness.'

'True. Hopefully I'll be gazing down at a body with a knife in its back and just drop in my tracks, whereupon Banbury will draw a chalk outline around me and I'll join my own cases.'

'Arthur, there you are! I thought we were supposed to meet in front of the clock tower? I gave up waiting.' A very odd-looking man was squinting at them from behind the Hook-a-Duck stall.

'Dudley Salterton!' Bryant exclaimed. 'Sorry, Dudley, I lost track of the time. John, this is a very old friend of mine. We went to school together in Whitechapel.' He hadn't seen the elderly seaside entertainer in years, and it was hard to tell if he'd got the right man. People described Salterton as *ageless* in a way that wasn't intended as a compliment. He seemed to exist somewhere between post-menopause and post-mortem. He dyed his hair and eyebrows a weird shade of gingery-brown and never shaved properly, leaving a patina of stubble around which a crust of stage makeup could be discerned, so that he looked as if he'd been inexpertly embalmed. He was wearing a too-short school tie and what appeared to be a red flannel dressing gown over a very old mismatched suit.

'I thought you only knew strange people in London,' May said from the side of his mouth as the trio walked away together.

'I did, but they started spreading out to all parts of the country,' Bryant replied with a hint of pride. 'Dudley is a ventriloquist. Are you still working with Barnacle Bill, Dudley?'

'No, I had to give him up. I left him in the shed a few winters back and he got woodworm. Did you ever use those lessons I gave you?'

'The ventriloquism? No, I forgot most of what you taught me.'

'Pity, you were very good at it. Gave me quite a fright, if I recall.'

'What have you been up to?'

'I was performing magic tricks at the Winter Gardens last winter until Health and Safety started giving me grief about keeping doves down my trousers. Then I took over the Punch and Judy show from my pal Arnold after he had his colon shortened.'

'Why?'

'Well, he couldn't reach up any more. The puppet booth is too high for him now.'

'No, I mean why the Punch and Judy show? I thought you hated children.'

'Oh, aye, I do. But I get a grant from the council for keeping English folk traditions alive. They pay me to put

170

the fear of God up ankle-biters twice an hour.' He released a high laugh that sounded like a seagull with a bone stuck in its throat. 'Mind you, I have to fight for their attention.'

'What do you mean?'

'Texting. The little buggers spend all their time taking photos on their phones and texting each other. Arnold used to give out oranges and walnuts at the end of the show. Not much point in doing that when the kids have all got these fancy mobiles. Punch and Judy is a play about the unstoppable power of the human life force. How can I teach kids that when they're busy blowing up aliens and texting folk on the other side of the world? They know it all now. Even Mr Punch cheating Death doesn't impress them.' He shook his head sadly. 'The truth is, Arthur, I can't keep up with them any more, even down here. There's no dignity in ending up like this, I can tell you. I can't be long, I only get an hour for lunch.'

'Actually, we came to see you with a problem. Do you still own the waxworks?'

'Aye, the place is falling down but I can't get rid of it. Part of me heritage, is that place.'

'Can we go in and take a look around?'

'If we're quick. This way.' Salterton crossed the road and brought them to the waxworks entrance. Now May understood why he had been dragged out here. His partner was suspicious of Robert Kramer because he believed the Mr Punch clues pointed to him. May was of a different opinion, and would have resisted making the trip if Bryant had forewarned him.

Salterton instructed a tiny old woman who sat behind the scratched Plexiglas of the entrance booth. 'Betty, let these gentlemen in on discount tickets, will you? They're under fifteen.'

'Don't make me laugh,' grumbled Betty. 'I caught a right little tearaway with his hand up Princess Diana's skirt just now. Couldn't have been more than ten. You have to have eyes in the back of your head.'

'You know, Betty, you could have been my assistant on stage, you've got the legs for it,' said Salterton.

'No, really, don't make me laugh,' said Betty. 'I mean it, I've just had my womb lifted. I'm not allowed to crack a smile for at least a fortnight.'

The waxworks had once been a private house, where Dudley's great-grandparents, a sturdy well-to-do Edwardian family from Kingston upon Thames, had entertained their summer guests visiting from London. Back in the 1930s the rooms had been stripped out and hung with red velvet curtains and waxworks of historical figures had been installed. After the Second World War the enterprise had struggled to compete with flashier fare on the promenade, and the building's fabric had deteriorated. Cary Grant and Elizabeth Taylor had been removed, Steve McQueen and Raquel Welch had been installed. Welch had recently been refitted as Keira Knightley, but these days the reality-TV celebrities came and went so fast that there was no point in changing most of the exhibits any more. Mice, moths, woodlice and spiders inhabited the damp drapery and warped floorboards, and the only paying customers now were bored children looking for something to make fun of.

'I've no money to fix the roof,' Salterton explained. 'I thought I might get a grant from the council, but times have changed since the credit crisis. We're all having to fend for ourselves.'

He led the way into the first room. 'We got rid of the historical figures and all the old film stars. Nobody's interested in Norman Wisdom and Diana Dors any more. I dressed up some of our old cast-offs with new wigs and clothes and I've given them new names. The Duke of Wellington and General Wolfe are now *Big Brother* contestants. Anne Boleyn and Mary, Queen of Scots have become *X-Factor* finalists. Nobody notices, nobody cares.'

The room had the spirit-lowering air of a hospital chapel. Half a dozen gruesome, ill-kempt figures were grouped in attitudes of supplication. 'They need a wipe-down,' said Salterton apologetically, 'but there's only Betty and me left, and she can't get about much.'

'Arthur, what are we really doing here?' asked May. 'I've been very patient, but I think I've indulged you long enough. If we hurry, we can catch the two-thirty train.'

'You asked me if I had any idea about the case,' Bryant countered. 'Well, I do. We need to understand a very devious and particular kind of mind-set. Dudley, kindly show Mr May your pride and joy, would you?'

22

MAMMET

Salterton perked up. 'So that's what you came to see me for. Come this way.' He led them to a narrow flight of stairs, turning on the lights as he went up. It was clear nobody ever came to this part of the building. 'Be careful. Some of the steps are broken.'

At the top landing, he unlocked a varnished oak door and groped for the light switch. 'We never let anybody up here because of the insurance. If anyone found out that they were on the premises – well, it's hard times, the local kids will break into anything nowadays and you can't find a copper for love nor money. I'm supposed to have a security system before the insurance will cover me, but where am I going to get the cash for that kind of thing?'

'Arthur, what is he talking about?'

Chemist signs made of rust-spotted tin decorated the walls. One read *Carson's Superior Nerve Tonic Dissipates Catarrh of the Bile Ducts*. Another showed a frighteningly elderly baby drinking from an unstoppered bottle beneath the headline *Baby Loves Formulated Mendalin Phosphate, the Only Cure for Unwarranted Secretions*.

'He's talking about those.' Bryant pointed to a series of dusty cases on crimson-painted pedestals. 'Go on, take a look.'

May made his way carefully across the room and wiped the dust from the glass with his sleeve.

'They were created for Queen Victoria in 1865,' Salterton told them. 'The height of the British Empire. They've been in our family ever since then. Some shyster from Sotheby's offered to put them up for auction, but I sent him away with a flea in his ear.'

May found himself looking at a collection of Punch and Judy puppets. The full cast included Punch, Judy, their Baby, the Beadle, Scaramouche, Toby – a real stuffed dog in its ruff collar – Pretty Poll, a pointy-haired Clown, a Courtier with an extending neck, an Archer, the Police Constable, the sinister Doctor, Jim Crow the Black Servant, the Tradesman, the Distinguished Foreigner, the Alligator, the Blind Man, the Ghost, Jack Ketch the Hangman, Mephisto, the Devil and, finally, Death himself.

'We think it's probably the most complete collection in the world,' Salterton said. 'The puppets got passed down from father to son, and each puppet master took on the royal coat of arms as the Queen's official Punch and Judy man, hired to perform before the children of nobles and heads of state whenever they came to visit Windsor Castle.' In the light of the puppet cases, Salterton seemed younger. His enthusiasm regenerated him. 'Everyone recognizes certain iconic figures, whether they're real or fictional. The devil with red horns and a tail, Napoleon with his hat, Alice in her blue dress, Nelson with his eye patch, the Knave of Hearts and Harlequin – and to those you can add Mr Punch here. It's the striped peascod doublet he wears that gives him the funny shape. He was once played by a live actor – Italian, of course, Pulcinella, anglicized to Punchinello, related to Don Juan – but he was really born in 1649. Then he became a wooden puppet, dancing about in his tall box opposite the Louvre.'

'Dudley Salterton has a secret,' Bryant told May. 'He's the world's leading authority on Punch and Judy.'

'*Mammet*,' said Salterton softly. 'It was the Elizabethan word for a puppet or idol. From Mahomet.' He unlocked one of the cases and carefully removed a Mr Punch, lovingly picking off specks of dust and stroking it like a puppy. 'He's always dressed in red and yellow, and you always see his legs. Everyone else in the show only appears from the waist up. The sets are here, too. Everything from Hampton Court Palace to the Bay of Naples. And props: Punch's drum, his beating-stick, his sheep-bell, the string of sausages and the gallows.'

May was beguiled and puzzled in equal measure. 'I don't understand Punch and Judy. It just seems to be all yelling and hitting.'

'The second commandment of the God of the Israelites was levelled against the power of the puppet. The dangerous thing about them, of course, is that they might become human. Many religious figurines were removed in the Reformation, but lived on as gargoyles carved into church walls and on misericords. *Punch and Judy* is a morality play about the absence of morality,' Salterton explained. 'Marionette players were banned by Oliver Cromwell, because many puppets have pagan histories. The Clown was originally Momus, the Harlequin was Mercury. We think Punch got his name from *Pulliceno*, a turkey-cock – a creature with a resemblance to Punch and his beaked nose. But the French say it comes from *Ponche*, short for Pontius Pilate, a character represented as a marionette in mystery plays, brought back for Christians to ridicule.' Salterton beamed at May, looking more than a little like a puppet himself. 'Many of the puppets in these cases first appeared in the shows given by Robert Powell, the great

Punch exhibitor, outside St Paul's Church in Covent Garden at fairs and market days. Punch is a clown, too, just as clowns look like puppets.'

'If we understand Mr Punch, we start to get an insight into the mind of the murderer,' interjected Bryant.

'He follows a long line of low tricksters, from Pan to Loki to Puck. But it was when he came to England that Mr Punch showed his real nature – and it was one that reflected the bullish Englishman of the times. The first English shows were called *Mr Punch's Moral Drama*, but Punch himself has no moral compass – he is nothing less than the ferocious spirit of England, condensed into a single creature. He's a man of the world and selfish, as all men are. He'll remove all obstacles in his way. This is what makes him so unique. He's not seeking revenge, he's not righting wrongs – he kills because he can, because others annoy him or block his path, and as he climbs the scale of adversaries, he finds himself unstoppable. He's a working-class man made good. Although he can be whoever you want him to be – a Quaker, a Republican, a Conformist, a Warrior, a Rake, Jupiter, Fate itself. In France he has a cat, in China he has a dragon. Sometimes in England he rode a white horse. But he must always triumph.'

'Like St George,' said May.

'Exactly. It's about sex, too. The length of the nose signifies lechery, as does the stick.'

'All this sounds rather cerebral. I mean, our killer wouldn't know about this stuff, would he?'

'Oh, Mr Punch is not an intellectual,' Bryant pointed out. 'He's pure unthinking energy. In his Italian origin he was a notorious coward and boaster, but in England he becomes a hero.'

'That's right,' Salterton agreed. 'Punch hates to be dog-bitten, henpecked, opposed, imprisoned, bedevilled, so he strikes out. He has no hypocrisy. He only deals in blood.

He kills the Baby because it cries. He kills Judy because she hits him, he takes out the Doctor's eyes, he tricks the Hangman into hanging himself and roasts the Devil to death on a turning fork. In one version he survives all the tortures of the Spanish Inquisition. He's been described as a cross between Sir John Falstaff and Richard III. Merriment and cruelty. Fear and amusement. It's a very English notion. Punch's confidence and presence of mind never desert him. And it's important that Mr Punch wins. There's a historical account of a pious showman who was pelted with mud for refusing Punch a victory over the Devil. I say Punch can be anything but really, at root, he's a Pagan.'

'I was terrified of him as a child,' May admitted. 'That creepy voice of his.'

'Here.' Salterton held out a serrated circle of pressed tin. 'It's called a swozzle, or a call. Put it on the back of your tongue and speak.'

May wasn't too happy about this, but gingerly inserted it in his mouth. He tried to talk but a peculiarly high rasping sound came out, and he nearly choked. He quickly spat the swozzle into his hand. 'God, I nearly swallowed it.'

'If you do swallow it, it doesn't hurt you,' said Salterton. 'That one was owned by my great-grandfather. He swallowed it hundreds of times.'

May turned pale. Bryant and Salterton laughed.

'There are all kinds of traditions surrounding Punch. The puppet must be made from birch or poplar. If there's a dog it must be a real one, wearing a flat hat and a ruff, and it must dance on its hind legs. The script is not written down, but passed orally from one generation to the next. And it usually contains words of a mystical nature. Dickens mentions the Punch cry of "Shallabalah" in *The Old Curiosity Shop*. Of course, the great secret to

Mr Punch – the great paradox, if you will – is that he is not the master of his universe at all. That honour belongs to the puppeteer, the man who controls him. And this marionette master remains invisible, hidden behind the curtains of Punch's life.'

'You're not just a seaside entertainer, are you?' said May. 'Who are you?'

'Tell him,' said Bryant. 'It's all right.'

Salterton smiled sadly. 'I was an academic employed in investigating the provenance of Victorian artefacts at the British Museum. I used to work with Arthur's old friend Harold Masters. But I left the museum under a cloud. After my wife died, I fell to drink and got myself in debt. I stole some small articles to pay my bills, and went to jail for my sins.' He returned the puppet to its case and carefully relocked it. 'But now fate has had the last laugh on me. I'm the penniless guardian of a priceless collection that I can never allow myself to sell. If I did, it would be broken up. I sit here in the damp and darkness, listening to the rain fall through the roof, and know that once again Mr Punch has come out on top.'

23

OPERATIONS

'Forget this rubbish about Punch and bloody Judy,'
Raymond Land warned the PCU staff. 'Let Bryant and
May wander around the country looking at puppet
theatres while we concentrate on the basics of criminal
investigation, before the whole of the bloody Met starts
laughing at us again.' Bryant had ill-advisedly left a
message apprising Land of his whereabouts. Perhaps his
note should not have read: *Gone to see puppets at the
seaside. Back soon.*

'Bring in the usual suspects from around Blackfriars and
Cannon Street. Run a check on the hostels, see if they've
had any trouble. Any offices that were working late, bus
drivers, cabbies, street sweepers, tube workers, anyone
who might have seen him. I want some answers today.
Who were Gregory Baine's enemies? Close friends? Work
colleagues? Talk to the girlfriend. Who's his family? What
were his movements last night? Come on, you all know the
routine. How the bloody hell did he end up underneath
Cannon Street Bridge? Was he killed before being strung
up? If so, how did the killer get his body there? Where did

he park? And the doll of the hangman, where was that bought?'

'We're already getting answers to some of those questions,' said Janice, checking her notes. 'Baine's girlfriend had dinner with him last night at the Square, which is a restaurant in Mayfair. He left very abruptly after getting a message from the maître d' at around nine-fifteen. We've questioned the waiter who took the call. Baine told his girlfriend he had to meet someone for a quick drink – didn't say who or why, but said he was heading over to Cannon Street. She reckons he was in a very odd mood when he left – preoccupied. His PA doesn't know about any privately arranged appointments, suggested I talk to Robert Kramer or the show's director.'

'Has Kershaw already ruled out suicide, then?' asked Renfield.

'No, but he thinks it unlikely that someone like Baine would have known about the drop from the bridge scaffolding. The street doesn't lead anywhere and gets hardly any traffic.'

'Were there other prints at the site?'

'Yeah, loads,' said Banbury. 'Workmen had been treading mud over it all day and it had been raining, so there was nothing salvageable. Suicides tend to go out in familiar surroundings. And if he'd chosen the bridge, why not just jump off? The tides are pretty lethal.'

'He might not have known that,' Renfield persisted.

'Giles found chemical residue on his face and reckons he may have been sprayed with pepper spray – like the ones you can buy for a handbag,' said Longbright. 'He's had water from the bridge dripping on him, so that's not conclusive.'

'Don't you have one in your bag?' asked Land.

'No, Raymond, I have a house brick. More effective. Baine had a fresh bruise on the side of his head, like he'd been slapped or punched, or he might just have walked into the scaffolding, blinded. He'd been led or walked along the planks and stepped off the end. Then he choked to death on the rope. He was a small bloke, but it would still have required a certain amount of strength to get him in place, so Giles is ruling out a woman unless it was someone with specialist training, like Meera here.' Mangeshkar had studied tae kwon do. 'Of course, a lot of actors keep very fit.'

'Meera, you were supposed to be keeping an eye on Judith Kramer,' said Land. 'Why are you here?'

'She wouldn't let me,' Mangeshkar replied. 'Her call.'

'Baine had been hammering the booze,' Renfield added. 'The girlfriend says he'd sunk a bottle and a half of Rioja.'

'Baine's neck was badly bruised when he dropped, but his shirt collar probably prevented it from snapping. Giles banged on for a while about the strength of the human spine but didn't add anything significant to his initial findings. It's unlikely that Baine walked any great distance – his girlfriend says he hated exercise. He didn't have an Oyster card on him and wasn't the public transport type, so we're checking taxis now.'

'Good. Anyone else?'

Meera tapped her notepad. 'The Hangman puppet – it doesn't belong to Robert Kramer. He says he still has his full set, minus the Punch, of course, which Giles has returned to our evidence room. I haven't yet found anyone who sells them. There's a Goth internet site that does something similar but they say they haven't received any special orders. Which probably means the puppet was either homemade or in someone else's private collection.'

'When I spoke to Robert Kramer, I asked him to talk to his doctor about reducing Judith Kramer's meds,' said Renfield. 'He said he'd done that anyway, because she wants to attend the funeral tomorrow afternoon. With any luck we'll be able to interview her afterwards.'

'Jack, you can't interview a mother about her dead son on the way back from his funeral,' Longbright objected.

'I don't see why not. I mean, there's never gonna be a good time, is there?'

'Forget it. I'll go later today, even if it means talking to her before her medication fully wears off. At least she can get it over and done with.'

'What about the phone number on the doll?' Land asked. He was quite enjoying being in charge for once, without Bryant being there to make fun of him.

'It was one of our own PCU contact cards,' Longbright answered. 'Whoever did this knows we're handling the case and is making fun of us, or trying to force us into action.'

'We're goading killers now?' asked Renfield. 'Have you ever thought that we might be making matters worse? Maybe if this unit didn't exist there wouldn't be so many crazies around trying to get at us.'

Land was flummoxed. 'No, you're wrong there, Jack. The world is full of weirdos—'

'Yeah, and we're encouraging them, aren't we? Our very existence is a red rag to a bull. We're bringing them out of the woodwork. Set up a unit to solve abnormal crimes and you get more criminals committing them and trying to outwit us. It's like we're a recruitment agency for psychopaths. Peculiar Crimes Unit – Nutter Magnet.'

This was one conversation Land did not want to get drawn into. 'Look, he – or she – obviously wants us to catch him – or her – otherwise he – or she – wouldn't be leaving clues.'

'Women are statistically less likely to kill,' Meera pointed out, 'so can we just stick with the male pronoun?'

'Actually, I think you'll find they've been catching up in the last couple of years.'

'You see?' cried Renfield, exasperated. 'Now you're talking about bloody statistics. Can we find out where this doll came from?'

'I've a list of other places that might be able to help us with that,' said Longbright. 'Hamleys toy shop stocks their own traditional puppets made by Pelham, and the Bethnal Green Museum of Childhood has a couple of experts who might be able to identify it.'

'Good, get on it,' Land said. 'The rest of you – traditional methods, witness statements, doorstep inter-views, dustbin duty.' Colin and Meera groaned. 'And come back with some solid connections. Find out where Kramer and all of his guests were last night. And no more nonsense about Punch and bloody Judy.'

Longbright returned to her office and opened up the time line of guests once more. Something had been bothering her for days.

She had made a list of smokers, all of whom had been out on the rear fire escape at some point in the course of the party. Gail Strong and Marcus Sigler must have done more than just pass each other on the fire escape. Larry Hayes, the wardrobe man, said he had tried to open the back door but it had been wedged shut. Yet it had opened easily a couple of minutes earlier, when Ray Pryce tried it. If Strong and Sigler had been outside holding it shut, perhaps they had been holding a little party of their own.

This particular line of enquiry seemed to be a dead end, not least because being on the fire escape had nothing to do with scaling a wall and prising open a locked window under the gaze of closed-circuit cameras, pedestrians and street traffic.

The more she studied the activity grid, the harder it became to discern an accurate pattern. Raymond Land was wrong – standard operational procedures would not be enough to unlock the investigation. She wondered how

Arthur and John were getting on. They hadn't yet been told about the discovery under Cannon Street Bridge. This latest development would either confirm their theories – or wreck them.

24

SCARAMOUCHE

The detectives caught their train home and passed back through the Kent countryside, which was alternately sodden and sunlit. As they crossed the flat expanse of the Medway River, May made an admission. 'All right, I can see why you wanted me to meet Dudley Salterton. We're looking for someone who understands perfectly why Robert Kramer is obsessed with Mr Punch. This is a mind game between the two of them. It takes a special kind of arrogance to even contemplate attacking someone in that manner.'

'Oh, I think we've already met the killer,' Bryant replied airily. 'The circumstances surrounding the taking of life are usually mundane or squalid. This was at a rather glamorous party. Ego, you see. The ego of someone who's taking on the world and proving they can win. Kramer prides himself on being a victor. And the trouble with being a victor is that there's always somebody waiting to challenge you.'

'No, it's something more than that,' May insisted, watching the flashing greenery. The fecundity of the

English countryside never ceased to amaze him. 'This great anger is driven by something very powerful indeed. A need for revenge, a desire to right a wrong – it's not just ego.'

Bryant sat forward with a crooked smile crinkling his face. 'Ah, now you're thinking like me. I wondered if you'd start to see things my way.'

'But I don't understand how someone can maintain two states of mind. How can you kill and deceive, and yet still go to work and smile at your colleagues as if there's nothing wrong?'

'Because that's what the most successful killers do, John. They hold two entirely separate mind-sets as one, and don't see any dissonance between the different states. Punch sees himself as a united persona, not a schizophrenic. He simply goes about his business, righting perceived wrongs and coming out on top, even if it involves murder. Killers have been known to operate in nursing homes where everybody loves them. In the 1940s, Dr Marcel Petiot injected at least twenty-seven people with cyanide while he was healing his patients. They say many successful City businessmen are trained to think in exactly the same predatory manner. Kramer sees himself as Punch, and so does the murderer. Punch wants to knock him down. You can't have two kings in one palace, as they say.'

'Then how do we separate our suspects? What can we do to force them to open up? If our killer thinks like Punch, he'll keep going, getting rid of anyone who gets in his way.'

'I have a few ideas. The sheer volume of suspects constitutes some kind of a clue. The killer is trying to cause anarchy, trying to break everything apart. And we are expected to watch. It's an act of bravura from someone with nothing to lose.' Bryant opened his mobile and rang Longbright's direct line. 'I have to be quick,' he told her. 'I think there are tunnels coming up. Did you do anything about Anna Marquand or did you forget?'

'I got thrown in a swimming pool,' said Longbright.

'Well, when you've finished messing about, could you go and see Judith Kramer? She'll probably respond better to you.'

'We've been trying to get hold of you. Your phones are off.'

'No, John's battery is flat and I put mine in the wrong pocket and got caramel fudge all over the aerial.'

'Gregory Baine is dead. He was found hanging from a noose under Cannon Street Bridge this morning. There was a Hangman puppet left beside him with one of our cards attached.'

'Baine? Are you sure it's him?'

'Of course we're sure. Why?'

'If there was to be another murder I would have expected it to be someone else. Judith was the obvious candidate, but I wondered about what's-his-name, the fat theatre critic who upset everyone.'

'Alex Lansdale.'

'Yes, him. Scaramouche, you see – the artful clown, usually described in the *commedia dell'arte* as "sly, adroit, supple, and conceited", although that would be favouring him with praise.'

'I don't understand. Why?'

'Oh, simple. In the play, Mr Punch stretches his neck.'

May had been listening. 'There's that song by Queen,' he said. 'You know, Scaramouche and something about fandangos?'

'That's right,' said Bryant. 'Traditionally, the hanged man dances a jig as he dies. But now you're telling me it was the producer. Pity there isn't one in the Punch story.'

'He's more of an accountant,' Longbright pointed out.

'Well, there is one of those,' said Bryant. 'You realize we

gave PCU cards to everyone who was interviewed after the Kramers' party? That's why it was attached to the Hangman puppet. The killer wants us to know he's part of the group.'

'But that makes no sense at all. Why?'

'Because if we're unable to make a prosecution even with the help we've been given, Punch will have proved his point. We'll be back soon. Get the kettle on. It's going to be another long night.'

25

GIRL TALK

Judith Kramer sat at her dressing table patting powder beneath her dark eyes. Dressed in a loose-fitting black V-neck sweater and jeans, she looked thinner and older than she had at the party. She had tied her hair back and donned plain silver earrings. The effect was severe and unflattering, like that of a New York hostess attending a charity function for want of something more useful to do.

'I'm expected to be presentable,' she explained, noting Longbright's watchful gaze. 'Robert likes his surfaces nice and smooth. He's very conscious of his image.'

'You don't approve?' Longbright asked, seating herself beside her.

'I support him.'

'That isn't what I asked.'

'That's what I'm here for, isn't it? To make him look good?'

'Mrs Kramer, I don't know you and I can't judge.'

'Oh, but everybody else does. They see the younger second wife come in and watch her struggle to be part of the actors' conversations. They're a likeable crowd, you know, but insular. If you didn't see Helen Mirren in *Phaedra* or Vanessa Redgrave playing Prospero in *The Tempest* they'll happily leave you on the outside. I'm afraid I only know Sir Ian McKellen from *Lord of the Rings*. I never saw him in *Waiting for Godot*, so apparently I'm not worth talking to.'

She sat straight and studied her skin in the mirror, as if suddenly realizing who she was. 'It seems odd not having to check on Noah every few minutes. Since last July he's occupied nearly every moment of my day, and now – emptiness. It's suddenly so quiet. I wasn't much of a mother. Didn't have the temperament for it.'

'Not everyone does. It's no sin.'

'I'm keeping Gloria on for a while, even though there's nothing for her to do. Robert blames her for taking the night off. And me, for letting the baby alarm turn itself off in my pocket. He has a long list of people and things he wants to blame, but Gloria and I are right at the top. He can't bring himself to look me in the face. It will always be like this from now on, and I suppose it will break us up. The guilt, the recriminations. I see Noah's face when I close my eyes, but it's already changing. Just a crying baby's face, you see, no real features. Like the horrible little wooden puppet of Punch's Baby. I never wanted them in the nursery, but they were put there because the room was lockable. Insurance. It's always about money with Robert.'

'If you'd prefer, I can come back another day. I realize this is a terrible time for you—'

'Frankly, I'm grateful anybody talks to me at all. Everyone around here is carefully avoiding the subject of the baby, as if I'll start screaming if they mention his name. I'm sorry – this really isn't like me. I feel outside of myself somehow. I guess that's the Valium I've been taking. What do you need from me?'

'I thought we'd get to know each other a little. Girl talk.'

'We're neither of us girls. Besides, I don't think it's very advisable. My husband wouldn't like it.'

'If you prefer, I can just listen. Why don't you tell me a little about yourself?'

'I'm not used to talking about myself. I'm better at listening, too. God knows I get enough practice in this house.'

'Try it, just this once,' said Longbright. 'I think you need a lighter lipstick. Here, use this.' She handed Judith a gold tube of Jungle Amazon Coral Dew that had been discontinued in 1970.

'All right.' Judith pursed her lips, applied the still-fresh lipstick and turned to face the detective sergeant. 'I come from a nice Hampshire family. If you don't like horses or yachting, we feed you then politely wait for you to leave the county. That's what I did. I came to London with a degree in media studies, which is the equivalent of a proficiency badge in knitting, and ended up taking a job in a telecommunications company, working for one of the directors who played golf with Robert. Robert was still getting over Stella, his first wife. She hadn't been dead for very long—'

'How did she die?'

'Pills and booze, nothing very original. She'd always been highly strung, had two modes of operation by all accounts, hysterical laughter and sobbing – very high maintenance. I think Robert disappointed her as well. Everyone said he was very cut up about her death, although I never saw much evidence of that. They lived in this palatial house in Smith Square. Robert had made his fortune in property and I hear she was a bit of a gold digger. Anyway, it was all about keeping up appearances, and they had a very grand lifestyle, but Stella couldn't handle it. After she died, Robert removed every trace of her from his life. He took down the photographs and burned them, threw away her letters, wiped the slate clean. That's how he copes. He can't be seen to lose at anything.'

'How did you meet? Just at work?'

'No. It was Boat Race Day and we were at a very grand party in Henley-upon-Thames, and we kept bumping into each other after that. We always seemed to be surrounded by crowds of people, and I thought, *one day I'll get him alone*, but I didn't. I never did, not even after we were married. Ridiculous how women think they can change men, and of course we don't. We simply become more and more prescriptive until they finally go away from us.'

'It sounds like you're being rather hard on yourself.'

'Am I? I honestly don't know what I brought to the party. He certainly didn't need me. All my friends thought he was a good catch. I have no idea what he saw in me then, and I still don't. Which is what makes it all so much worse.'

'What do you mean?'

'Please dignify me with a little intelligence. I'm not stupid, I'm just not very interested in the theatre. I know that you know. I've seen who you've been talking to. It was me who continued the affair, not Marcus. I needed someone to talk to, and it was obvious Robert would never be my friend. But by then the wedding preparations were already under way and I couldn't back out. I suppose it suited my purposes, but if a woman says that, everyone thinks she's a bitch. Strange how it's fine for a wealthy man to keep a mistress.'

'You think your husband has a mistress?'

'Of course he has. Why else would he slip off after the theatre shuts and come home at four in the morning? He doesn't even bother to wash the perfume off. I suppose it's the lack of effort he puts into deceiving me that makes it so galling.'

'Do you think he's in love?'

'I very much doubt it, if his track record is anything to go by. He's spending more nights with this one than anyone else he's seen, but I think that's simply because he doesn't want to come home to a wife and a crying baby. Well, he won't have to worry about that now. The affair will come to an end eventually, he'll be in a bad mood for a few weeks and then he'll come creeping back to me with a new pair of diamond earrings, something obvious like that, and I'll still have Marcus. I'm sure you know all this anyway. Actors are such gossips, and you did take statements from them.'

'We heard plenty of unsubstantiated rumours.'

'I assume one of them concerns the paternity of my son.'

'Yes. You don't have to tell me any more, unless you think it has a bearing on the case.'

'For all I know it might. I assume you're like a priest? You can't repeat what's said outside this room?'

'I can if it incriminates you in the case under investigation.'

'I imagine it incriminates me for stupidity, if nothing else. Marcus is – was – Noah's father. The baby wasn't planned, but Robert was desperate for a son, so I thought it would all work out – until now.'

'You think someone did this to get back at you?'

'Well, what do you think, Detective Sergeant? Let's see now, who would be the most upset to find out that Noah was not his son after all, but the product of his unfaithful wife and her lover?'

'That's a very serious accusation, Mrs Kramer.'

'Everything I've ever done has been about survival. I suppose I thought that having a child with Marcus would help me to survive a loveless marriage. I hadn't counted on my husband finding out the truth.'

'You can't be sure that he has.'

'It certainly looks that way, doesn't it? You should see him this morning. He looks like he's just met his own ghost.'

'You mean because he's upset about Mr Baine.'

'They used to be best friends until Robert started thinking that Gregory was cheating him. Gregory was always getting them into financial scrapes. I imagine Robert is very upset, because he won't have his money man to bail him out this time. Even if he finds another producer, it'll be a nightmare trying to put everything right. I heard there's no question of cancelling the play. They're going on.'

'My boss thinks your husband really believes in the Punch legend,' Longbright observed. 'Do you think he does?'

Judith Kramer paused to think, qualifying her words. 'He certainly believes in good and bad fortune. That's why there's a puppet in the play that comes to life. It appealed to Robert. He was raised in a very odd family. His mother filled his head with all kinds of nonsense. You'd be surprised how superstitious successful men often are. For all I know, he honestly believes Mr Punch stepped down from his hook and murdered his child. I assume that was the desired effect, and it has been achieved.'

Longbright studied the sallow face before her and could see that Judith Kramer was still suffering from the effects of over-medication. 'How is your husband coping?'

'You've spoken to him, you should know. I'm not sure anything really touches him. His main goal in life has always been to make something of himself. Now that he's achieved that, I can't imagine anything else matters.'

'I've read his statements. The only thing that puzzles me is his move from property into the theatre.'

'Why?'

195

'Theatre people seem – irrational. They're not known for their pragmatism.'

'Well, of course they're steeped in odd beliefs. They see ghosts and touch wood, ban the mention of *Macbeth* and wish each other bad luck before performances. If anyone whistles backstage they have to go out of the room, come in, turn around three times and swear in order to lift the curse. But have you ever noticed? The more money people have, the odder they become, and my husband is extremely rich – or at least he was until Gregory died.'

'There's no indication that your husband is in any way involved. I have physical evidence against that.'

'What kind of evidence?'

'I can fully account for his time at the party, and I hear he has an alibi for last night. He was with you.'

'Was he? I don't think I noticed. Anyway, I didn't say he would do it himself.' Judith gave a bitter laugh. 'Robert never does anything himself. He'd hire someone to handle the problem for him. I'm surprised he proposed to me in person.'

'A lot of men are like that.'

'Oh, my husband is unique, I assure you. Robert purchased the Punch and Judy puppets just after his first big sale. It was very important that he beat everyone else at the auction, and he didn't care that he paid far too much for them. There are lots of ugly stories about how he made his money. In one of these tales, he set up a holiday flat-share website for students, bringing a million contract users to it on the promise that he would never charge them for the service. Then he sold the site to a company that immediately started charging them via a loophole he had deliberately left in their log-in forms, and sued them when they defaulted.'

'He wasn't at all bothered by that?'

'I suppose he has the morality of a typical City boy. They're all opportunists, aren't they? It doesn't pay to be sentimental. Anyway, with the money he made, he bought a Victorian theatre called the Putney Empire from two widowed sisters, on another supposedly unbreakable promise – that they could stay as sitting tenants in the property next door while he restored the building's fabric to its former glory.'

'I assume he didn't keep his promise.'

'No. He cheated the building regulations, paid off the council, hired some thugs to kick the sisters out and tore both the theatre and their house down. I heard they died penniless, although that may be an exaggeration. While the case dithered in the courts he rented the site as a coach park. He used the money from the vehicle leases to build a block of flats and opened his first nightclub. He was just twenty-one years old.'

'If nothing else, it sounds as if he's been consistent.'

'Robert has every version of the Punch story on his bookshelves because he believes in its message. *Morality is just sentiment, challenge the world with righteous anger*; that's how he thinks you should live your life. I wonder just how much of his tainted wisdom he'd have imparted to Noah if he'd lived. I wonder if I'd have liked my son once he'd grown.'

'How is Marcus?'

'He's rather more like Robert than he realizes. He doesn't have time to think about anything or anyone other than himself. Not even the child he fathered. I don't really mean that as a criticism, it's just the way he is. Maybe one day he'll look back with regret. Once he starts to age. I don't suppose I'll still be with him. It's exhausting loving someone more than they love you. But since Monday's . . . event . . . I don't think I want to see him any more. I don't know what I want.'

'These are early days.'

Judith moved the conversation away from herself. 'I

suppose you see a lot of tragedy in your job. You're trained for it.'

'Yes, but if there's one thing I know, it's that this part is the worst, and it slowly gets better, to the point when you'll look back and see something harmful and distant – like a fading thunderstorm.'

'That's a poetic thought.'

'I have to ask you, Mrs Kramer. Do you think—'

'You're going to ask me if I think my husband could break the law and get away with it.' Judith gave her appearance a final check and turned from the mirror. 'I know he could, because as far as I can tell, he's been doing so all his life. He never seems to have any regrets. Do you know what's wrong with all the people who pass through this house? Nobody ever cries. There's no real emotion here, it's all hidden away. And I've broken yet another rule by bringing it out. Oh, and did I tell you I mentioned the Scottish play on the night of my son's death? So I brought a curse down on the house. I'm starting to see why Robert's first wife killed herself. It must have seemed a viable option.' Judith Kramer wiped her cheek, closed the lipstick and handed it back. 'Thanks for the girl talk.'

26

DISINFORMATION

There was something wrong with Leslie Faraday's chair. It squeaked every time he tipped it back. Faraday had sat his broad bottom on it every day of his working life for the last fourteen years, and took it with him when he moved departments. Like its owner, it was noisy and had an over-stuffed red seat. It tilted and swivelled and had fat wooden arms that helped to support his increasing girth. Faraday leaned forward and punched out his PA's internal number.

'Miss Queally, could you get maintenance to come up here with an oilcan?'

There was a sigh of impatience. 'I'll do what I can.'

'And can you bring in the file on the PCU?'

'Which one? There are so many.'

'Just dig out the latest. And brew some fresh tea, will you? I'm spitting feathers.' The portly Home Office liaison officer unsheathed himself from the chair and gave it an experimental wiggle. It squealed in protest. Sighing, he went to the window and looked down into the tiled Whitehall courtyard, at the palms and ferns, the pacing executives on their BlackBerrys. He saw the same view every day. It was like being in prison, only with more paperwork. It seemed he had spent his life peering out from cages: through the bars of his nursery pen at his family home in Norwich, through the mullioned windows of his prep school in Cambridge, through the stained glass of his college chapel in Bristol. He was happily institutionalized, and if someone was to open the door of his office and boot him unceremoniously into the outside world without his black umbrella and initialled briefcase, he suspected he would creep around the back of the building and return via the service bay, to remain in place until the day he died, after which he would be technically freed from his contract.

He knew, as soon as he heard the news, that Oskar Kasavian would be over to see him. He dreaded visits from the Home Office Internal Security Supervisor. Where Faraday bumbled and caused offence, Kasavian focused and targeted and made others fearful. He reminded his staffers of a Stalinist apparatchik preparing to erase malefactors from history. His laser glare made subordinates fidget, and his reports damned the innocent along with the guilty. Faraday stood at the window watching him crossing the courtyard on his way to the building, his coat flapping like a vampire's cape. Was it pure coincidence that the pale sun chose this moment to cloak itself in cloud?

Faraday searched his desk for evidence of inefficiency, knowing that Kasavian would home in on his faults like an airport Alsatian sniffing out drugs. He tried to remember if the supervisor had a favourite biscuit (this trait alone providing an insight into the smallness of the civil servant's mind) but came up empty, for he had never seen Kasavian nourished by anything other than night and misfortune.

In a fug of panic, Faraday searched his hard drive for anything untoward. Luckily, that embarrassing fracas after his off-colour remarks at the Down's syndrome fundraising dinner, and his display of support during an NHS recruitment campaign for an organization funded by the tobacco lobby – those mistakes could be written off as mis-briefs. But the latest PCU mess was harder to dismiss. He was struggling with a way forward when the door whispered itself open and Kasavian glided in.

Oskar Kasavian had no time for pleasantries or platitudes, even as a wrong-footing device; he preferred to plunge in, shake things up and leave before the inevitable tsunami of blame and recrimination began. 'I understand the Peculiar Crimes Unit is investigating Gail Strong. I assume you know who she is.'

'Yes, she's the granddaughter of the Lord Commissioner of the Treasury and the daughter of the Minister for Public Buildings.'

'Well done. Before I come to ask how this happened, perhaps you could explain why you thought it was in the nation's interest to allow this investigation to proceed without recourse to a higher authority.' He spoke slowly and clearly, like a judge pronouncing a death sentence.

Faraday had trouble following that train of thought. His palms were sweating and his jacket felt suddenly constricting. He wracked his atrophied brain for an answer but came up with nothing positive, because the truth was that it had happened before he was even aware of the circumstances. He had read about it in a free newspaper on the way to work, like everyone else. He knew that the most important thing to do now was appear confident and sure of his facts, so he stuttered and waffled.

'The thing is, none of us realized Miss Strong was directly involved. I mean, the PCU's cases get flagged up whenever they come in, but the notes just cover the outline of the investigation, they don't go into detail. Jack Renfield has refused to keep us apprised of the situation ever since we fell out with him. The first we heard about the extent of Miss Strong's involvement was when the minister called.' *To scream at us for letting her name get into the news again,* he remembered.

'I have to assume you understand the implications of this situation,' said Kasavian slowly. 'Even you can't be that stupid. There is a credit crisis. There are those who consider the minister's daughter to be a reckless, dim, spendthrift little tart, photographed falling out of night-clubs while those who pay her father's salary have their benefits cut.' Kasavian studied Faraday's blinking face. 'I'm making this too difficult for you, aren't I? Let's put it this way. Given the situation, do you think the general public will be for or against the minister when he tries to railroad through the latest round of spending cuts later this month?'

He watched Faraday's mouth open and shut like a beached sea bass. 'Still too complicated? Then let's try this. What do you think will happen if you now try to divert the Peculiar Crimes Unit away from investigating the Right Honourable Gentleman's daughter?'

A look of horror dawned on Faraday's plump face.

'That's right, we'll be seen to be perverting the course of justice with the tacit approval of a government minister. An incredible insight into the workings of the public mind. And all because you didn't act in time. So what happens next? Well, there are several possibilities, not including the one where we encourage you to fall on your sword.'

'It wasn't my fault,' Faraday stammered.

'Of course not; your stupidity is largely genetic and a by-product of your education. I suppose I could let you flounder around looking for a solution, but I think it would be better for all of us if I tell you exactly what to do. First and most obviously, you're going to remove Gail Strong from the investigation by shipping her off to some flyblown country where communications technology consists of two baked bean cans and a length of string. Then you're going to discredit the Unit by getting them to pin the blame on the wrong person.'

'How will I do that?'

'By encouraging Arthur Bryant to run with his instincts. He's as mad as a bat and will follow any lead you give him provided it makes no sense whatsoever. Come up with something that will appeal to his inner crackpot. Here's a little starter for you. Robert Kramer is an opposition party donor. He pays them out of an offshore fund he set up with his accountant called Cruikshank Holdings. We've been looking to use that against him when the time was right. According to my sources, the PCU already thinks he's the most likely suspect in the case because of his bad relations with his wife. Bryant has harboured suspicions about Kramer from the outset. Now you just need a way to confirm them.'

'You want to secure a conviction against a man who might be innocent?' asked Faraday, appalled.

'I didn't say that. But it would suit everyone if he was arrested, whether it turns out that he's innocent or guilty.'

'I'm not sure I understand—'

'If he's innocent, the Unit will be blamed for wrongful arrest, and I can act against them. If he's guilty, we remove a source of party revenue, taint the system by association and find another way to blame the PCU for not acting sooner.'

'Why is it so important to you?' asked Faraday, undergoing a nanosecond of lucid thought. 'Why are you so intent on closing them down?'

Kasavian looked as though he'd been struck in the face with a codfish. Could this insignificant little time-server actually have the temerity to be growing testicles? 'Because,' he said, very slowly, as if explaining to a simple child, 'there is no room in the government's structure for a stalactite.'

'A stalactite?' Faraday repeated in confusion.

'A calcified accretion from years gone past. You can't control these people. They stray off-message and de-stabilize the system.'

'Then why don't we simply slash their budget?'

'What budget? Their salaries are minimal, their operational costs are negligible, they're being studied by the IPCC as an economic test case and the Chief Inspector of Constabulary himself upholds them as a shining example of independent policing. With so much background attention on them, anything we do will be thoroughly examined, which is why you have to proceed with caution. There must be no trail back to us. Your safest bet is to employ an intermediary – and I think I have the very person you need.'

Kasavian wrote an email address on a slip of paper and handed it to Faraday. 'Destroy that after you've entered it, and erase your file path after each electronic communication.'

'I don't know how – um, Miss Queally might know how to, er—'

'I expect a result from you before the weekend is out.'

'We can't get to Arthur Bryant this way,' Faraday objected, reading the slip. 'I don't think he's easily swayed by the opposite sex.'

'Who said anything about Bryant? I want you to use this woman to go after John May. He's the only person Bryant listens to. She'll plant her information, May will feed it back, Kramer will be arrested and when the lady in question is summoned back for a deposition, she'll have mysteriously disappeared.'

And with that he was gone, slipping from the room

without, it seemed to the civil servant, either turning his back or opening the door, like a wraith passing through a castle wall.

27

SOURCE

Arthur Bryant dug out an old penny and inserted it in Madame Blavatsky. 'I say, come and see this, Raymondo.'

Land reluctantly dragged himself over to the glass case containing the tattered medium. 'This is all a load of old rubbish,' he complained, but watched over Bryant's shoulder.

There was a clonk, and Madame Blavatsky's eyes glowed to life. Her gears creaked and groaned as she reached out a grubby, rubbery hand, dropping her prediction into the slot beneath her. Bryant pulled out the card and read it.

LIFE AND DEATH ARE INDIVISIBLE

'Not very exact, is it?' said Land. 'I don't think she's going to be helping us much in the investigation.'

'She's right, though. Two dead bodies and two living puppets.' Bryant rolled his eyes at Land suggestively.

'Why am I even listening to you? I should have prevented you from taking control of this unit years ago. It's your fault we've ended up in a building once rented by Aleister Crowley. Now you want me to believe inanimate objects can come to life and murder people.'

'Well, you're not getting results using traditional investigative methods, are you?' Bryant took out his gobstopper to see if it had changed colour, then reinserted it in his mouth. 'Did you find out where all the guests at Kramer's party were around Gregory Baine's estimated time of death?'

'Many of them were travelling at that point of the evening. We're checking their Oyster cards and looking at CCTV footage, but nearly half are unaccounted for. The whole thing is a nightmare.'

'Poor old sock, you're not cut out for this sort of thing, are you?' said Bryant. His gobstopper rattled annoyingly against his false teeth. 'For years we've tried to protect you from involvement in our work, and now you've got stuck in and made a mess of things. I'll be happy to help you out, but you have to let me work in my own fashion. You've started from the wrong end. Turn the case around the other way. Forget about what the witnesses did or didn't see, and start with the killer's mind. Why would you wait until there was a house full of people to murder someone? To increase the number of suspects. Why would you leave the PCU's business card at the site of the second death? Because, having met them, you're sure they're on the wrong track and you want to keep it that way. Why direct attention to the Punch and Judy dolls? Because Robert Kramer believes in their power.'

'You're already losing me.'

'You have to believe very strongly in something before you act upon it. Ray Pryce was surprised by Kramer's interest in his script – Kramer was interested by the idea of the dummy exacting revenge. His fascination with the Punch legend arose because he sees a mirror image of

207

himself in it. Strong men are always looking for analogies that explain why they're so driven. Remember the Thatcher generation? When the bankers openly admitted they believed greed was good, back in the eighties? Do you know what the top-selling book was in the City of London during that time? Machiavelli's *The Prince*. Those captains of industry saw in it a reflection of themselves.'

'So you think it's Robert Kramer?'

'I didn't say that. It's one of two leads I'm pursuing, but you wouldn't like the other one. As far as I can see, Kramer is the only one with a real motive and the ability to hide his feelings that deeply. His relationship with Gregory Baine was strained to breaking point. Baine was Kramer's partner and strongly disapproved of his expansion plans. The pair of them own a dodgy company that Baine has been draining money from.'

'How do you *know* all this?'

'It's not difficult. I checked their company registration and followed up reports in the financial papers. Kramer is subject to fits of anger. We know that from talking to his wife and to Ray Pryce, who saw them fighting in the theatre. Now, let's suppose Kramer follows his role model. He revels in being pugnacious, amoral, murderously strong-willed. He determines to remove all obstacles to his ultimate victory.'

'But what does he hope to achieve?'

'What does anyone with that mentality hope for? Power over others. And what is the one trait that marks such men out from those whom they consider to be their inferiors? Aggressive, overreaching self-confidence. Which is why he even dares to link Baine's death to our unit.'

'Well, when you put it like that . . .' Land rubbed his chin, thinking it through. 'But if he's that smart, how do we nail him?'

'By understanding how he did it,' said John May,

appearing in the doorway. 'I think I have a lead.'

'Wait, I'm not saying he did it,' Bryant backtracked. 'I'm merely proposing an academic theory. Now, if you'd like to hear my further thoughts on the matter—'

But Land and May had already gone.

Lucy Clementine had sea-green eyes, long legs and raven-wing hair. Her smile was so bright and perfect that if the room slowly dimmed on her it would have been the last thing to disappear, and the sight that everyone would most remember. She sat in the Ladykillers Café in a short black skirt and suit jacket, stirring honey into her lemon tea, listening to May.

'I can't tell you anything more than that, because the matter remains under investigation, but if you really can shed light on the case I'd be grateful.' John May's weakness for pretty women manifested itself in the gentlest and most charming of ways; he found himself believing almost anything they said. If a woman told him she was cold, he would raise the heat to an unbearable degree. If she told him she believed in astrology, he would follow her horoscope for weeks. And now that Brigitte, his partially present, wholly difficult ladyfriend, had decided to extend her stay in Paris, he was more susceptible than ever.

Lucy was a government employee in a division he was not familiar with, something called the Department of Social Resources. She said she had decided to email May after reading about the case in the *Daily Telegraph* that morning.

'I worked for Mr Kramer at his property company, Cruikshank Holdings. It wasn't an easy job. He was nice most of the time, but had – well, let's say anger management issues. He used to be extremely unreasonable with his wife.'

'Did you ever see or hear him lose his temper?'

'Yes, several times. The worst was just after Judith – I mean, Mrs Kramer – told him she was pregnant. She came to the office one evening – they were going out to dinner – and they had such a terrible argument that she went home in tears. After she'd gone, he told me he didn't want to become a father, that it would interfere with his career. He used to keep these creepy dolls in his office, Punch and Judy puppets, and I remember something he said that really bothered me.'

'What was that?'

Lucy looked up at May with sadness in her eyes. 'He said that Punch had the right idea when he beat the baby to death.'

'You clearly recall hearing him say those exact words?'

'Yes, I do. But I don't know whether he meant half the things he said. I think he liked to shock people.'

'What was he like to work for?'

'Very charismatic but a bit frightening – his energy amazed me. He could go out to a fund-raising night until two in the morning and be at work the next day at six a.m. I was in awe of him. He told me he was superstitious. That was why he owned the puppets.'

'What do you mean?'

'He believed in what they represented. Some evenings, if we were working late, he would open a bottle of wine in the office. He would invite me to sit and have a glass with him.'

'And did you?'

'No, I don't drink. But I would listen to his stories. I think he felt lonely, even though he was married. He once explained the whole Punch story, how it was a metaphor about the making of the modern world. He called Punch "the unpalatable face of heroism", and said that this was the way all successful businessmen would have to behave one day.'

If May was surprised by the luscious Ms Clementine's rehearsed glibness, he didn't show it. 'It sounds as if believing in such things was very important to him,' he remarked.

'I think he was always looking for ways to understand his life. I heard he became rich at a very early age, something to do with creating a website for students. When you make so much money at that age, it's bound to affect your behaviour, isn't it?'

As May took his leave, he thought about the Hangman figure found by Gregory Baine's body. Somebody who had attended Robert Kramer's party knew about his fascination with the story of Punch, or believed it themselves. And now they were using it to show him how little power he really had over his own life.

Which meant that Robert Kramer might not be the main suspect at all, but the main target.

Arthur had said he was developing two theories. If one involved the investigation of Robert Kramer, what, May wondered, was the other?

28

PERFORMANCE

The New Strand Theatre stood at the corner of Adam Street and York Buildings, just off the Strand itself. The white stone edifice had been constructed in 1920 along clean, elegant lines and peaked with inspirational statuary. It was now entirely filled with offices. The double-height ground floor had belonged to a travel company that had gone bankrupt in the credit crunch, and the building's landlord had decided to put the entire six-floor property on the market. Robert Kramer had seized his chance and purchased it, transforming the atrium into a gold and crimson mock-Edwardian theatre seating an audience of 450.

Arthur Bryant settled himself in the middle of the second row with a bag of cheese and onion crisps and watched the theatre fill up. The audience for *The Two Murderers* was unusually young and mixed. While the middle classes went to the National to see plays about politics and society, a more raucous crowd yearning for sex and sensation headed for West End shows that delivered value for money.

Ray Pryce's script was unashamedly populist. The play began in a grand Victorian Gothic mansion filled with suits of armour and stags' heads, where angled shadows strafed the floor in expressionistic patterns. In the first act, the ageing lord of the manor caught his wife in a clinch with the handsome gardener and imprisoned her inside the wall of his ancestor's torture dungeon before the illicit lovers turned the tables on him.

Soon the convoluted plot called for a wax dummy of the lord to come to life, and for the wife's lover to break it open and reveal the real lord imprisoned within. The twists compounded themselves in a satisfying Golden Age fashion, and soon the titular murderers were being placed in torture devices and bodies were returning to life, all part of some grand plan to trick the lord into handing over his estate.

It was neo-Jacobean tosh, of course, but well constructed and packed with stylish jolts. Bryant could see why the snobbish critic Alex Lansdale had taken against it so strongly.

'Excuse me, can you put those things down?' said the woman in front of Bryant, turning round to point to his bag of crisps. 'You're spoiling my enjoyment of the play.'

'Madam, your fox fur collar is having the same effect on me, but I restrain myself from complaint.' He bit into a crisp as noisily as he could and raised his knees against the back of her seat, giving her a good thump. Someone was being strangled onstage. Della Fortess screamed and clutched her breast before falling to her knees. Bryant grinned. At the blood-spattered close of the play, as everyone else sat in stunned silence, Bryant applauded loudly and bellowed 'Bravo!' until everyone turned round to stare at him.

'So I hear you enjoyed our little melodrama,' said Ray Pryce, stopping Bryant in the foyer as the sickly-faced audience fled to tell their friends how awful the play had been, and how they should definitely go and see it. The writer had been watching the performance from backstage.

'You heard me?'

'We could hardly avoid hearing you. You were laughing when everyone else had their hands over their eyes.'

'Well, I enjoy a good murder. Marcus Sigler is very good, isn't he? That part where he flew into a murderous rage – how does he manage to achieve that level of fury night after night?'

'He reckons he harnesses his inner anger – thinks about something that torments him. Stanislavsky and all that.'

'Tell me, how did you do the bit where the dummy came to life? I thought that was very realistic.'

'I only came up with the idea on paper,' Ray admitted. 'It's Ella Maltby's job to make it work. She built the props.'

'She knows her Victoriana.'

'It's a passion of hers. An obsession, almost. Ella has some very strange ideas. That's why our director picked her for the team.'

'What kind of strange ideas?'

'You should see her house. She's a real-life vamp. She has a collection of African juju dolls, and some ancient Sumerian figurines that are supposed to have the souls of the dead inside them. She used to be a doll maker. Ella told me she genuinely believes that inanimate objects can become human.'

'Makes a change. In my job I usually encounter the reverse. Sounds right up my street, in fact.'

'Yours, perhaps, but not Ella's girlfriend's. She walked out on her, couldn't bear to be in the place a minute longer. Said it gave her the creeps. Ella's been behaving very strangely ever since. She's stopped socializing with the cast and stays away from the theatre unless she's absolutely needed.'

'That's odd. When did this start?'

'Let's see, her girlfriend left last Sunday night.'

'The night before Noah Kramer was murdered.'

'I'm sorry?'

'Oh, nothing, I'm just thinking aloud. Perhaps I should pay a visit to Ms Maltby.'

'She won't like it,' Ray warned. 'Ella won't let you in without a very good reason.'

'I'm a police officer, I can do whatever I want,' replied Bryant. 'It's fabulous being me. Look, I'll show you.'

On his way out, he stopped by the concession stand. 'Can I take one of these?' he asked, indicating the programmes. 'I'm a pensioner.'

'I'm afraid senior citizens have to pay just like everybody else,' said the old lady behind the counter.

'Well, I'm also a police officer, so I'm taking one of those as evidence. Chuck it over, Gran.'

'Charming.' She reluctantly withdrew a copy and passed it to him. 'Some of the older ladies in this cast remember the days when we had a nicer class of people in here.'

'I'm sure you did, back in Victorian times.' He turned to Ray. 'See? With your unpleasant turn of mind, you should think of enlisting in the force. The perks are great.' Bryant opened the programme and began reading it. There were monochrome photographs of the cast members and, on the next page, the production team. 'Every single one of these people was in attendance at Robert Kramer's party,' he told Ray, 'and most seem to be hiding some kind of secret. But which of them is a murderer?'

'It's like a whodunit,' Ray said, sounding amazed. 'I thought that sort of thing only happens on TV.'

'Most investigations are whodunits,' said Bryant,

buttoning his coat, 'but most are solved before they've barely begun. This one is different.'

'In what way?'

'Oh, the murderer is keeping pace with us. It's not an investigation now. It's a race.'

29

AUTOMATA

Alma Sorrowbridge always baked industrial quantities of cake and bread before heading to her church on Haverstock Hill, and the smell of hot ginger and corn bread lured Bryant from his bedroom. He drifted into the kitchen in his patched, tasselled dressing gown and seated himself half asleep at the table like an impoverished Edwardian lord waiting to be fed.

'Oh, so you are still here,' said Alma, carrying in a tea tray of spiced pancakes and eggs. 'I was beginning to think you'd moved out without telling me.'

'Why would I do that?' asked Bryant. 'You feed me.'

'Not for much longer.'

'What are you talking about?'

'In case the packing crates in the hall have escaped your attention, we're moving out.'

'Don't be ridiculous. We've hardly been here five minutes. I'm still cataloguing my police manuals; I'm only up to 1928.'

'We lost the court hearing. They're tearing this place down and building an apartment complex. I keep telling you but you don't listen. No one wants an eyesore like this in their nice upmarket neighbourhood.'

'Well, can't they rehouse us temporarily and move us into one of the new apartments?'

'The starting price of the new flats will be £1.5 million each. Have you got that kind of money knocking around? No, I thought not. I blame Jude Law and Gwyneth Paltrow. When they moved in around the corner, the house prices shot up. But if you have got any savings tucked away in your mattress, now would be the time to get them out.'

'I'm not sure I care for this new sarcastic side of you,' Bryant said. 'Can't we talk about it another time? I'm in the middle of a case.'

'You're always in the middle of a case. I've been telling you about the court proceedings for months, but I knew you had your hearing aid turned off. I tried to get you along to the hearings, remember? It's too late to do anything now – we have to go. The Compulsory Purchase Order was approved.'

'Oh, this is ridiculous. I can't be expected to stop everything and move house when there's a murderer on the loose.' He had a sudden thought. 'Hang on, I haven't anywhere to go.'

'No. That's because you haven't got any friends.'

'I did have some, but most of them died or went mad. Well, what are we going to do?'

Alma folded her arms across her generous bust. 'We? What makes you think I want to move with you?'

'Don't be absurd, you'd never live with your conscience if you abandoned me now. You've seen what I'm like without you. I nearly burned the house down drying my socks on the gas stove. When I'm left by myself, things have a tendency to explode.'

'Just as well I've made us some arrangements, then. You

won't like it, but I don't see that we have any choice. I've found us a place.'

'Where?'

'Number seven, Albion House, Harrison Street, Bloomsbury.'

'The Gray's Inn Road end of Bloomsbury? But that's wonderful! Home of Dickens and Virginia Woolf and Brasenose College.'

'It's a council flat.'

Bryant thumped the side of his head theatrically. 'I'm sorry, for a moment I thought you said it was a council flat.'

'I did and it is.'

'But I'm a professional. I have a salary. I can't throw myself on the mercy of the state—'

'And you can't afford to live around here any more. Neither can I. Think of the advantages. You'll be able to walk to work. And the manager assures me that it's a nice quiet block. There's even a small garden. I put our names down when I first heard about the purchase order.'

Bryant looked around in alarm. 'Will there be room for all my books?'

'Most of them. There's a spare room. Some will have to go. You could keep your reference manuals at the Unit.'

'But—'

'We have no choice, Mr Bryant. You weren't interested in attending the meetings, and I couldn't fight to keep this place without you.'

'I'm so sorry, Alma. I've failed you.'

'It's all right, I'm used to it. The first thirty years were the hardest. Go on, have some corn bread.'

Bryant munched and thought for a minute. 'You know, it might be a good thing. We'll meet new people. Common people with ordinary lives, the ones who watch talent shows on television and take their children to football matches. I can get to know them, find out about their habits. Make a proper clinical study of them.'

'I don't think that would be a good idea. They may not like being studied,' said Alma. 'Let's see what the neighbours are like first.'

'When does all this happen?'

'The removal van is arriving on Monday. Don't worry, everything will be taken care of. The flat has just been painted for us. I'll write down the address for you and give you a set of keys.'

'What would I do without you, Alma?'

'You'd be thinner, for a start. It's a bit late to get sentimental. You do your work and I'll do mine.' She began pouring fresh tea.

'What is your work?'

'Why, looking after you, of course.' She gave a shrug. 'It's a disgusting job but somebody has to do it.'

London experiences most of its foggy mornings in May and October, but on Friday morning John May stepped out onto his balcony on the fourth floor of the converted warehouse at Shad Thames to find a cool grey mist eddying over the still green surface of the river. Near the shore, a police patrol boat nosed a corridor through the vapour like an icebreaker. Seagulls dropped and wheeled from the milky sky, reminding those below that they lived on an island in a cold grey sea.

He missed Brigitte. She was hardly bothering to return his emails and phone calls. He knew that her job at the Paris Tourist Board required her to attend a great number of social events, and felt sure that she was meeting younger, more eligible men who possessed the added benefit of being born Parisians. Here he was on the wrong side of the Channel, fooling himself into thinking that a glamorous French divorcée still preferred to be with him. *Men are worse than women when it comes to worrying about their own attractiveness,* he thought glumly. *I'm old, it's as simple as that, and I'm going to be alone. Other people learn to manage. I've always put my career before my relationships. Perhaps I'm like Robert Kramer in that respect. And I'd better learn to deal with it, because it won't get any easier.*

He ground fresh coffee beans – a breakfast ritual he had developed after seeing Michael Caine do it in *The Ipcress File* – then chose a new white shirt and a ribbed grey silk tie, because looking smart at least made him feel younger. He envied Arthur, because his partner had obviously not looked in a mirror since the year of the Coronation and seemed entirely happy in his own rumpled skin. *Vanity is a form of self-harm,* he decided, slipping into his black suit jacket. *It's time to concentrate on something more important.*

Lucy Clementine's testimony against her old boss bothered him. She had clearly meant it as a condemnation, but why? What had she to gain now, when she no longer worked for him? Ms Clementine had turned up too conveniently. It felt as if someone was pushing Kramer at them and making sure they stayed on target.

The more he thought about the detestable Robert Kramer, the more he seemed to be a victim. It was a gut instinct born from years of experience. *Every investigation reveals a worm in the bud,* May thought, *and you often end up hating the people you're meant to defend, and vice versa. I really should talk to Arthur about my mixed feelings.*

As he came out of the building, he found Arthur Bryant sitting on a traffic bollard opposite his front door. He had his hat pulled down over his ears and was dipping a Mars Bar in a polystyrene cup of tea. 'Ah, I was wondering how long it would take for you to finish your ablutions,' he said, dunking the last of his chocolate. Bryant had a habit of appearing when May was thinking about him as if he had been psychically summoned.

'I didn't know you were outside. You could have come up.'

'No, I was having a plate of pork sausages over the road at your transport caff. I wanted to get an early start but something's gone wrong with Victor's carburettor. I thought we'd take your BMW.'

'Fine by me. Where are we going?'

'I need you with me, but I don't want you to get annoyed again.'

'Why do you think it will annoy me?'

'Trust me, it will. We're going to play with dolls. I've arranged an appointment at Pollock's Toy Museum in Whitfield Street.'

'So long as it brings us nearer to catching a killer, I'm all yours,' May said magnanimously, digging out his car keys.

'How did you get on with your contact?' asked Bryant as they turned into Charlotte Street.

'Interesting. Lucy Clementine worked for Kramer and hates him enough to suggest that he killed his wife's child.'

'Yes, I rather thought she might,' said Bryant, burying himself deeper into his coat.

'What do you mean?'

'Take no notice of me. I shall keep my mouth zipped until I have further evidence. Let's talk to Mr Granville. Pull in here.'

'It's a double-red zone, Arthur.'

'You really have to stop worrying about these minor legal details. Don't you get it? We're old, we can do whatever we like. Come along. We're late.'

Pollock's Toy Museum was named after Benjamin Pollock, the last of the Victorian toy theatre printers. When it moved from the teeming streets of Covent Garden in 1969, it was relocated in an old corner house in a shaded back street behind Tottenham Court Road.

The museum on the corner of Whitfield Street was built over a working shop that specialized in Victorian puppets and theatres. Bryant peered in at the nicotine-coloured window display, which had not changed in decades. Bright red and yellow proscenium arches, trimmed from cardboard, reflected a world long vanished. In the narrow winding staircases and corridors above the shop, glass-eyed dolls and balding teddy bears stared out from corners. The existence of such a place in the modern world was a testament to the determination of its owners, who were resolved to keep the gateway of childish imagination open.

Nimrod Granville was one of the few men working in London who made Arthur Bryant appear healthful. Tussocks of snowy hair were clumped about the freckled, corrugated flesh of his pate, and a pair of ridiculous half-moon glasses were perched upon his spectacularly hooked hooter, lending him the appearance of Mr Punch himself. These days he remained seated on a high wooden stool behind the counter, and the shop's dimly lit interior played havoc with his ability to read the boxes that contained the shop's toy theatres, but Dudley Salterton had recommended him to Bryant as the capital's last working expert on Victorian theatrical toys. Granville asserted that his longevity was due to a regular intake of Guinness and a sixty-a-day cigarette habit that had begun when he was twelve years old. Consequently his breathing sounded like a gale blowing through a fence and he was required to stop every thirty seconds to get his wind back.

'I hear you've found the Madame Blavatsky,' he said. 'Dudley called me, very excited. We thought she had been lost in the Blitz.'

'I didn't realize she had a reputation,' Bryant replied. 'She still works.'

'Those things were precision-engineered to last, and the oil doesn't dry out in them because the cogs are sealed within vacuum glass. She's worth a bob or two.'

'Oh, I wouldn't sell her.'

'Good man. She's a creepy old thing, isn't she? Of course, I've only seen pictures. I'd love to come and try her out. I've always been fascinated by automata, ever since I heard about the Turk.'

'What's the Turk?' May asked.

'It was a mechanical chess player constructed in 1770 to impress the Empress Maria Theresa, a turbaned man on a wooden box filled with brass machinery. The Turk could beat human opponents at chess, and also performed something called the Knight's Tour, which was a puzzle requiring the player to move a knight to occupy every square of a chessboard just once. The Turk was a sham, of course, but a rather beautiful one. The machinery appeared to go all the way to the back of the cabinet, but this was optical trickery. The last third of the cabinet housed a tiny man who was a chess master. But the illusion was a complex one involving deceptive sounds, magnets and levers that worked brilliantly. It eventually ended up in America and was destroyed in a fire. There have been reconstructions, but the Turk was the first and best of the automata. The French made brothel automata in the late nineteenth century that simulated lovemaking. And these days I hear the Japanese have developed life-sized robotic dolls that respond to the human voice, powered by tiny microchips.'

'Have you ever heard of a Mr Punch puppet that could operate in this manner?' asked Bryant.

'You'd think he would be an obvious choice, wouldn't you? But no, there's not been one to my knowledge. Punch is out of favour these days. Not politically correct. But then he was never intended to be. Most people don't really get what he was about.'

'What do you think he was about?'

'Anarchy,' answered Granville. 'Chaos, pure and simple. It is a mad world, and the only way to survive in it is by behaving more madly than anyone else. Punch exists beyond good and evil, right and wrong. I suppose you could say he's a god. He remakes the universe in his own image.'

'You must meet people who love this sort of thing,' said Bryant. 'Collectors, academics. You wouldn't happen to have a list of them, would you?'

'I can make you up one. We keep a file of regular visitors. I won't be a minute.' Granville eased himself from the stool with some difficulty and tottered over to a gigantic ledger, which he proceeded to pull down from the shelf.

'Do you want me to give you a hand with that?' asked May.

'Thank you, I can manage,' said Granville, looking as if he was about to be flattened. Clutching the immense tome, he staggered over to a corner of the counter and slammed it down.

'This isn't going to help us,' May whispered to Bryant. 'So far I've learned about mechanical dolls, robots, puppets and wax dummies, and absolutely nothing about the case at hand.'

'Not so.' Bryant shook his head. 'We're much closer to understanding what we're up against.'

'Would you care to enlighten me?'

'Not really.'

'Here we are,' Granville exclaimed, thrusting a piece of paper at Bryant. 'If I can be of any further help, do pop in.'

'Well, that was a waste of time,' said May as they left

the museum shop. 'Let's get back to some proper policing.'

'I think we have one more stop to make,' said Bryant, showing his partner the slip of paper. 'Look who's a regular visitor to Pollock's.'

Ella Maltby, the New Strand Theatre's set designer and props manager, was listed at the top of the page as a collector of dolls and automata. 'According to Mr Granville's records, the last item Maltby purchased from the museum shop was this.' He unfolded a sheet of photo-copied paper and showed May the picture on it.

May found himself looking at a puppet of the Hangman.

30

MORBIDITY

Ella Maltby lived in a redbrick Jacobean-style house over-looking the north end of Hampstead Heath. It rose in magnificent isolation on the brow of the hill, rendered almost invisible by the profusion of damp greenery that surrounded it. Here kestrels, tawny owls and woodpeckers made their homes in the trees, and London, blue and misted, was spread out below, its glass financial towers placed to one side, like condiments at a picnic feast.

'This is probably the grandest building I've ever attempted to enter legally.' Bryant looked up at the door with approval. 'It makes Hampstead Golf Club look like Bethnell Green Slipper Baths.'

'I wonder why she works if she lives in a place like this?'

'I don't know. Ray Pryce said she was very odd. Let's find out just how very odd.' He gave the iron bellpull a tug.

'Is my tie straight?' May turned to Bryant with his chin forward.

'It's fine. I don't know why you feel the need to

straighten a piece of silk dangling from your neck whenever you visit a woman.'

'I don't want to look an utter scruffbag like you.' May looked down at Bryant's knees and recoiled. Blue and white striped material was sticking out of his trouser bottoms. 'Please tell me you're not wearing pyjamas underneath your strides?'

'It was cold when I got up, so I just put another layer on. Is that so wrong?'

'I can't believe you have to ask.'

The door was opened by Ella Maltby herself. She was clearly unhappy and unprepared to find the detectives standing on her doorstep.

'Ms Maltby, we need to talk to you about a purchase you made from Pollock's Toy Museum six weeks ago,' said Bryant.

'You'd better come in before anyone sees you,' Maltby said, looking behind them.

She led the way into a wide, oak-panelled hall hung with cobwebbed chandeliers. When May studied them, he realized the cobwebs were stage effects that had been carefully sprayed onto the candlesticks.

'Well, they say you never can tell what's behind an Englishman's front door,' said Bryant in a not entirely complimentary tone.

'I am not English and I'm not a man,' Maltby pointed out. 'I am German, originally from Hamburg. My father anglicized our family name after the war.'

'Ah, a Jerry, yes, well, I imagine he would. We had quite a few family friends who visited Hamburg. Didn't stop, just flew over it and returned to base. Never mind, forgive and forget, eh?'

'Give me strength,' May muttered under his breath, but Bryant was on a roll.

'It probably explains your fascination with torture, I

mean with the Hun being a notoriously cruel race, but you gave us our royal family, even though we dumped the Saxe-Coburg and Gotha surname because it was simply too embarrassing.'

Maltby froze Bryant with a cold stare. 'You wanted to talk about a purchase.'

'A Hangman doll, I believe.'

'That's correct.'

'What puzzles us is this: Robert Kramer is a collector of Punch and Judy memorabilia. Bit of a coincidence that you are, too, isn't it?'

'I'm not,' Maltby said. 'I bought the doll for Robert while I was buying the rest of the props for the play. That way it goes through the business books. They're rare and very expensive.'

'Kramer already has a complete set of puppets.'

'Not true. There's no single agreed set of characters. The productions varied across the centuries and the only surviving sets that match are in museums and private collections. They hardly ever come up for auction. The only way to collect them now is to buy the characters piecemeal. Mr Granville had heard of an original Hangman going, so I obtained it for Robert.' She looked from one detective to the other. 'I'm assuming this has something to do with the death of Robert's son?'

'A puppet of the Hangman was found beside Gregory Baine. Nobody's told you?'

'I had no idea. What happened?'

'He was found hanging under Cannon Street Bridge.'

'I assume he killed himself.' She sounded curious but not surprised.

'Why would you think that?'

'Everyone knows he had money worries. He asked for a loan, but Robert turned him down.'

'Where were you on Wednesday night?'

'Here at home, by myself.'

'Where did you last see the puppet?'

'In Robert's office at the theatre. I think he intended to keep it there. It was certainly there on Monday, before the party.'

'You're quite close to Robert, aren't you?'

'It pays to be. He employs me.'

'Friendly with his wife?'

'Not especially. She doesn't talk to other women.'

'How about the mistress?'

'I didn't know she had one.'

'Robert Kramer's mistress.'

'I didn't know *he* had one.'

'Why don't I believe you?'

'You're a policeman. Do you believe anything?'

'Sorry to hear about your girlfriend, by the way. Left you, did she?'

'It's common knowledge.'

'Anyone else at Robert Kramer's party you're especially friendly with?'

'I don't know any of the others that well. I keep my distance.'

'Why's that?'

'They're not my kind of people.'

'I heard they don't much care for you. They think you're weird. Your girlfriend did, too.'

'I imagine they all do.'

'Why do you think that is?'

'Because of my . . . predilections.'

'And what are those?'

'Come and see for yourself.'

Maltby led them to the staircase at the end of the hall and started to descend. 'I'm a model maker,' she explained. 'That's how I got into props and set design.' At the bottom of the staircase, Bryant and May found themselves faced with a double-width wooden door covered in square iron studs, closed with an iron ring. She grabbed the ring and twisted it. The door swung wide with a theatrical groan.

The detectives found themselves inside a dungeon, complete with perspiring grey stone walls, a full-sized rack, a gibbet, thumbscrews, a scold's bridle, a brazier with a red-hot branding iron sitting in it and various implements of torture. But more alarming than this were the full-sized mannequins that writhed in agony in the contraptions, burned, scarred, pierced and stretched. A hooded figure with a bare chest stood beside them holding tongue pincers. Another was posed standing over a screaming naked girl with a pair of eye gougers in his hand.

But the tableau that interested Bryant most was the one that featured a corpse hanging from a perfect hangman's noose.

'And you wonder why your girlfriend walked out,' murmured Bryant.

'I kicked her out,' Maltby replied hotly. 'She told me I needed psychiatric help. I'm a model maker, not a psycho. I just make these scenes for the skill of it. I build dioramas for the London Dungeon. I wanted to work for Hammer Films, but their heyday was before my time. They employed highly skilled craftspeople. You wouldn't have turned around and told them they needed psychiatric help, would you?'

May suddenly realized what his partner had been doing since they arrived. Knowing that Maltby had isolated herself from everyone, he had set out to goad her into providing some angry answers, and had got them.

'Missing any rope, are you?'

'No, I don't think so.'

'Ray Pryce said you believe souls live on in the models you make.'

'He would say that. He's a writer; they all exaggerate. I guess in a sense I do put myself into my figures. After all, they're all modelled on real people. I don't do all this by myself. I have an assistant. We hire models and use their features in order to get exact likenesses. So you do come to think of them as being alive.'

'I imagine it's a lucrative field. Unusual jobs often are.'

'I come from a long line of model makers. My great-grandmother worked for Madame Tussauds, and so did her mother. Madame Tussaud developed her craft by making wax death masks of aristocrats who had been executed during the French Revolution. She arrived in England at the start of the nineteenth century and put her waxworks on display at the Lyceum Theatre, just off the Strand. My skill with wax is what got me the job on *The Two Murderers*. I'm supplying exhibitions all over the world.'

'Well, she didn't seem crazy to me,' observed May as they left the house. 'If anything, I thought she was pretty damn smart. She's about craft, artistry – and making money.'

'I'm afraid I have to agree with you,' replied Bryant glumly. 'My biggest problem is that I can't see what she would have to gain by killing. But her fascination with the morbid fits a certain pattern.'

'I'll do some checking into her background, look for the usual signs, but we're going to need more than circumstantial evidence if we're going to make anything stick to anyone. It sounds like they all had access to the Hangman puppet.'

'Did she have any unexplained absences during the party?'

'She's another smoker. I think she slipped out for a snout a couple of times, but wasn't gone long in either case. Sounds like we can't prove where she was when Gregory Baine died.'

'Too many suspects, and none of them entirely fit – yet. Bloody annoying.'

They returned to the Unit and worked separately for the rest of the day. After the Unit had finally closed for the night, Bryant told his partner to put on his coat and follow him to the King Charles I pub. He appeared to be troubled by something; his brow was even more rumpled than usual. Over pints of Bombardier, he explained his problem.

'I think we can rule out Robert Kramer now,' he began, leaving a foamy moustache on his upper lip. 'I'm afraid we have to assume you were fed a dud lead by the Home Office.'

'How do you work that out?'

'I realized that Kramer doesn't fit the pattern. He might have reached the top by behaving in an immoral manner, but he certainly isn't an anarchist. If anything, he's an arch-conformist. He abides by the status quo. He doesn't want to upset the ordered world, he simply wants to exist in its upper echelons. He might assume he has something in common with the myths of strong leaders, but he behaves in the prescribed manner of all rapacious businessmen.'

'Well, he's all we have right now, even though he has no motive for killing his own partner.'

'I read the email Lucy Clementine sent you. Fond of detailing her boss's bad behaviour, isn't she?'

'If she's right, we've got enough to hold Robert Kramer on suspicion,' said May. 'We're not subject to the rules governing the Met.'

'You won't get a confession out of him. He'd fight every step of the way.'

'You sound as if you don't want to make an arrest.'

'Of course I do, but we can't afford another mistake. You've no concrete evidence, only hearsay. We need more

233

proof than the word of a disgruntled former secretary. He fired her, John. Lucy Clementine sued Kramer for wrongful dismissal and settled compensation out of court, but the amount she received was the lowest that could have been awarded.'

'How did you find this out?'

'I didn't. I got Dan Banbury to run a background check on her. What he found was that she had no background.'

'You mean someone erased it?'

'Afraid so. Their mistake was taking out the whole of the period when she worked for Kramer. It would have been more convincing if they'd left something in. Her testimony is compromised.'

'Why were you suspicious?'

'The Department of Social Resources is housed in the same Whitehall Home Office building as the Department of Internal Security – the department that's run by Oskar Kasavian.'

'It could just be a coincidence.'

'And it might not be. All I'm saying is, you can't trust your source.'

'Then what do you want to do?'

'The same as you. I want to get to the truth before anyone else is hurt.'

'You think it will happen again if we don't stop it?'

'I know it will.'

'What makes you so sure?'

'Our murderer is winning. Nobody has been arrested. He's getting exactly what he wants.'

'But we don't know what he wants.'

'I have a shrewd idea now. I just don't know which one of them it is.'

'Still going to play your cards close to your chest, then.'

'I have to. If I'm wrong, I can't afford to drop us both in the *merde*. It would be better if I took the fall.'

'So what happens next?'

'We need to keep a close watch on everyone who was at that party.'

'You know we can't do that. We don't have enough staff.'

'If we don't, somebody may die.'

'Then we have to decide who to prioritize. I'm assuming Judith Kramer is high risk.'

'You mean because she collapsed after the death of her son she can't possibly be guilty.'

'Someone set out to hurt her by killing her child.'

'But she wasn't hurt by Gregory Baine's death.'

'Giles says he can't entirely rule out suicide. There's still the idea that Baine might have killed himself over his debts. If I had to choose the person most at risk right now, it would be someone involved in the love triangle. Marcus Sigler or Kramer himself.'

'Really? Interesting. That's not who I would have picked.'

'Then who do you think is the most exposed?'

'Ray Pryce, the writer, because he's as nervous as a cat and knows more than he's letting on. I think he saw something at the party. What did he witness that he's not telling us?'

'OK, anyone else?'

'Yes, that obnoxious critic, Alex Lansdale.'

'The *critic*?'

'Of course. We're looking for a very unusual killer. Someone who's a careful planner, but also capable of murderous rages. Remember what Janice said about Mrs Kramer? That she always felt stranded on the outside. Nearly everyone else there was directly connected with the play, but one man was a traitor and did his best to close it down – Lansdale. That puts him on the wrong side.'

May drank up and set his pint down. 'Call me

old-fashioned, but I think we should protect the women first. Everyone who attended that party is technically a suspect.'

'Not true, John. The timings have ruled at least three of them out.'

'Nevertheless, we need to keep them all close by. What do you think?'

'I think I'll have another pint,' said Bryant, peering through the bottom of his empty glass.

31

DESPAIR

DS Janice Longbright returned to Bermondsey late, because she wanted to catch the Hagan family by surprise. She was required to make the visit in the company of another officer, and took Jack Renfield with her.

The lights were on in the corner house behind Jamaica Road. 'Who's in there?' Jack asked as they approached.

'Five teens, three girls, two boys. One of the girls is fifteen and has a new baby. Their father lives there with his girlfriend. I think the original mother took off some years ago. And there are the grandparents – his, I think. None of them have ever held down legal jobs, the father and the grandfather have both served time for armed robbery, the oldest daughter has a soliciting record, the youngest son was admitted to a methadone programme at the age of fourteen. Anna's mother reckons her daughter's first mobile was taken by one of the boys. She saw him running away. The police searched the place and found nothing. The family know their rights.'

'They always do,' said Renfield. 'It's usually their one area of expertise. Let's get this over with.' He rang the doorbell, stepped back and looked at his watch, counting down.

'What are you doing?' Longbright asked.

'There's going to be a thirty-second gap while somebody checks us out from upstairs. That's the trouble with families like the Hagans. The sheer bloody predictability of their behaviour.'

Sure enough, half a minute later the door opened and they found themselves faced with the kind of man who was physically incapable of looking innocent. A shaved head, a bulldog face, a thick tattooed neck, the body pitched forward slightly on the balls of the feet, the arms barely restrained at his sides.

'What do you want?'

Renfield mentally checked Longbright's list. This was obviously Joseph Hagan, the father, middle generation, an eight-year jail sentence behind him. 'Joe, we need to talk to your boys for a minute. Are they around?'

'You ain't coming in.'

'We don't need to come in. But we're not leaving until we talk to them.'

'You ain't from round here, neither. Show me your ID.'

Renfield flashed his PCU badge. He hated its design. He would probably get more respect from waving his coffee loyalty card around. 'It's about Anna Marquand.'

'She been complaining again? Her bloody mother wants to learn to keep her mouth shut.'

'Anna Marquand is dead.'

Joe's voice dropped. If nothing else, he had respect for the dead. 'I'm sorry, I didn't know that. But it's nothing to do with us.'

'I didn't say it was. Natural causes, very sudden.'

'She been buried yet?'

'No, not yet. The coroner's inquest still has to be closed.'

'But if it's natural causes—'

'The Unit doesn't operate under normal police and medical jurisdiction.'

'Let me know when it is. We'll send flowers.'

'OK, but I'd still like to speak to Ashley Hagan.'

'Why?'

'I've got him ID'd for nicking her mobile phone.'

'ID'd? Round here? You sure?' Joe Hagan was clearly certain that no one was brave enough to make a complaint.

'He was identified by Anna's mother.'

'That old cow sits at the window all day looking for trouble. You can't believe a word she says.'

'Probably not. Listen, I'm not going to get a search warrant over a bloody phone, but I have to talk to him, just to say I did, OK?'

Joe blew out through his teeth, thinking. 'All right, stay there.'

For once, Janice was glad that Renfield had accompanied her. She felt sure Hagan's attitude would have been more obstructive and antagonistic with her. After a few minutes, Ashley Hagan came downstairs. Longbright immediately saw his past laid out before her. He was a user. She could discern the shape of his skull beneath his yellowed skin. His arms were covered in tattoos, the designs clearly traceable to around 2008. They'd been created to hide track marks. Since then he had probably switched to the backs of his legs. His eyes were turned off. He would steal anything, say anything when the need arose again.

She had seen his type a thousand times before. But he wasn't the man who attacked her at the lido.

'You're Ashley Dean Hagan, twenty-two years old, yeah?' said Renfield, checking his pad. 'You know Anna Marquand of 14 Hadley Street, Bermondsey? Just say yes, lad.'

'I seen her. Course I seen her. She's like eight doors along. She had a fight with my sister over bins or summink, I don't know. I seen her, though.' Ashley's speech was rapid-fire and anxious, the kind of speech you used when asking a punter for money and needing to get the sentence out quick before they turned and started to walk away.

'You were seen taking her mobile phone, so let's not even argue about that. But she's dead and I want to know—' He got no further. Ashley fell back and ran towards the rear of the house with surprising speed. A second later Renfield launched himself inside and Longbright followed.

They ran through the house to the kitchen door, already thrown open, and out into a small square yard filled with children's toys. Two chained bull mastiffs started jumping up and barking.

Ashley was already over the rear wall. He had climbed on a crate left there for the purpose and had kicked it aside with practised ease as he went over.

Longbright had seen this kind of manoeuvre many times before and knew what to do. She doubled back to the front of the house and followed the side wall around. Families like the Hagans had chosen their position as carefully as English chieftains building fortresses. The intention was to confuse, but any officer worth their salt could see that only one direction led to escape. The boy needed to find crowds, not empty roads where he would stand out. And the only crowded area around here was the tube station, which meant cutting through to Jamaica Road.

Longbright was ahead of Renfield, behind Ashley Hagan. She surveyed the scene ahead and saw his leg vanishing from sight. Renfield was strong but packed weight – the boy would be able to stay ahead of him. She was faster. Turning into Jamaica Road, she saw the streaming traffic and knew he would run out into it with the feral awareness of a fox or cat.

He was dead ahead, vaulting the central railing, and she had no choice but to follow. A gap in the cars allowed her halfway.

Renfield was closing behind. Hagan was all the way across. The new glass station shone in a row of unlit shops. She took a chance and ran, ignoring the squeal of tyres on tarmac, knowing she had just caused a truck to shift its load.

A train had just come in and Hagan was trying to lose himself in the discharged commuters, but people moved aside because of the way he looked, revealing him.

He was already over the barrier, and now Longbright knew there was a real chance of losing him, but as he pushed down the escalator, opening the gap between them, the moving staircase suddenly slammed to a stop, sending everyone forward. She looked back and saw that Renfield had hit the red emergency button.

Three people had fallen but nobody seemed hurt. Hagan was blocked by a tumble of luggage that had pitched forward across the stairs. Locking an arm around his neck she pulled him back, checking his right hand to make sure it was free of a weapon. Renfield grabbed his arm and twisted it behind him, and together they pulled him from the escalator.

Longbright was surprised to see that Ashley Hagan's face was wet with tears. The boy could not raise his eyes to hers and seemed barely capable of standing, so they sat him against the corridor wall, one on either side.

'Get your breath back, son,' said Renfield.

'I didn't know she was dead,' he moaned. 'Yeah, I took the phone, but it wasn't – I mean, I didn't want to sell it. I took it 'cause it was hers, you know?'

'What do you mean?' asked Longbright.

He wiped his nose on the back of his sleeve. 'She was – special, you know? She stood up to my sisters. My sisters are bitches, and she stood up to them. An' they wanted me to hurt her, but I couldn't so I just took the phone and kept it, because it was hers. 'Cause she was decent and I wanted – I can't believe she's dead. I don' know how—'

'She cut herself, a stupid accident,' Longbright told him, bluntly. 'Because she was still shaken up after being mugged.'

'Wait, she can't be dead. She can't have died.'

'What do you mean?'

'We're talking about the same thing, right? This was months ago.'

'No, it was this week. She was attacked on Monday night and her phone was stolen from her shopping bag along with some keys.'

'But that wasn't me. I took her phone after she had the fight with my sisters, that was back in February. I've still got it at home. I can show you. Her mum will tell you it's her old phone.'

'Where were you on Monday night at around nine?'

'I was at the clinic waiting to see my doctor. There was a long wait – the nurse knows me, she'll tell you—'

'What time did you leave?'

'About ten-fifteen. They'll tell you.'

'Give me the address.'

Ashley Hagan dug into his pocket and handed over a grubby, creased card. 'I can't believe she's dead,' he said again, looking for something he could not find in their faces.

'I'm sorry for your loss,' said Longbright, touching his shoulder. 'Stay with your family tonight. Remember what she meant to you. Don't let her down by doing something she'd have hated.'

* * *

'The bloke who attacked me was older, heavier,' Longbright told Renfield on the tube back. 'He had a lot of upper body strength. He wasn't wasted away like Ashley. I think he must have got away with whatever was in Anna's locker.' She turned to look at Renfield. 'You don't suppose this has anything to do with Arthur's stuff, do you? His memoirs?'

'I don't see how. The old man's indiscreet, but he wouldn't put anything in there that was worth all this hassle.'

'Civil servants have topped themselves over leaking sensitive material. Look at David Kelly. Or they've been killed by the Russians.'

'You lot always seem to think there's a conspiracy going on.' Renfield said it disapprovingly.

'That's because sometimes there is.'

At London Bridge they changed to the Northern line and flopped down into seats. The train was almost empty.

'So, where did you learn all that stuff?' Renfield asked.

'All what stuff?'

'The way you talked to Ashley Hagan. That *don't do anything she'd have hated*. You know, being nice. He's scum.'

'He was a kid once. Now he's half dead and in despair. He hates his family and he'll never be able to get away from them. Kicking him around isn't going to change anything.'

Renfield had been a desk sergeant with the Met, where they behaved differently. He sat back, lost in thought as the train rattled through the tunnel, heading north towards King's Cross.

32

OLDER LADIES

Saturday morning dawned but nobody noticed. It barely grew light. The sky had tilted and was moving fast. The racing clouds bulged so low that the spires of St Pancras threatened to tear them open. The lack of a rush hour today meant that most of the shops and offices in King's Cross were shut, but the lights were on at the PCU. A seven-day policy had been placed in effect while the investigation remained active.

Unusually, Raymond Land was the first one in. Last night Leanne had sent him an email saying that she couldn't join him on their sailing holiday in the Isle of Wight because she had accidentally made a double booking. This morning she had gone off to a retreat in Wales to practise tantric yoga with an old family friend. In a way Land was quite pleased, because he needed to get the investigation closed, and was a lousy sailor.

He made himself a cup of coffee, then wandered into Bryant's room and stood before the case containing Madame Blavatsky. Looking around to check that he was alone, he felt in the coin slot for an old penny, inserted it and waited.

The medium's eyes glowed and buzzed. Her cogs turned and she withdrew a card, jerkily reaching forward to drop it into the metal tray. Land plucked it out and turned it over. It read:

NOBODY DOES YOGA IN WALES

'Ah, there you are, *mon petit oiseau tôt*.' Bryant was standing in the doorway with a dreadful grin on his face.

'What?' said Land, shocked, tucking the card behind him.

'Early bird. You. In early.'

'Ah. Yes. Couldn't sleep.' Mortified, he hastily dropped the card back into the tray.

'Just as well. There's a lot to get through today. We went to Ella Maltby's house yesterday.'

'Remind me?'

'The set designer. She has a dungeon filled with people being tortured. Wax mannequins.'

'How extraordinary.'

'Yes, but it doesn't exactly move her forward as a suspect. Questions, questions everywhere. The most obvious one – is the case closed?'

'What do you mean?'

'Did Gregory Baine hang himself? If he did, why did he take a Hangman doll with him? Could it be he committed suicide because he felt guilty about Noah Kramer's death?'

'Why would he have had reason to kill a child?'

'You see, another unanswered question. Anyway, he didn't kill himself, I'm just being theoretical.'

'You don't know that.'

'Yes, I do. Dan tells me the bulbs were burned out in the safety lights by the duckboards beneath the bridge. With the best will in the world Baine wouldn't have been able to find his way to the hole in the boards and attach a rope. It was prearranged by someone else. And where are the motives? What are they? Revenge, profit, love – hate? Well, that one's obvious, at least.'

'It is?'

'Hate. Somebody hates Robert Kramer very badly indeed. They kill his child. They kill his best friend. The pair owned a company together, Cruikshank Holdings. That's what gave the game away.'

Land looked lost. 'What do you mean?'

'The name Cruikshank.' Bryant widened eyes and raised hands, expecting Land to get it. 'Obviously Kramer chose it. George Cruikshank was the greatest-ever illustrator of Punch and Judy. His book is still the key text on the subject. I found details on the register at Companies House. Cruikshank Holdings operated out of the Cayman Islands. It was their nest egg, and Baine was in charge of it. He'd been making some heavy withdrawals. The rumour is that he played the Stock Exchange and hit a losing streak. Oh, Robert Kramer has the business sense but Baine was the money man. His death effectively destroys Kramer's financial power, because Baine has been prevented from making the money back. There's nobody else in yet – mind if I smoke?'

'Oh, go on then, just this once. It'll help get rid of the smell of damp.'

Bryant enthusiastically stuffed his pipe with Old Mariner No. 2 Rough Cut British Navy Shag and lit up. 'What's the matter, old boot? You look like you have the cares of the world upon your shoulders.'

'It's just—' For a moment, Land thought about confiding in Bryant. Then he came to his senses. 'Nothing. I just want to get the case closed.'

'Weren't you supposed to be going on holiday today?'

'I changed my mind. The case is more important.'

'That's impressive. Not like you.' He cascaded a grace-ful funnel of blue smoke into the air. Land coughed.

'There's a terrible smell of burning rope on the landing,' said John May, unbuttoning his coat and throwing a copy of the *Guardian* onto his desk. 'Or someone's hair is on fire. Oh, it's you, Arthur.'

'Raymondo's letting me smoke today. I feel most privileged.' Bryant swanned to his desk, wreathed in smoke, and flicked open the programme of *The Two Murderers*.

'Well, it's good to see both of you in the same place for once,' Land said. 'It seems to me the more time you spend together, the closer we usually get to a solution.'

'I think he just complimented us, John. That's a first. I had no idea you were capable of pleasantries, Raymondo.'

'I don't see why not, I was well brought up. Some of the older ladies in our family—'

'Oh, my lord! Older ladies!' Bryant sat up suddenly, catapulted by his chair.

'What's the matter?'

'*Older ladies*! I'm a total idiot!' He climbed onto his desk and began pulling at a dusty leather-bound volume at the top of the bookcase.

'Do you want me to get that?' asked May, concerned.

'What did I say?' asked Land, but nobody was listening to him now.

'Why did I not think of it at the time? Somebody take this from me.' Bryant passed Land the volume and toppled off his desk, just in time to be caught by May. The book was *Twentieth-Century British Theatre, Volume 2* by A. A. Gingold. Bryant began feverishly searching it.

'What on earth's he so excited about?' Land asked May, bewildered.

'I really have no idea,' May admitted.

'Here it is,' Bryant announced. 'Of course. It all fits together perfectly. But we may be too late.' He squirmed around in his chair, trying to get his arms into his coat.

'For goodness' sake, let me do it.' May threaded one of his partner's arms into a sleeve.

'Have you got your car here?'

'No, I got the tube in today. Why?'

'Then we need a cab. Hurry.' With half his coat still trailing on the floor, Bryant was pulling him towards the door like a dog that had been offered a walk.

Out on the street it was just starting to rain. 'Damn, the taxis will vanish in seconds,' Bryant complained. 'Wait, there's one.' He threw himself into the street, slipped in front of the taxi and nearly disappeared under it.

'Where to?' asked the driver.

'The New Strand Theatre, Adam Street. Fast as you can.'

'Are you going to tell me what this is all about?' asked May as they fell back in the seat.

'Echoes,' said Bryant enigmatically. 'There are echoes everywhere. I thought there was something vaguely familiar about that blasted play when I saw it. Then when Raymond mentioned the older ladies in his family – you see, I was coming out of the performance and bumped into Ray Pryce. He mentioned that Ella Maltby kept wax dummies. And Maltby told us that the talent had always been in her family. Then I went to get a programme and had a bit of a row with the seller—'

'Why am I not surprised at that part?'

'—and she said the older ladies in the cast remembered the days when the theatre had a nicer class of clientele – then I remembered the book.'

'Arthur, I struggle to make sense of you at the best of times, but you've completely lost me.'

'And I thought *older ladies*? There's only one older lady

in the cast – Mona Williams, the one who kept flirting with me during the interviews – and the programme seller must mean her. So I was wrong, it's not Alex Lansdale, he's not the one.'

'He's not the one what?'

'The one who's in danger. It's Mona.'

'Why are we going to the theatre?'

'Because according to Janice's notes, that's where she is this morning.' The taxi got stuck in traffic halfway down Gower Street, but the driver turned off sharply and gunned his way through Holborn, coming into the other end of the Strand in record time.

'That was a nifty piece of driving,' said Bryant, throwing a note at him. 'You'll go far.'

'Not if it involves going south of the river,' said the cabbie with a laugh, roaring off.

'Stick!' said May. 'You've forgotten your walking stick!'

As they watched, the cab screeched to a stop, reversed, stopped and Bryant's walking stick was thrust from the open window. The pair raced into the theatre.

33

BRIDLE

The foyer of the New Strand Theatre was unlit, and the doors to the main auditorium were locked.

'There must be someone here,' said May, 'otherwise the front doors would have been closed. There's probably a cleaner.' He looked at the stairs, and realized that Bryant would have trouble getting up them quickly. 'Stay here and keep an eye out. I'll go up.'

He took the stairs two at a time. Theatre auditoriums are, by their nature, buildings without windows. Moments later, May found himself in oppressive darkness. The air in the closed theatre was still and dead. All sound was muffled. He stopped to listen. In the distance, an ambulance siren seesawed along the Embankment. Nothing in here, though.

He searched for a light switch but realized that the lighting panel would have to be housed inside a central office, where the general public could not touch it. The corridor at the rear of the dress circle curved away into velvet limbo.

He felt his way along the wall, trying to be as quiet as

possible. Somewhere above him a floorboard creaked. He froze and listened. Nothing. As he moved forward, he groped for his radio and turned it off.

At the end of the rear corridor he found a set of doors to the upper circle and swung one open. Small windows set into the staircase wall afforded him a little light. Reaching the floor above, he pushed carefully against the brass panel on the door.

The steeply raked rows of seats descended below him. May knew that one mistake in the dark would send him headlong down the stairs. He wished he had brought his Valiant – the old usherette's torch used to go everywhere with him, but they had been in a hurry to leave.

A foot scraped, and there was a small but definite displacement of air behind him. He felt the flat of a hand on his back, pushing hard, and suddenly there was nothing beneath his feet. He fell into darkness and silence.

'What happened?'

'You bashed your head on the armrest of a chair,' said Bryant, leaning over and studying him with interest. 'It was padded, but still gave you a nasty bruise.'

May tried to sit up, but it felt as if someone had stuck a knife in his eye.

'It's a pity you let him get away,' Bryant complained, holding a wet handkerchief to May's forehead. 'He must have been standing right behind you.'

'I didn't do it on purpose. Ow!'

'That's good, it hurts. Your nerves are still working.'

'How did he get past you?'

'I heard you shout and fall, but it took me a while to get up the stairs. I imagine he came down the other side. This is Mrs Blimey, she's the cleaner here.' He pointed to a middle-aged woman in a fake leopard-skin headscarf, curlers and a flowered apron, standing beside a mop and bucket. She appeared to have stepped out of a British stage farce from the 1950s, a character actress like Irene Handl. 'You all right, ducks?' she asked solicitously, suspending an alarming ledge of bosom above his eyes and dropping fag ash on his shirt.

May's eyes swam. He felt sick and fell back. When he awoke again, the cleaner had transformed herself from a cheeky landlady-type into a glum, tiny Filipino with an unwavering gaze.

'The skin's not broken. I just wanted to make sure you're not concussed.' Bryant was helping him sit up. 'That's it. Lean on me.'

'What did I miss?' May winced as he pulled himself to his feet.

'Quite a lot, it appears,' said Bryant. 'I'm afraid we were much too late to do anything for her, though. She's in the back row of the stalls. Been there overnight, by the look of it. Giles will give us an accurate time of death.'

'You're talking about Mona Williams.'

'Are you up to seeing her?'

'Give me your arm.'

With his walking stick in one hand and May's sleeve in the other, Bryant led the way. The lights in the main auditorium were now on and Colin Bimsley was talking into his handset by the door.

Mona Williams had been sat upright in the final row of stalls seats. There seemed to be some kind of rusted metal contraption strapped across her face. Six brass sections were held in place with bolts. 'It's a branks – a scold's bridle,' said Bryant. 'A muzzle. The iron curb-plate here sticks into the mouth and presses down on the tongue. The underside of it is studded with small spikes. They first turned up in Scotland, around the mid-1500s if memory serves. They're designed to punish gossipy women who can't keep their mouths shut. Unfortunately, Mona

Williams panicked and choked to death on her own vomit.'

'I've seen this before,' said May. 'In one of your old books.'

'You've seen it more recently than that,' Bryant reminded him. 'There was one in Ella Maltby's waxwork dungeon.'

34

GUIGNOL

'You're enjoying yourself, aren't you?' said May, watching Dan Banbury at work. The stubby crime scene manager was on his knees between the theatre seats, enthusiastically dusting the arms of the chairs with fingerprint powder.

'I don't enjoy death, Mr May, you know that. But I do enjoy uncovering the provenance of crime. I like to know what happened. My curiosity always got me in trouble as a nipper. Whenever I saw a dead animal in the woods, I'd always try and find out what killed it. I used to go to strangers' funerals, just to discover what they died of.'

'That's the sort of thing serial killers do when they're young.'

Bryant had slouched down in one of the seats, his huge overcoat riding up about him. 'He came in from the back,' he said absently. 'She was already sitting facing the stage. You might lift a footprint from the aisle carpet.'

'What makes you say that?' asked Banbury.

'An empty theatre is like a church for her. She feels safe

here, she comes here to think. It was preying on her mind, you see.'

'You mean she knew something,' said May.

'She may even have arranged to meet him, to get the matter off her conscience,' Bryant suggested. 'Come on, Dan, what happened next?'

Banbury examined the back of the seat for a minute. 'OK, he came in, saw her in the seat and dropped the bridle over her head. It's heavy – she fell back, making the scratches here.' He pointed to two fine channels dug into the top of the wooden seat by the base of the cage. 'From the marks I'd say he held her there while he talked to her. Maybe he was just trying to warn her, to frighten her into silence. But she panicked. You can see where her shoes have kicked out at the base of the seat in front. She suffered from excess acidity; there's a tube of Tums in her bag. She struggled and hyperventilated, then threw up.'

'Check the bridle for dabs,' May suggested. 'If he cared about her enough to warn her away, he might have tried to get this thing off her head when he saw she was choking.'

'I already did. I think he wiped it afterwards.'

'No puppet this time.' Bryant was peering under the seats. 'Because this was an unexpected development. He hadn't allowed for it. Colin, go and arrange for Ella Maltby to be brought in, will you? Take someone with you but talk to her personally. Find out if the scold's bridle is missing from her display. And call in Neil Crofting, the old character actor.'

'Why do you want to see him?' asked May.

'He was Mona Williams's best friend. If anyone knows why she died, it'll be him. Colin, get Meera to warn Mr Kramer that there'll be no performances today. His theatre just turned into a crime scene.'

Bimsley set off for Hampstead, leaving the detectives

with Banbury. Bryant beckoned to his partner. 'Come and sit down for a minute. Dan doesn't like us messing up his floor. Besides, it's relaxing watching other people work.'

For a while they sat talking to and about each other, not always listening, scattering seeds of conversation like an old married couple. May was waiting for his partner to explain his thought processes.

'Come on then, out with it,' he said finally. 'How did you know about this?'

'Well, I didn't at first. I thought it would be the critic.'

'Explain.'

'Alex Lansdale trashed the show, but turned up at Kramer's party. They were seen talking together. Therefore he must be a friend of Kramer's. Kramer is under attack. Those he loves and trusts are being removed.'

'Why is he friends with a man who has spoken out against the play?'

Bryant felt in his coat pocket for a sheet of paper. Unfolding it and removing the half-sucked sherbet lemon that had become stuck to it, he handed the page to May. 'Read the review again. It's not what we first thought it was. Look at the key phrases I marked. Read them aloud.'

May read aloud. ' *"iPod generation – overmiked sound – no appeal to older audiences – superb Gothic set – drenched in gore – multiplex action movie – soap stars – nudity – teens will flock."* Kramer didn't want the usual old-school audiences to attend because he knew they'd hate it. He wanted a younger crowd with plenty of loose money in their pockets. Ray explained that most of the marketing budget for the show has been on social networking sites. That's what gave me the idea.'

'So he bought his critic and told him what to say.'

'Exactly. At first I thought that if somebody was just trying to stop the production, they'd go after Lansdale. If the critic had died, there'd have been no way to keep a lid on this whole thing. His paper would have told their readers.'

'How did you come to realize Mona Williams was in danger?'

'When I came to see the play, the programme seller said something odd. She said, *Some of the older ladies in this cast remember the days when we had a nicer class of people in here.* First of all, there's only one older lady in the show, so she had to mean Mona Williams. Second, *We had a nicer class of people in here*? But the New Strand is exactly that, a new theatre – there *were* no days when it had nicer clientele. But of course the clue is in the name. If there's a New Strand Theatre there might have been an old one. So I consulted my old theatre books, but failed to turn anything up. Then I realized I was looking for the wrong additional word – not the *New* Strand Theatre but the New *Strand* Theatre. I tore the pages out to show you.' Bryant handed May yet more crumpled sheets. 'There was a theatre here before, right on this spot. The auditorium was boarded over and converted to offices, but I'm guessing it was still intact when Kramer bought it. He realized what it was when he had the survey done, and hit on the idea to open it up again.'

'But why hasn't anybody else picked up on the fact that it used to be a theatre? And surely it would have been worth more as offices?'

'Not if you get the right audience for a new play. You can license it for different productions all around the world. As offices, the ground floor would have provided a nice atrium, but that's just wasted space. This one could be packed with 450 people who would pay nightly to be here. Kramer needed the right script to launch the theatre. He wanted to get in a younger crowd, so he commissioned Ray Pryce.'

'Why Ray?'

'Why not ask him yourself?' Bryant pointed behind him just as Ray entered the stalls.

'I got your text, Mr Bryant, although I had trouble understanding it.'

'He doesn't know how to use predictive,' May warned.

'Oh, my God, what is that?' Ray peered over the corpse's boxed-in head and leapt back.

'Mr Bryant, can I ask you to keep the public out of this site?' said Banbury.

'I'm afraid it's Mona Williams. Ray, explain to my partner how you convinced Mr Kramer to stage your play, would you?'

Ray had trouble drawing his eyes away from the bridled actress. 'I told him it would outrage everyone. Controversy is a sure way of firing up the box office. There's no such thing as bad publicity.'

'Now tell him the rest. Tell him how you plagiarized someone else's work to worm your way into Kramer's good books.'

Ray looked shocked, and started stammering. 'I don't know what you mean.'

'Come off it, chum. I know you copied the play.'

'It's not plagiarism, not in the strict sense.'

'*The Two Murderers* follows the script of *Les Deux Meurtriers* almost word for word.'

'I'm clear of the seventy-year rule.'

'You haven't exactly gone out of your way to acknowledge the original, have you? Does Robert know?'

'No, but—'

'The seventy-year rule,' May repeated. 'An author has to have been dead for seventy years before his work comes out of copyright.'

'That's right,' said Ray, shamefaced. 'I found the script right here in the building.'

'Now perhaps you'd like to tell my partner about the Grand Guignol,' Bryant prompted.

'OK, sure.' May could see that Ray was not nervous because he was standing near a corpse, but because he had suddenly had the spotlight of suspicion turned on him. 'The Grand Guignol was built in the Pigalle, in Paris, at the end of the nineteenth century, by a man called Oscar Méténier. It was a kind of vaudeville of horror. It staged a programme of one-act plays that featured murder of all kinds – matricide, infanticide, kidnap and rape. The scenes were graphically depicted on stage. They were so realistic that audience members regularly used to pass out.'

'And where did the name of the theatre come from?'

'From "Guignol", the Punch and Judy puppet character from Lyons.'

'The plays were often taken from the police blotters of the times,' Bryant added. 'True crimes, staged to delight and horrify Parisian audiences. Sex and violence for the chattering classes. Now explain what happened over here, if you would be so kind.'

Ray glanced back at the body and blanched. 'Can we go somewhere away from – her?'

'I'm sorry. Of course.' The detectives took him out to the foyer. 'Pray continue if you would,' Bryant asked.

'Well, it's simple. The Grand Guignol of Paris was a huge success for the next twenty years. So it was brought across the Channel and staged in what was then known as the Little Theatre, later the New Strand Theatre, here in Adam Street. But right from the start there was a problem. We had a Lord Chamberlain who censored plays and he refused a licence to any play he considered dangerous to the morals of the public. So the Grand Guignol at the Little Theatre highlighted the psychological cruelty of the characters, rather than showing blood and sex.

'In a way, that was worse. In two years they staged eight

series of plays, and many more were turned down. Altogether, forty-three plays were seen here. Most of them were psychological studies of damaged people. Stanislavsky created emotional memory exercises for actors – the idea was that you give a more convincing performance by inhabiting the character and making it believable from a psychological point of view. As a result, the theatre attracted famous names, even though it drew adverse critical reviews and caused a scandal. Noel Coward wrote a play for the Little Theatre called *The Better Half*, and Dame Sybil Thorndyke appeared in many of them. For four years, young Londoners came here to be shocked. Eventually, the Lord Chamberlain got fed up with what he considered an affront to human decency, and the theatre company had to close. The place changed its name and carried on for a while, but it was never really successful again.'

'So that's why nobody remembers the old theatre.'

'He banned all the plays from public performance. Odd, really, when you consider that the English stage has a history of horror, from the blinding of Gloucester in *King Lear* to the gruesome tortures of *The Revenger's Tragedy*, where the Duke's lips are burned away with acid and his eyelids are torn off so he has to witness his wife's adultery. The Little Theatre was low theatre in the Lord Chamberlain's eyes and there was a danger that it might appeal to the lower orders. So he came up with a solution. He allowed plays to be performed in their original French, because he thought only the middle classes would come here then and they were less likely to be corrupted.'

'How did you find out about the play?'

'I was working in the building.'

'Doing what?'

'After I finished working for the government, I became a night watchman. One evening I was asked to clear out a load of old boxes from the basement, ready for the dust-man in the morning. There was a bunch of playscripts inside. I was sitting behind the desk with nothing to do, and some nights Mr Kramer came to look at the building with his producer. I had time on my hands, so I rewrote a few of the plays and submitted them as my own work. I didn't hurt anyone. These things are ancient history. I just modernized them and bumped up the levels of sex and violence.'

'You acted with questionable legality,' said May, 'but we have bigger problems now.'

'Are you going to make an arrest?' Ray asked.

'You'll know at the same time as everyone else,' May replied. 'I'd make myself scarce if I were you. This place is now off limits.'

Mona Williams's body was delivered to Giles Kershaw while Banbury cleared the crime scene. The detectives watched what appeared to be a second Grand Guignol play being performed in front of the proscenium arch, then returned to North London.

'I think we know what we're dealing with now,' said Bryant, waving his walking stick at a taxi. 'Robert Kramer is clearly the target, not the suspect.'

'But why?'

'Because he has a secret, something he hasn't revealed to us in almost a week of questioning. This secret is so great that someone wants him to suffer very badly. They took his child, and that should have been the end of the matter. Then they went after his money man, his best friend, destroying his financial empire in the process. Kramer knows someone is out to get him. But here's the interest-ing thing. Despite his secret being known to another individual, he doesn't know who his own enemy is. Intriguing, no?'

'A woman,' said May suddenly.

'Hm. I was thinking about that possibility.'

'The harming of a child by throwing it about. Frightening an old lady, but not intending to kill her. It feels like a woman somehow, one who'd been angered by Kramer's behaviour. Particularly if we say that Gregory Baine's death was suicide.'

'I see what you mean. Kramer's enemy finds out that Mona Williams knows something which can give the game away. But she's an old lady, she'll frighten easily – she can be scared into silence.'

'The plan goes wrong. And revenge is not properly dealt. Kramer's still around and his life continues; nothing seems to touch him. He's not as broken up over his child as he was meant to be, because he's not the father. He's not destroyed by Baine's death, because for all we know there could be another offshore company designed to protect his finances from Baine. So there could still be another attempt to hurt him.'

'But why doesn't this enemy simply kill Kramer if he wants revenge?' Bryant asked.

'Where's the pleasure in that? Someone needs to see Kramer suffer. Merely being rid of him won't take away that gnawing anger. The killer wants to watch the pain slowly building in the victim's eyes. Nothing is working out as it was intended to. Hardly anything has gone right. Something else is bound to happen now.'

'Women,' repeated Bryant. 'There are four in the case. Della Fortess, the female lead; Ella Maltby, the set designer; Jolie Christchurch, the front-of-house manager; and Judith Kramer.'

'Incredible,' May marvelled. 'Last week you parked your car to get a bag of boiled sweets and spent the rest of the day trying to remember where you'd left it, but you can remember the name of everyone in the investigation.'

'I have a system for finding Victor now,' Bryant replied.

'I only park in places where I upset people. That way I can always find someone who remembers my car. Hang on, I've left one female out. Gail Strong.'

'Ah, the disreputable Ms Strong. I'm not sure I believe a word she's said to me so far. Maybe we should talk to her again.'

'After we've grilled Ella Maltby about her scold's bridle.' Bryant made a strange sound between a sink gurgling and a cow waking up. This noise usually indicated that he'd had an idea.

'What's the matter?'

'I've just had another thought. According to my *Twentieth-Century British Theatre*, when the Lord Chamberlain banned the plays he destroyed the reputation of the theatre's owner, who died in penury. You don't suppose someone at that party was a descendant of the original owner, looking for revenge against Kramer now?'

'Incredible as it may seem, no, I don't,' said May.

'OK, it was just a thought.'

The taxi sloshed through gutters filled with rainwater, wending its way into the deepening northern light.

35

LA RONDE

In the warehouse that had become the headquarters of the PCU, Bryant took one suspect and May took the other. Ella Maltby sat in the common room with her arms folded and her boots turned outwards in a gesture of defiant unhelpfulness.

'The bridle in my props room is one of three we made,' she explained icily. 'When Ray brought the scripts to us, we first chose a different play, and it featured a scene where the village gossip was locked into a bridle. Robert was never really happy with the second act, and eventually we junked it in favour of *The Two Murderers*.'

'What happened to the other two bridles?'

'I imagine they stayed in the props room at the theatre.'

'Aren't you in charge of that?'

'Yes, but I didn't have to keep track of them; they weren't exactly lethal weapons.'

'They were, as it turned out.'

'You know what I mean.'

'Who had access to the props room?'

'Everyone. I mean, we wouldn't keep it locked unless

there were weapons involved in the production. Anyone who needs to get into the backstage area of the theatre has to sign in at the stage door.'

'So access is strictly limited to cast, crew and theatre staff.'

'That's right.'

'And at the time when Mona Williams was attacked, you say you were—'

'At home. By myself.'

Bryant had nothing more. Banbury had found no prints on the bridle and had not been able to lift anything from the stalls carpet. 'All right, you're free to go, but don't go far,' he told Maltby. 'At least you could have come up with a decent alibi this time. No wonder you haven't got any friends. Janice, make her sign something, then kick her back onto the street.' He wandered into May's interrogation.

'This reminds me of *An Inspector Calls*,' said Neil Crofting. 'Mona was terribly good in that. I shall miss her. A real trouper. What do you think happened?'

'We're pretty sure someone tried to intimidate her and went too far,' May told him. 'You were by her side on the night of the party. Did she see or tell you anything unusual?'

'Let me think. I'd had rather a lot to drink. She usually gives me far too much information, a running commentary on the state of her innards, what she doesn't like about the leading lady, how Andrew Lloyd Webber is killing the theatre, why she can't eat sprouts before a show, that sort of thing. We were like an old married couple.' He wiped a misted eye. 'She chattered a lot, the usual tittle-tattle about the company. Mona was a terrible old gossip. Loathed the director, thought he was an idiot. It's hard to believe she's gone. She made a lovely Ophelia in her time. *There's rosemary, that's for remembrance*. She had the legs for it, you see.'

'What did she talk about specifically?' May prompted.

'Well, various people came up to pay their respects – she was a bit of a *grande dame*, after all, waiting in one spot for everyone to circle past her and pay respects like a remnant of the Hapsburg Empire, then she relayed the talk on to me. She said Russell was drinking too heavily, Della had a yeast infection, Ray was complaining his nicotine patches didn't work, Marcus had been seen backstage with Judith, Ella was being a bore about her ex-girlfriend, that sort of thing. But the big scandal was that Robert's wife and mistress were both in the same room. And I don't think Judith had an inkling.'

'You know his mistress?'

'It wasn't common knowledge, but we both knew because we've worked with Robert in the past, and we recognized the signs.'

'What sort of signs?'

'The ones that tell you when a man is about to become infatuated again. We were there going over our scenes on the night Robert first met her. And we could tell from the first moment what was going on. You could see the sparks from the stage.'

'Who is his mistress?'

'Gail Strong,' said Crofting, as if it was obvious. 'She set her cap at him. A disgraceful display. I suppose he was flattered, a man of his age.'

'When was this?'

'Oh, a couple of months ago, way before she joined the play. I think she'd been introduced to him through her father. And then at the party I remember Mona saying something that struck me as odd, just before everything went wrong.'

'What was that?'

'She said, *That completes the circle*. You know, like *La Ronde*. And I asked her to explain, but she wouldn't.'

'She meant exactly what she said,' said May. 'Gail Strong was seeing Robert Kramer, Kramer's wife was seeing Marcus Sigler, and then at the party we think Marcus and Gail had sex.'

'But did Marcus and Judith know about Gail?'

'Perhaps not, but somebody does. Did Mona Williams have any enemies?'

'Mr May, you reach a certain age when you don't have enemies any more, just people who find you mildly annoying. You become invisible. Mona had got to the point where she only existed on stage.'

'You can't think why anyone would want to kill her?'

'No, of course not.'

May sat back with a sigh. 'Arthur, is there anything you want to ask?'

Bryant was rooting through his pockets and looked as if he'd been caught out. 'Ah, yes – I have this written down somewhere but I can't find it – bladder complaints.'

'I'm sorry?'

'You said she talked to you about her innards. Any bladder complaints?'

'Well, I suppose the usual, at that age.'

'Only it would make sense if she had.'

'Arthur, *you're* not making any sense, as usual,' said May.

'It's very simple,' said Bryant impatiently. 'The only reason Mona Williams was threatened was because she knew the killer's identity. Now, she didn't know it before the party because the first death hadn't yet occurred. Maybe she worked it out later, but she saw or heard something at the party that revealed the killer's identity to her. And at some point this realization also hit the killer. I seem to remember from the chart Janice gave me that Mona Williams visited the loo three times. On several occasions during the evening there was a queue in the hall. In those kinds of situations, people tend to talk to each other. I'm wondering if somebody told her something they shouldn't have.'

'Well, Mr Crofting, I think we can let you go for now,' said May. 'You've been very helpful.'

Bryant watched the old actor don his coat. 'I thought you were marvellous in *The Crucible*. I saw you when I was a child.'

Crofting eyed Bryant coldly. 'No, I don't think it was that long ago,' he said, and left.

Bryant trotted off to the kitchen to brew tea, chatting to May as he went. 'We're missing something very obvious in this tangle, aren't we? Something in plain sight. I should have been able to figure it out in an instant. After all, we're not dealing with a particularly sophisticated killer. Rather the reverse. A baby shaken to death, an accountant knocked over the head and hanged, an old woman intimidated. And the crude symbolism of the dolls, everything intended to frighten Robert Kramer – but nothing ever does. Have you spoken to him in the last twenty-four hours?'

'He's annoyed about the theatre being closed but has negotiated it down to three days. They'll reopen on Tuesday.'

'You see? Nothing touches him. And he leaves nothing to chance. Which brings me to Gail Strong's father.'

'Her father? What about him?'

'Kramer's not a nice man, we agree on that? He was horrible to his first wife, he cheats on his second and he has a string of compliant girlfriends who can be relied upon to keep their mouths shut. So why would he choose Gail Strong? She has a high media profile and seems physically incapable of behaving herself. She's a liability.'

'He's probably just infatuated with her.'

'He may well be, but if she proved to be a nuisance he'd drop her like a hot brick. He'll have made sure she knows nothing about his business dealings, but she could still make life very difficult for him.'

'Unless he needs something from her,' May suggested.

'My thought exactly. He's not sleeping with her because he's in love.'

'Then it's her father he's after.'

'He introduced them. He's in charge of building licences. The original licence for theatrical performances would be attached to the building, and if Kramer needed to get the licence of the theatre extended, Gail's father would be the key to that.'

'But surely if her father finds out that Kramer is having an affair with his daughter, he won't be disposed to grant a licence application.'

'We don't know what Kramer is capable of doing. He'll use her to get what he wants, then dump her. It's more business than pleasure. I don't suppose we'll get any more answers from Kramer or his wife, not unless we allow Jack Renfield to torture them – something he'd probably relish the opportunity to do. I think we need to bring in Gail Strong.'

PCs Colin Bimsley and Meera Mangeshkar were sent to Gail Strong's Notting Hill apartment together to bring her in for further questioning. They were sent as a pair because there was a likelihood that Strong would have reporters and photographers hanging around on her doorstep, and someone would have to distract them.

'Have you noticed we get all the crappy jobs?' Meera complained. 'Go through the bins, sit on a roof all night, update the reports. Bryant tried to get me to make him a cup of tea the other day, but I told him to bugger off.'

'I don't mind making him tea. I always feel guilty when he does those big wet puppy eyes and looks helpless.'

'You're a pushover.' Mangeshkar swiped herself out through the tube barrier at Notting Hill.

'I don't know why we couldn't have taken your Kawasaki,' said Bimsley.

'Because I didn't want you pushing yourself up against me every time I braked, thank you. What number is it?'

Bimsley pointed. A pair of overweight men were loitering outside one of the terraced houses with coffee cups and telephoto lenses.

'OK, let's avoid these creeps. See if there's another way we can get her out of the building.' Meera punched out Gail's number on her mobile. 'No answer. She was there half an hour ago.' She approached one of the photojournalists. 'Oi, you waiting to get pictures of Gail Strong?'

'What's it to you?'

'I'm a police officer, that's what it is to me. Sling your hook before I run you in.'

'You got no right to order us around.'

'Terrorism Act. This is a High Alert area. I can bang you up without even bothering to invent a reason.'

The men grumbled, but gathered their equipment together promptly.

'Have you seen her?' Meera called. 'Did she go out?'

'What, you want our help now?' The photographer spat at her feet and waddled off.

'Come on.' They crossed the road to the front porch of the house. Meera checked the bells and rang the top one. They heard it buzz somewhere above their heads. Colin stepped back to examine the top floor windows. 'No sign of movement. How are we going to get in?'

'Cover me.' Meera put her elbow through a square of glass and felt for the lock.

'Blimey, Meera, that's B and E.'

'She could be hurt. What would the old man do?'

'Break in, you're right.' Bimsley followed her up the darkened stairway.

On the fourth floor, they found the door to flat 160D ajar.

'Someone's forced the lock.' Meera pointed to the damaged hasp. The pair advanced cautiously into the dimly lit flat, searching each room. The kitchen and lounge were undisturbed, but someone had recently been here. A Lily Allen CD was still playing, with four tracks left to go. 'Colin, in here.'

It was hard to tell if the bedroom showed signs of a struggle or whether Strong was just untidy. Shoes had been kicked off and clothes were scattered over the floor.

'Fire escape, over there,' said Meera, leading the way to the back of the house. The rear door on to the black iron escape was shut but unlocked.

Colin studied the back gardens. 'There's a gap in the fence. It goes straight out into the road behind. The photographers wouldn't have seen a thing.'

'You're forgetting something. She's trouble. If she'd been abducted she would have made a hell of a noise.'

'She's small. He could have knocked her out and carried her.'

'Let's call it in. I'll get to the neighbours, see if anyone saw anything. Although around here the only people who are ever home are the Filipino nannies.'

Meera dashed off as Bimsley double-checked the bedroom. 'Three deaths and a kidnapping,' grumbled Bimsley. 'The old man's going to go nuts.'

36

KNOWLEDGE

Janice Longbright stood and stretched. She had taken on the Anna Marquand case as a favour to Arthur but had reached a dead end. If Ashley Hagan hadn't stolen the girl's mobile, who had, and why? She stared at the shopping bag on her desk and tried to imagine what had happened. In desperation, she emptied it out on the desk again. A half-litre bottle of Gordon's gin, a volume of poetry, a packet of Handi Wipes, some tomatoes, a tin of beans.

Anna had come up to town and given Arthur his book, then caught the Northern Line south to Tooting Bec, then back up to London Bridge, where she changed for Bermondsey. Leaving the station, she had walked home with her shopping bag, where she was attacked. All pretty straightforward.

No, not straightforward.

Her attacker had been after something more. Longbright had a habit of keeping passwords on her mobile. She knew she shouldn't, but who could remember every user name and code phrase? What if Anna had done the same? What if he had already searched their house? How did he do it, and when? No, that didn't work because Rose Marquand never went out, and nobody had broken in. Besides, he had taken Anna's keys and found out that there was another lock-up, which was why he had gone to the pool. But had he actually found anything?

Longbright called Anna's mother.

'I can't talk to you right now,' said Mrs Marquand. 'I've got all this washing up to sort out, and then the laundry. I have trouble getting around with my back and there's so much clearing up to do.'

'I thought you had Sheena helping you.'

'So did I, but she buggered off.'

'What happened?'

'Bloody little thief. I went upstairs and found her going through Anna's bedroom. All the drawers open, all her papers out. You can't trust nobody no more.'

'What about her safe?'

'Wide open. I was going to call the police but she ran out of the house. This was yesterday morning. I haven't seen her since and her mobile number isn't working.'

'Is there anything missing?'

'Not that I can see. Anna had files for all her clients and they're numbered, one to thirty. It looks like all the files are still there.'

Except one. Arthur told her he'd let Anna look after the disc, because he was likely to lose it. Anna knew what was on it. Her attacker had been through the shopping bag and the lido locker – maybe he hadn't found it after all. Maybe she'd been too smart for him. So what the hell had she done with it? Longbright rang off and went next door to see Bryant.

'Arthur, are you free for a moment?'

'For you I have all the time in the world.' He aimed her at a ratty armchair she had not seen before. 'It was in the

273

attic,' he informed her. 'I found a swastika flag down the back of the seat but apart from that it's very comfortable. You should come up there with me – there's all kinds of strange stuff stored away.'

'Was there anything in your memoirs that could have been considered dangerous?'

'Anna removed the most contentious passages. There were some bits about past prime ministers that weren't very flattering. A few mentions of missile bases, Russian spies, the pensions scandal—'

'But does any one thing stick out above all the rest? Anything worth killing for?'

'You think Anna Marquand was murdered? It was blood poisoning. You can get that from virtually anything.'

'I know, but it's the timing that makes me suspicious. Look, I know it sounds crazy, but Anna's mother was befriended by a girl who just turned up on her doorstep one day offering her services as a carer. Then, when Mrs Marquand caught her going through Anna's belongings, she fled. If someone had been monitoring Anna's electronic mail, they would have known what she was working on. I want Giles to talk to his opposite number at Bermondsey mortuary. I need to know if there was any-thing at all suspicious about Anna Marquand's death. I think there was something in your memoirs that could be considered a danger to national security, and Anna knew what it was, even if she didn't realize the importance of it.'

'That's the trouble.' Bryant shook his head. 'I've only got Anna's edited final version of the book to go on – some of the notes were written, some were dictated. I simply can't remember what might have been in the original. Talk to Giles anyway, see if he can pull any strings with the coroner.'

'Are you sure there's absolutely no possibility of you

remembering all the things you wrote about?' Longbright pressed.

'I suppose there might be one way,' said Bryant. 'Hypnotism. If I was put under, I might be able to recall what it was. And I know the very person who could do it.'

37

BACTERIA

'You're a bit out of your jurisdiction, aren't you?' said Dr Leo Hendrick, resident coroner at the Bermondsey mortuary. The young Jamaican's borough was a tough beat that suffered a statistically disproportionate level of violent crime, but he was fast building a reputation as the most ambitious medical officer in town. 'I suppose we should be flattered, a specialist coming south of the river to see us at work.'

'It may be nothing,' Giles Kershaw admitted, setting down his briefcase. Clearly, Bermondsey had more money than St Pancras; the building was new and fitted with state-of-the-art equipment. Hendrick received him in a carpeted visitors' room that was as smart as a hotel suite.

'It was kind of you to see me. We just wanted to run something by you.'

'Yes, I read your email. Not being rude, but it sounds to me like you think I made a wrong call, and you're fishing for a different verdict that's a better fit with your investigation.'

'Not at all. I'm perfectly happy to let your diagnosis

stand. But there's been some additional information about the case that we thought you should know.' He explained about the coincidence of Anna Marquand's property being searched and her role in handling sensitive information for government departments.

'Why was I not told of this?' Hendrick complained, checking Anna's notes on his laptop.

'This kind of information doesn't just drop into the case files,' Giles explained. 'It's part of the PCU's brief to make such connections.'

'When Anna Marquand came in, there was nothing in the patient notes about her background. Her address told me she's from a low-income housing estate. She suffered from a stomach ulcer but seemed healthy enough apart from that. Sometimes it's hard to tell what these girls get up to. We have to make some assumptions.'

'She went to Nuffield College, Oxford. Surely that should have given you a clue to her background. She was an academic.'

'A university background is no signifier of class. She could have had a college education and become a junkie. She had tetanus. It's a soil-based infection, Mr Kershaw. In other words, dirt. *Clostridium tetani* is very hardy. The spores get into a wound and spasm the muscles, locking the jaw and forcing air from the body. It's found in the environment, not transmitted from person to person. More common in developing nations than over here. Soil, dust, animal waste – apparently there was a neighbour-hood dog her mother sometimes let in. There's a potential source, right there. The bacteria enters through puncture wounds. I've seen it caused by rusty nails, insect bites, a wooden splinter, a torn nail. IV drug use, obviously, but she wasn't a user. The only wound on her body was a tiny nick from the bread knife.

'I checked the knife blade and found traces of the toxin

Tetanospasmin on the serrations. There were further traces on the bread board. It seems fairly clear to me that the knife had fallen on the floor at some point earlier in the day and had been replaced without being washed. My assistant spoke to the mother and she remembers picking it up from the kitchen floor not long after the dog had been allowed in there. The Marquands have a small garden. If the dog sometimes did its business on the path and the mother rarely cleaned up the mess . . . well, poor hygiene. It's unfortunate, but hardly uncommon.'

'It's my understanding that tetanus takes a while to become established,' said Giles. 'Anna Marquand died quickly.'

'There are exceptions to every rule,' replied Hendrick impatiently.

Giles thanked the doctor and took his leave, but he was not convinced. On his way back to the station he rang Longbright. 'Something feels wrong,' he told her. 'Didn't you say there was a packet of Handi Wipes in Anna's shopping bag?'

'That's right. There was a small plastic bottle of anti-bacterial stuff in her handbag, too.'

'Then I think Anna knew what her mother was like and was careful at home. I don't think it's very likely that she would have used the knife without washing it first. Wait. The shopping bag was taken away from her and returned.'

'That's right. The mother says Anna came out of the house and found it on the back step.'

'Can we get everything in it tested?'

'I'll do it right now.'

Longbright ran the bag up to Banbury, who was working in the makeshift laboratory he had been rigging on the floor above. She explained the problem as Dan debouched the shopping items. 'Give me a couple of hours,' said Dan. 'I'm sorry, I should have done this at the outset.'

'You had no reason to be suspicious then,' Longbright reminded him.

At six-thirty p.m. he came down to find her. 'You were right. It's in the bread,' he said.

'The bread wasn't in the shopping bag I gave you.'

'No, it was in the shopping bag originally, but she took it out to make a sandwich. I just had the remains of the loaf brought over from the house. It was still in her mother's cupboard, untouched. The cut on Anna's finger was incidental. She *ingested* poison. Not tetanus but strychnine. It's quite similar in chemical structure. Hendrick wouldn't have expected to test for that. He went with the most likely cause of death.'

'We should call the supermarket and warn them.'

'No, I mean it's *in* the bread. Injected into it. I found a pinprick in the plastic covering that corresponds to an indentation on the crust, both with traces of poison. It got to her internally. Anna Marquand had a bleeding ulcer. The poison killed her in a fairly short space of time. So I think you can call Giles and tell him the cause of death was strychnine poisoning. The mugger took the bag and returned it with a lethal addition.'

'This is much bigger than a mugging,' said Longbright. 'The girl in the house, the man in the alley. There are others involved.'

38

HYPNOTIZED

Maggie Armitage, Grand Order Grade IV White Witch of the Coven of St James the Elder, Kentish Town, was having problems of her own. 'We've got sprites,' she complained as she opened the door to Arthur Bryant. 'Come in but be careful. They're everywhere, getting into the cupboards and breaking things. They're especially fond of custard.'

'Are you talking about mice?' said Bryant, checking to see if he'd brought his hearing aid. He rarely used it in the PCU building because it kept picking up old episodes of *Hancock's Half Hour*, which was very distracting.

'No, these are white and made of discarded ectoplasm, but they have little legs and can really shift. They appeared after a séance and now we can't get rid of them. I can't see them but Daphne swears she can, ever since her accident. She says they moved into the back of the television, but something has repelled them. The poor quality of programmes, I imagine. It's nice to see you, give me a kiss.'

Bryant proffered his cheek and received a lipstick brand.

'How are you getting on in your new building? Had any manifestations yet?'

'What of?'

'Oh, the usual things that get left behind after a séance. Spirit dregs. Every building keeps a ghost imprint of its past and for over a decade yours was full of people contacting the dead, so you must have all sorts of things floating about in there. Don't you hear strange noises at night?'

'All the time, but I think it's mostly Raymond swearing.'

'The signs of manifestation include speaking in tongues, the gift of prophecy and damage to skirting boards,' said Maggie. 'I'll come over with my thermal scanner one evening. I suppose you're here wanting information. There was a time when you'd pop by for my banana treacle trifle, but these days you just use me as a resource.'

'I'll have some trifle if it's going, but I do have a question for you. Do you know anything about stage magic, how the effects are achieved?'

'A fair bit. Shakespeare was a dab hand, Banquo's ghost pointing an accusing finger at his killer, that sort of thing. Early melodramas often materialized pale, melancholy figures from behind folding doors. Sometimes they burst sachets of blood under their white gowns. But I think the Victorians did it best. They had phantasmagoria, magic lantern shows which projected images of the dead onto smoke, looming menacingly over the spectators. And in 1863 there was Pepper's ghost, of course.'

'What was that?'

'Oh, that was a marvellous effect by all accounts. Professor John Pepper lit a sheet of glass so that it looked like people were walking through walls and gliding across the set. Thanks to the illusion, the London stage was soon awash with disappearing ladies, dancing skeletons and babbling severed heads. And they came up with something called the "ghost glide". An actor would ascend through the floor of the stage, moving forward without taking a single step. Of course, most mediums were more like stage magicians than real psychics. Why do you want to know?'

'We're dealing with a very peculiar case.'

'Well, that is your remit, isn't it? The peculiar?'

'It was never meant to be,' Bryant admitted. 'Anyway, it's not why I'm here. I have another problem. I need you to hypnotize me. I have to recall something I've forgotten.'

'Oh, that's easy enough. Didn't I regress you to your past lives once?'

'Yes. You went back too far. I couldn't speak, remember?'

'Oh that's right, I think I turned you into protoplasm. It's not my fault you're so susceptible. Go and make yourself comfortable on the chaise longue, I'll brew us some seaweed tea. What exactly do you need to remember?'

'I gave all my file notes to the girl who was helping me with my memoirs. I told her I remembered everything, but I don't. Now she's dead and I need to find out what it was in those notes that killed her.'

'Well, that's as clear as mud. You weren't there when her soul departed, were you?'

'No.'

'Good, I can't be dealing with a case of possession tonight, I haven't got enough salt. You need to recover what you wrote, yes? So let's go back through the process. Hang on a minute.'

She returned with bowls of tea the colour of a rough sea and a covered plate. 'Take a couple of these first. They'll help you relax.'

'What are they?' Bryant peeked under a tea towel.

'Custard creams. They always work for me. Now, you need to find yourself in a comfortable place.'

'I can't, I'm in your house.'

'I mean, imagine you're on a beach.'

Bryant closed his eyes, laced his fingers and lay back. 'All right, Hastings.'

'Not Hastings. Not somewhere with a burnt-down pier and a juvenile delinquency problem. Pick somewhere warm, safe and relaxing.'

'All right, I'm at home with Alma, sitting in front of the fire, reading my copy of *London's Disused Underground Stations 1920–1959 Volume 3*, the annotated version.'

'You don't have to tell me everything, just imagine it. It's warm and you're feeling sleepy. Your heartbeat is slowing down—'

Bryant opened one eye. 'Is that a good idea?'

'It's fine. You're relaxed. You're starting to fall asleep.'

Bryant promptly fell asleep.

'No, you're not supposed to actually fall asleep. Wake up.'

Bryant released a snore. His head lolled. Maggie slapped his face gently. Then harder.

'Ow. What's happening? Did you do it?'

'You fell asleep.'

'You told me to.'

'Let's try again. I'm going to count back from ten to one, and you will feel yourself sinking deeper and deeper into a state of relaxation.'

Maggie counted back and Bryant slipped into a light hypnotic state. In fact, he relaxed so much that he almost vanished into the sofa. Bryant had always been open to new ideas and beliefs. He was highly susceptible and in many ways naïve, but she loved him for his refusal to become regimented in his habits and thoughts.

'You are in your office, assembling your notes and thinking about your memoirs. They are laid out in front of you on your desk. What cases are you considering for inclusion in the first volume?'

'The Palace Phantom, the Deptford Demon, the Belles of Westminster, the Battersea Cat Batterer, the Flying Dragons of Soho, the Blood Thrower of Belsize Park, the Butterfly Killer, and that strange business in the Elephant and Castle Odeon that led to the building being demolished. We called it the Fall of the House of Usherettes—'

'Apart from the criminal cases, was there anything that would have breached the Official Secrets Act or any freedom of information rulings? Try to see yourself typing up the pages, and wondering, *Should I be putting this down on paper?*'

'Oh, I never think that. Put it all down, I say.'

'Didn't you have a problem with the Ministry of Defence?'

'What kind of problem?'

'I don't know. You came round here and told me about it.'

'When was this?'

'About seven years ago.'

'Oh, that's right. The researchers.'

'Tell me about them.'

'They were working on a secret project down in Wiltshire. Some kind of weapon. The work had been out-sourced to a private company jointly owned by US and UK executive bodies. There had been a high number of suicides over the year, research scientists, all males in their twenties, mostly Asian. None of them had shown suicidal tendencies before, and all were working on the same project.'

'What was your involvement?'

'We'd been called in by an independent think tank to look at the situation. I handled the assignment personally, as a favour. I didn't involve John. I delivered a report, but no action was ever taken. My findings were ignored.'

'What did you find out?'

For the first time, Bryant hesitated. 'I'm afraid I can't tell you that,' he said slowly.

'How much of this did you put in your notes to Anna?'

'I'm not sure. I never include the boring bits. I probably edited it a little. Oh.'

'What?'

'I gave her the file of background material, just for fact-checking. I meant to go through it, just to make sure there wasn't anything sensitive. But then we got involved with the Highwayman case and I didn't get round to it.'

'How would an outsider find out what she'd read?'

'John explained it to me. If she'd grown curious enough to run searches online they would have been flagged up in the Cyber-Defence Security Department of the MoD. They could have traced the requests right back to her.'

'You think they would do that?'

'Of course. Defence of the realm. Oh, what have I done?'

'All right, you are rising back to the surface now as I count down to zero, and you will remember everything we discussed. When I reach zero you will be awake.' She brought Bryant back to full alertness.

'Don't you see?' said Bryant, attempting to pull himself up from the couch, scrabbling for his hat and coat. 'It means they knew where she kept her files. They knew she had a stomach ulcer. They knew how to get to her, and to her mother. They planted the girl in the house to look after Mrs Marquand. But they still haven't found what they need. I wish I hadn't come to you, Maggie. You've made me realize something terrible.'

'What's that?'

'I killed her. It's my fault Anna Marquand is dead. Defence of the realm.'

And with that, he was gone.

39

CRUELTY

The hunt for Gail Strong was in full swing. Renfield and Longbright were working as a team, dividing the search into quadrants. 'Every home of everyone who was at the party,' Jack told the others, handing out their assignments. 'Every garage, vehicle, lock-up and attic. Every private place they don't want us to know about.'

'How are we going to get them to tell us things like that?' asked Mangeshkar.

'You'll just have to use your charm, won't you?' Renfield snapped. 'Any sensible questions?'

'It might be worth trying offices, any place they've got keys to,' said Bimsley.

'Good thinking. Where's Dan?'

'He's over at Gail Strong's apartment.'

'OK, Janice is going to cover the theatre. Meera, you're always complaining about getting the crap jobs. I'm taking you off the property searches and putting you on something trickier. Go through Gail Strong's social network sites, Twitter, Facebook, anything else she's on, and talk to her closest friends. She might not be very likeable but she's a smart girl; she might try to leave us a clue as to her whereabouts. See if there's anything she's particularly associated with apart from shopping and partying. Nicknames, passwords, emergency contacts, anything we should be watching out for.'

'But she's got millions of online friends,' Meera complained. 'It'll take for ever.'

'That's OK,' Renfield replied, 'nobody's going home until it's done. We may be able to save her life.'

'It's better than house searches,' Colin suggested cheerfully. Meera shot him a poisoned glance.

May left the briefing session and went back to the office he shared with his partner. 'Why aren't you sitting in on this?' he asked, leaning against the door jamb.

Bryant was slumped at his desk, surrounded by his beloved books. 'I can't – not while there's this mess with Anna Marquand to sort out.'

'There's nothing you can do right now,' said May. 'I sent a beat constable from Bermondsey to keep watch on Mrs Marquand.'

'I must find that disc.'

'You don't know where it is and besides, even if you did, you still wouldn't know exactly who was behind her death. MoD outsourcing transfers a multitude of sins away from its centre of operations, you know that. Whoever it was will have covered their tracks by now.'

'Not if I can find the disc and let them know I have it,' said Bryant doggedly.

'I honestly don't know how you're going to do that, Arthur, but if I think of anything I'll tell you. I'm going back to help them look for Gail Strong. She could still be alive. Anna's gone. We have to prioritize.'

Gail Strong's father hit the stratosphere when the PCU was forced to inform him that his daughter was missing, presumed kidnapped. Raymond Land locked himself in his office to field the endless unhelpful calls from officials. Gail Strong's father had appointed various senior officers with the Met and the City of London to take immediate action and do something, anything, but nobody could tell them exactly how they might help. Whitehall was able to dam up press interest, but nobody knew how long that would last. Once the paparazzi regulars who stalked her street realized that she had disappeared, it would only be a matter of minutes before the story hit the internet.

Bryant sat at his desk and told himself to snap out of it. John was right; sometimes his partner shamed him. Arthur knew that the living took precedence over the dead. Anna could not be brought back, but perhaps Gail Strong could. He was convinced that the answer was right before him; there was something he had seen and missed, something right in front of his tired blue eyes.

His attention drifted to *The Dreadful & Remarkable History of Mr Punch*, which lay open at the page of Punch beating the Devil himself. He had been focusing on the wrong thing; Punch and Judy were only involved because of Robert Kramer's obsession with the puppet play.

This was about the Grand Guignol. The Little Theatre. The New Strand. It had begun with Punch, but was really about the staging of lurid set pieces. The murder of a child. The hanging of a banker. The terrorizing of an old woman. There was another term for the Grand Guignol.

The Theatre of Cruelty.

Which was why Robert Kramer had not been killed – he was being tortured, made to suffer by someone who hated him so deeply that his death would come as an anticlimax, and that moment had to be delayed for as long as possible. Kramer's legacy was being removed piece by piece. His child's life had been taken, his livelihood threatened and now his girlfriend stolen away, but nothing had had the desired effect. It was a question that must be going through the killer's mind: what was there left for Kramer to really care about? What other ways were there to hurt him?

Dan Banbury rocked back on his heels and tried to think. It didn't make sense. He had covered all the entry and exit points, all the heavily trafficked areas in the bedroom, kitchen and hall, and had found nothing but Gail Strong's own prints. A few stray fibres had turned up, but nothing male, and it had to be a man if the girl had been rendered unconscious and carried out down a steep, narrow fire escape. The majority of fibres that passed his way were suggestive of gender.

He rose and took another look around the room. This time he searched every drawer, labelling and numbering the items as he went. Then he called Bryant.

'She wasn't kidnapped,' he said bleakly. 'I can't find any trace of a secondary presence here. She's got an awful lot of clothes and it's impossible to tell what's missing, so I had a word with her cleaning lady, who put everything in specific places. Sure enough, there's a set of clothes missing.'

'It could mean her kidnapper took spare clothes for her,' said Bryant.

'No. Her passport's still here – smart move – and so are things like her handbag, makeup and toothbrush, but she could replace those. The most telling thing that's missing is her MP3 player. *"I live for my music. Life deserves to have a beat," says Mayfair socialite Gail Strong*, headline from one of her press cuttings – she actually collected them; more insecure than we thought. There's no music anywhere here. She's somewhere in the British Isles. Think about it. She has a history of getting into scrapes and running away.'

'This makes things worse,' muttered Bryant.

'What do you mean?'

'If the killer hasn't taken her, it can only be because he knows she means nothing to Kramer. He's playing us all. Look at us, running around with no idea what to do next. He's extending his theatre of cruelty to all the players, and he's loving it.'

'Wait – this girl who came forward with information about Kramer's cruelty, you said she was a plant?'

'That's what we think.'

'Has it occurred to you that Gail Strong might have been sent away by her father? He's politically well connected. He could easily have arranged it.'

'That's the problem, Dan. Every step we take just reveals more duplicity. I don't know who or what to trust any more.'

Bryant replaced the receiver and sat back, massaging his brow, forcing himself to think. His mind refused to function. Perhaps he was losing it. There was simply no way forward now. It was up to the others to turn up something. Unless he fully understood the method of destroying Kramer, he had no solution.

What is important to a man like Robert Kramer? he thought. *Love? Money? Fame? What can you take away from him that he values above all else? What could I lose that would destroy me? That's easy, the Unit. But what would it take to devastate a man like Kramer?*

Punch was an unrepentant sinner who took the world by the throat and shook it. Some fleeting fear brushed the back of Bryant's heart and was gone. He had a terrible feeling that the final act was yet to be played out, and that he was powerless to stop it.

40

PRIDE

Bryant reached home in a state of mental exhaustion. Dropping his keys into the bowl on the hall table surprised him, because the bowl wasn't there, and neither was the hall table. Alma had succeeded in clearing the house in his absence.

All the rooms had been emptied except for one part of the lounge, which now looked like the stage set for a Fringe production of *Death of a Salesman*. Seating himself in the only remaining armchair, he watched in silence as Alma trotted in and placed a tray of haddock and poached eggs before him.

'You're a very strange woman, you know,' he told her. 'So self-sufficient. What do you get out of it?'

'I'm a good Christian, Mr Bryant. I believe if you help people in this life, it will do you good in the next.'

'Apart from the fact that that's Buddhism, you're telling me you're just paying in good deeds, like having a bank account, so that you can make a withdrawal in the future.'

She folded her arms and regarded him with an assessing gaze. 'You don't understand and never did. People go to work and come home and think that's it, that's all the good they can do, but it's just the start. There are real sins in the world, Mr Bryant – you know enough about those. I try to make up for some of them, in my own small way. I have my church work, and I know you do good even though you have a funny way of going about it, so I look after you.'

'Then let me ask you something,' said Bryant. 'What do you consider to be man's greatest sin?'

'That's easy. The sin of pride. It's the tricky one, it keeps on changing form. But if you took your nose out of your books for a minute and looked at what's happening to the country, you'd see all these silly kids around you, thinking they're going to become celebrities when they have nothing to offer the world. When I was a little girl me and my sisters wanted to be doctors and nurses, explorers, teachers. We wanted to give something, to do our duty, not to be idolized for doing nothing.'

'Surely that's just overconfidence,' said Bryant.

'It's another name for pride. It's when a man thinks he's greater than God. Like this man Robert Kramer.'

'What do you know about him?' asked Bryant in surprise.

'I read the papers. I've heard you talk. Not even showing remorse for his dead son. That's what a man like him needs to lose, his pride. But it's the one thing he'll never give up.'

Bryant's blue eyes widened at her. 'Alma, you never cease to amaze me,' he said. 'I think you've just helped me to understand our killer.'

'Well, thank the Lord for that,' she said. 'Eat your haddock. And give me that scarf for the wash, it's filthy.'

John May had given up trying to get hold of Brigitte in Paris, and was just about to go to bed when Bryant rang.

'I think we've got it around the wrong way,' Bryant told him without any preamble. 'We should have been studying the victim, not the perpetrator. We need to catch him by surprise, tear him apart and look inside, understand what makes him tick. I asked myself: what must Kramer be made to lose? What does the killer most want to take away from him? And Alma came up with the answer. His pride. That's what he's after. Mr Punch, the ruler of his own world, needs to be taken down from his pedestal and made to beg for mercy. Nothing the killer has done so far has worked. So what will he do next?'

'Go after Kramer himself,' said May, completing the thought.

'Exactly. I should have thought of it earlier but I got distracted by Gail Strong's so-called disappearance. I'm sending Colin and Meera over to Northumberland Avenue right now. By the way, Dan was right about Ms Strong. She checked into a boutique hotel in Devon, using a credit card to secure her room. She didn't think they were taking a payment, but they ran a check and it flagged. Not a smart move. Devon police are going to keep an eye on her.'

'So what do you and I do?'

'Get a few hours' sleep,' said Bryant. 'We're going to need it.'

Meera parked her Kawasaki under the bridge at the Embankment and walked to Northumberland Avenue with Colin. Rain was just starting to gloss the road ahead and speckle the roofs of passing taxis. Many of the streets around Trafalgar Square were now awash with neon but this road had retained its dark, deserted look. 'Where do you want to locate?' she asked. 'I'm not sitting in a shop doorway watching you eat Pad Thai from a box.'

'I don't see we have much choice,' Bimsley replied. 'The offices opposite Kramer's gaff are closed for the night and the nearest café is down there under Charing Cross Bridge. We won't be able to keep an eye on the apartment from that far away.'

'Then why don't we just park ourselves in the foyer of his building?'

'John doesn't want us to show our hand.'

'I can't see why not. If you ask me, I don't think they know what they're doing. We've turned up nothing. Why is that? Maybe Kramer chucked his own kid out the window and frightened the old dear, and his banker just saw how things were going and took his own life.'

'Why do you always think they're not on the ball?' Colin asked. 'You're always having a go at them – too old, too slow, don't know what they're doing. We've still got a higher success rate than the Met.'

'Everyone's got a higher success rate than the Met. My old mum could solve crimes quicker than them. It's the way they operate, keeping us in the dark, going off without explaining, it makes me so angry—'

Colin laid a calming hand on Meera's arm. 'Meera, *everything* makes you angry. Have you not noticed what an angry person you are?'

'I'm under stress, my parents hate me being in this job, my sister's a walking disaster and I can't get a bloody date because I'm always at work.'

'Look, it's raining, it's miserable, come here and give me a cuddle, just a friendly hug.'

'No, Colin, that's not a good idea.'

'Why not? We're mates, aren't we? What would it take to get a hug from you?'

Meera thought for a second. 'Well, you know how we're all technically in line for the throne? Like, if fifty-four million people died, you'd be Queen?'

'Y-e-es,' said Bimsley uncertainly.

'It would be like that.'

Colin looked down at his rain-splashed boots. 'Are you telling me that you'd only give me a hug if every other eligible man in the country was dead? That's really, really hurtful.'

'Why do you always have to show your feelings? People don't want to see them all the time. Why can't you be a bit more like me?'

'I can't help it, Meera.' Colin looked crestfallen. 'I can't change, even for you. I don't have any other face but this one.'

She looked at the rain dripping through his spiked fair hair and her heart started to melt. He looked like a Disney dog someone had decided to drown instead of rewarding. She reached out a hand to touch his shoulder.

'Colin—'

Suddenly, the ground-floor door of the building opposite opened and Robert Kramer came out. Colin checked his watch. It was 11.42 p.m. 'He's leaving, look.'

'Where does he keep his car?'

'He has a space in the NCP at the next corner.'

'Back to my bike.'

They ran across the road, heading to Meera's Kawasaki just as Kramer disappeared beneath the yellow neon of the car park entrance. A minute later Kramer's black 500 Series Mercedes pulled up at the barrier and he fed it a ticket. Meera moved out behind him with Colin riding pillion. She stayed two cars back, hoping that the night and the rain would reduce their noticeability.

The Mercedes dropped to Victoria Embankment and headed along Upper Thames Street to the City of London. It clipped the lights on the one-way system at Tower Bridge, leaving Meera stranded.

'He's over there in the far left lane,' shouted Colin. 'Get closer or we'll lose him.' Meera accelerated and skirted round the shining wall of oncoming traffic, catching him up.

She tailed Kramer over the bridge and left towards the Rotherhithe Tunnel. The Mercedes picked up speed. 'I think he's spotted us,' she called back, roaring ahead. Behind them, a police car siren sounded and lights flashed in Meera's wing mirror. An officer was waving the Kawasaki off the road.

Meera had no choice but to slow down and park and the Mercedes sped off. The officer behind them strolled over. 'Turn the bike off. You're in a bit of a rush, aren't you?'

'Yeah, and you've just ruined our night's work.' She sullenly threw open her badge and waved it at the cop. The patrol officer peered at it but did not seem convinced. 'Peculiar Crimes Unit? Is that a made-up name? Off the bike, both of you.'

'It's a specialist investigation unit,' said Colin.

'Oi,' the patrolman called back to his co-driver, 'ever heard of the Peculiar Crimes Unit?'

'Yeah,' called his mate, 'they're the bunch that put the mockers on one of our cases this week, the girl in Hadley Street. They screwed us over.'

The patrolman returned the badge. 'In that case, I'm glad to return the favour,' he said with a grin, swaggering back to his patrol car.

41

PITCH

Robert Kramer saw that he had lost the motorbike, and doubled back. He turned the sat nav back on and followed its instructions, coming off the M25 somewhere near Dunton Green. He headed south into the Kent country-side. The roads grew narrower, the overhead branches grew denser and soon there was only an intermittent signal on his mobile phone.

His headlights picked up the distant homes of the rich, buried behind hedges, beyond fields. He passed an ancient granite church, a dead pub, a handful of dark houses, then nothing but black and green country roads for miles.

The sat nav told him he had almost reached his destin-ation, but there was nothing to be seen outside: no turn-off, no signpost, only spattering rain and the dark treeline at the horizon. He slowed down, searching the hedgerows, and found a car-width space with a twin tyre track running through it. Nosing the wide-bodied Mercedes along the lane, jouncing over the tufts of grass, the branches snatching at his wing mirrors, his headlights picked up some kind of farm building ahead.

He pulled up in front of it and opened the window slightly. He felt the spit of rain and smelled pig dung. It was several degrees colder here than in town. He rarely made trips into the countryside and would not have come tonight but for the message left at the theatre.

He was wearing light brown handmade shoes and did not wish to get them stained. Collecting a torch and treading carefully, he made his way to the barn door and tried the handle. It opened easily. Inside were machine-rolled bales of hay; some kind of farm machinery, all red metal and spikes; and what appeared to be a stage area, surrounded by lit candles in curved glass pots, the ones you could buy in cheap hardware stores.

'Well, you got me here,' he said aloud, looking up. 'Now what?'

Somewhere from the rear of the barn he heard piano music start playing – tinny and unreal, presumably an iPod hooked up to a portable system. He walked forward onto the makeshift stage and squinted into the musty darkness. 'Is this supposed to frighten me?' he called. 'If the music is meant to tell me something, you're wasting your time. How did you know I would come here?'

'I knew you wouldn't be able to stay away,' sang a strange, distorted voice.

'What is that – Auto-Tune? Or are you meant to be Mr Punch? Dear God, tell me you're not using a swozzle. There can't be two of us, you know. Anyway, I think you've misunderstood me. It's not an obsession, just – a role model. I could have picked Flashman or Moriarty or Julien Sorel from *The Red and the Black*. Patrick Bateman. Hannibal Lecter. They all rise above mere morality to make something more of themselves.'

There was no reply.

'Yes, that's right, I read books. You didn't know that, did you? That's what we have to do these days, find a role model. It's not easy making a success of yourself any more. You can't just sit around waiting for a war.'

He walked while he spoke, trying to work out where his adversary was hiding. He stopped to listen, but there was no sound other than the warped piano music and the patter of rain on the barn's corrugated iron roof. The candles guttered, extending shadows. He paced in a slow circle around the lights, carefully placing one polished shoe in front of the other, his hands linked behind his back, like Prince Philip attending the opening of a new factory.

'But a funny thing happened when I was a little boy. I grew up in Brighton, and every Sunday afternoon I used to go to the beach to watch the Punch and Judy show. Not because I liked the show – it was always exactly the same – but there was a girl there I cared for. Her father was the Punch and Judy man, so she had to sit there and wait for him. She had a kind of – what do you call them? A page-boy cut, like French girls have, shiny black hair that came to points below her ears. I used to sit behind her and study that soft white neck. I wanted to reach forward and touch it with my tongue. I suppose she was two or three years older than me. I was ten.

'Well, one day I was sitting behind her and it had just started to spit with rain, and Mr Punch had come on and was beating the hell out of his wife with a stick, and everyone was laughing, and I reached forward, closer, and – very lightly – touched her neck with my tongue. And she turned around and slapped my face. And all the kids started laughing at me. Well, they probably weren't, but you know how sensitive you are at that age.

'I followed her around for weeks and she never knew I was there. One day I waited while she bought an ice cream and watched as she walked down the alley back to her horrible little pebble-dashed council house with seashells set into the garden walls, and I kicked her legs from under her and pelted her with stones I had brought from the beach. I broke her teeth and blacked her eyes with them, and then – well, let's just say I enjoyed my first sexual experience.

'Next Sunday the Punch and Judy man was gone. He never came back. Well, somebody had to become Mr Punch. Life kicks you in the teeth and the only way you can win is by kicking it back. There, I've only told one other person that story in my entire life.'

He stopped and looked up into the rafters. It sounded like a pigeon scuffling. Something was moving about among the beams. Dust sifted down, glittering in the candlelight.

'Now I think you'd better tell me what you want. Before you're arrested, I mean. The detectives who interviewed us after the party, they seem to have put a tracker on my car. I bought this little device at the spy shop in Park Lane that tells you whether there are any abnormal electromagnetic pulses near you, quite useful. They should be here very shortly.'

'Why did you come?' sang the voice.

'Why? I would have thought it was obvious. I want to know why you would go to so much trouble as you have, but not try to hurt me.'

'I want you to admit your guilt.'

'For what?'

The sound above Kramer grew suddenly louder. Wood cracked. A fresh flurry of dust and cobwebs fell. Something heavy dropped down, a large dark shape that barely missed his head.

It slammed onto the plywood sheets at his feet.

He found himself looking at the body of a woman. For a moment his breath froze inside him, but he took a step closer and the brief spasm of fear melted. The dummy had cracked open, spilling a mixture of what appeared to be dried red beans and sawdust. The effect was unnerving, like an eviscerated corpse.

'Do you understand now?' asked the voice.

Kramer laughed. 'Is that what this is about? You drag me all the way out from bloody London to stage *this*? Christ, it's a good job you never tried for a career in the theatre – sorry, I forgot – you did, didn't you? I think I'm going to have to fire you now, though. I don't think our working relationship will be able to survive this.'

Kramer walked closer to the dummy and knelt to examine it. 'Ella will be very upset when she finds you've stolen one of her dummies. She would never have dressed it up in this tacky outfit. Do you want to tell me what your connection is with this creature? Or do I have to guess? Were you two having an affair?' He rose to his feet, angry now. 'Oh, for Christ's sake you can come down now and ditch the am-dram. I knew I should have hired a decent director. You should have stuck with telly, Russell, it's where you belong. You know your problem? You're the director but you just can't get the right reaction from your audience.'

The pitchfork seemed to have no one behind it. It came out of nowhere, thrown in anger, but found its mark. One of the tines pierced Kramer's throat, and the one below it entered his chest very close to his heart. The third tine only grazed his armpit, but the damage had been done.

Kramer gave a small gasp of surprise and fell forward onto the fork, punching it deeper into his throat. His expensive new handmade shoes had slipped away from him on the plywood floor.

He hovered there in a fulcrum, then toppled to the side. He was dead before the PCU officers managed to open the barn door.

42

ESCAPE

Jack Renfield had run the London Marathon four times, but he had been lighter in those days. He had seen the figure burst from the back of the barn and had taken off after him. But he didn't know the terrain and couldn't see where he was going. He knew he might break his ankle at any moment as they charged across the roughly ploughed, rock-strewn field. There were drops and ditches all around.

He fell once, then again, and wished there was someone other than Bryant and May with him. Looking up he could still see the figure hopping and flailing over the earth trenches, heading for the cover of tall trees. If he reached them there would be no chance of finding him.

Renfield lifted his aching legs higher and jumped over the deepening ridges. The figure he was pursuing looked like a scarecrow come to life, presumably because of the greatcoat that flapped about him. Perhaps it was a woman – a girl, even – the figure was light and had immense agility. The chase was played out in total silence, with only the rain and the wind talking in the trees. A large bird beat past him, knocking him back. Renfield was not easily stopped, and climbed up on his feet again, now caked in reeking mud.

But there, just ahead, was an insurmountable problem. A black, wide line crossed the field – a deep-sided brook too wide to jump. He knew he was likely to break a leg if he threw himself in and would not be able to get up the sheer earth bank of the other side. He watched helplessly as the hopping figure reached the treeline and vanished inside it.

'Don't stand any closer or I'll brain you,' said Dan Banbury. The CSM had been on his way home to Croydon when he received the call, and was quickly able to divert his route. Bryant had been about to walk on the plywood boards but thought better of it. Instead he was forced to lean forward from behind Banbury's tape line.

'Nice pitchfork shot,' remarked Bryant. 'Would he have survived if he'd fallen the other way?'

'Yes, probably. Bad luck. Slippy shoes. Expensive leather soles. He'd have lived if he'd been wearing trainers.'

'Any dabs on the handle?'

'Given the history of this case, what do you think?' Banbury gave him a withering look.

At the front of the barn, May was talking to medics from the Kent Ambulance Service. They were attempting to find a staffed regional local police constabulary, but so far had had no luck.

'The dummy's a bit of a giveaway,' said Bryant, opening a packet of Rolos. 'You'd better put a call out for Ella Maltby, John. And see what's happened to Renfield.'

'We're in a barn,' said Banbury. 'I'm not going to look for fibres and specks of dirt, the whole place is made up of them. There's half a foot of mud in here. I've got at least six sets of prints made by wellingtons.'

'Just do what you can.' Bryant unstuck caramel from his dental plate. 'We'd better find out who this place belongs to. A local copper would be useful. John, you having any luck?'

'We're still trying,' said May. 'Can I send the med team in yet?'

'Dan, can we take out the body?'

'Yeah, I've got all I need there.'

The detectives watched as Robert Kramer was unpinned from his position on the barn floor and removed. 'I don't understand,' said Bryant. 'We should have caught him before this happened. I honestly thought both victim and criminal were equally duplicitous, but now I can see I made one fundamental error.'

'What was that?'

'Anger takes many forms. Kramer wasn't forced to come here. It means he was arrogant enough to think he could deal with whomever he was meeting. I'd assumed we had got in the way of a victim and an attacker who were equally matched. They say cruelty is the English disease, don't they? But from here it looks as if they had very different temperaments. Kramer had the coldness that allowed him to retain perspective. His killer is someone whose frustration makes him prone to outbursts of violence. Now he's finished what he set out to achieve. It's over. We've lost him.'

'It has to be somebody who was at the party, so if he tries to vanish, we'll know who's gone.'

'Yes, but if he's smart he'll stay in plain sight and brazen it out, just as he has been doing, and then we'll never get to discover the truth. I honestly thought we could stop him before he acted again. Four deaths. It's a total disaster.'

'Jack chased someone across a field and got cut off by a stream.'

'A stream? Tell me you're joking. He couldn't cross a stream?'

'It's pitch black out there and raining hard, and there was quite a drop by the sound of it.'

'Did he at least get a good look at him? Where's the nearest light?'

'Sevenoaks. Nine miles away. No, he didn't. Couldn't even be sure it was male. Just somebody running in a big coat and boots.'

'Well, here's a how-de-do. Dan, have you got anything else?'

Banbury looked up from his position beside the dummy. 'You could say so.' He held up something in a pair of tweezers. 'He makes his own labels. Stitched into the top of the dummy's spine.'

'What does it say?'

'*An Ella Maltby Original.*'

'That does it. Let's get back to London. We can stick Maltby in one of the lock-ups in Islington and resume in the morning. Make sure she's not left alone.'

'You're sure this is over, Arthur?'

Bryant folded his sweet wrapper into his pocket, thinking. 'The target of all this torture is dead. The killer is, we hope, about to be apprehended. There's nothing more we can do except watch the Unit crash and burn after Kasavian gets wind of this. I guess we should all start looking for jobs again. Oh, and by the way, I'm having my home taken away from me tomorrow. All in all it's the end of a perfect week.'

43

ADMISSION

The Sunday morning sky was milky and soft, its light blurring the buildings and fading the edges of the streets. It was the kind of early summer's day London excelled in, burning off to a clear blue hemisphere by eleven, clouding again by three, finally clearing for a golden sunset.

At seven a.m. in the warehouse at 231 Caledonian Road, the Unit staff began sleepily arriving. Meera boiled spiced tea and Longbright made fresh coffee. Colin brought croissants and sausage rolls. Bryant stood on the tiny back balcony sucking at his pipe, his forehead creased in thought. Renfield was on the top floor hitting a punch-bag Bimsley had rigged up from the ceiling. And Ella Maltby was brought down from Islington police station for questioning.

'I have never seen such unprofessional behaviour in my life,' said Maltby's lawyer, Edgar Digby, an oleaginous young man with a mane of slicked black hair, a Turnbull & Asser shirt and an air of outraged entitlement. 'You take my client to a police station and leave her there for collection by your unit without any explanation of her rights or what's going on, and now you expect her to cooperate with you?'

'We had to act quickly in the interests of public safety,' May explained. 'Your client is the chief suspect in an investigation involving four deaths. Her explanation for her whereabouts during the times of these events is uncorroborated, and items belonging to her were found at the sites of three of the crimes. I think you'd better let her answer our questions, because any further silence from Ms Maltby is merely going to build the case against her.'

'My client's silence is no indication of her guilt. Under British law—'

'Drop it, Edgar,' said Ella Maltby. 'Let's hear what they have to say.'

'Robert Kramer was killed last night, and this was found beside his body.' May opened the plastic bag containing the dummy. 'Your label is sewn into the back of it.'

'This is our most popular model,' said Maltby. 'We sell them all over the world. Madame Tussauds have around thirty, which they use in background scenes. The New Strand Theatre has two. Let me see.' She took a look inside the bag. 'These are supplied naked. Our clients add the clothes.'

'Dan, get the skirt and jacket off and find out where they're from,' said May. 'In your statement you say – once again – that you were home all evening.'

'Yeah, I don't go out much. Is that a crime?'

'Did you talk to anyone?'

'No, I was working on some new designs. I don't email or use the phone when I'm working, it's too distracting.'

May knew he was on shaky ground. Ella Maltby's car had not been driven in days. Banbury had found no mud or dirty clothes at her house. There was nothing to indicate that she had left her home in twenty-four hours. 'Somebody is clearly anxious to place you at the crime scenes,' he pointed out. 'Do you have any idea who that might be?'

'Is this the part where you ask me if I have any enemies?' Maltby scoffed. 'No, I don't to my knowledge. People just dislike me in general. I'm not a sociable woman, but to my knowledge that's not a punishable offence either.'

'We're going to get nowhere here,' Longbright whispered in May's ear. 'Let her go. Jack can arrange for someone to keep an eye on her.'

'You're right,' May sighed. 'I'm stuck. How can this have happened? We have four bodies and no investigation. This is humiliating.'

After Ella Maltby's release had been secured, May went back to his office and sat on the edge of his partner's desk. 'I hate to say this, Arthur, but for once I really need one of your crackpot ideas. We're getting nowhere.'

Bryant looked at him steadily. 'How much are you prepared to trust me?' he asked.

'Right now, I'll go anywhere.'

'All right. What do we know about our killer? He's very angry, and very good at hiding his temper most of the time, but sometimes it erupts and becomes uncontrollable. He lost control with Noah, and again with Kramer himself. That means we might be able to goad him into an admission of guilt. Remember, everything hinges on what took place that first night at the party. What could have happened to make the killer calmly go upstairs and attack a child? And how the hell did he do it, assuming he did and a puppet didn't just come to life and shake a baby to death?'

'I don't know, but I imagine he saw the puppets and they gave him an idea.'

'I suppose so. Then he followed the idea through, thinking it was a way to rattle Kramer. And now that everything's behind him, he thinks he's got away with it.

But he can never stop being vigilant, because he knows we're after him and will stay on his case – at least, for as long as we and the investigation are still open. But it could happen again; he'll have the confidence to act on his anger, knowing that he managed to deceive everyone before. What we have to do now is lure him out into the open.'

'How do you propose to do that?'

'I thought at first we could attend Robert Kramer's funeral, because I assumed Judith Kramer was going to invite all his colleagues, but I hear she's not. It'll be a small, private family service, and she's specifically asked for none of us to be in attendance. We can override that, of course, but we'd have to keep a low-key presence.'

'I hear she's taking her husband's death surprisingly well.'

'That's not much of a shock, is it? He was having affairs and she was in love with someone else. In a way, his death has solved everything for her.'

'You don't suppose—?'

'She killed her own child? I don't know. Janice doesn't think so. We know Judith was at home in bed when Gregory Baine and Mona Williams died, and that her child's nanny was sitting with her, so unless she was working with an accomplice like Marcus Sigler . . .'

'This is all guesswork, Arthur. It won't get us anywhere. Without Kramer and his producer the show will shut and the players will all disperse. We have no powers to keep them close by.'

'I know. That's why with your help I can take action before it's too late.'

'What do you propose to do?'

'We're going to throw a little end-of-show party. *The play's the thing wherein I'll catch the conscience of the king*. Killers often lack social skills, but theatre folk are social animals. Therefore we have to put them in a social situation where they feel comfortable. If we handle it correctly, no one will dare to stay away for fear of drawing attention to themselves. If we can't force our murderer out into the open and goad him into admission, we'll have lost him for ever.'

May shook his head. 'Oh, I can't wait for Raymond to hear about this,' he said.

44

INTRUDER

On Monday morning, Janice Longbright took time off from the investigation to visit the Marquands' house in Bermondsey once more. She had not been able to concentrate on the Kramer case for days, knowing that someone was prepared to kill in order to keep Arthur's memoirs hidden.

Whoever was behind the plot knew the players well. They had followed Anna Marquand's routine, and knew enough about Bryant to understand that even he would not be able to remember what was in his notes. All he possessed was a book of proofs with the most contentious details missing. Everything hinged on finding the disc that contained the missing sections of the manuscript. Rose Marquand's helper had not been able to finish searching the house – now it was up to Longbright.

She arrived to find Mrs Marquand in a state of extreme nervousness. 'I just called,' she told Longbright, 'but the police said they were too busy to deal with it right now.'

'What happened?' asked Longbright, coming in, but she

could already see. The kitchen window had been smashed and opened.

'I can't move about quickly. I heard the glass break and tried to get back here. It was that Hagan boy. I scared him off.'

'How do you know it was one of the Hagans?' Longbright asked.

'Who else could it be?'

'When was this? Did you see where he went?'

'It was about ten minutes ago – that's what I'm trying to tell you. I don't know where he went. He didn't go off down the garden. I think he might still be in the house. I've been too frightened to move from here.'

Janice searched the ground floor, then went to the foot of the stairs and listened. There was no sound from upstairs. The house was less than a decade old and nothing creaked. She peered up and watched the light in the hall above, searching for shifting shadows. She rarely felt nervous when she understood the kind of person she was dealing with, but the anonymity of the intruders invading Rose Marquand's house made her uneasy.

'I don't think there's anyone here now.' She looked through the rear hall window and saw the magpies hopping into the garden. Rose had been complaining about them. Suddenly Longbright realized what she was looking at: Mrs Marquand had strung CDs on her clothes-line. It was a tried and tested deterrent. The glittering discs were meant to scare off the birds.

Instead of venturing upstairs she went to the back door and out into the garden. She recognized the spidery hand-writing at once. Bryant's disc was there, strung on the line along with Shirley Bassey and Neil Diamond. As she was trying to free the clothesline she looked up and saw the face in the window, watching her. A man whose outline was familiar, late twenties, heavy, well over six feet tall, cropped hair and scrub beard, hard army build. She knew in an instant that the tables were about to turn.

Unable to free the line from the tangle of knots Mrs Marquand had made, she pulled out her penknife and sawed through the nylon, catching the CD in her hand as the back door opened and he came running for her.

She saw his boots leave the grass and the distance he covered was astonishing. He barrelled into her with such force that she was knocked off her feet. Before she could begin to rise, she sensed she was in serious trouble. His grip felt mechanical, his bulk unbelievably solid. He closed his hands around her wrists and forced her back. She brought her knee up between his legs but he closed his thighs, blocking her.

Then he punched her in the side of the head.

The disc jumped out of her hand and rolled across the wet grass. She felt herself blacking out. Without even climbing from her he was able to reach back and seize the disc. As he concentrated on slipping it into his zipped pocket, she brought up her elbow and smashed his nose.

Turning his attention back to her, he punched her hard in the solar plexus. Longbright vomited into the lawn, the pain burning across her ribcage. He was astride her now, studying her. Wiping his bloody nose, he raised a fist over her face and brought it down.

She shut her eyes hard, readying herself for the blow, knowing he would shatter bone.

But nothing happened.

There was a dull thud, and she felt his weight suddenly ease from her. When she opened her eyes, she saw Mrs Marquand standing beside them with a brightly painted concrete gnome in her hands. There was blood dripping from its pink hat.

Longbright's attacker was out cold. Blood oozed thickly from a cut on the back of his head. She shoved him aside with difficulty and dug her hand into his padded black nylon jacket.

'That's not one of the Hagans.' Mrs Marquand set down the gnome. 'I don't know who he is.'

Longbright found the CD, but nothing more. He was carrying no wallet, no personal belongings of any kind. She tried his outer pockets and his trousers, her fingers closing around a slender slip of paper in his back pocket. As she rose with it, the garden swam before her. The side of her head was already starting to swell and there was a searing pain in her stomach. Mrs Marquand held out her arm and helped Longbright inside. Longbright knew she had to make a call to ensure that the intruder was taken into custody, but she needed to sit down for a moment – just thirty seconds, to get her wind back.

Helped to the lounge sofa, she fell into soft cushions and closed her eyes. She awoke nearly ten minutes later. Mrs Marquand had locked the back door and was standing by it.

'What's the matter?' asked Longbright, puzzled.

'He just got up,' she whispered, peering out. 'I thought I'd killed him.'

Longbright looked through the lounge window and saw the empty patch of grass where her attacker had lain. The garden gate hung open. She unlocked the door and ran outside, but the alley beyond the garden was already empty.

Remembering the slip of paper she had taken from him, she pulled it from her jeans and read it. Her heart sank.

Most modern offices in Whitehall operated on electronic swipe cards which had to be returned after you had visited the building, but a few of the older departments still used visitor slips. You signed yourself in, adding the time, date and the name of the person you were visiting, and were meant to return the slip as you left, but most people forgot to do so.

The white slip had a government crest on it. Underneath was a name: Mr T. Maddox, timed in at 7.45 p.m. a week ago, at the Department of Internal Security, Home Office, 50 Queen Anne's Gate, London SW1.

Next to the box that read 'Person Visiting', the receptionist had written *Oskar Kasavian*.

45

GENESIS

'You cannot throw a cocktail party for a bunch of murder suspects and charge it to the Unit!' Raymond Land shouted, outraged. 'In all my time serving at this lunatic asylum, this is the stupidest idea I've come across, even worse than that suspect line-up you held on the Somerset House ice-skating rink.'

'I was thinking we'd serve Bloody Marys,' said Bryant, not listening. 'And little sausages on sticks. Mini-burgers are always popular.'

'Could we have some decent Indian snacks?' asked Meera.

'And chicken wings with barbecue sauce,' Bimsley added.

Land shut his eyes and held up his hands for silence. 'For the last time. We are not. Having. A. Party!'

'There's a little more to it than that,' said May. 'We're going to tell the invited guests we've made an arrest. They'll think the pressure is off and they'll drop their guard.'

'Who are you going to palm off as the arrestee?'

'An outsider. An unfamiliar name. We're going to make

316

the killer think we've been misled. Arthur has the whole thing planned.'

'I know it sounds completely crazy, but just listen to him,' Banbury suggested.

'Nobody's going to know we're behind this,' said Bryant. 'If you agree, Ray Pryce will help us rig the whole thing up, script the event with exits and entrances. Nobody would dare stay away. The show closes without Robert's company funding it and it's the last time they'll all be together. After this, they'll be going their separate ways. It's traditional to end a run with a farewell party. The timing's perfect.'

'How are you going to arrange it?'

'Tomorrow night there was going to be a charity performance of the play to raise money for the Variety Club of Great Britain. The idea is to now go ahead with the performance. The crime scene has been cleared, so the obligation can be honoured. There'll be a dedication to Robert Kramer at the end; it's an old theatre tradition. Marcus Sigler will say a few words, and so will Judith Kramer. Ray will send a text to everyone hinting that there's going to be some kind of revelation during the course of the after-show party. We'll reveal that we've arrested someone as a potential suspect. John and I will have some carefully worded questions prepared, and we'll be watching everyone. And we want the facts of the investigation to be subject to full disclosure – no withheld information.'

'You absolutely can't do that.' Land was outraged. 'It's unethical and contravenes just about every rule in the book. Besides, what if still nothing happens?'

'Then we'll be no worse off than we are now.'

'We'll just be messing with a few people's heads,' said Meera. 'It's worth a try, isn't it?' With a shock, Bryant realized that, for the very first time, the entire team was behind him.

'All right,' said Land finally. It was worth giving in just to stop them all staring at him. 'But we'd better have someone stationed there in case this goes wrong.'

'I'll put Fraternity DuCaine on standby,' said Longbright.

An hour later, Ray Pryce came by to sort out the invitation wording with May. 'How's this?' he asked. 'I'll personalize all the texts. I'll tell them that you and your partner wanted to thank the company and pay your last respects to Robert. I'll mention that you're going to be on hand to explain that you're now ready to press charges.'

'And you think everyone will accept?' asked May.

'How can they not? They all have to be here tomorrow in order to complete their contracts. We've even had an email from Gail Strong asking if she could come back for the final show. A bloody cheek, after walking out like that.'

'What time does everyone finish work?'

'The play ends at nine forty-five, so I guess the last one will be out of the theatre by ten-thirty.'

'Then we start the party at eleven. My partner has come up with the perfect venue.'

'I hope you know what you're doing,' said Ray. 'I could take notes about this to use in my next play, except that nobody would believe me.'

'I know what you mean,' said May, indicating his partner. 'Welcome to my world.'

The weather worsened steadily through the day. Longbright had applied anti-inflammatory cream to her blue-black bruise, but the side of her face was still painful. She listened to the sound of tapping buckets as she sat in her office and ran through the contents of Bryant's disc.

She had decided not to worry her boss with the news that she had managed to retrieve his disc. He was locked in his room with May, planning something. She settled down and prepared to search through four hundred pages of small-point type. After five hours without a break, she was still unable to find any disclosure so contentious that someone would be prepared to kill to hide it. The answer had to lie in some footnote or sidebar to the main investigations under discussion, something seemingly innocuous. She tried to think of a way of isolating the information. What would the Ministry of Internal Security find so damning in the Unit's old cases?

Using a technique she had learned from Bryant, she decided to tackle the problem from an entirely different perspective. Oskar Kasavian had been transferred to the department from the Ministry of Defence a couple of years ago. She ran a search on Kasavian's background but was shut out of the MoD's files, so she called up his CV through a public access request. It meant that her enquiry would be logged at HOIS, but that couldn't be helped.

The CV contained no detailed information, just a list of dates and employment statistics. She was about to shut it down when one date jumped out – a period spent at Porton Down, the military science park in Wiltshire. Porton Down was home to the MoD's Science and Technology Laboratory, DSTL. It was an executive agency that had been set up by the Ministry of Defence itself. It was common knowledge that the site housed Britain's most secretive military research institute, but access was denied to journalists without written permission from a variety of senior officials.

She scanned back through the pages of Bryant's memoir and found what she was looking for: the suicides of eleven Asian workers, all based at a company outsourced by the DSTL. The case had made news headlines at the time, until all details of it had suddenly been pulled. Their dates fell within the period that Kasavian was employed there.

She scanned through the disc and found what Bryant had written. He mentioned the case in reference to an entirely separate matter – a mentally ill man who had killed a number of women in London pubs. That investigation had been solved and closed, so why had he mentioned Porton Down at all?

Then she saw it, a small reference number directing her to an addendum at the end of the chapter. She went in to see Bryant.

'You shouldn't have come in today,' Bryant said. 'Your poor face.'

'I'm fine. It looks worse than it is. Arthur, what is Project Genesis?'

Bryant's aqueous blue eyes sought focus as he remembered. 'It was a bioscience initiative. I always felt it was linked with the deaths of some technicians.'

'The drownings – you think the MoD had something to do with them?'

'Let me put it this way: the deaths could have been avoided. I think they were probably suicides, but they were caused by the stress of the situation. You have to remember that an awful lot of people worked there under conditions of absolute security.'

'But why would they all pick the same method of death?'

'I talked about that with our old pathologist, Oswald Finch, at the time. He reckoned many scientists see drowning as a painless, clean method of taking one's life. The whole thing came to our attention because of a man named Peter Jukes. He was project leader for chemical and biological security at the MoD's Wiltshire laboratory. He was found dead in suspicious circumstances. I requested his notes from the Home Office, but the Defence Secretary refused to acknowledge that there was a case. Supposedly Jukes had been suffering from depression and had long been recognized as a security risk. It was said he drowned, but there were anomalies in the case. At the time, military contractors were desperately trying to spend out the year-ends of their budgets before the axe fell on their departments. Project Genesis was closed down.'

'What were they trying to do?'

'I can't remember the details – what we heard was mostly rumour – but it was something involving gene splicing. The management had been exaggerating their progress to the MoD, and it turned out their technology wasn't quite as advanced as they'd led everyone to believe it was. So the unit was shut and the staff dispersed.'

'Then I have some bad news for you,' said Longbright. 'I think someone's opened it back up again. You mentioned the Porton Down case in your notes.'

'You think that's what they were after?'

'You flagged it yourself. You showed your hand by contacting the MoD. That's why Oskar Kasavian has been trying so hard to close us down all this time. He's desperate to discredit you. He's been monitoring us. And then he discovers that an outsider – a well-connected writer and editor to boot – has the information. The situation was containable so long as it remained inside the Unit, but suddenly he discovered a leak. She probably ran fact-checking enquiries from her computer. I'm willing to bet that Mrs Marquand's so-called carer copied Anna's entire hard drive and then wiped it.'

'You think Kasavian acted on his own initiative to kill the story?'

'It looks that way. He mustn't know that we know. We need the advantage over him.'

Bryant ran a wrinkled hand through his side tufts. 'OK, let's get through the party. I'm not a woman.'

'Sorry?'

'Can't do two things at once.'

She left him studying the spreadsheet Banbury had created from the activity at the Kramers' party. As she walked away, a chill ran across her back. *Things are coming to a head*, she thought. *There's danger here for all of us. Nobody is safe now.*

46

PARTY!

'The London Dungeon. This is your grand idea, is it?' said Land, looking up at the swinging sign that dripped with painted blood. The rain was pounding down on the deserted pavements, as hard and heavy as the spray from a thousand showerheads. Bryant had ducked under the cover of the doorway. He peered round the corner like an exhibit planning an escape.

'I thought it would appeal to their sensibilities,' he replied. 'Plenty of Ella Maltby's gruesome tableaux inside.'

'And hardly any light. What if you do catch one of them out and he makes a break for it? How are you going to find them?'

'There are only two exits. We'll have Meera and Colin, and Jack and Fraternity positioned in front of them. We're putting them in guards' uniforms. Nobody will even notice them.'

'This is the most deranged thing I have ever let you do,' said Land wearily. He checked his watch. 'They'll be here in a few minutes. Well, I suppose we're committed now. Show me how this is going to work.'

Bryant led the way inside, past a skeleton in an iron gibbet. 'They're geared up for parties,' he explained, pointing to a table laden with wine and glasses.

'Wait a minute, who's paying for all this?'

'I got it out of petty cash. Listen, Raymond, I wouldn't be doing this if I thought there was any other way. I think the killer has finished his work but won't be able to resist turning up for one last gloat. Robert Kramer was made to suffer and now he's finally dead. I should have been able to save him. I should have acted on my instincts but I held back.'

'For once I really wish you'd done something crazy earlier,' Land admitted.

'This is our last chance. You've seen this sort of thing before, people who turn up to watch the ambulance services removing the bodies of the victims they've killed, murderers who stand by as the houses they've set alight burn down. Our killer shared his victim's sense of the macabre – that's why he continued to use the puppets. Tonight we will get to the truth, or the Unit will go down trying.'

A few minutes later, just as Bryant had predicted, the guests began turning up. The show's female lead, Della Fortess, was still in her closing scene costume, a black diamanté basque hidden by a long red overcoat.

Neil Crofting, the veteran actor who had been Mona Williams's best friend, looked years younger in jeans and a sweatshirt.

By contrast, Marcus Sigler, the male lead of *The Two Murderers*, looked sickly and unwell.

Unsurprisingly, Judith Kramer was putting in an appearance under sufferance.

Ray Pryce was already inside, helping May to learn his lines.

The director, Russell Haddon, turned up with an

extremely young woman on his arm who was protruding from her minuscule dress, and appeared to be under the mistaken impression that she was attending some kind of premiere.

Ella Maltby, the set designer and props wizard, strolled in as if she were coming home, and in a sense she was.

The wardrobe master, Larry Hayes, arrived with his suspiciously pretty male assistant.

The corpulent *Hard News* critic, Alex Lansdale, came with his publisher, Janet Ramsey.

Lastly, Mohammad al-Nahyan (carpenter) and Jolie Christchurch (front of house) arrived together.

Just before the doors were shut, Gail Strong made her entrance alone. She looked lost and far less confident than she had a week earlier at Robert Kramer's party.

'Who are all these extra people?' Land asked. 'I thought you'd only invited the suspects.'

'I invited everyone from the office to make up numbers and be on hand if there was trouble,' said Bryant. 'Plus, they heard there was a party.'

'Obviously we had to invite everyone who was there on the night Noah Kramer was killed,' said Ray. 'It would have looked really odd just to have half a dozen people sitting under statues of torturers drinking cheap white wine.'

'I'm sorry,' Bryant apologized. 'The Unit budget wouldn't run to good plonk.'

'Well, now what happens?' Land demanded.

'We crank up the music and let them get a few glasses down. Then John makes his announcement.'

At first, the guests stood uncomfortably beneath the exhibits, keeping to their usual groups while John May and Ray Pryce circulated between them. Bryant sat at the back of the room watching carefully. Russell Haddon's girlfriend was called Naida, and seemed to be drunk already. Gail Strong and Marcus Sigler were most notice-ably different. They stayed clear of each other, and seemed to be eyeing everyone else with suspicion.

May checked his watch and turned to Bryant. 'OK, let's get this started.'

Ray Pryce stepped up onto the low dais that stood at the rear of the room and called for everyone's attention.

'Ladies and gentlemen, I know it seems odd to be having a party without Robert here to play host, but, in spite of the week's extraordinary events, we couldn't let the pro-duction close without marking the occasion in some way. The Unit detectives investigating these dreadful deaths were anxious to meet with you so that they could make themselves accountable and answer as many of your questions as possible. I'm sure you're anxious to know what happened to Robert, and where the police now stand with regard to ending the investigation. They'll be at your disposal during the course of the evening, and they hope that by doing this we can achieve some sense of closure and be able to move on with our lives. I've been asked to explain that anything said in this room tonight will operate under Chatham House Rules – in other words, all information goes no further than here.'

'That goes particularly for you, Janet,' said Bryant, noticing the editor of *Hard News*, who looked furious.

'In order to encourage a spirit of openness and to make sure that no one is tempted to mention what passed here this evening, we'll be keeping the main doors locked until midnight. After that, you are all free to go.'

Everyone started talking at once. If nothing else, it seemed like an outrageous and somewhat morbid offer from the police.

Bryant and May stepped out into the crowd and waited as the first tentative guests came forward. Within moments, everyone was asking them questions. Was it true that Robert Kramer had been staked through the heart? And that Mona Williams had been treated as if she were a witch? Was witchcraft involved? Had necromantic rituals been performed at the theatre? Had the show been cursed? What about their producer, had he taken his own life or had someone made his death look like suicide? And what were Ella Maltby's dolls doing at the scenes of the crimes?

After the first barrage of questions, Bryant noticed a fresh element creeping into the conversation – veiled accusations. Someone had heard that Maltby was a little too fond of her dolls. Someone said the killer was probably the playwright, because he had a creepy turn of mind. Someone had spotted Russell Haddon having a huge argument with Mona Williams about her overacting the day before she was found dead. Someone suggested that Judith Kramer was more cunning than she appeared to be.

'This is going to get ugly very quickly,' Longbright warned. 'How are we going to stop them fighting?'

'Between you and me, I think that's what Arthur wants to encourage,' said May.

'How's it going?' asked Ray, coming over. May had noticed that the actors were shunning the writer now that it was clear he was helping the police. 'They all seem to have a lot to get off their chests.'

'They'll have more when they see this.' May unfolded a large spreadsheet Longbright had printed out. 'It's the cross-referenced time line of everyone's movements at the party. We're going to show it to them. Give me a hand.' He shook out some drawing pins and together they hung it along the nearest wall.

'How does this work?' asked Ray, pulling out his glasses and perusing the colour-coded graphs.

'What happened to your spectacles?' May pointed to the tape holding one of the arms in place.

'Oh, I had to repair these. Mona sat on them at the

Kramers' party. I'm having another pair made. She was always doing things like that.'

'Was she now?' said Bryant. He turned to the spreadsheet. 'Well, there you are, you're the red stripe here, two trips from the main lounge in the course of the evening, one for a smoke and one for the bathroom, both witnessed, and by two different people, Mona Williams and Marcus Sigler, which clears you. But take someone else – Neil Crofting, say, two trips from the room also, only one witnessed, by Ella Maltby – or Russell Haddon, two trips, neither remembered by anyone at all.'

'Does that make Russell more of a suspect?'

'Only in terms of opportunity. He has no motive I can think of. And that's the trouble. Nobody here really has a proper motive for killing the child except Robert Kramer, and in his case we would have to assume he would only have done it if he'd known then that the baby belonged to his wife's lover.'

Gradually, the crowd shifted over to examine the huge spreadsheet, their sense of curiosity mingled with outright suspicion.

'What do we do now?' asked May in desperation.

'I don't know about you, but I'm going out for a pipe,' said Bryant cheerfully.

'I thought you weren't letting anyone out.'

'I'm not. There's a small bricked-in area at the back of the building. It opens into a courtyard with sheer walls. Nobody's leaving that way.

'Ladies and gentlemen,' he announced, 'if the smokers amongst you would care to follow me, we can grab a quick drag and a gasp on the patio.'

The release of tension in the room was palpable as the crowd split in two, one half heading for the patio.

'Bloody hell, I need a drink,' groaned Renfield, wiping his forehead.

'Not until after midnight,' said May. 'You're on duty.'

'Do you honestly think anything's going to come of this? Let me tell you, I'm putting in for a transfer after this shambles is over. At least the Met officers were professionals. You lot are like a bunch of bloody children. Men and women are dying out there on the London streets and we're all in here playing some elaborate version of Cluedo, looking for Colonel Mustard in the sodding library with the lead pipe. I've had it. Actually, why wait? I wish to tender my resignation, right now.'

'I don't think you want to do that, old stick,' said Bryant, wandering past with his unlit pipe in his mouth.

'You can't stop me,' Renfield warned.

'Maybe not,' Bryant agreed, 'but I'd give it a few minutes yet, just to watch the fireworks.'

'What fireworks?'

'The metaphorical ones that will go off when I do my Hercule Poirot impersonation and announce who the murderer really is.'

'Wait a minute.' May stopped him. 'You mean you know who it is?'

'I have a most definite suspicion. Have had for quite a while. But now I need proof.'

Raymond Land grabbed Bryant's arm as he led the smoking pack through the room. 'On the dot of midnight the street doors of this place will be opened and it will be over,' he hissed. 'That's it, investigation suspended, all files get packed up and shipped off to Islington CID.'

'There's still another twenty minutes to go,' said Bryant, flicking the brim of his trilby. 'Care to join me for a pipe?'

47

ELEVENTH HOUR

Bryant stood in the centre of the patio, watching everyone with a raven eye. He was smiling cheerfully, as rumpled as a mariner's map, the battered ringmaster of a duplicitous circus revolving around him in a sinister carousel, and he missed nothing. He strained to hear all of the conversations at once, watched every gesture, every nuance, every flicker of the eye. When anyone glanced at him he returned their gaze and held it questioningly. When anyone brushed his sleeve he flinched theatrically and stared back. He spoke but was processing information. He was determined to keep all his senses aware.

Questions crowded his brain: why dress the dummy in the barn in women's clothes? Was it meant to represent Judith Kramer? Why had Mona Williams been threatened? And how the hell did Noah Kramer fall from the window? Bryant had all the answers, but none of the proof. He needed the admission of guilt – one tiny movement that would lock the wheels of justice into place.

We saw what we thought happened, not what happened. We saw what someone else wanted us to see.

Bryant made a silent bet with himself. *If you can't solve this by midnight, you have to retire, it's not fair on the others. Let somebody fitter, fresher and younger take the reins.*

He checked his watch. Just twelve minutes left to go.

'By Godfrey, he's cutting it fine,' grumbled Land. 'Isn't there anything you can do?'

'I've done everything within my power,' said May. 'I don't understand it. I keep asking myself the same questions over and over. The whole thing should have been wrapped up within minutes of Noah Kramer being found dead. The guilty party must have been on site, watching us and calmly carrying on as normal, as if it was just an acting exercise, a mannerism copied from TV footage of a serial killer. Do you know what I thought? When I heard that Marcus Sigler was the boy's father, I became convinced that Robert Kramer had killed his own son. But then what? The killer knows that the elements of the case don't make sense, which is why he's safe.'

'It is galling,' Land agreed. 'Someone has been telling us lies and there's nothing we could do to stop them.'

'Unfortunately the electronic equipment hasn't been invented that can properly prove a falsehood. The fundamental flaw in policing is its reliance on public information. If that information is corrupt, so is the entire case. It looks as if the criminals have finally learned to outrun us.'

'Well, we had a good innings. I must say, I'm very disappointed by your partner. He spent part of the day asking actors about their stage performances. What good could that do? Honestly, if Arthur had come up with something utterly outrageous right at the last second, I'd have forgiven him so long as it put this lunatic behind bars.'

'Oh, it's no lunatic, that's the problem,' May told him.

'He set out to destroy Kramer and did so. And now he's walking away, happy in the knowledge that there's nothing any of us can do to stop him.'

'Did you know, Gail Strong was sent away on Home Office instructions?' said Land. 'Her father got her off the hook. What a scumbag.'

'There are so many different levels of guilt. Arthur was right, this entire city is complicit. Nobody is innocent.'

Janice Longbright glanced at the watch Bryant had bought her for her thirtieth birthday. The date dial ran backwards for some reason, but the time was accurate. Seven minutes to midnight. Her nerve endings were buzzing. *If we have to close the Unit for good*, she thought, *at least I'll be able to place an accurate time on the moment when the decision was made.*

When she couldn't take it any longer, she headed for the bar and ordered herself a large gin and tonic.

'You're not supposed to drink before midnight,' said Renfield, leaning next to her.

'Jack, I'm watching my career collapse here, and so are you.' Ignoring his protestations, she ordered him a beer. She raised her glass to his. 'This should be a relief, but I just feel terrible. I can't believe we failed. In the past we always managed to come up with something at the last minute.'

'Hey.' He stooped and lightly kissed her bruised cheek. 'I've been wanting to do that for ages. Slap my face if you want, I don't care. We won't be working together any more after this. I just tendered my resignation.'

'Hey, did you just see that?' said Colin Bimsley. 'Renfield just got a snog in with Janice. What's going on?'

'It's four minutes to midnight,' said Meera. 'We're under orders to open the doors at twelve. The old man's given up and gone outside with his pipe. And you were convinced he was going to crack it. I should have put money on this.'

'Don't gloat, Meera, it's really bloody ugly, OK?' He turned away from her, genuinely upset.

'I'm sorry, but I saw this coming. We should never have been given the case. It was a family problem, the husband and wife could no longer stomach the sight of each other, both having affairs, other people meddling, the husband kills the baby in a rage, kills the producer for nicking his funds, muzzles the old bag to shut her up—'

'Then stabs himself to death with a pitchfork, thrown from the other end of a barn. In front of a life-sized dummy of his wife.'

'No, I saw the dummy – it didn't look like his wife.'

'Then who did it look like?'

'His first wife.' Meera shrugged. 'I found some photos of her online – very frumpy. Same Marks and Spencer skirt.'

'Did you tell the old man this?'

'No, of course not.'

'I think you should. He specifically asked us if we'd come across anything odd.'

'Well, it's too late now. Almost midnight.'

'There's still – three minutes left.'

'Right. Tell you what, if the old man pulls something out of the hat now—'

'You'll what? You'll go out on a date with me?'

'No, stupid. Just—'

'No, come on, Meera, put your money where your mouth is, he's got the time it takes to smoke a cigarette left. If he still manages to nail someone before midnight, you'll go on a date with me.'

'All right,' agreed Meera, safe in the knowledge that she had already won, 'you're on.'

* * *

Bryant pulled on his pipe and watched the embers turn crimson. 'That stuff will kill you,' said Ella Maltby, joining him in the courtyard.

'Doesn't matter, I'm ninety-five per cent dead anyway,' Bryant replied. 'Our brains start atrophying when we turn eighteen. Can I ask you something?'

'Fire away.'

'How did the dummy get to the barn? I mean, it's a bulky object, not heavy but awkward. Did you take it there?'

Maltby held his eyes for a long moment. 'I guess we must have done. At least, our delivery firm would have. It was bulky because it was one of our pregnant models.'

'Pregnant?'

'That's right. The order came through from the theatre.'

'Whose name was on it?'

'The producer's. Gregory Baine had to sign off on everything we bought. It's the producer's job to balance the budget.'

'The clothes as well?'

'Everything.'

'Interesting. You don't suppose the dummy killed him, do you? Like Mr Punch killed the baby?'

'Now you're making fun of me,' said Maltby. 'I'm a craftsperson, not a witch.'

'Fair enough,' Bryant replied. 'You can't blame me for asking.'

'Sorry, can I borrow a light?' Ray Pryce stepped between them. Bryant lit his cigarette for him. 'I guess the evening didn't go as planned. It's midnight.'

'Yes, I'm a bit disappointed about that,' said Bryant.

'Just a bit?' Ray held the cigarette between them, its smoke wafting across their faces. 'I should think you're devastated. What a terrible way to end a career.'

'Nobody said it was the end of my career.'

'Your boss has been telling everyone that the Unit is finished. He seems quite pleased about it.'

'He always is.' Bryant looked down at Ray's cigarette. 'What brand is that?'

'Oh, my brother gets them abroad. They're pretty strong. Want one?'

'No, no.' Bryant checked his watch. There were only a few seconds left before the doors had to be thrown open.

'Tell me,' he said. 'I suppose you watch actors all the time, don't you?'

'I have to. They're the ones who translate my words into actions.'

'But that's not strictly true, is it, because you're new to the business. Which would explain it.'

Ray looked puzzled. 'Explain what?'

'The way you hold your cigarette.'

'I'm not sure I understand what you mean.'

There came a cheer from inside; the dungeon doors were being opened.

'Well, I guess that's that,' said Ray. 'We're free to go.'

'I'm afraid not.' Bryant sucked on his pipe until the bowl glowed demonically. 'I'm arresting you.'

'I think not, Mr Bryant. You're a dog who has had its day.'

Ray turned to go, then looked down. He found himself attached to the courtyard's waste pipe by a pair of handcuffs.

48

STRUNG UP

When Colin Bimsley was seven years old his father bought him a black and white cat which he called Bargepole because it kept knocking things over. One day, Bargepole decided to get closer to the blackbirds that lived in the elm tree at the end of the garden and got stuck in its boughs.

Colin's father suffered from a rare syndrome that affected his spatial awareness. It created an imbalance in the inner ear and was a hereditary condition but, luckily, young Colin had shown no sign of developing the same problem. Until he decided to climb the elm tree.

For once he reached the cool, breeze-swept branches at the top where Bargepole had become lodged, his sense of distance and equilibrium deserted him. The ground telescoped away into the distance and Colin was left as stranded as the cat.

Every time he reached out to Bargepole, trying to lure him nearer, the cat growled in fear and backed further away. What the boy had failed to notice was that he was now in the more precarious position, extended on a sapling branch that could not hold his weight for long. As he felt it break, he glanced back at the ground and saw it rushing towards him like the bottom of a roller-coaster loop. The fence to the railway broke his fall, and his right leg.

The memory of falling never left him. His old nemesis reappeared whenever his diminished spatial awareness struck, and it did now, with a vengeance.

Colin was halfway up a flight of service stairs leading from the brick arches of Tooley Street to the railway line above when sweat broke out across his back and forehead. Ahead of him was Ray Pryce, running with a section of rusted iron downpipe manacled to his wrist. It shouldn't have happened – but nothing in the case should have happened the way it did, and now they were dealing with the consequences.

Colin fell back against the wall, watching in horror as the stairs rotated beneath his feet. He could not move. From the corner of his eye he saw Jack Renfield and Fraternity DuCaine ascending towards him. All he could do was point upwards.

Renfield and DuCaine powered up and out into the rainswept corridor that ran beside the train lines. The southern routes of London Bridge station fanned out in a vast grey swathe. The bright windows of carriages flickered past, heading for Kent and the coast. Pryce was running hard, but DuCaine's powerful long legs quickly closed the gap. Renfield could see an escape route; at the end of the alley there was an open section of the fence that led to a buttress of the railway arch. Ray Pryce would be able to get out, but it was a long way to the street below.

Fraternity had almost caught up with him when Ray slipped through and out onto the brick promontory. 'Leave him,' Renfield called, 'he can't go anywhere.'

Fraternity answered by jabbing his finger down: *Look*.

Renfield peered over the side and saw a decorative pillar ten feet below. If Pryce jumped to it, he could jump once more to the pavement and run back into the tunnels beneath the lines. There was a good chance that he would be able to evade capture. 'No,' he shouted, 'you can't let him jump!'

But it was too late, and Fraternity was still too far away. Ray saw the pillar and made his move. He was light and managed the fall easily. Now he just had to jump again, and then he would be home free. Renfield fatally hesitated, knowing he should head back down the stairs, but was too far behind. Fraternity was there one second, gone the next. He had jumped, too. Renfield watched as Ray made the second leap.

And right at that moment, something entirely un-expected happened. He stopped in midair, hovering above the street with his arms over his head. It seemed insane, impossible, but there he was, suspended over the road.

Bryant, you've got the luck of the bloody devil, Renfield thought, unable to stop himself from grinning.

Ray Pryce had jumped between a pair of all-but-invisible metal guy ropes that ran between the arches. They had been used to suspend signs for the London Dungeon's last exhibition. Pryce had passed between them but the length of pipe had not. Trapped by his left wrist, desperately trying to ease his weight by holding onto the other guyline with his right hand, he swung helplessly back and forth, unable to move.

A few moments later, he was surrounded by various surprised members of the PCU.

'You're too late,' Ray shouted down at them. 'It's over. I did what I set out to do. You know I did. Whatever happens now, remember this. I won.'

49

TEMPLE MAGIC

'Why on earth did he run?' Longbright wondered. 'Why didn't he simply shrug off your accusation? He's a master liar. He makes stuff up for a living.'

'The handcuffs,' said May simply. 'I've seen Arthur use that trick before. He only does it when he's desperate. To some people it's something tangible, like holding a gun. Maybe a part of him wanted the final chapter in place. It could only truly be over with his arrest.'

'A poetic idea,' said Bryant, 'but he still saw an escape route and took it. He realized that the pipe was rusted through, stuck his foot against the wall and pulled hard, then ran.' He sauntered to the centre of the room and looked about. 'Well, go on then, I know you're all dying to ask.' He loved an audience, especially when he knew things they didn't.

'Talk about leaving it to the last minute – no, the last *second*,' said Banbury.

'I just couldn't be sure,' Bryant admitted. 'Would anyone begrudge me a pipe on this occasion?'

He didn't bother to wait for a reply. Wind and rain

buffeted the windows of the common room. The storm was so violent that they could hear the roof creaking. It was nearly two in the morning but nobody wanted to go home. Instead, Dan Banbury, Colin Bimsley, Meera Mangeshkar, Fraternity DuCaine, Janice Longbright, John May, Raymond Land and Giles Kershaw were gathered together on the threadbare sofas with a few beers, waiting to piece together the thinking that had resulted in Ray Pryce occupying an Islington police cell.

'Go on then, stop milking the suspense, what caught him?' asked Meera.

'The annoying thing was that I suppose I knew from Wednesday morning – subconsciously, I mean. I told you your time lines weren't going to help, but they did. The answer was right there in front of me all the time, pinned to the wall. Marcus Sigler, Ray Pryce and Gail Strong were the three on the fire escape. But Sigler's and Strong's times didn't match. Strong reckoned she was there a few minutes after Sigler – she said she saw him coming in, but according to the guests in the lounge she and Sigler left the room at the same time. If Sigler wasn't in or outside the toilet, he was on the fire escape smoking, so how could he and Gail Strong not have seen each other?'

'We know that one of them was lying, we already established that,' said May.

'Yes, but I wanted to know why. And the answer lay in Janice's suspicions, which led me back to the testimony of the actress Mona Williams, who said that despite the fact that Marcus Sigler was conducting a passionate long-term affair with Mrs Kramer, Gail Strong had been giving him the come-on that night, right from the moment she set eyes on him, and they left the room together. They made out on the fire escape and lied to protect themselves. Sigler and Strong came back in, and Sigler saw Ray Pryce passing them in the corridor, so he asked the writer to back up his new story. What he didn't know was that Pryce had just committed murder.'

'What gave him away?'

'Arrogance,' answered Bryant, sucking hard on his pipe and filling the room with the scent of burning hay. 'He had to rub my nose in his success. He should have simply kept out of my way.'

'I don't understand. What did he do?'

'He asked to borrow a light, and then smoked in front of me.'

'Is that all?' Land was horrified. 'Please tell me you have something that will stand up in court.'

'Don't worry about that, old sausage. The cigarette was just the final tip-off. Everyone knows Ray Pryce is a smoker. He's talked incessantly about his nicotine patches and trying to give up. He barged in while I was talking to Ella Maltby and stood right in front of me, with his cigarette – herbal, incidentally – like this.' He indicated the method with his pipe, holding it a few inches below his chin. 'But nobody smokes like that. I talked to actors who don't smoke, and one of the first things they have to learn is how to smoke convincingly. Actors always need to do something with their hands, so they like smoking roles. Smokers know they annoy non-smokers and become wary around them, so they always hold their cigarettes away to one side.'

'I fail to see—' Land began.

'Yes, Raymondo, you usually do, but we're happy to cover for you. When I looked at Ray Pryce standing so close, I suddenly realized he was a non-smoker. Now, if that was the case, it changed everything. On the time line for the Kramers' party that Janice provided, Pryce is marked down as leaving the room to smoke a cigarette. So the trip was wrong.'

'But Marcus Sigler saw him on the back staircase,' objected Banbury.

'Marcus lied to cover the fact that he was on the staircase with Gail Strong. At Strong's request he changed his timing so that nobody could place them together. So where did Ray Pryce disappear to? He went upstairs to the baby's room.'

'Why?'

'We'll get to that in a minute. Let's just say that he was extremely angry, and very good at hiding it. Now, we know the nursery door was unlocked because Judith and Robert Kramer both expressed surprise when they got upstairs and couldn't open it. So Pryce slipped inside and approached the cot, and the baby started to cry.'

'Was he intending to kill the child right then?'

'That's hard to say. It'll be interesting to hear him in court. I think he had murderous intentions, but maybe they failed him when he saw the child. Well, he needed to shut Noah up, but already his sense of self-preservation was working and he was worried that someone would find out that he had been in the room. He didn't want to leave prints. And he wanted to silence the baby. So he grabbed the Mr Punch from the wall behind him and waved it about, hoping to amuse the boy.

'And when Noah cried even harder, Pryce let Mr Punch pick up the baby. He wrapped the figure's hands around the child and rocked him, and the rocking turned into throttling, and then Noah Kramer was silenced. So he ran to the window and shoved it open, and let Mr Punch shake the baby out into the street. Downstairs, on the fire escape, Marcus Sigler heard what he thought was a can of paint sliding. What he'd heard was the window going up above him. Pryce stepped back, threw the dummy on the floor, and the rain squalled in, soaking the rug. The water raised the nap of the rug, lifting impressions. If you want to remove chair marks from a carpet, you just put an ice cube in each dent. I got that tip from *The Good Wife's*

Guide to Housekeeping, 1935. Right, so Pryce was back on the door side of the empty cot. The deed was done. But what if somebody came up? He needed to buy himself some time. The Yale key was in the door, but of course there was no way of locking it from the inside without remaining in the room. Except that there was.'

'I really don't see how.' May frowned.

'Come on. Ray Pryce is a writer. He spends his life coming up with outlandish ideas. And now he had a brain-wave. A few minutes earlier, Mona Williams had sat on his glasses and broken them. The right arm had snapped off. He had put the broken glasses in his pocket.

'It was such a simple idea. I tried it myself and it works perfectly every time. He stuck the arm of the glasses through the hole in the end of the key, closed the door and went outside. Then he simply ran his credit card down through the gap in the door. It was enough to flip the key, and now that it was no longer upright, the arm of the glasses simply fell out onto the floor. He had been gone no longer than the time it takes to smoke a cigarette.

'Next, the Kramers break the door down and rush in, and the guests come up to see what's wrong—'

'—and Pryce retrieves the glasses' arm from the floor,' said May.

'Precisely. He had achieved exactly the effect he was hoping for. Retribution from Kramer's own role model. Pryce must have gone to bed that night thinking he had destroyed his nemesis. But he was wrong. Because while he was here, sitting in the hallway waiting to be interviewed, Pryce accidentally overheard that Robert wasn't the baby's father – and of course, the thing nobody realized is that Robert already knew it. Of course he knew: he'd been to see his doctor because he and Judith had been having trouble conceiving, and the doctor had explained about his low sperm count.

'Pryce had failed. Judith was devastated, but Robert Kramer seemed barely touched by the tragedy. Pryce had to try something else. But what? What did Kramer care about so much if it wasn't the life of a child?'

'Money,' said Meera.

'Hit him where it hurts. Get rid of the financier and watch the empire collapse. Oh, and stick a Punch and Judy doll there, to make sure Kramer knew the two tragedies were linked. How perfect to mirror Kramer's obsession with the Mr Punch story and exact a theatrical revenge! The ancient Greeks used something they called "temple magic". They would make heavy doors open by themselves via secret systems of pulleys and ropes, and used hidden tubes and secret passages to make the Sibyl whisper through the walls. Pryce knew that the effect was as important as the act. So this time he concentrated more on the staging. He lured Baine to a melancholy, darkened spot and a lonely, awful death.'

'Baine had a lot of alcohol in his bloodstream when he died,' said Kershaw. 'From the state of his liver, I'd say he'd been drinking hard for a year.'

'Do you mind?' said Bryant. 'This is my story. The credit crunch had caught Baine on the hop and he'd dipped his hand in the till to try and keep things afloat. So, once again, fate undermined Pryce and produced the wrong effect. If anything, he did Kramer a favour by getting rid of Baine. Then things got even worse. Mona Williams remembered sitting on Pryce's glasses just before he left the room – and he remembered that he'd given her the scripts.'

'What scripts?' asked Land.

'The ones he'd found from the original Grand Guignol at the New Theatre. The ones he cribbed from. And there it was in another play, *The Mystery of the Locked Cell*, staged in 1923 with Dame Sybil Thorndyke, written by none other than the master himself, Noël Coward. In it,

344

the murderer seals a room by inserting a steel rod in a key and twisting it from outside.

'And Mona did what she always did. She started gossiping. So Pryce needed to frighten her into silence. He waited until she went into the theatre for her "thinking time", and, in the gloom of the stalls, dropped the scold's bridle on her. But it had the wrong effect. It terrified her and she choked to death. Has there ever been a series of crimes that have gone so horribly wrong? Meanwhile, Robert Kramer sailed through it all, untouched.

'So, in desperation, he lured Kramer away to confront him with his misdeeds. And this, too, went wrong. We don't know what Kramer said, but presumably he shrugged off the scare tactic used on him—'

'The dropped dummy,' May pointed out.

'That's right, the dummy, another hopeless failure. Kramer probably laughed in his face. Which was when Pryce exploded and chucked the fork at him. Even worse, Kramer's shoes slipped and he fell on the fork and died. Pryce wants us to believe that he achieved what he set out to do, but he failed in every possible way. His victim cheated him right until the very end.'

'I don't understand,' Land persisted. 'Why did Pryce drop a life-sized dummy on him in the barn? Who was it meant to be? Isn't that a ridiculous thing to do? What's the motive for all of this?'

Bryant removed his pipe from between his teeth and gave a ghastly grin. 'The oldest motive in the world. Revenge. This is about the memory of blood. Blood in the sense of blood relations. Dummies are representatives of people. This particular dummy was intended to be the first Mrs Kramer. Robert Kramer didn't know she was pregnant when she died. He would have had a real heir after all. And the significance of the first Mrs Kramer? It's very simple. She was Ray Pryce's mother. Pryce knew and, in his own absurdly roundabout way, was trying to tell Robert that he knew.'

'His mother?' May repeated. 'How did you find out about that?'

'Remember I told you this was about the victim, not the murderer? I had a bit of a root about in Kramer's background and her name kept coming up. Stella Kramer was a writer, too – or at least she tried to be. She wrote about the experience of giving birth for a weekly magazine. She wrote about her unhappy childhood, and anything else she thought might sell. It was hard to separate out the facts; at first I assumed she was making everything up. And after a while, thanks to a few carefully planted denials by her husband, so did everyone else. I followed the paper trail as her articles dwindled to bitter letters in the local press and the salient facts are clear. Ray was born out of wedlock and raised by foster parents, but Stella stayed in touch with him. She met him in secret and told him all about her disastrous marriage to Robert. He advised her to leave, but she couldn't. The couple's fights eventually made the *Evening Standard*, but Stella came off badly. Kramer's bullying drove her to suicide. And Pryce sat impotently by, penniless and powerless, unable to do anything about it as Kramer grew richer and stronger. Pryce tried to make a living as a writer and failed. There was nothing he could do but watch and nurse his hatred.

'All this changed on the day he discovered the box of scripts. Suddenly, fate stepped in and gave him the power to act. He palmed off one of the plays as his own and went to see Kramer. He slowly wormed his way into the inner circle. Did he, like Hamlet, plan to stage a version that re-enacted a parental death? No, because we all remember what happened to Hamlet.

'But, like Hamlet, he bided his time and waited for an opportunity to strike. There's a good chance it would never have happened, if it hadn't been for Robert Kramer's ill-chosen remarks about his first wife at the party, which Ray overheard.

'It was the last straw. He stormed upstairs and attacked the baby. I kept looking at Janice's chart, but for ages I couldn't see the error because everyone was accounted for. Then I realized that it was impossible. Somebody had to have made a mistake. But it took more than one person to make a lie; it took the perpetrator and the witness, and I couldn't work out which of the corroborators was lying. Of course, I should have seen it, because now it's obvious. And there's an ugly little sidebar to this. Robert Kramer happened to be Jewish, and Pryce attacked him with his own puppetry. The Mr Punch model conforms to the physiological concept of the cephalic index – the mockery of Jewish facial features. Ray Pryce has a prior conviction for an anti-Semitic attack dating back to his time in foster care. I enrolled him in the case to keep him close, just as Kramer had with his enemies.'

Bryant sat back and contentedly puffed away at his pipe. Everyone, including his partner, stared at him in amazement.

Colin turned to Meera. 'You have to go on a date with me now,' he said, grinning.

347

50

THE SIBYL

Raymond Land came in soon after dawn. He had woken to find there was no breakfast because Leanne had gone to Wales and he didn't know how to use the microwave, or where she kept the eggs, or where the saucepans lived, so he caught an earlier train and breakfasted at the Ladykillers. The little café was empty at eight a.m. – most shops and offices in the area opened at nine-thirty – so he had time to sit and reflect over his morning tea.

Perhaps, he thought, *just perhaps I've been wrong all this time, waiting to be transferred to a place where life is easy and the sun always shines. Perhaps that's not what life is all about. Perhaps you only get a sense of yourself when everything has to be fought for. It's less pleasurable here but more exciting.* Watching the two detectives the night before, battling their way to the end of the case, he felt he was seeing them at the top of their game. He could feel the gravitational pull of London life, the magnetic energy that raced around them, the essence of awareness that sparked everything into activity.

He had felt truly alive.

But he couldn't let Leanne down. She dreamed of holidays to Barbados. She wanted to spend days by a pool beneath an azure sky. She didn't want to have to take an umbrella and a scarf every time she left the house. She didn't want to be married to a man who divided his time between paperwork, pubs and putrid corpses. She needed pampering. How could he deny her dreams?

With a heavy heart, he dug out his keys and let himself into 231 Caledonian Road. He absentmindedly stroked Crippen, who was waiting on the stairs. The glossy black cat rubbed its back against his legs and followed him along the labyrinthine corridors to his office. Land disconsolately noted the newly painted walls in an odd variety of mismatched colours – the nice plain white had turned out to be undercoat. Who on earth had chosen heliotrope? He stepped over the lethally warped floorboards and breathed the smell of beer and stale pipe smoke that hung in the air. Nobody else was in yet.

He went into the office that Bryant and May had commandeered. May's desk was obsessively neat, the electronic gadgets arranged in rows, recharging, a few piles of paperwork squared off to the corners of his workspace.

Bryant's half of the room was the opposite. A black candle had dripped rank wax over his chased-silver Tibetan skull, making it smell even worse. A piece of mouldering tannis root dangled from a carapace over his filthy, barely used computer. Wavering stacks of esoteric books threatened to fall. A stuffed weasel with only one eye leered from a bowed bookcase. Two dozen minor Indian gods carved from coloured chalks were randomly scattered over his ink-stained papers. The receiver of his telephone had somehow been burned and had become fused with its base. An odoriferous lime and purple chemical compound was sprouting in a Tupperware dish. The power point under his desk had been held open with the blade of a kitchen knife so that he could leave a light burning over his hydroponic marijuana plant. A hardback book lay open by his keyboard. Land idly examined the chapter Bryant had been reading. *Knife Wounds 6: Identifying Weapons from Entry Stabs Section B: Cuts to the Face & Eyes*. He sighed wearily.

His eye fell upon Madame Blavatsky. She seemed to be perfectly at home in here. He wandered over to it, checked the coin slot and dug out an old penny. Dropping it in, he watched as the seer rummaged awkwardly for a card and dropped it into the delivery tray. He reached in and picked it up.

It read:

YOUR WIFE IS HAVING AFFAIRS BEHIND YOUR BACK

Startled, he shoved the card back in the tray.

He looked back at Madame Blavatsky. 'Don't be so ridiculous,' he said aloud.

The clairvoyant winked at him grotesquely. One of her eyes was shorting out, causing her hand to tremble. Suddenly she spoke. 'Your wife, Leanne, is not in Wales, Raymond, she's at the Regent Palace Hotel with her Spanish flamenco instructor. You will find them checked in under the name of Cheryl and Roger Boothby.' Blavatsky's voice was low and ominous and seemed to come from a place far within the cold earth.

'How do you know this?' Land asked.

'Don't be stupid, I'm a clairvoyant. I see all.'

'What should I do?'

'I tell you nothing you have not suspected before. You must face your demons.'

'How do I do that?'

'Go there at once, before they leave the room. Confront her. Take back control of your life. The power is in your hands.'

'You're right,' said Land, suddenly filled with conviction. 'By God, you're right. I should have done this a long time ago.' He turned on his heel and quickly left the room.

Arthur Bryant emerged from his place inside the old armchair that he had turned to face the wall. He yawned and stretched.

'I say, I say, I say,' said Madame Blavatsky. 'Did you hear about my clairvoyant friend Madame Raya? She won the lottery. I said to her, "Well done, Medium Raya."'

'What on earth's going on?' asked John May, coming in and throwing his newspaper onto his desk.

'Oh, years ago Dudley Salterton taught me ventriloquism,' Bryant replied. 'I went to see Maggie Armitage to get my memory back, and her treatment made me remember his lessons. I got bored sticking little hints on Madame Blavatsky's cards – Raymondo's so hopeless I knew he'd never get the message – so I made the old dear tell him about Leanne. He's gone off to sort her out. He completely fell for it.'

May made a sound of disapproval but was not really surprised. 'Arthur, you are completely incorrigible.'

'I should hope so. It's one of the few benefits of my age. Anyway, I've nothing better to do. Ray Pryce is behind bars. My desk is clear once more. Except—'

'I know,' said May. 'But you're not going to be able to sort this one out. It's far too big.'

'I know, but I have to find a way, John. I can't leave her murder on my conscience.'

'You wouldn't be fighting an individual over Anna Marquand's death. You'd be taking on the entire British

351

government. You're not a political animal, Arthur. You'd be beaten.'

'I wouldn't do it alone,' said Bryant.

'No,' May agreed. 'I wouldn't let you do it alone. We're a team. But whatever the outcome, you know it would be our final investigation. It would be the end of us.'

'Yes, I know that. But still, I think I have to do it.'

'Then I'll do it with you,' said May. 'We'll find a way to put things right somehow.'

'There's always another fight, isn't there?' said Bryant. 'You strip away one mask and find another beneath it.'

'That's this city for you. It's filled with infinite impossibilities, but it has survived for more than two thousand years, and it'll still be here long after we've gone. There's one small consolation.'

'What's that?'

'It will remember your name, Arthur. You did something with your life. London remembers all those who make a difference.'

'So you think we should go out with a bang?' Bryant asked. He raised one dangerously mischievous eyebrow.

'Why not?' said May, unable to contain a rueful smile. 'That was the way we came in, wasn't it?'